"ALWAYS A ROLLING STONE"

ALAN GREENHALGH

"ALWAYS A ROLLING STONE"
Reprinted 2014.

This is a true story. In many instances fictitious names have been adopted to protect the privacy and reputations of those involved. Incidents and events are based upon the author's interpretation which is entirely subjective and may not match that of the persons who figure in this story.
It is not the intention of the author to cast aspersions on, judge or give offence to the any person. Should any person resent or take offence at what they imagine to be a portrayal of a particular person, persons or situation with which they feel or imagine they are familiar, such instances should be treated as unintentional and coincidental and the author unreservedly apologises in advance for giving offence.

Interior Book Design and Layout by
Alan Greenhalgh

ISBN 978-0-9775844-7-5

DEDICATION

I dedicate this book to my family, past, present and those as yet unborn and to my beautiful wife, Chris who has supported me throughout all the wonderful years of our marriage.

ACKNOWLEDGEMENTS

My wife and soul-mate Chris who was also my editor and kindly agreed to wade through this work and provide invaluable guidance.

***

FOREWORD

Always a Rolling Stone is a true story. Finding sufficient content for the story was no problem. However, deciding what to exclude presented a real quandary. Packed with amazing incidents "Terry's" fourteen years as a policeman was but a small part of his often tortured life journey and provided so much material that there was no possible way to include everything. Therefore, I have taken a random selection of policing incidents in the hope of providing the reader with some incite in to police life during the sixties and seventies. Although his police service helped to mould the man "Terry's" story is much more than the memoirs of a former policeman.

Obviously, the names of the characters and some key places are fictitious to protect individual privacy. However, the persons figuring in A Rolling Stone may feel that they can identify themselves and various other characters within the story from the events described. Please let me say my recollection of events and my opinion as to each character's behaviour is entirely subjective and invariably warped by personal emotion. While I have struggled to portray sensitive incidents non-judgmentally and with compassion if I have not succeeded then that is a reflection on my failings as a human being and not a criticism of the characters who make up this story. If I give offence let me apologise in advance, as I bare no malice of ill-will toward those whose paths and "Terry's" have crossed.

I hope you enjoy Always a Rolling Stone.

CREED

In this life, I seek no fortune, fame, might or power.
I yearn to make a lasting mark, before my final hour;
To realize my secret destiny, before the sands of time,
Filter through the hourglass, like worthless bits of grime.

Although I'm born a simple man, with skills and talents few,
There beats within my aching chest, a heart that's kind and true.
And in my head, there is a call, to grow bloom and flower.
Love is my guiding force; I won't quell or cower.

I need a goal, a cause, a plan, something for which to aim,
I know this life has meaning, and to me it is quite plain.
Some folk have sought to limit me, and squeeze me in a box,
To dance to any other tune. I 'm deaf to all their knocks.

If I listened to the critics and those that seek to judge;
Potential I would never find and life would be a drudge.
Unlike the tortured bonsai tree so stunted in its pot,
I'll emulate the mighty oak and show them what I've got.

And as I journey on my way, I'll keep my goal in sight,
To leave a lasting legacy of deeds both just and write.
And, when I lose the final race against the ticking clock,
There at my earthly resting place please write upon my rock;
"He loved to dream and find truth. He never quit his quest,
'Tho trekking many roads in life, he always gave his best!"

— Alan Greenhalgh

CHAPTER ONE

It was a serene suburban Sunday morning in spring. The distant rattle of trams interspersed with noisy kookaburras mocking from the wooden power poles filtered through the wooden casement window of the bedroom awakening the three boys from their innocent slumber. Although it was only 6.00 am they had been in bed since 7.00 pm the previous night and they were eager to embrace the bright sunny day which beckoned them through the flimsy net curtains of the single bedroom window. Past experience had taught them not to get out of bed before their parents awoke so they whispered quietly at first so as not to disturb their parents slumbering in the adjoining bedroom. However, becoming increasingly animated, the boy's voices soon increased in volume as they bickered over the spit races conducted on their bed heads. As usual, six year old Terry was coming last behind eight year old Michael and ten year old Paul who by sheer size and seniority always dominated. They simply forgot their father Henry enjoyed to a lie-in on Sunday and the chattering emanating from their shabby, cramped bedroom eventually penetrated the adjoining brick wall disturbing his slumber.

The three boys stopped talking as the bedroom door opened. *Oh no. We've woken dad up,* Terry thought fearfully. His terrified gaze went to the open doorway. *That's strange. Dad's smiling.*

Relieved to see their father's apparent good humour, the three boys returned his smile.

"Come out you lot," Henry beckoned, his wide grin displaying broad white false teeth hastily grabbed from the glass of Steradent where they had soaked overnight. The boys bounced off their beds, scrambling across the worn linoleum to the dining room, eagerly hoping for some rare treat from their father.

"Stand in line!" Henry's smile had vanished replaced by a black, angry, maniacal look they knew only too well. Henry produced a wide, leather razor strop from behind his back. Grabbing Paul roughly by one arm, he dragged him forward while tugging his upper body downward. With his free hand, Henry ripped Paul's pyjamas down to reveal bare white thighs.

"No dad! No dad, please," Paul screamed in terror.

"I'll teach you to be quiet," Henry roared, whipping the strap repeatedly across his eldest son's legs. Large red welts burst across the tender flesh as Paul howled in pain.

Aware of that they were next in line for the cruel punishment, Michael and Terry screamed and pleaded to no avail. Shoving Paul back into the bedroom, their father grabbed Michael who hopped and struggled to escape the flailing strop. "Keep still," Henry demanded as his anger raged.

By now, Henry was out of control. The boys' terrified screams only served to fuel his anger to a greater frenzy. WHACK. WHACK. WHACK. The cruel leather cut deep into tender flesh until all three children were sobbing, deeply traumatised by the severity of the punishment and the betrayal of their father's grinning countenance.

This episode was simply one of the many reasons that Terry didn't remember his childhood with any fondness. Although he treasured some moments, by and large it was a miserable time. Born in the working class western Sydney suburb of Ashfield, he lived in Leichhardt for the first ten years of his life, where poverty and cramped, squalid living conditions were normal for the majority of the inner-city residents. As an English migrant, his father Henry, was proud to announce that *he* wasn't "a ten pound Pom." Alluding of course to a period of post war migration in which thousands of people from the British Isles arrived in Australia under the scheme of assisted passage. Under this arrangement, an individual could pay ten pounds[1] to the Australian Government for the right to a berth on a ship packed with like-minded individuals hoping for a better life in the distant colony. Henry looked with scorn on "The Poms" who availed themselves of this opportunity. He looked with even greater scorn on those who complained about their lot when they didn't immediately find things the same as, "back 'ome".

Henry originated from the village of Bury, just outside Manchester England, which was in the post war years, a bleak miserable place. During his younger years, Terry intended to visit his father's birthplace because he wanted to understand what made the man tick. When the opportunity arose to visit England

---

[1] $20.00

in his adult years, he travelled north from London, passing through Manchester. Although he was to some extent prepared by the pictures and stories he'd seen on television, when he eventually got as far as Manchester he changed his mind. Although the smoke stacks of the cotton and steel mills from his father's era no longer belched forth coal fumes, Terry's preconceived picture of the area was vindicated by the actual reality. The squalor, dour-faced factory workers and incessant rain were sufficient for him to understand how someone raised in the era of the Great Depression and the Second World War could turn out mean, ill tempered and violent.

Terry remembered his father as a man of medium height, with a head of thick straight hair, combed to one side and parted, which was the fashion in those days. His heavily lined face sported a brow deeply furrowed like a sheet of corrugated iron. He rarely smiled and was possessed of a jaundiced and pessimistic outlook on life, rarely finding qualities worthy of admiration among those who made his acquaintance. Unfortunately, Henry's children also seemed to fall into this latter category. Mostly, Henry showed little interest in his offspring, apart from deprecatory comments resulting in their poor self-esteem. However, when their behaviour impinged negatively upon his world, he reacted with sudden and frightening violence.

On another occasion, when Henry came home from work in a mood more foul than usual, his hard, strong hands reached for Terry, gripping either side of the small boy's head. Terry did not understand what he had done but something had obviously incurred his father's displeasure. Lifting his youngest son clear of the floor, he hurled him across the room. Terry fell in a crumpled heap, too shocked to whimper in protest.

"Leave him alone!" Judy's shriek brought her husband to his senses. Henry flopped into his favourite chair and he reached for the newspaper, reading sullenly as Terry scrambled to safety.

Although he could be excused for harbouring deep resentment, Terry didn't hate his father. He never bore him any malice, despite thinking as a child that the perpetual ringing in his ears (tinnitus) was quite normal. The unrelenting sound akin to an angry mosquito was a result of the iron-fisted clobbering to his skull, or from being thrown across the room by his head. No, he didn't hate him, but by God, he was terrified of him!

The youngest of three boys, Terry constantly lived with the knowledge that, from the time of his birth, he was the cause of great disappointment in his father's life. Henry had desperately wanted a girl and his new son's huge blue eyes, blonde hair, milky fair skin and disarming smile were insufficient consolation for the Lancashire migrant. The knowledge that he was unwanted and the beatings were the root cause for Terry's self-loathing and sense of worthlessness he was to carry with him for many years.

The gift of intuition was Terry's compensation for average intelligence. This gift was to stand him in good stead throughout his life. Terry was also able to read people skilfully, quickly empathising with most people's viewpoint.

Somehow, even as a child, he understood that each of us is the product of our upbringing and conditioning. Although Terry would have been unable to articulate that sentiment during his childhood, he sensed that his father must have had a very unhappy life to make him what he was. He could also understand that he had inherited much of his father in his own personality. He hated that and always would as he battled throughout his life to suppress the omnipresent snarling dog of anger lurking within.

Sometimes it seemed as if his father hated the entire world. The seething resentment bubbling red-hot beneath a thin veneer of indifference easily overflowed like lava from a sleeping volcano. Just like that lava, the anger was not selective; it engulfed everything in its path with frightening speed.

One summer afternoon when Terry was only eight years old, he was playing 'chasing' with Paul and Michael while they waited to be called in for dinner. It was a favourite game of the older boys, who knowing Terry was not as fast or as agile, mercilessly exploited this disparity. As usual, he was the one doing the chasing while in the way of children everywhere, Paul and Michael did their utmost to provoke him. Dodging and weaving around the footpath outside 14 Cromwell Street, they successfully managed to avoid the clutches of the smaller boy who was becoming increasingly frustrated. As Paul ran past him, Terry lunged but missing his brother, stumbled and fell onto the hard concrete footpath. As he fell, he instinctively put out his left hand to break the fall. A white-hot pain lanced the length of his arm. Getting to his feet, tears poured down his cheeks as he supported the arm with his right hand to lessen his unbearable agony. Strangely, the left arm would not respond when he tried to move it. Seeing Terry's pain and plight, Paul erupted into sadistic laughter. To Terry, the sight of his brother laughing unsympathetically hurt him as much as his arm.

Clutching the injured limb, Terry staggered inside, his face pale. Hearing the sound of her son's anguished wails, Judy ran to the back door to meet him, almost fainting at the sight of her youngest son's arm. Stooping to comfort him, she placed one arm around his shoulders and soothed, "Oh, you poor darling. Let me see if I can fix you up."

There was no doubt in Judy's mind that her son's arm was broken. There were tell-tale bumps beneath the swollen flesh, which was painful to touch. While Terry sat quietly shaking, she carefully fashioned a makeshift splint from wooden school rulers and a Kellog's Cornflakes box.

"Here, swallow these." She placed the aching limb in a sling and handed Terry two white tablets.

He swallowed his mother's favourite cure-all, choking on the bitter tasting Aspro tablets while with a poker face Paul stood watching.

"I think we need to take you to the Children's Hospital when your father gets home from work," she told him anxiously.

For some reason, Henry was later than usual. Perhaps he'd been required to work overtime. Eventually, the little beige Austin A40 utility pulled into the back yard. Judy breathed a sigh of relief. As Henry walked in the back door and dropped his Gladstone workbag on the floor, she hurried to meet him. "Henry, I think Terry has broken his arm. We'll need to take him to Hospital."

Henry grunted bad-temperedly. He was in no mood for domestic problems and resented the disruption to his nightly routine. "Let me have a look," he said disbelievingly.

Terry's strained white face clearly reflected the pain and shock. He stood quietly with the splinted limb supported by its sling.

"Give me your arm," Henry growled, grabbing his small son's injured limb. Wrenching it unceremoniously upward, he straightened the bandaged arm, pulling it from the sling for a better view.

"Yaaa!" Terry's involuntary screams dispelled any further doubt as to the severity of his injuries.

11

Henry dropped the arm like a red-hot brick. "Get in the car!" he snarled, showing no remorse for inflicting further pain.

Looking daggers at Henry for his cruelty, Judy pulled Terry to her protectively. "Perhaps now you'll believe him," she stated crossly. Although Judy would willingly suffer many personal indignities in silence, she was fearless when the welfare of her children was at stake.

They drove in silence to Camperdown Children's Hospital, Terry sitting on his mother's knee in the small cabin of the utility truck. Henry parked the vehicle in the car park and waited in the cab while his wife and son made their way to the entrance. The overheated waiting room smelled of disinfectant and floor polish. There were few vacant seats with the room packed with crying children and worried mothers. Judy approached the desk and after providing the relevant details, they sat waiting their turn for treatment. It seemed an eternity before a nursing sister bustled into the room.

"Master Terry Flatley!" she called loudly in her cold clinical voice.

Judy got to her feet, "Yes. We're here. Come on Terry!" She helped her son into the examination room.

A kindly young intern immediately sent Terry for X-rays. A further period of waiting followed before the doctor swathed the broken limb in sticky white plaster bandages.

"Well, young man. You made a nice mess of that didn't you? You've managed to break your arm at the wrist and above the elbow. You'll soon be right and you can collect lots of autographs from all your friends," he smiled.

Several hours had elapsed by the time they returned to the car park and Henry drove them home, his face like thunder. One look at his wife's face was sufficient for him to know better than to comment.

Terry had not been the only one to suffer his father's cruel remarks, iron fists and angry stentorian voice. Paul and Michael also bore physical and mental scars of that uncontrollable anger and psychological abuse!

His oldest brother Paul had been a tall dark haired boy with thin sharp features, dark eyes and a sombre introverted personality. Possessed of an intelligent and inquiring mind, he loved gathering facts on a plethora of subjects, which he meticulously recorded and quoted through the gift of instant recall. The eldest son also loved electronics and chemistry, often constructing crystal sets[2] and model aeroplanes, or conducting various experiments with an amateur chemistry set.

Terry was unable to recall Paul having any friends. His brother's meticulous and studious nature meant he seemed to have his nose perpetually buried in a book, branding him as quite different to most boys his age.

One early example of Henry's cruelty toward his oldest son was to leave an indelible stamp in Terry's memory. This incident occurred when Henry was laying a concrete slab to park his truck behind their grotty little rented house in Leichhardt. His three boys had gathered on the back step to watch him wield the trowel and smooth the cement. Henry was a very adept handyman and always seemed to do everything to perfection. The wet glistening surface of the concrete was as smooth as glass.

"Don't get off the step or touch the concrete!" Henry had commanded, his tone leaving no doubt as to their fate should they disobey. The boys sat meekly, watching in fascination. They dare not even whisper for fear of in some way incurring his displeasure.

Paul who was four years Terry's senior, was for some reason overcome with the urge to touch the wet grey strange looking substance that their father had laboured long and hard to prepare. It seemed like a split second after his little hand had touched the surface that the steel trowel ceased its wet, gritty sliding. With a glint of sunlight on shiny steel, the trowel flew through the air like a lethal missile. Henry was kneeling only three metres away and he hurled the tool with all his might. The trowel struck Paul on the wrist, glanced off and clattered to the ground. A stunned silence followed as the boys looked aghast at the exposed white bone and cherry red sinews of the older boy's wrist.

Shocked by this sudden display of violence, Paul did not cry despite excruciating pain. Gripping his wrist instinctively, to stem the blood flow, he retreated inside. Judy silently bandaged the gaping wound as Henry continued working without explanation or apology. Although stitches were called for, Judy was

---

[2] A crystal set is a very simple radio receiver requiring no electricity. Due to the weakness of the signal, it requires headphones make the signal audible.

understandably reluctant to incur Henry's wrath by suggesting medical intervention.

Judy was a kindly, sensitive woman with curly brown hair and large hazel eyes. She was of timid disposition and possessed romantic imagination. Judy and Henry had met when she was only eighteen. A pretty, though naive and overly protected country girl from Kerang in Victoria, Henry's strength and decisive personality seemed to promise her security and the chance to realise her dreams for a quaint English style cottage with picket fence, roses around the front door and the sound of happy laughing children to love. The reality had been much different but Judy dare not admit the mistake to her mother. Emily, on learning of her daughter's intention to marry Henry had issued the stern instruction, "You've made your bed my girl. Now you've got to lie on it!"

Loyal to Henry, she tried hard to please him, making the best of the union by justifying his meanness and brooding nature with an ingenious and inexhaustible array of excuses. Little did she know that she was deceiving nobody but herself.

Henry's belief that, "Kids should be seen and not heard" was one of many tenets that he had inherited from Grandma Flatley. Grandma was an eccentric, stick figure of a woman who spoke with a broad Lancashire accent. "Ooh eeh, by goom lad!" was often a preface she used to some little gem of wisdom.

Grandma smoked Capstan, cork tipped, cigarettes. Her fingers were heavily-stained with nicotine and her lank, grey hair was tinged yellow, from the rising smoke of the butt on which she sucked with obvious relish.

Grandma spread newspapers on her floors to keep them clean and used to give Paul, Michael and Terry two shillings apiece when they visited. Although Terry didn't ever recall her being nasty toward him, there was something about her appearance and character that held him in awe.

Terry never knew Grandfather Flatley. Grandma said that he was a merchant seaman and that he had run off. *Probably to get away from Grandma*, he guessed. Grandma lived alone and the family went occasionally to visit her out of a sense of duty. She kept a brood of black chooks in her back yard and Terry considered the bloody chooks to be as batty as she was!

A huge rooster with gleaming plumage and exceptionally long spurs ruled fiercely. The winged devil used his spikes to great effect to keep his harem in order, while aggressively defending his territory against all and sundry. Finding the highest perch, his beady eyes challenging, he'd immediately launch himself in a flurry of squawking feathers at anyone foolish enough to open the gate.

In Terry's opinion, there was some similarity between that rooster's personality and that of his father, although, he was sure his father didn't have a harem!

Terry's brother Michael was the middle child in the Flatley family. Two years Terry's senior and much shorter in stature he was much closer in appearance to Terry than Paul. Possessing blue eyes, blonde curly hair and fair skin, Michael was undoubtedly highly intelligent and blessed with the ability to assimilate information quickly and without recourse to study. He was well aware of his superior intelligence, adopting an air of disdain toward those who could not match his mental agility. Michael, although more outgoing than his older brother, still tended to be introspective. He rarely incurred his father's displeasure, cunningly avoiding trouble and gauging the volatile mood of the undisputed head of the household with the accuracy of a barometer warning of a pending storm.

On one occasion, Michael naively entered the wire netting enclosure at the rear of Grandmother's tiny suburban yard in Padstow. Whether he entered the pen to collect the eggs or through childhood curiosity, it was never established. With wings flapping wildly, neck arched and legs pounding, the ball of feathered fury launched itself at the curly blonde head presenting such a tempting target. With beak and spurs, it pecked and clawed for all it was worth. The vicious bird might have been poultry in name but there was nothing paltry about the attack. Michael's terrified screams brought Grandma running. Grabbing the little boy, she pulled him to safety through the open gate. With squawking chooks running hither and yon in panicked confusion, she re-entered the pen and kicked the gate closed behind her.

The feathered despot stood its ground, beak open, wings spread and with a blood- curdling screech, it challenged the old woman.

"You horrible, nasty beast! This time you're for the chop."

Grandma executed a well-placed kick to the rooster's crop with her slippered toe, sitting the bird back on it's magnificently plumed behind. Stooping quickly, she seized the feathered fiend by the throat in strong leathery hands. Carrying it at arms length, flapping and screeching in protest to the nearby chopping block, she quickly dispatched it with one quick stroke of the axe.

Watching aghast from a safe distance, Terry's young stomach churned at the sickly stench of hot blood and feathers wafting on the slight breeze, while Paul, who detested mess of any description, hastily retreated inside away from the grisly spectacle.

Somehow, the recalcitrant rooster escaped. With wings flapping and legs pumping, it ran in ever decreasing circles, gushing blood from its headless body before finally collapsing against the fence where it lay quivering. Dropping her bloodied instrument of death, the geriatric assassin retrieved the carcass. Holding it aloft by its scaly spurred legs, she called to little Michael, "Ooh ee by gum. Now we'll fix your poor wee head. This one won't be bothering you any more."

Although the murderous bird no longer posed any threat, the traumatised boy was not having the grisly carcass near him. Shocked into silence by the swiftness of the execution, his screams of terror began afresh.

Throwing the limp headless carcass beside the kitchen door, Grandma ushered the boy inside where she bathed his scratched, blood specked and tousled blond head. "You'll feel better with a good dinner inside you my lad," she assured him.

"What's for dinner Grandma?" he sniffed.

"Lovely roast chicken of course!"

Waste not, want not was Grandma's oft- repeated maxim. She could not understand why little Michael paled at the thought of eating his attacker and her other grandsons could not bring themselves to touch the tough stringy meat.

* * *

The Leichhardt in which Terry grew up in during the 1950's was a typical inner city working class area, with terraced and semidetached houses, each separated by wooden paling fences. The harsh Australian sunshine had bleached the splintery hard wood palings to a dull grey. White ants and dry rot infested supporting posts, causing the fences to sag and lean at precarious angles. The unmistakable electric whir and metallic clatter of tramcars was a major contributor to the din of city traffic. An unsightly maze of power poles and electric cables festooned the streetscapes of grey buildings, peeling paint and hoardings proclaiming the merits of Dickies Towels, Vincent's A.P.C. Powders and Peter's Ice Cream.

In the post war era, the population of Sydney consisted of mainly second generation white Australians. Materials of all description were in short supply, electricity was unreliable and blackouts a regular occurrence. In an attempt to expand Australia's economy, the Liberal Government led by Prime Minister Bob Menzies attempted to increase the population under the infamous "White Australia Policy." As a result, migrants from Europe arrived in large numbers. Australian born citizens regarded the new arrivals with narrow-minded suspicion labelling Italians as, Dagoes, Greeks as Wogs and viewing any other non-English migrants with the same distrust as aliens from outer space.

Australia later honoured Menzies with a knighthood, remembering him as a statesman although his nickname at the time was, "Pig Iron Bob." The derogatory title resulted from his pre-war error of judgement in selling scrap metal to Japan. According to most Australians, the Japanese returned the metal in the form of bullets, fired at the fledgling country's soldiers during the Second World War.

A bread delivery man referred to as "The Baker" (although God only knows why, he didn't actually bake the bread.) delivered loaves by horse and cart. Running from house to house with a large basket of fresh round top crusty loaves of white bread, while his horse plodded slowly along, pulling the cart. The clip clop of steel shod hooves echoed from the black macadam surface of the quiet streets. Occasionally, the horse would stop to allow the baker to catch up and refill his basket before moving off, head down, shaggy hooves rising and falling in their measured tread.

Sometimes, the baker stopped to allow the children to feed the old Clydesdale a carrot, or pat its' long grey head. Kids watched the horse snuffling explosively in the chaff bag, noisily snorting the dust from its wide black nostrils as it munched a much-deserved feed of the dry shredded hay.

Milk arrived mysteriously at night when all self- respecting children were tucked up in bed. Mothers left aluminium billycans on the footpath outside the front gate and chalked the number of pints required on the pavement, placing the lid tightly on the can to prevent neighbourhood cats helping themselves, or a stray dog's urine fouling the milk should it cock a mangy leg against the front fence.

The Flatley house was one of many possessing an ice chest to protect perishable food against the simmering heat. Although refrigerators were in use by the more affluent, they were a luxury the working class could not afford.

The iceman used to come once a week in his dilapidated truck, with its splintered wooden deck all black and shiny from the slithering blocks of melting ice. The boys awaited his arrival with excitement. When the opportunity arose, they sneaked slivers of ice on which to suck as he separated the blocks with a heavy steel ice pick.

The iceman would hoist the slippery glistening block onto a sack draped over his shoulder. Holding it in place with metal tongs, he hurried through the narrow hallway of the house, dripping his way across the worn linoleum floor to the white enamel Meters ice chest on the back verandah.

His father always kept a bottle of beer in the ice chest, along with the butter, meat and other perishable items, which were stored there against the fierce summer heat. Sometimes Terry would sneak a swig from that bottle, revelling in the bitter sweetness of the bubbly, forbidden brown beverage. Beer never tasted as good in adult years as those illicit mouthfuls stolen from the tall brown glass bottle!

Among Terry's few treasured and vivid memories of "life in the slums" were the rabbito and the rag and bone man.

Both drove a horse and cart. The rabbito would come once a week calling out loudly, "Rabbito." "Rabbito." The apron-clad housewives, Judy included, hurried out to select the skinned and repulsive looking carcass of a fresh rabbit. (When later recalling those times, Terry often thought that newborn babies have a remarkably similar appearance.) "Underground mutton," Henry called it disparagingly but Judy made a delicious roast dinner with this cheap source of meat. The three boys would pick the fragile white bones clean of the strange gamy tasting flesh.

The rag and bone man trundled down Marlborough Street beside the house, shouting, "Bottle O! Bottle O!" On hearing the familiar cry, Terry climbed onto the paling fence with scant regard for the easily dislodged splinters, glimpsing the rattling cart and the gaunt Grim Reaper-like figure perched high on the seat before it vanished down the hill.

For some reason, the rag and bone man always stood on the seat of his four wheeled, rubber tyred cart. Whether it was to make his voice heard, or whether he suffered from ♠ "Farmer Giles" as his father termed the embarrassing and painful complaint.

Terry was puzzled. *How this strange creature could make a living from buying beer bottles? Why did everyone refer to him as a "rag and bone" man? I've never seen anyone sell him any bones!*

Whatever the answers to these childhood mysteries, there is no doubt he was one of the earliest recyclers!

Of course, Judy and Henry never sold any bottles to him! Even though Judy didn't drink and Henry made a bottle of beer last about a week, they didn't want the neighbours to think they were alcoholics! Attitudes to drinking were very different in those days and any discarded bottles were carefully wrapped in the Sydney Morning Herald so that they wouldn't emit a tell tale clink when the battered, galvanized iron garbage bin was tossed up and emptied on the garbage truck each week by the "garbos."

Strangely, even in Terry's pre-pubescent years, he detested his life and the area where the family lived. Although he had never been anywhere outside the city, somehow he knew there was a better place to live and the concrete jungle was not for him!

Due to the strict disciplinarian upbringing and the atmosphere of fear that constantly prevailed in the home, Terry's life was hellish at the hands of his older siblings. He was at the very bottom of the family pecking order. His father dished out the whacks and created the atmosphere of pure fear while both Paul and Michael sought relief from their mistreatment by dishing out additional physical and mental abuse to their younger brother. Had there been a cat or a dog, which was impossible in the Flatley house due to their father banning pets, it would have been

---

♠ Rhyming slang for piles or hemorrhoids.

a natural transition for Terry to take his suffering out on that poor unfortunate creature. However, due to a love of animals this would have been unlikely.

The name calling, teasing, belittling comments, constant put downs and beatings at the hands of Terry's brothers took place at every opportunity when their parents were out of sight. So bad was the torment, he seriously planned how to survive if he ran away, dreaming of living on fish caught and mussels cut from the stout wharf piles at Balmain and Haberfield The rational side of his juvenile mind told him that option was not feasible. Instead, he chose to make a solemn personal vow of silence, pledging at the tender age of seven to never speak unless it was necessary. Bitter experience had taught him that being punched or hit was less likely if he kept quiet.

Although he became a solitary child with few friends, Terry managed to get into a fair bit of trouble at school. In the absence of evidence to the contrary, he readily adopted the belief system fed to him in constant reminders of his stupidity and inability to catch a ball. Indeed, the mere mention of cricket, rugby or anything that involved physical co-ordination or interaction in a team situation filled him with dread. The lengths he would go to avoid such activities were testimony to a well-developed imagination and cunning. Wagging school every sports day became normal.

Swimming and athletics were an entirely different proposition. With nobody dependent upon him to achieve victory, running races and swimming were just good fun.

During the cooler months when the swimming baths closed for the winter, school sports comprised of basketball and rugby. On sports afternoons at Leichhardt Primary, the kids all assembled in the playground after lunch and the teacher called the roll.

"Right you lot! Line up and wait for the bus." Mr Reid ordered. A beanpole figure of a man with a long stern face to match his disposition, all the boys feared Mr Reid. His favourite pastime seemed to be caning any child who incurred his displeasure. It was not difficult to end up on the receiving end of the long whippy cane, as he strutted with it locked across the small of his back by arms crooked rigidly around the weapon, which was his constant companion.

"Psst! Derek." Terry called urgently to his partner in crime. "Now! Let's go." With the teacher's back to them, Terry and Derek darted unnoticed into the nearby toilet block. Half-closing cubicle doors, they squatted on toilet seats with their legs off the floor, waiting.

A shadow in the doorway signalled the arrival of the school mafia in the guise of Mr Reid's personal prefect. Terry pictured him bending down to look under the toilet's partitions. "Nah, there's nobody in here," the boy muttered before turning on his heel eager to board the bus.

"Right, they've gone. We're off too!" Terry called to his friend as the sound of the bus's diesel engine receded in the distance.

With the little rat-faced Derek running beside him, Terry headed for the wharves of the harbour side suburbs of Haberfield, Balmain and Abbotsford, keeping to the back streets.

Each week, they explored the wharves, canals and shoreline around the upper reaches of the harbour, revelling in their freedom. They searched for crabs in the muddy little beaches and fantasised about running away from home and living on fish caught from the murky, polluted lower reaches of the Parramatta River which flowed into the world's most magnificent aquatic sanctuary. It was an exciting world for a small boy with all manner of watercraft plying the waters. The smell of seaweed and salty river mud, the excitement of hiding from all adults who would no doubt report their truancy, the chance to play and exercise the childhood mind and the delicious secret they shared, were to remain vividly in Terry's memory forever.

At the appropriate hour, Derek and Terry resignedly trudged home with leather satchels flung over skinny shoulders, bravely concealing their disappointment that the adventure had finished for another week. Amazingly, they avoided detection, keeping their secret well into adult years.

Leichhardt was a tough, working class area during Terry's childhood. With parks where kids could play safely being almost non-existent, the street or tiny backyards became battle scenes for games of 'Cowboys and Indians' or, 'Rubbish Tin Cricket'. There were few bought toys, and fertile juvenile minds improvised with what ever they could scrounge. Wondrous things eventuated from sticks, old packing cases, cotton reels and jam tins. In fact, any old junk salvaged from garbage bins, vacant lots or woodsheds was highly prized. Springy oleander boughs when stripped of their leaves quickly became an effective bow and arrow. Children had many hours of fun playing "Cowboys and Indians," or firing arrows at a variety of targets including the cheeky brown sparrows that came down to peck in the dry dust. Thankfully, the little birds were always too quick for juvenile archers who never managed to inflict a casualty.

Rubber bands and fencing wire were fashioned into "gings" or shanghais and hidden carefully from the disapproving gaze of parents. They fired various dangerous projectiles including fencing staples, nails, stones or pieces of bent wire with remarkable accuracy and occasionally frightening consequences! Some sense of responsibility usually prevailed and the majority of children never aimed at each other or where they were likely to break windows, streetlights or power pole insulators, although rumour had it that some of the 'tough' kids did.

Terry had another mate, Kenny Burton, a snowy headed, stocky boy with almost an albino appearance. Kenny lived up Marlborough Street. His house was just across the road from the Leichhardt Police Station where the boys watched the cops coming and going on shiny black Indian Motorcycles with stub nosed sidecars sporting a thin gold line pin-striping.

When the factory workers gathered noisily in the pub in Norton Street, to toss down huge glasses of frothy Millers Lager, fights would break out. There'd be one cop on the bike and another sitting in the sidecar and they'd race to deal with the fracas.

Sometimes they watched the "D's" (plainclothes officers) in shiny black Humber Snipe cars, or a uniformed constable dragging a protesting drunk into the lock up.

Everyone regarded the coppers in awe and fear. Kenny and Terry would cross the road rather than walk directly past the police station. Community policing and public relations were unknown and invariably the administration of justice came in the summary form, with a cuff around the ear or a large boot placed strategically in the miscreant's backside.

Kenny's house was next to a narrow laneway, which ran through to the next street. Behind Kenny's was a vacant two-storey house with broken windows and a small yard overgrown with weeds. For some reason the weeds grew higher in a rectangle at the centre of the yard. Kenny and Terry walked down the alley and peeked through a rusty corrugated iron and paling fence.

"Betcha it's haunted!" Kenny said delighting in scaring them both, one Friday afternoon after school.

"Yeah! There's probably bodies buried in the yard. That's why the weeds grow so high there," Terry speculated.

"Come on. Let's go and have a look inside," Kenny dared.

"You go first. The murderer's probably waiting inside to get you and cut your head off!" Terry mused, looking at the forbidding dark interior his imagination running wild at the prospect of all sorts of horrible deeds perpetrated in the grim building!

"Come on. I'll race ya to Nina's. She might have some broken biscuits!" Kenny decided, suddenly changing the subject to avoid showing his fear of the dreaded house of horrors.

Terry didn't hesitate. The anticipation of sweet pieces of broken biscuit dolled out at the local corner shop, was a much better option than having your head chopped off by an axe wielding maniac lurking somewhere inside that silent and menacing structure.

Nina Foye's tiny crowded shop on the corner of Cromwell and Marlborough Streets was directly opposite Terry's home at 14 Cromwell Street. With a mop of curly brown hair and thick rimmed, circular glasses, she presented an owl-like appearance. Huge glass lolly jars filled with jelly babies, chocolate freckles and soft jubes lined the counter. The smell of Arnott's' biscuits permeated the shop from the square metal tins stacked along the back walls. Nina sold the biscuits by weight, carefully placing the crisp sugary treats into brown paper bags. With the biscuits packed loosely in the metal boxes, breakages were inevitable but then Nina would occasionally take pity on a small hungry and calculating child, dishing out fragments of broken milk arrowroot or a sugar-coated Nice biscuits. The shop was the epitome of heaven for small hungry children.

Occasionally, Terry or Kenny managed to scrounge a few pennies by collecting and cashing-in empty soft drink bottles for their deposit. Half a penny (pronounced "Ha penny") would purchase four aniseed balls and sixpence represented a small fortune.

"I've got thruppence!' Kenny boasted proudly.

"Where did you get that!"

"That's my business!"

"I bet you stole it!"

"Did not!"

"I bet you did! I bet you've been nicking milk money again!"

"Did not. Any way don't ya want an ice block?"

"Course I do," Terry said, suddenly realising that Kenny held the bargaining power. If he were not nice to him, Terry would miss out. "What flavour are you going to get?" Terry inquired, hoping to get back into favour.

They sat on the kerb outside Nina's, sucking on their icy treats. Sticky drops of melting syrup running down grubby hands, they watched fascinated as little black ants scurried back and forth, stopping to drink the manna, which had miraculously fallen onto the concrete wasteland of their world.

"I seen some good junk on the footpath in Allen Street yesterday arvo," Kenny announced. "Must be time for another 'pick up'."

"It's saw. Not seen." Terry automatically corrected Kenny's grammar.

Judy always took great care to ensure her boys did not slip into the local idiom of poor grammatical pronunciation or use of the vernacular. Kenny said things like, "chimmley instead of chimney and "ain't," instead of is not. He dropped his aitches and often used terrible words like, "bloody" and "bugger."

Kenny didn't seem to notice Terry's attempts to educate him. "I reckon we could find some bloody beaut' wheels," he continued.

Every year, the Leichhardt Municipal Council invited residents to place unwanted household items on the kerb for collection. All manner of fascinating items would appear in heaps outside houses, representing a veritable treasure trove of old iceboxes, unwanted furniture, stoves, drums, crates, broken down lawnmowers, piles of newspapers, broken alarm clocks and anything that was of no further use. It was a time of great excitement and anticipation for small boys. Particularly prized were old perambulators, strollers or anything that yielded useable wheels.

"Yeah. Maybe we could even find some old bike wheels. Just imagine how fast they'd go!" Terry's imagination worked overtime with the exciting prospect of building a "billy" cart exclusively theirs.

"Let's go tomorrow morning and see what we can get."

"Okay. See ya after breakfast."

Henry worked as an odd job man at Forsyth's Rope Factory. Every Saturday he worked overtime. Catching the tram two blocks away in Norton Street, he'd leave the house early and wouldn't be home again until midday. Judy was more than happy for Terry to go to Kenny's where he would be out of her hair for a while.

"You be careful now and make sure you're home before your father gets back from work!" she instructed needlessly. There was no way Terry was going to arrive home after his father. If he got back from work and Terry wasn't there all clean and scrubbed, he'd get a hammer-fisted clout around the ears. Henry believed raising children was somehow not his responsibility and resented any disruption to his ritual of a quiet beer, dinner and reading old copies of "Popular Mechanics."

Paul was tinkering on the back verandah with copper wire and an old tuning condenser from a radio. He was too busy attempting to construct a crystal set to take any interest in his annoying little brother. Michael had gone to play at a mate's house but probably would have stayed home, had Terry disclosed his plans for the morning. Terry wanted the first pick of the treasures that were on offer. Besides, Michael would take over, not only the exploration and quest to construct a cart but Kenny's friendship. Terry had learnt early from bitter experience, the old adage, "two's company but three's a crowd."

Kenny was waiting at the front gate. "G'day mate!" he greeted cheerfully. "You ready to go?"

"You bet!" Terry replied enthusiastically.

As they headed down Marlborough Street, women in floral aprons, their hair in the ubiquitous curlers were throwing items out onto the kerb line. In the heat of the summer morning, their old valve type wirelesses blared from open front doors.

"I like Aero plane jelly. Aeroplane Jelly for me.
I like it for dinner, I like it for tea.
A little each day is a good recipe."

"You'll wonder where the yellow went,
When you brush your teeth with Steradent!"

Where the occupants were obviously at home, the boys continued past, confining their search for junk where there was less chance of admonishment. A boy about ten years of age rounded a corner from the opposite direction, dragging a rope attached to a billy cart laden with sundry junk. With his hair shaved into a crew cut style, which was fashionable for the era and a pair of bracers holding up baggy khaki shorts, his freckled face lit into a big grin of recognition.

"Hi ya Ken. You lookin' for some wheels?"

"G'day Blue. Yeah. Ya seen any?"

"Yeah. Ya better be quick though. Have a look down that way near the Cyclops factory," he said pointing. "There was a 'pram with four good wheels and the tyres were okay."

"Ta Blue. See ya Sport"

"Yeah, see ya tomorrow arvo. You still want to play cricket?"

"You bet. What about you Terry?"

"No. Sorry, but dad won't let us out to play on Sundays." This was true but unlike most kids, Terry didn't want to play cricket. The rock-hard leather ball stung and bruised his fingers whenever he attempted to catch it. Not wanting to be seen as a sissy.' he was quite glad to have a valid excuse for avoiding the inevitable ridicule that accompanied his ineptitude in every ball game in which he was involved.

"I forgot. You're old man's a real mean bugger!"

"No he's not. He just thinks we shouldn't go out on Sundays," Terry sprung to his father's defence, "We gotta respect other peoples' right to peace and quiet 'cos it's supposed to be the Lord 's Day of rest." This was a strange statement from Terry given the Flatley family never attended church and he was just parroting his parents justification for not following their faith more diligently. Harry and Judy both professed to be Anglicans but they categorised all church goers as hypocrites. "They tell lies, steal, run each other down all week and then profess to be Christians just because they go to church and sing hymns," Judy would grumble. "You don't need to go to church to be a Christian."

Bluey trudged off, the paraphernalia on his cart rattling and clanking and Terry wondered what his parents would say when he arrived home with a pile of other people's trash. Terry knew his parents wouldn't be too happy if he dragged a lot of stuff home and deposited it in the back yard. A few wheels and a crate to make a billy cart would probably be acceptable, or the odd old alarm clock, but nothing more.

As they neared the large brick Cyclops bicycle factory, they spotted a tattered cane perambulator lying on its side among a pile of rusty corrugated iron and some planks of hard wood.

"Whoopee!" shouted Kenny. "Give us a hand." He began dragging the iron sheets to one side cursing as the jagged rusty metal sliced a finger.

"Bloody, bugger, damn!" He swore using the full extent of his vocabulary of curse words.

"Let's have a look," Terry pulled a snotty piece of rag that he carried as a handkerchief from a pocket to bind Kenny's wounded digit.

"Piss orf! I don't want your germs!" Kenny pulled his hand away and sucked the blood, spitting it onto the weedy verge.

After the initial pain subsided, Kenny re-joined Terry in extricating their prize. They righted the pram and Terry selected a plank of wood. "This'll make a good belly board."

"Here's a crate for a seat," Kenny added, tossing his lank white hair back from his forehead.

The boys quickly dragged the old pram bearing the necessary components for a sturdy cart, to the back yard at 14 Cromwell St. With his father's shed securely padlocked as usual, preventing access to his more than ample collection of tools. Kenny ran off home, returning a short time later with a rusty claw hammer, a hand drill and a crosscut wood saw.

They bashed away at the metal base of the pram and after what seemed like hours and many blood blisters later, managed to break the welds securing the axles to the pram's sturdy frame. They attached both axles to wooden planks, hammering the nails in and bending them over each side of the axle. The rear axle they attached to the belly board with copious nails extracted from packing crates. They secured the front axle with a single bolt to the other end of the belly board and tied on a loop of sash cord enabling the contraption to be steered with either their feet or hands.

Judy brought polony and sauce sandwiches and cordial into the yard and admired their handiwork. "Don't leave that lying around where your father will trip over it," she warned, although she was clearly proud of their efforts.

After washing their filthy hands at the concrete trough in the laundry at the back of the house, Kenny and Terry stuffed the white bread into hungry mouths, eager to try out the cart on the hill outside the side gate. The sound of their delighted screams as they careened down the long sloping footpath soon brought other children from the neighbourhood. It wasn't long before other carts appeared and impromptu races organised to find the fastest cart.

There were many spills and grazed knees but it was all part of the fun! That cart held together for weeks. When the tyres wore out, they fashioned new tyres, using garden hose and wire. Nails that worked lose were replaced until there were so many holes in the wood they couldn't find another place to hammer in a nail. Eventually the wood splintered and broke. The cart eventually joined the kindling heap, with its buckled, sorry looking wheels ending their days in the garbage bin.

* * *

Life for the working-man in post-war Sydney was far from easy. The sweatshop environment of a rope factory was dusty, noisy and offered little opportunity for advancement. Wages were poor and producing rope not exactly in the classification of fulfilling a higher calling or purpose.

Henry left home before the children awoke and returned in the early evening, ill-tempered and tired. When he walked in the front door, his expectation was for dinner to be ready, the table set, his three boys scrubbed and silent and a cold beer waiting in the icebox. Failure to meet these expectations would invoke terrible consequences.

Henry never asked about his son's day and took no interest in their schooling or childhood aspirations. As head of the house, he ruled with all the compassion of a Third World Dictator.

One afternoon after school, Terry went to play at Derek's house about a mile from Cromwell Street in the next suburb. Derek had a sister, Eileen, a mousy little girl who wore glasses. Her long straight brown hair was tied in bunches either side of her head. Although Eileen was quite plain, her smile lit up Terry's young life. She was his first girlfriend, although there was no way he would have acknowledged her in the playground or in front of his mates. Terry's admiration had to remain secret, even from Derek. Publicly he did not even dare glance in Eileen's direction and would even cross to the other side of the street if he saw her in public in case anyone noticed his childhood infatuation. Having a girlfriend was bad enough, but a girlfriend who wore glasses? The teasing would have been unrelenting.

Terry had been unable to work out how he could conduct a clandestine childhood love affair without speaking to Eileen. Her willingness to be friendly was all too obvious and a source of tremendous embarrassment for him. That the relationship was doomed under the imposition of such impossible restrictions was not immediately apparent to his nine-year-old brain. However, he was helpless. Complete and blind infatuation decreed he go to Derek's house to be near his sweetheart and cast furtive admiring glances in her general direction.

Unlike the Flatley family, Derek did not live in a rental house. Derek's father was in the process of renovating their old brick semi-detached bungalow. In some rooms, the calcimine walls had been stripped back to expose the bare bricks. Their furniture was Spartan and basic but the home clean and tidy. Most surprising to Terry was the fact that Derek's dad actually liked children. He was a ruddy faced, plump man who often whistled and sang about the house. Terry was unable to understand such freakish behaviour as he thought all men were supposed to be bad-tempered and cold-hearted characters like his father.

Eileen was learning to play the piano. Terry had never seen a piano before. The instrument took pride of place in the lounge room, its ivory keys contrastingly beautiful against the gleaming black lacquered cabinet. No-one seemed to mind when he depressed the keys experimentally. The fascinating sound emitted by each key was sheer delight and his childhood imagination soon took over. While Derek and Eileen watched, he ran his fingers over the keyboard in total absorption, instantly becoming a great concert pianist, at least in his own mind.

Whether others appreciated Terry's musical efforts is open to conjecture. It is more probable that he created such an unbearable cacophony that after half an hour or so, Derek's mother sought respite.

"Terry, hadn't you better be on your way home? It's nearly six o'clock!"

Terry fell to Earth from his musical heaven. *Oh no, dad will be home!*

Stricken with terror he ran home without stopping. Breathlessly, he burst into the house, desperately hoping for permission to plead his case. Henry was sitting at the table with Judy in her usual place on his right. Paul and Michael were silently eating the dinner of mutton chops, mash potatoes, peas and gravy. Pale faces freshly washed and hair combed, they were striving with some degree of success for invisibility, desperately praying that they would not be included in the inexorable wrath that must follow Terry's absence. A palpable sense of foreboding filled the dingy room.

"I'm sssory." Terry stuttered as he entered. "I ...," He got no further. His father flew from his seat, the wooden chair tumbling, clattering backwards on the worn linoleum floor. With his lined face black with rage, a rumbling roar seemed to rise from his very boots. Henry's heavy backward blow from an iron-hard fist crashed into the side of Terry's head. The force of the impact knocked the slight boy across the room. Hitting the dining room wall, he fell to the floor stunned.

"Where have you been?" The tone of the voice left him in no doubt that it was pointless trying to explain. Nevertheless, failure to respond would invoke further retribution.

"I am sorry," he stammered lamely. "I forgot the time."

"Go to bed." With the release of his volcanic rage, Henry was suddenly and strangely calm.

Tears burnt Terry's cheeks. His head throbbed but the shame was far worse than any physical pain. He retreated to the laundry where he washed his hands and face with the cake of yellow Sunlight soap on the side of the concrete wash trough. Creeping quietly past the dining table, he entered the bedroom he shared with Paul and Michael. After pulling on striped flannelette pyjamas, Terry dropped onto lumpy kapok mattress and buried his face in the pillow. Although he should be hungry, food was the furthest thing from his mind.

Although this was certainly not the first or last time Terry suffered from his father's explosive temper, he was never late again.

Henry's ambition and detestation of his lot eventually drove him to seek an alternative to the meagre wages offered by Forsyth's Rope Company. Participation in the dinner table conversations was taboo. However, like permanently attuned electronic tracking stations, juvenile ears tuned in, hoping to catch any communication from the distant galaxies of the adult mind. The three boys quickly deduced that change was in the air.

"It look's like we can get it for a fair rent, Judy," Henry announced after sitting down at the table one evening.

What 'IT' was Terry had no idea but curiosity was instantly aroused. *Were they going to move house from the cramped and dark abode he had always known as home?* There seemed to be an excitement and air of anticipation about their father that they hadn't previously experienced. Perhaps they were at last going to get away from the flaking paint, damp, stained walls and cracked linoleum floors to something better.

"It could be the chance of a life time, Henry!" Judy stated encouragingly.

"It will mean tightening the belt for a while." Henry announced.

How they could "tighten their belt", any more was beyond Terry's comprehension. *Are we going to go hungry, wear clothing made from old flour bags drink from jam tins and eat stale bread and dripping as dad always threatened?*

"We'll manage. The kids will help at home won't you?" Judy turned to smile benevolently upon the three boys, oblivious as to their lack of involvement in the family plans.

Three heads nodded in unison. *How could they dissent?* In any case, change was always exciting even if it meant the threat of starvation.

"We'll have to buy a truck," Henry added another condition to the Great Plan.

"It will work out. I'm sure of it. There aren't any shops close by and people are sick of the rubbish that's sold down Parramatta Road."

At last! Some inkling of what's afoot. Terry thought.

"It's close to home. I'll go to the markets early in the morning and get the best produce and you can open the shop until I get back. We'll start a fruit and vegetable round to get extra customers. We'll do that on the quiet days when we can shut the shop without losing trade." It seemed that their father had already made up his mind.

"Paul can take charge until we get home. Michael and Terry will get the dinner ready and set the table!" Their mother volunteered her son's involvement excitedly.

Terry's heart sank at the prospect of his older brother having any more control over him. He rubbed his thin arms in anticipation of the extra bruises that surely must follow this careless delegation of increased power.

In the spirit of true enthusiastic entrepreneurs, Judy and Henry launched the greengrocery business! Henry bought a brand new Dodge truck, its' rear tray covered by a canopy with canvas side curtains. He arrived home one evening shortly after its acquisition, grinning like a child with a new toy.

"Come on get in. I'll take you for a ride!" Their father's unexpected generosity was totally out of character. Paul, Michael and Terry eagerly clambered up into the high cabin. The smell of new upholstery and the throb of the powerful engine under the gleaming, green bonnet held Terry in awe as he struggled to peer over the dashboard.

Where did they get the money to buy this? Terry puzzled. The family seemed to struggle to find the money for rent each week. Judy appeared to have only a couple of dresses. "The Sydney Morning Herald" when torn into squares served as toilet paper and the boys regularly ate dripping on toast for breakfast. Torn up sheets were used for handkerchiefs and although they never went hungry, luxuries such as fruit and milk were strictly rationed. Terry knew nothing about the nefarious, financial minefield of hire-purchase agreements.

Unfortunately, Judy and Henry's lack of entrepreneurial and business skills failed to match their imagination, enthusiasm and hard work and their entrance into the world of commerce was doomed from the start. Henry who had previously left home before dawn now left home at 2.00 am, driving to the Sydney Markets where he bid for fruit and vegetables to sell in their tiny, leased back-street shop. They also plied the streets of the inner western suburbs in the Dodge truck, slowly building a mobile base of customers to supplement their reliance on the sporadic passing trade. Each night after they shut the shop, they would arrive home to eat whatever the boys had learnt to cook. After dinner, their mother would send the boys to bed while Henry spread the day's takings on the kitchen table for counting and calculation of the meagre profits.

The hard work and long hours took their toll. They had seriously underestimated the problems associated with on-selling extremely perishable produce and the resultant financial rewards and anticipated success failed to materialise. One evening, the sound of raised voices drowned the tinny clink and rattle of coins on the wooden table.

"Get him out here!"

"No Henry. You don't know it's him. It might have been lost!"

"He's stolen it, I tell you!"

The bedroom door burst open. Seized by rough hands and dragged bewildered and frightened into the kitchen, Terry stood trembling in his pyjamas. Piles of notes bound by elastic bands and coins wrapped in brown paper bundles covered the table. Henry proceeded to tear the sheets from his bed, overturning the mattress and dragging the pillow from its' thin cotton cover.

"Where is it?" His father demanded. "We're ten quid short. What have you done with it?"

What is he talking about? The injustice of being wrongly accused left the small boy open mouthed and bewildered. *How could he think I would steal ten pounds? That was a fortune. What would I do with so much money? I would never do such a thing!* Terry cried silently.

God knew he was no angel and he got into his share of mischief but stealing mum and dad's hard-earned money was unthinkable.

"I told you he didn't do it!" Judy offered in Terry's defence.

His father swung his right arm. The sound of the open-handed slap to the side of his mother's head rang off the walls. Instantly regretting his display of rage toward his long-suffering spouse, Henry turned to his youngest son. "Get back to bed!"

Terry slinked back into the bedroom and closed the door. He had never seen his father strike his mother before and that his father could have such a low opinion of his son's honesty shocked him more than he could imagine.

Whether the financial impost was too great or whether repossession was imminent, Terry never discovered; but the new truck disappeared within days. An old Chevrolet milk truck appeared in its place. The previous owner had removed the doors to facilitate ease of access. In place of the doors were canvas flaps to protect against inclement weather.

Henry constructed a makeshift canopy over the flat deck from wood and corrugated iron. When it became necessary to transport the family as an entity, Paul sat on one side, Michael the other and as befitting his inferior status, they assigned Terry to the middle where he was unable to escape prodding elbows.

Shortly after the arrival of the milk truck, Henry announced that the family was going into share farming. Henry kept the old truck. They loaded their few pathetic possessions into the back for the move to Castle Hill, which was at that time, a market gardening area on the outskirts of Sydney.

Henry and Judy had entered into a verbal agreement to share the profits from growing carnations on a two and a half acre property. The owners occupied one of two houses and assigned the Flatley family to the second dwelling, a tiny two-bedroom cottage constructed from asbestos cement sheeting. By mercilessly culling their few sticks of furniture, they squeezed into the poky rooms. Conversion of Paul and Michael's beds into bunks and the use of apple boxes for dressing tables completed the process.

Henry continued to operate the fruit and vegetable round on a part-time basis providing a small income. By planting a disused patch of land with peas, beans, carrots, parsnips, potatoes, and silver beet, they subsisted while awaiting harvest of the carnations.

The entire family laboured on the small farmlet, drawn on by the promise of future wealth. They hand weeded and spent countless hours pinching the centres out of plants to maximise the blooms. Backs ached from the toil but because Henry seemed happy for the moment, the family relaxed. At times, he even smiled and joked with them. Such good fortune was incredible!

The necessity for hard work left no time for friends or play. The walk to and from school was approximately a mile (or one and a half kilometres in the language of today.) Enrolment at the Castle Hill Primary School brought Terry instantly to the attention of the reigning playground bullies as he strove to establish a place in the educational jungle of a new school.

"Hey you! Curly top with the high duds. Come over here!" The reference to 'high duds' referred to Terry's hand-me-down, oversize, grey school shorts, held up by a pair of bracers which pulled the waistband up beneath his armpits. With his blotchy, freckled pudding face challenging and hands on hips, the juvenile thug taunted the nervous and defenceless new arrival.

It was Terry's first day and he knew instinctively that this was an opportunity for the older boy to demonstrate a position of superiority and dominance. The group of boys gathered behind the fat thug left him in no doubt that this kid was going to be trouble.

"What do you want?" Terry looked around for some sign of support. There was none. Mysteriously, there was also no sign of the teacher on playground duty.

"You! That's what I want. I'm going to f... you!" Unaccustomed to such crudity Terry recoiled in shock.

The bully strode toward him closely followed by his jeering henchmen. Terry turned and ran, not knowing where he was going but in no doubt this fat, ugly creature did not simply want to play. A hubbub of shrill pre-pubescent voices increased in intensity as the group spread out to cut off his escape. He had only covered a few short paces before a pair of strong arms wrapped around his legs in a well-executed rugby tackle. He fell to the asphalt. As he struggled to rise, fists rained to his head and back, knocking him down. The weight of bodies held him fast.

With his face pressed into the hot dirty bitumen, Terry felt the obese lout kneeling between his legs. There was no mistaking the hot prodding of the youth's erect organ against his buttocks. Hands ripped at the waistband of his shorts as his attacker frenziedly tried to pull down his pants for the ultimate humiliation.

Suddenly the weight of bodies lifted as he screamed piercingly in an attempt to attract attention. Perhaps it was the shock of being party to a brutal attempt at homosexual rape or perhaps the co-offenders were frightened of the possible consequences; what ever it was, Terry was not going to waste time on speculation. Rolling onto his back, he punched and kicked wildly and blindly. He felt a foot make contact with soft flesh and heard the sharp intake of breath as his tormentor pulled back clutching his lower abdomen. Leaping to his feet Terry ran toward the shelter of a classroom. The group scattered as the school bell rang a blessed reprieve.

Being older, Paul and Michael travelled by bus to respective High Schools, not that Terry was about to share his plight with them. He did not complain to his mother who had her own problems, or to the teachers, who seemed blind to the unspeakable acts perpetrated daily in that playground. In any case, he was too ashamed and did not know how to articulate what took place.

Terry was unable to recall the names of the children involved or their leader. As with all bullies, the fat boy was a coward and acted in consort with a faceless group of brats. When reflecting later on what transpired, Terry could not help but wonder whether these individuals grew to become rapists, child molesters and thugs. For his part, he rapidly developed a finely tuned instinct for self- preservation, ensuring he did not leave himself vulnerable in future.

With the constant pampering and attention, the carnations grew bushy. The boys became excited as the time for harvest drew near. At last, they would get new bicycles their parents had promised when the money came in. Terry toiled eagerly alongside Paul and Michael in the long rows of spiky grey foliage. The opportunities to taunt and tease were minimised by omnipresent parents ensuring life was finally bearable.

With no explanation or warning, Henry announced one day that they were leaving.

How can we leave? We were going to be rich. The carnations are ready to flower and all our hard work has been for nothing! The incredulous thoughts remained unspoken. It wasn't Terry's place to question the wisdom of his father. His father must have had a good reason for such a drastic and sudden decision.

"We're going to live on a sheep station. Dad's going to become a mechanic and look after all the tractors and vehicles!" Judy announced.

They quickly forgot their disappointment at the prospective loss of shiny new bicycles and a prosperous future, as they eagerly awaited the next new adventure. Terry's only hope was that his father would continue to be more cheerful and not revert to the former state of ill -tempered violence.

CHAPTER TWO
A NOMADIC EXISTENCE

At 3.00 am on an autumnal morning, the three boys squashed into the back of the old Chevy between tea chests, cardboard cartons and the family's paltry furniture collection, which almost completely filled the rear tray of the ancient truck.

When Henry embarked on a journey, he liked to start early and refused to stop unless it was to refuel or to attend to some mechanical emergency. With the canvas side curtains rolled down and fastened, Judy and Henry had some protection against the early morning chill. Paul, Michael and Terry huddled under the corrugated iron canopy as the rushing wind eddied around the rear of the cabin. Terry tried to sleep and managed to doze fitfully beneath a threadbare blanket pulled around his shoulders.

He awoke nauseous, with the first rays of the morning sun warming his cheek. The brown rolling countryside spread either side as they headed south through the Goulburn district and dirty grey sheep dotted the landscape. This was Terry's first sight of open country. He instantly felt a strange new sense of freedom and belonging. Despite his upbringing in a treeless environment of concrete and asphalt, somehow he had always known that a better life waited outside the fumes and bustle of the metropolis.

The family continued southward through Canberra, marvelling at the symmetrical layout of the streets, the green lawns and neatness of Australia's capital city. Lake Burley Griffin sparkled in the sunlight. Weeping willows dangled long green stems into the placid waters and forests of blue gum trees blanketed the surrounding hills. After the crowded dirty Sydney streets, it was the most beautiful sight any of the boys had ever beheld.

Stopping briefly in the main street of Queanbeyan, Judy went shopping for essential supplies.

"Better make sure you've got everything you need to last a month! We can't just go running to the corner shop from now on," Henry instructed.

Judy explained to the boys, "We'll be living abut thirty miles from town and Henry will only get one day off a month."

It's thirty miles from town! Terry could not believe they could be so far away from houses and shops.

While Henry disappeared through a doorway under the wide verandah of the local pub, Judy went shopping with Paul and Michael. Terry remained on the back of the truck, fascinated by the sight of a real Australian country town. It reminded him of something from one of his comics about the Wild West, as farmers and graziers from the surrounding district congregated to take advantage of Saturday morning shopping. Wide brim hats, open neck shirts and burly sunburnt arms seemed to be the order of the day. Sheep dogs ran frantically to and fro on the back of trucks and utility vehicles parked either side of the wide roadway, barking their canine challenges to all and sundry. A cattle truck rumbled past, brown cows shuffling and pushing, the smell of dung and urine pervaded the air. It was all so new and strange.

Judy returned after a while, followed by Terry's two older siblings. They heaved on board, brown paper bags of groceries, a sack of flour and other essentials. Henry also appeared with a faint odour of beer wafting past as he climbed behind the steering wheel. "Willow Flats, here we come!" he announced, a wide and very rare grin displaying the whiteness of his false teeth.

The macadam road south from the town changed quickly to a rutted, dusty track. A plume of reddish yellow filth rose up from the wheels, enveloping the back of the truck. Terry's teeth seemed in danger of rattling loose from his gums as he shifted position to ease the jarring through his spine. It seemed as if every nut and bolt in the antediluvian vehicle would be shaken out. He peered ahead through the rear window of the truck. Rocks jutted through the hard surface of the road and Henry fought the steering wheel as he attempted to steer a path through the worst of the corrugated gravel. Their speed slowed considerably as they caught up with the dust of an unseen vehicle travelling ahead. It was impossible to see but a few feet in front of the blunt nose of the old Chev. A film of dust soon caked their faces and covered everything with a talcum like dust.

After an hour of torture, they passed a group of tall pine trees on the left side of the track. Old milk cans and forty-four gallon drums mounted on posts stood sentry at the roadside, silently announcing their arrival at Willow Flats Station.

Henry slowed the truck and swung off the road, stopping in front of a wide wooden gate barring access to a narrow, graded dirt road. Terry could see a number of cottages surrounded by fruit trees and neat vegetable gardens on one side. Post and rail fences marked cattle yards and a milking shed atop a low rise.

"Come on, Dopey! Open the bloody gate." Henry commanded.

Paul responded to the derogatory nickname. Scrambling to stretch his muscles still aching and stiff from the long trip, he dropped his lanky frame over the side of the truck. He released the rusty brown chain securing the heavy gate and swung it in a wide arc to permit their entry.

They went by two more cottages on the right and off to the left glimpsed a two-storey stone house with a steeply sloping roof. "Wow! That looks pretty flash," Terry remarked.

Henry stopped the truck near a long stone building with whitewashed walls and the ubiquitous red iron roof. Terry guessed correctly that these had once been used to stable horses. Through the trees and neatly trimmed hedges, he was able to make out an old colonial style residence of immense proportions. More white washed walls, wide verandahs, lush gardens and smooth lawns, spoke of wealth and serenity. Sulphur-crested cockatoos squawking overhead from towering pines were a rude interruption to the otherwise peaceful scene.

Henry and Judy walked to the homestead. The murmuring of voices floated back to the truck for a while before they returned. Henry gestured across the river flat toward the red roof of a substantial whitewashed stone dwelling surrounded by a high netting fence.

"That's ours," he stated simply.

The boys turned in unison to look. *A real house with room for a garden!* Terry thought incredulously, his fatigue vanishing with the realisation they would have their very own house.

Their assigned accommodation was a solid, one hundred year old, stone building; its immense walls built by convict labour in the days when bullock drays plied the road to the mining town of Captain's Flat. There were two huge rooms, one boasting a large wood-fired baker's oven. A gigantic fireplace dominated one end of the second room. Four doors of thick white painted planks, each concealing a bedroom, lined the southern wall. Waiting expectantly in a recess at one end of the big farm kitchen, a green and white Metter's fuel stove seemed to demand the chance to provide a cosy glow.

"Mrs Brunner told us that this used to be an inn for travellers in the old days. Horse drawn carriages would have to stop on their way to Braidwood and Bungendore with prisoners who were being transported. The long stone building that is now used as the Groom's quarters, provided overnight accommodation for convicts. You can still see the bolts in the walls where they were shackled to stop them escaping," Judy's excitement created an atmosphere of intrigue.

"Willow Flats is owned by the Falcon family. Mrs Brunner is the Manageress who is in charge until young Mr Falcon is old enough to take over running the property," Judy continued. "You'll have to mind your P's and Q's. By the way, the homestead is out of bounds!"

Terry's jaw dropped as he imagined a matriarchal figure with servants bowing and curtseying as she made her appearance among the minions who ran her Empire. When he eventually sighted the lady in question, she did in deed carry with her a haughty air and manner, leaving others in no doubt as to their inferior status.

Terry was soon to learn that eighteen thousand acres required a complex team to ensure successful management. In order to maintain Mrs Brunner's demanding lifestyle, the homestead employed the services of a cook, housemaid, gardener, groom and full-time bookkeeper.

The actual operation of the farm was in the hands of Dan Hart, the overseer. Beneath him in the rigid hierarchical class-conscious society, were various personnel such as, a tractor driver, stockman, jackeroo, carpenter, and rabbito and of course Henry, the station mechanic.

Each weekday, Mrs Hart would drive a Volkswagen kombi bus taking the Station children to schools in Captain's Flat.

Captain's Flat, or 'The Flat' as it was known, was a mining town of some two thousand people who owed their existence to the underground mining of copper, silver, lead zinc and gold. Situated at the headwaters of the Molonglo River, the fledgling village had derived its' name from 'Captain,' the leader of a bullock team that once grazed upon the river flat. The town boasted a public school and a private school for children from

Catholic families. There was considerable animosity between the Catholic children and those who attended the state run public school. State school children sang, "Catholic kids stink like pigs!" to taunt their primly dressed private school counterparts.

At fifteen, Paul had reached the legal minimum age for employment. Henry, in his eagerness to reduce the family's financial burden, arranged employment for Paul as the homestead's gardener.

Michael, two years Paul's junior, was a very intelligent boy who found schoolwork easy. Michael never had to study and as a natural high achiever, topped his grades at the Captain's Flat public school. Perpetually in the academic shadow of his brothers who revelled in every opportunity to decry his stupidity, Terry struggled, yet to become aware that his only impediment to progress was his poor self-image.

Autocratic, cane-wielding males dominated teaching during the nineteen fifties. Classes were large with in excess of forty students. Learning was by rote and individual tuition non-existent. Woe betide any child with special needs, whatever the reason! Although he struggled hard, a huge inferiority complex coupled with long absences due to sickness, ensured Terry dropped behind his peers. For some reason ill-health seemed to dog the youngest Flatley who contracted nearly every childhood malady, along with such other life threatening diseases as, scarlet fever, peritonitis and I.B.S.[3]

The mining community threw up all manner of ill-bred, hard-bitten individuals who spawned children of similar ilk. Once again, school bullies dominated. The only difference this time was Michael also became the focus of attention. For once, Terry and he were by the necessity for self-preservation, united in their stand.

The educational system also hid its own share of bullies and child abusers, masquerading as teachers. Each day children assembled in the playground for marching classes. Colonel Bogey and similar themes blared from the loudspeaker system.

"Left, right, left, left. Left, right left." Striding alongside, ever vigilant for any individual whose lack of co-ordination made him out of step, one particular member of the school's male Gestapo

---

[3] Irritable Bowel Syndrome

delighted in administering liberal doses of corporal punishment. Not unexpectedly, Terry was one of those who became the subject of a well-placed boot to his rear-end on more than one occasion.

It remains open to conjecture whether the system endeavoured to churn out soldiers or productive members of society. Whatever its aims and objectives, it certainly bred hatred and resentment against those who abused a position of authority!

Once a year Captain's Flat school mustered its pupils for inter-school sports. A single-track railway line serviced "The Flat" providing a means by which ore could be moved on a daily basis from the mine. The line ran through to the community of Bungendore providing the obvious means to transport children to the sports day. On the big day, a steam locomotive pulled ancient wooden carriages packed with rowdy children the forty miles between the two communities. For some obscure reason there was little adult supervision and near anarchy prevailed on board the train.

Michael and Terry found themselves together in a compartment with the inevitable school bully and his usual pack of juvenile henchmen. With the compartment having no interconnecting door with the other carriages, there was no escape, other than to jump from the moving carriage.

Being the school dullard, the lout who on this occasion forced his unwelcome attention on fellow travellers, was some years older and of superior size and strength. He had no doubt engineered events to place him in a compartment occupied by smaller, vulnerable boys.

The train had only just gathered speed when the junior sexual deviant's predilection for homosexual acts became apparent. Encouraged by his co-conspirators, several boys bared their genitals rather than face a severe beating for non-compliance with group depravity. Rampant groping and fondling among the group ensued. Knowing they could not avoid similar attention, Michael and Terry rushed into the tiny toilet cubicle. Slamming the door, they slid the flimsy bolt home.

There was an immediate pounding and immense pressure against the plywood partition. Aware that the lock would not resist such force, they placed their backs against the door. With legs and feet braced against the toilet bowl, the two frightened boys resisted a howling onslaught of booted feet and angry fists until one hour later, the train reached its destination and provided their freedom.

If they thought that was the last of it, they were sadly mistaken.

The luxury of flushing toilets had not yet reached "The Flat," with the boy's latrine consisting of a flat roofed shed, located at the far end of the playground. The choice of location was no accident. The ammoniac stench ensured a blind man could find the convenience without difficulty.

A black, tar-coated drum placed under one end of a galvanized metal trough served to hold the stinking contents of a make shift urinal. Similar drums with wooden seats occupied a number of tiny cubicles. Invariably, the drums overflowed. When made aware of the unhygienic predicament, teaching staff chose unfortunate boys to replace the full drums with empties as punishment for minor misdemeanours. The mess resulting from this process was unpleasant, unhygienic and unavoidable.

One day, Terry stumbled into the cubicle as the lout from the train was in the process of replacing the brimming pisspot. Avoiding his gaze and holding his breath against the acrid, urine fumes, Terry entered a cubicle and unbuttoned his shorts. He sensed a presence behind him and before he could turn, a clenched fist slammed into the area of his left kidney. His knees buckled and he dropped to the filthy concrete floor. Blowflies rose from the filthy mess in the drum, a few inches from his nose. Strong hands pulled at his hair, forcing his head backward. A stabbing pain shooting through his back rendered him speechless.

"I've got a job for you." The youths' face hovered within inches of his.

The weight of the brimming urinal drum was beyond Terry's strength. As the brute stood glaring, the contents slopped over Terry's shoes as he dragged the drum to one side. Fearing far worse consequences for his resistance to the youth's advances on the train, Terry averted his gaze. No help was forthcoming, as any boy who entered the shed immediately fled at the sight confronting them.

"Put a clean drum under there. Then mop the floor with your shirt."

Eyes smarting and the bile rising in his throat, Terry meekly complied with the first part of the demand. With the older boy's attention momentarily diverted, Terry seized the opportunity he needed to dart beneath flailing arms and escape to the fresher air of the playground and safety. For the next few days, he carefully avoided the redheaded thug whom the whole school feared.

One morning as Terry walked from the little school bus to the playground, his friend Michael Johnson met him. The stocky, dark haired boy could barely contain his excitement, hopping from one foot to the other. 'Hey Terry. Have you heard the news?"

"No Mick, What's up?"

"Big Bluey Proctor's in gaol."

"What?"

"Yeah. He stole a car last night and broke into some shops. The cops caught him and carted him off. I reckon that's the last we'll see of him."

"Jees, that's the best news I've heard for a long time. Maybe he'll get a taste of his own medicine in the home for naughty boys."

With the redheaded thug's departure, the entire school seemed to breathe easier. No longer would small boys suffer at the callous hands of the young thug. Even the teachers appeared more relaxed, not having to worry about how they were going to control his antics.

Station life was less dramatic than Terry's school life. In the tranquil surroundings of the closely-knit Willow Flats community, the family quickly settled into a comfortable routine. Judy worked at the homestead, helping with the cleaning. With wood chopping and various other chores assigned to the two younger children, Michael and Terry soon boasted a productive vegetable garden. The silty black river loam yielded easily to the spade and responded well to an infinite supply of manure.

The old house proved difficult to heat. With eighteen-inch thick stone walls, it could have been an excellent wine cellar. However, it was still a palace compared with 14 Cromwell Street. After some trial and error, Judy mastered the old fuel stove, turning out an abundance of scones, cakes pies and hearty roast dinners. Although the stove warmed the kitchen, they could never chase out the chill from the remainder of the house. Once or twice, they attempted to get a fire roaring in the sitting room's enormous fireplace. Large enough to walk in standing up, the immense cavern like hole gobbled up entire tree trunks, sending the majority of the heat up the chimney. They gave up trying, shutting the door on that room, instead choosing to shiver under thin and tattered blankets in bedrooms, which being situated on the southern side of the house, never felt the warmth of the sun's rays.

Terry made friends with the children of other station employees. Together they carved tunnels in the firm sandy banks of the Molonglo, built rafts and rode the bucking calves in the cattle pens. They rounded up sheep to be killed for the station's meat supply and explored the hills and upper reaches of the timeless river, filling leisure hours with unprecedented healthy fun and excitement.

For the abused and sad little boy from Sydney's slums, Willow Flats life represented a vitally important time of catharsis.

The Molonglo Valley was rich in mineral deposits and the evidence of earlier mining activity abounded. On one particular expedition to the upper reaches of the river, Dennis Hart, the son of the overseer and Terry discovered a disused gold battery rusting away on the riverbank. The boy's own excavations sometimes produced mineral samples. Alas, early prospectors had long since scoured the Molonglo bare and their efforts failed to produce any trace of gold, let alone a prized gold nugget.

Until the arrival of white men, the Molonglo had been a placid, meandering stream, its gin-clear waters sparkling, as it wound through timeless eucalypt forests and giant ghost gums. Abundant native fish and bird life provided a veritable Garden of Eden for aboriginal peoples. However, European settlers quickly recognised the areas' potential. Cracking whips echoed through the valley as bullock teams dragged mammoth hardwood logs to provide timber for construction and housing. Grubby white tents appeared like strange mushrooms, as optimistic miners sought fortunes from the rich mineral deposits of the gentle river lands. In the quest for wealth, white men denuded the deep soils of the river flats to provide grazing land for sheep and cattle. In a desire to replicate England, gums gave way to graceful exotic willows, tickling the languid surface with their long green fronds.

With the discovery of valuable minerals, optimistic prospectors flooded the area. While a few lucky souls found wealth, many starved. Others managed to eke an existence from deposits of alluvial gold. The river formed the very life-blood of the district. Unfortunately, as is often the case, the most valuable asset became victim of man's greed and lack of foresight.

As with the deflowering of a beautiful virgin, the country's beauty remained but its innocence had been lost forever.

Australia is the land of extremes. Ignorance of this fact and failure to work with nature and not against it, resulted in a disaster during the winter of 1956! Torrential rains created a myriad of tiny rivulets pouring unchecked down the deforested hills, into the headwaters of the Molonglo. With the erosion of scarce topsoils, water levels rose until the river's banks brimmed with a coffee coloured tide of churning mud.

A wall of clay constructed across the river valley stored vast tailing deposits from the Captain's Flat Mine. Among these deposits were heavy metals, arsenic, mercury, cadmium and other toxic substances from the mining process. With the pressure of water against the barrier becoming too great, the ooze began to push through the yellow clay in small cascading trickles. These rapidly grew in size and strength until the wall suddenly yielded to the force of nature. Like the contents of a giant saucepan of porridge upended into the headwaters of the Molonglo, thousands of tons of filthy poisonous sludge burst free, tumbling into the ravine.

The impending tragedy was unstoppable. All along the river flats from Captains Flat to Queanbeyan, the lush soils were contaminated and rendered useless. As the waters receded, everything died, including the grass, the trees and all fish life. The blue flash of Kingfishers diving into the languid pools became only a memory, along with the other water birds and native animals dependent upon the river for their survival.

Without the roots of tussocks and grasses, subsequent floods carried away the top soils, laying waste to vast areas of valuable grazing land. The magnificent river became an open sewer and its river flats a desert monument to man's greed.

It was to be more than forty years before nature healed the running sore.

"Don't swim in the river. You'll get sick!" Judy often warned, alluding to the invisible but potentially lethal heavy metal contamination.

Her pleas were in vain. How could any adventurous eleven-year-old boy resist the delight of diving naked into quiet, crystal-clear pools on a warm summer day? The yellow mud scraped from the river bottom was fun to plaster over tender white skin or throw in mock battles. They were unable to smell or see anything in the water that could harm them. In their minds, it was just grown-ups trying to spoil their fun.

Despite the barren river flats and rotting willows struggling for survival along its banks, Terry developed a lasting affinity and love affair with the Molonglo Valley. With warm summers, plentiful food and a father who for the first time in Terry's young life seemed to have lost his rage, life was good. The family even travelled together on the Station tractor, which they occasionally borrowed to cart firewood. This otherwise tiresome chore became a fun-filled picnic into the picturesque hills surrounding the valley.

Yes, life was worth living at last; at least for the moment.

Once a month they would all board the old Chev truck for the journey into Queanbeyan to replenish the larder. On these shopping expeditions, the boys received a few precious shillings pocket money to spend as they pleased. It was also a chance for Henry to grab a well-earned beer while his wife shopped.

"Steve, is coming with us tomorrow," Henry announced, poking at the glowing embers in the old wood stove.

Judy looked surprised. It was uncharacteristic of Henry to offer assistance or favours. He was normally a solitary man who did not make friends easily. He was often quick to criticise all and sundry and very few could meet with his approval.

"That's nice dear," she replied, busying herself with the shopping list. She was nobody's fool. If Steve was getting a ride, her husband obviously had a reason. It had been weeks since Henry had enjoyed his customary evening glass of ale. She guessed that having Steve along would provide him with an excuse to disappear into the pub while she shopped.

Saturday dawned clear and sunny. After an early breakfast, the family piled into the ancient truck. Despite sitting idle under the crudely constructed shelter Henry had made for it next to the rainwater tank, the Chevy's engine fired immediately.

"Good girl Betsy!" Judy patted the dashboard fondly.

The engine growled in response. Henry pushed the gear stick forward and released the clutch. The truck rumbled slowly along the rutted track to the main road. It seemed to Terry that the old jalopy was almost eager to be free after being inactive for nearly a month.

Thirty miles of dust, ruts and bumps passed uneventfully beneath the wheels of the faithful vehicle. As was their habit, they parked in Queanbeyan's main street a short distance from Henry's chosen watering hole, the Queanbeyan Hotel. As Judy expected, Henry and Steve lost no time in heading to the public bar from which emanated a rumble of masculine voices.

"Come on boys. There's lots to do," their mother commanded wishing Henry would for once help with children. Trailing along behind her they obediently pushed through the bustling throngs at the local supermarket, casting wide-eyed glances at the delightful array of treats on offer.

"I think that's everything!" Judy eventually announced, ticking off the last item on her shopping list. They made their way back to the vehicle, struggling under the weight of a month's provisions. Henry and Steve were nowhere in sight.

"Hop in the back. Your father will be along soon." The three boys climbed under the crude canopy and sat down to happily munch on lollies purchased with their hard-earned pocket money.

Nearly thirty minutes elapsed before the two men returned. Henry seemed to be having some trouble with his legs and an uncustomary grin split his normally stern countenance.

"Have you got all the tucker Judy?"

"Are you alright to drive?" Judy ignored his question huffily.

"Get off me back, Haversack." Henry joked. "I'm fine!"

Even to the three boys it was evident that Henry's behaviour was unusual. The unmistakable odour of beer wafted from the cabin as the two men climbed aboard. The truck lurched forward and Henry lost no time in pointing its nose in the direction of the road to Willow Flats.

As they rattled out of town and the dust plume rose behind the vehicle, Terry glanced through the window into the cabin of the truck. Judy was sitting in the middle and her head obscured any chance of sighting the speedometer. However, it was obvious from the engine's whine and the swaying of the chassis that their speed was considerably greater than normal.

Must be okay. Dad's a good driver, he reminded himself silently and settled down to suck on a red and white humbug.

In the cabin, above the noise from the engine, the thump of tyres on the bone jarring potholes and corrugations, Judy called to her husband. "Slow down Henry. We're going too fast!"

"It's okay Luv. I know the road like the back of my hand." Henry depressed the accelerator a little more as if to emphasize his point. The noise from engine increased to an urgent roar.

"There's a track winding back to an old fashioned shack,
Along the road to Gundagai.
Where the blue gums are growing and the Murrumbidgee's flowin'
Beneath that starry sky."

Judy sang to hide her fear hoping her inebriated spouse would see some common sense.

They negotiated a long rise with a blind crest and plunged down the steep slope into a deep gully at the bottom of which, the road curved sharply to the right.

"Where my daddy and mummy are waiting for me,
Where the pals of my childhood once more I will.......""

Her voice trailed off and she reached forward to brace herself against the dashboard.

As they neared the bottom of the dip, Henry pumped the brake pedal to slow the heavy vehicle. The narrow tyres bit obediently into the lose gravel which rolled beneath the treads. Henry, suddenly realising the bend was upon them too quickly, slammed his foot hard on the brake pedal. He furiously yanked the steering wheel to the right in a desperate attempt to turn the nose of the truck away from the ravine. The front wheels locked as the tyres finally found purchase on the rocky surface. As the nose of the truck answered the command and turned back toward the road, the rear of the truck continued to slide toward the drop. The right rear wheel lifted first, followed by the front right wheel. Suddenly all four wheels were off the road and they were tumbling down the bank. Sitting on the back, Terry watched as the lollies in his paper bag spilled out and pass his vision, seemingly in slow motion.

When the dust settled and the crashing racket subsided, Terry opened his eyes. Somehow, he was sitting on a tree stump. He didn't know how he got there and could not recall anything since the truck had commenced to roll.

The truck! Where is the truck? Panic rising from the pit of his stomach, his eyes followed a trail of debris and broken bushes from the road to where the truck lay on its roof. The front wheels were spinning slowly and steam rose from the now silent engine. The only sound to break the stillness was the clicking and popping of hot metal as it contracted. Groceries, cans of food and an assortment of items were scattered down the slope from where they had left the road.

Terry breathed a sigh of relief on sighting Paul and Michael wandering dazedly about the dry gully. Then he remembered, *What about mum and dad.* As he got shakily to his feet, the canvas side curtains of the truck popped open. Steve crawled from the wreck first, closely followed by his mother, her face ashen and one eye beginning to close from a large bruise on her cheek. Henry appeared from the opposite side of the wreck and stood with his hands on his hips, surveying the scene. He showed no concern for the welfare of his family or passenger.

"Looks like she's pretty well buggered!" Steve remarked unnecessarily in his slow drawl. His tall skinny frame stooped to retrieve a battered bushman's hat, which he whacked against skinny legs concealed beneath faded denim jeans. Placing the hat on his thatch of jet-black hair, he rolled a cigarette and surveyed the scene, unruffled by the rollover. At twenty-five, the tractor driver's leathery face belied his youth. Deep crows feet from squinting into the sun, entrenched the corners of his sapphire blue eyes.

"You could say that." Henry gave a sardonic grin at the understatement. "What the hell are we going to do now?"

Oil dribbled from the overturned truck. A myriad of glassy diamonds from the broken windscreen sparkled in the dust. The crushed roof of the cabin bore clear testimony to their good fortune to have escaped more dire consequences. The flimsy wooden canopy under which the boys had been sheltering had entirely disintegrated. Corrugated iron sheets and splintered timbers littered the ground.

Ignoring her initial shock and the pain of various bruises, Judy's only concern was for the welfare of her three boys. After assuring herself that they were unscathed, she bustled about, retrieving the remnants of their precious food supply. Henry, now jolted into sobriety, sighted a plume of dust signalling the imminent arrival of another vehicle. Climbing quickly up the steep bank to the road, he waved his arms to hail the passing motorist. A battered Holden utility slid to a stop. A head as bald as an egg, protruded from the driver's window, its owner's sunburnt face creased in concern and shock.

"Jesus, mate! Is everybody okay?"

Henry nodded. "Thanks for stopping. We're all right but we're going to need a tow truck. Can you give me a lift back to town?"

"By the looks of that, you're going to need more than a tow truck. I'd say she's about buggered mate. Hop in. What about your missus and the kids?"

"They can wait here until I get back."

The Good Samaritan cast a doubtful look at the bedraggled group. "Won't be long lady!" He called as he let out the clutch and spun the nose of the ute around.

After piling their spilt belongings in a tidy heap, Judy, Steve and the three boys sat silently under the shade of a nearby tree, the first tremors of delayed shock beginning to run through bruised limbs. Henry returned an hour later, riding in the front of a tow truck. In a practiced and business like fashion, the operator backed up to the edge of the road. Alighting from the cab, he seized the hook dangling from the towing arm and slid down the bank to the battered wreck. The three boys jumped to their feet, crowding around to witness the old truck's fate.

"Stand back." The tow truck driver warned. With a whirring noise, the winch took up the slack. The old Chev rocked slightly and toppled over onto its side with a crash. The winch continued turning, once more drawing the wire rope taut, pulling the sorry looking shambles over until it teetered at the point of balance. The rope suddenly slackened. The old Chevy righted itself, bouncing on its ancient springs like a wounded beast shaking itself after a fall.

"You won't be driving her anywhere!" The towie pointed to the twisted chassis. "My guess is, she's not worth repairing. Come on, I'll take you home and then I'll dump her at the wreckers."

Somehow, Terry had grown to love the old truck as if it was a living thing. *What a sorry end through no fault of her own*, he mused sadly.

On the family's return to Willow Flats, Henry was concerned that Mrs Brunner would soon learn of events via the grapevine. Despite the lack of telephones, news somehow travelled swiftly in the Bush. Henry who prided himself on his sense of responsibility, worried she would dismiss him for his uncharacteristic stupidity.

On the following Monday, Judy presented herself as usual for her cleaning duties at the gracious homestead.

"My, my Dear. How did you get that terrible black eye?" the haughty Manageress enquired knowingly.

"I walked into a door," Judy replied lamely.

Mrs Brunner cast her housekeeper a sideways look before walking away. Amazingly, the subject never arose again.

Entertainment in the small community largely depended upon the ingenuity of its inhabitants. Television had not yet reached Australia. Reading or listening to plays or quiz shows on the wireless were popular past-times. Henry insisted the three boys be in bed by 7.00 pm each evening, as he couldn't tolerate normal childhood chatter. In any case, it was safer for the lads to be in their rooms where they were unlikely to incur his displeasure.

Paul's electronic skills resulted in the construction of two crystal sets. He and Michael retained control over both sets, permitting Terry to listen to programs in his bedroom via a pair of war surplus headphones connected to the set in Michael's bedroom via wires strung along the outside wall of the house. When the atmospheric conditions were right, "Life with Dexter," "Pick a Box with Bob Dyer" and "The Goon Show," kept them entertained until they fell asleep. Sometimes Michael waited until the evening to wield the power having control of the set gave him. In the middle of Terry's favourite shows, he'd suddenly disconnect the wires to Terry's headphones. Knowing Terry couldn't raise a fuss without risking a thrashing from their father gave Michael immense pleasure.

Undoubtedly, the highlight of station life was the weekly movies. Each Saturday, station families gathered at 7.00 pm in a large room at the front of the Carpenter's house. Furnished with an array of old sofas, kitchen chairs and hard benches, a movie projector and screen dominated the makeshift theatre.

In the front row, four white canvas deckchairs with comfortable cushions occupied pride of place. Reserved strictly for Mrs Brunner and her family, to go near those chairs was unthinkable and akin to an act of heresy.

Each Saturday, as the clock approached 7.30 pm, an expectant hush fell over the excited, chattering assembly. With everyone dressed in their best clothes for the important occasion, they waited the arrival of the Queen of their little Domain.

The first to arrive in her entourage was young Mr Falcon, followed by the Station Overseer and his wife. After a respectable delay of two minutes, the Great Lady would sweep into the room, in the manner of a diva making a grand entrance from stage right.

Clad in an elegant evening gown, complete with a fur stole, Mrs Brunner cut a regal figure. Nodding almost imperceptibly to greet her minions, she placed her ample posterior carefully in the allotted throne. Not until she sat, would the remainder of her group dare to take their places. The lights dimmed, the projector commenced to whir, celluloid spilling its hidden wonders before the enthralled gaze of the little audience.

Richard Widmark was Mrs Brunner's favourite actor. They saw every picture in which he starred. John Wayne came a close second and Johnny Weissmuller, third in Tarzan and Jane.

It was during Terry's days at Willow Flats that the marvellous new invention, television, first came to Australia. During this time, Russia launched the first satellite into orbit. Along with millions, Terry craned his neck under the mantle of stars, staring toward the heavens, watching in fascination as the tiny speck of light that was Sputnik, traversed the night skies. He was not to see his first black and white television set until two years later.

Judy often sang in the kitchen as she prepared meals and there was plenty for growing boys to occupy their time. Terry was starting to catch up with schoolwork and with Paul employed, Michael now sought his younger brother's company. For a short time, life was comfortably normal and predictable. That was until the bombshell announcement!

"You had better start packing your things. We're going to live at a little place called, Cookardinia."

Terry paused from licking the wooden spoon his mother had used to stir a chocolate cake. His jaw dropped. *What was mum saying?*

Noticing his astonishment she continued, "Dad's got a new job. He hasn't been getting on with Mrs Brunner!"

Why on earth, couldn't he ever get along with people? Terry wondered silently.

Paul looked up from a book he was reading, "What about me, mum?"

"You can either stay here as the gardener. Mrs Brunner is very happy with you, or you can come with us."

"But, I thought dad was happy here!" Michael protested.

Judy heaved a heavy sigh. It was always her task to make the life changing announcements. It was as if her spouse didn't know how to communicate with children or thought them irrelevant.

"I know dear. But dad's had enough. He can't stand things here any longer."

It was no good pressing their mother for further explanation. If their father had made up his mind, that was the end of the matter. The decision was not open for discussion or question. The bottom had just fallen out of Terry's world again. Willow Flats had been his dreams come true. Nothing could replace the wonderful river, the rolling tree covered hills and the friends he had made.

Like Bedouins, they packed their belongings and searched for another elusive oasis.

A Post Office, community hall and hotel, which had closed its doors, were all the tiny hamlet of Cookardinia could boast. Located in the wheat belt of southern New South Wales, the countryside was flat and almost featureless with a sea of brown wheat stretching in all directions to the horizon. The occasional line of ubiquitous gums marked the boundary between farms and not a beloved watercourse with all its secret delights that Terry had grown to love so much. He felt a sinking nausea in the pit of his stomach as his eyes searched the paddocks for something of interest.

There's not even a creek or a hill, he thought despairingly. *How could dad bring us out here?*

It was the height of summer. The heat was scorching. Swarms of bush flies descended on sweating faces, seeking moisture. These pests refused to be shooed away, crawling up nostrils, into mouths and permanently forming a black cloud around every living thing. As if the torment from these creatures was not enough, huge blowflies buzzed around the interior of their worker's cottage, blindly crashing into windowpanes and dive bombing unprotected food. It was a minor miracle if they completed a meal without fishing drowning flies from a plate or cup. With no flyscreens, there was nothing to do but live with the problem.

After the abundance of good sweet drinking water at Willow Flats, they were to soon learn bathing was a once a week luxury. The water for washing and baths came from the farm dam. Shared with livestock, it was a filthy brown colour and it was a moot point whether one was any cleaner after the experience. Rainwater tanks provided the only drinking water sporting lively mosquito larvae wriggling in every glass drawn from the tap.

"They won't hurt you. There just wrigglers!" their father scoffed as the boys wrinkled their noses in disgust.

When Henry rapped on the side of the house tank, it was apparent that the water level was low. With no rains expected for months, every contaminated drop was precious.

"We'll have to strain the water and boil it to be on the safe side," Judy decided. "Oh, and you boys be very careful when you go outside. There's lots of snakes around here!"

"We've got to find a job for Paul. I'm not going to feed him while he sits around," Henry grumbled.

It had been Judy's decision to allow Paul to accompany the family on their move. Henry was annoyed and disappointed that Paul had not stayed in gainful employment at Willow Flats. It didn't matter to Henry that the shy, intelligent boy had more potential than that offered by pulling weeds and picking vegetables. To Henry the only thing he cared about was once again assuming the financial burden of feeding a growing adolescent.

At the first opportunity, Michael and Terry enrolled at the tiny Cookardinia School, a single weatherboard and iron classroom sitting among the wheat fields. Mr Burrell a stocky, but kindly, middle aged chap presided over the entire roll of twenty-seven children ranging in ages from six to fifteen years. A luxuriant growth of grey bushy hair framed a square face creased with laughter lines. A pair of spectacles perched permanently on the bridge of his nose completed the impression of a wise, benevolent, old owl from a child's fairy tale. The kids all loved him and the congeniality of the atmosphere was a welcome change from Terry's previous experiences in the N.S.W. state school system. Lessons were by correspondence. The relaxed atmosphere suited Terry who willingly applied himself to his assignments. Encouraged by Mr Burrell, he progressed at a rapid rate. He couldn't wait to get home and share the good news.

"Mum, Mum. Guess what?"

"What darling?"

Terry waved his end of year report card. "I came third in my class!"

"Why, that's wonderful," Judy replied, delighted with her son's achievement.

"He didn't tell you that there's only three in his class," Michael chipped in, spoiling the moment.

Electricity had not yet reached the back blocks of Cookardinia. The farm relied upon a noisy diesel generator. Its omnipresent chugging just another source of annoyance, added to a long list including, water shortage, flies, isolation, heat and the boring featureless terrain.

Noelinel household electrical appliances were useless with the feeble 110 volt electricity supply. There was insufficient power to light more than a single globe in their Spartan farm cottage. Each evening, at 8.30 pm the station owner turned off the generator to conserve fuel. At this point kerosene lamps became their only source of light.

In the spirit of resilience that children possess, the Flatley boys made the most of their situation and sought pleasure in simple things, such as feeding fallen fruit to a placid jersey cow grazing in the paddock near their home. They were in the height of summer. Harvesting was in full swing and occasionally a magnanimous farmer allowed Michael and Terry to ride in the cabin of one of the big Sunshine combine harvesters that threshed wide trails through the endless fields of golden wheat and oats. They'd watch in fascination as the enormous rotating boom knocked the heads off the grain and the machine spat a constant golden stream into the hopper behind them. When the hopper became full, they would stop and discharge its contents into sacks. The boys watched in admiration as, without complaining, fit muscular men lifted and stacked each bag onto the waiting trucks, toiling for hours in the midday heat.

With Christmas approaching, there was palpable excitement at the little school. Every year Mr Burrell busily organised a play to celebrate the end of the school year. In an amazing feat of ingenuity and diplomacy, he ensured the inclusion of every child. Displaying inventiveness, the school verandah became an improvised stage. He produced foot lights, using kerosene tins to reflect the white-hot glare from pressure lamps lining the verandah edge.

In the preceding weeks, mothers busily sewed costumes for the budding thespians and a few enthusiastic fathers found time to construct the set.

This year the school was going to produce The Christmas Story. Terry was unable to contain his pride at his selection to play one of the three wise men. Entering into the spirit of things, and with limited materials at her disposal, Judy fashioned an Arabian costume from old sheets.

"Your father's very tired. Mr Scofield is a real slave driver." Judy as usual, did not want her boys to think unkindly of their father and proffered a credible excuse for his lack of interest in the pending performance.

Although they had never sighted the station owner, Mr Scofield had become an ogre to blame for all their woes. Attuned to the nuances of dinner table discussions, the boys quickly sensed that things were not working out as well as Henry had hoped. Although Henry's role entailed the maintenance of farm machinery, he had soon discovered to his chagrin that the job description extended to much more. In the seasonal urgency associated with harvesting, necessity dictated all hands work from daybreak to dark, loading and stacking heavy sacks of grain and carting bales of hay. There was little if any doubt that Henry was fatigued, but he wasn't the only man working in the heat and dust all day. Still, his disinterest in the school play was no surprise.

On the opening night, the brown dusty schoolyard filled with an assortment of vehicles as proud parents gathered to view the much-rehearsed production. The occasion provided a welcome relief from the relentless work of the harvest. It was a rare chance to socialise with old friends and neighbours.

Brown moths fluttered in the glare of the footlights. Children darted around the legs of grown-ups as they chatted and gossiped in little groups before the makeshift stage. Cicadas clicked a noisy chorus from the windbreak of tall pine trees. Paper Christmas decorations hung limply in the oppressive evening heat. Despite the conditions, the atmosphere was festive with a bonhomie known only to country folk.

Mr Burrell appeared on the verandah. On his cue, the school bell rang, commanding silence.

"Ladies and gentleman. Welcome to Cookardinia School's end of year production." The stocky schoolmaster paused theatrically, adjusting his spectacles as he surveyed the hushed assemblage. "Your children have worked hard to bring you tonight's entertainment, so please give them some encouragement. We bring you, The Christmas Story!"

After a hesitant ripple of polite applause, a sextet of boys and girls waiting in the shadows raised recorders nervously to young lips. A shaky rendition of "Silent Night" squeaked plaintively across the quadrangle in competition to the cicada's incessant racket. Obediently, the audience moved to take up positions of vantage on the hard plywood stackable chairs arranged in rows before the stage.

Dressed in his robes, a charcoal beard smearing his face, Terry watched the performance of Mary and Joseph from backstage as he waited his chance to participate. A strangely comforting feeling filled his chest. The privations of hard farm life faded into insignificance with the sudden realization that, among these warm and friendly country folk he felt accepted. Little did he know that his world was about to be turned upside down once more!

As the sun cast the first bright rays across the hard stubble of the harvested paddocks, an almost surreal stillness hung over the harsh landscape. There was not a single breath of wind. Sounds usually associated with the commencement of daily farm life, were absent. The early morning flocks of cockatoos, normally carpeting the dry land searching for grain, had disappeared. Even the blowflies were silent.

The iron roof of the cottage emitted small explosive sounds as it expanded in the white-hot glare. The mercury in the thermometer hanging from a nail on the porch began to climb steadily. Christmas Day promised to be scorching hot.

Adam Scofield strode purposefully across the parched yard separating the homestead from the worker's cottage. He was dressed in a sleeveless khaki shirt and moleskin trousers faded from frequent washing. His battered, stained, war surplus, slouch hat, shaded his weather-beaten countenance bearing a permanent scowl. Reaching the cottage of his hired help, he stopped and lifted a sun-tanned leathery fist to pound impatiently on the door. After a moment, the door opened as Judy appeared, hastily pulling a patched, well worn, dressing gown about her shoulders.

"Where's Henry?" he demanded.

"He's still in bed, resting."

"Well, tell him I need him at once to fix a pump!" Scofield announced, thin lips drawn tight, like a scar beneath the beak of his hooked nose. He had no time for the normal pleasantries and protocols associated with civilised greetings.

"It's Christmas Day!" Judy replied indignantly, shocked at his rudeness.

"Machinery doesn't care what day it is. If the pump's not fixed, there'll be no water for the stock. Get him our here, now!" Turning on his heel, he strode away as if expecting Henry to follow like an obedient sheepdog.

"And, Merry Christmas to you too," Judy called sarcastically.

Judy retreated into the cottage, her face flushed with anger. Henry was already pulling on his clothes. "Did you hear that Henry? That man is so rude! He didn't even have the common decency to say good morning, or to use my name, or to wish me a Merry Christmas. I swear he must be the most ill-mannered person I have ever come across. He seems to think that he owns you!"

"It's just 'cos he never stops working. He expects everybody to do as much as he does. He forgets that we're employees and don't have the same dedication to the place. I'd better get down there. The sooner I get it fixed, the sooner I get back." Henry reasoned.

Upon Henry's departure, the three boys appeared, knowing they were now safe to show themselves. Until the head of the house got up, it was not a good idea to make any noise. Christmas morning was no exception. They hurried to the small pathetic looking pine branch stuck in a bucket and decorated with crepe paper, streamers and silver tinsel. Judy somehow always managed to provide a small Christmas present, despite the paucity of their circumstances.

The sight of such youthful excitement quickly dispelled Judy's annoyance. She hugged her boys in turn, tears of sadness dampening her cheeks. Oh, how she wished she could give them the World. "Merry Christmas boys," she sniffed.

Unaware of her mood, the three boys chorused, "Merry Christmas mum."

As the clock approached midday, there was no sign of Henry or Mr Scofield. Judy's temper was beginning to match the heat in the kitchen. Aromas from the ancient fuel stove bore promised a hearty dinner of roast leg of lamb, mint sauce, potatoes, pumpkin, parsnip and sweet potato. A huge sherry trifle and a dish of homemade ice cream already waited in the kerosene refrigerator. The dining table adorned with the best tablecloth and silver cutlery reserved for special occasions, contrasted with the foulness of Judy's mood. For the umpteenth time, she glanced at the old wind up alarm clock, ticking loudly on the mantelpiece.

"If your father's not back soon, I'm going down to fetch him!" She muttered testily, more to herself than to the boys.

"Terry, the wood box is nearly empty. Will you go out to the wood heap for me?"

"Sure mum."

Terry picked up the box and singing to himself, sauntered down the path to the wood heap, a short distance from the house. In his excited anticipation of the special dinner, he was oblivious to his mother's mood. He placed his hand over his face, peering between his fingers to lessen the searing pain from the sun's glare. It was as if someone had opened the door of a giant blast furnace.

Terry reached the neat piles of sun-bleached firewood and set the box down next to the hardwood stump, scarred from a thousand axe blows. He became aware that his bladder was full and turned to enter the old 'long drop' dunny nearby. An overpowering pong from the dark latrine pit, mingled with a furnace blast of built up heat. After holding his breath for several long moments against the stench, his lungs seemed about to burst. Clutching a handkerchief to his nose to filter the smell, he sucked a precious mouthful of putrid air. Then, with the business at hand completed, he burst from the tiny, oven-hot confines of the cubicle and inhaled deeply in the clean summer air.

A soft hissing noise, which was foreign to his ears, attracted Terry's attention. Turning to look back toward the direction of the toilet, his skin contracted with goose bumps and the hair on the back of his neck bristled. An extraordinarily long, black, tiger snake was sliding menacingly toward him. A forked tongue flicking rapidly, the reptile slid through the chicken netting of the dividing fence.

Galvanised into action, Terry abandoned the quest for fuel, which had placed him in such dire peril. In one bound, he hurdled the heavy hurricane wire gate, separating the cottage from the wood yard and the odoriferous dunny. He covered the thirty or so yards to the house with the ability of an Olympic athlete.

"MUM. MUM!" Ashen faced and wide eyed, he burst into the kitchen. "Th...th....there...there's a b....b...bloody big sn...snake near the dunny!"

His mother dropped the wooden spoon she was using to stir gravy in the baking dish. Wiping house worn-hands on her floral apron, she headed to the garden and seized a sharp spade.

Hearing the commotion, Paul and Michael ran after her, not wanting to miss the excitement. Terry tailed along at the rear. Numerous warnings on the dangers of snakes had instilled in him healthy respect for the loathsome creatures. This respect had quickly turned to an almost paralysing fear at such a close first-hand encounter.

"It was over there." Terry pointed shakily toward the place where the angry reptile had menaced him.

They stalked toward the fence, treading carefully. Paul clutched the axe from the wood heap. At the sound of their approach, the snake swung a black ugly head to meet the threat. Leaning over the fence, Judy jammed the blade of the spade hard down behind the evil creature's head. Pinning it tightly to the ground, she quickly realised that if she lifted the spade, the angry snake would strike through the netting at her legs.

"Paul! Paul! Help me." she shrilled.

Clambering between the top strands of rusty barbed wire, Paul confronted the snake, axe raised. Writhing and thrashing, the snake struggled to be free from the metal blade pinning it to the dirt, a yellow underbelly and stripes distinguishing it as one of the world's most venomous reptiles. The axe flashed once in the sunlight, as Paul swung the heavy steel blade in a downward stroke. Despite cutting the long scaly body in two, it continued to writhe and twist in its death throes. The axe descended several more times before they were satisfied that the twitching remains posed no further threat.

"Blimey! It must be at least six feet long." Paul blasphemed, stretching the reptilian carcass over the fence.

The episode with the snake served as a catalyst for Judy's next actions. Throwing the spade angrily to one side, she stomped off across the paddocks in search of her absent spouse.

She found Henry and the boss labouring in the relentless heat at the bottom of a farm well as they strove to repair the broken pump. The boss looked up quizzically at the sound of her approach.

"How much longer are you going to be?" It was more of a demand than a question as her patience had run out.

The boss's jaw dropped. *How dare a mere woman challenge my authority in such a fashion? Who does she think she is this wife of my station hand?*

63

"A fine Christmas this is turning out to be. If you don't let Henry knock off soon, Christmas will be over!" Judy turned on her heel and marched back to the cottage without waiting for a reply. The door had barely closed before Henry followed her inside in an uncharacteristic display of submissiveness. When Judy finally put her foot down, even the mightiest of creatures trembled!

They ate Christmas Dinner silently. There was no mention of events at the well.

A few days later, Henry came home crestfallen.

"What's happened now?" his wife queried. "Why are you home so early?".

"I've just been given the boot." With three hungry mouths to feed, Henry was at his wit's end. "What are we going to do now, Judy?"

"Well, you know Mrs Brunner thought the world of you. She was very upset when you gave your notice. I think you've just got to swallow your pride and ask her if she will take us back."

Henry gave her a withering look.

"It's no good looking at me like that. You know we've got nowhere to go and that's the best option."

They returned to Willow Flats, where the Flatley family took up residence once more in the much-loved old stone house. Armed with the knowledge that Henry harboured a low opinion of her, the relationship between the prodigal mechanic and Mrs Brunner assumed a new level. Where he could previously do no wrong, he had now fallen from grace. Perhaps it was subconscious, but Mrs Brunner chose revenge in subtle ways. Previously spared from unpleasant and mundane tasks, they were now part of his expanded job description.

Henry's mood deteriorated in direct proportion to the increase in simmering tensions between him and his employer. Life in the Flatley household was no longer as carefree and contented, as the dark cloud hovering over Henry's head followed him home each day. The 'Sydney Morning Herald' positions vacant columns received his regular and constant attention. Outward mail from the Flatley house increased exponentially as copious job applications flowed from Henry's pen. Although Terry was aware of his father's sullen mood, he was oblivious to the changes in the wind. However, he received the announcement that they were once more on the move, philosophically exhibiting little surprise.

This time they would not return to Willow Flats.

At twenty eight thousand acres, Jiggalong was ten thousand acres bigger than Willow Flats. Located in western New South Wales, on the banks of the Lachlan River, the station mainly ran sheep, and some cattle. The terrain was much hotter and dryer than the temperate Southern Tablelands area Terry had loved so much. However, it proved to be more interesting than the flat, dry plains of Cookardinia.

"At least it's got a river," he observed upon their arrival.

The deep muddy brown waters of the mighty Lachlan River flowed within a few yards of their house. In a significant feat of engineering, huge levy banks constructed either side formed a deep trench to contain the flood prone waters. Giant gums leaned drunkenly overhead, thrusting tortuous roots into the sticky mud.

When the boys attempted to reach the water's edge, they found the going slippery and difficult. They quickly abandoned any plans for a soothing cool dip in the river as their feet sank deeply into the brown ooze, covering them to their thighs. In comparison to the placid friendly Molonglo, the Lachlan's deep black waters seemed treacherous and threatening.

"The boss has promised us our own house cow for milk," Judy informed the boys.

"You'll have to take turns at milking her every day," Henry added.

Their very own pet cow. Terry was thrilled.

"When are we going to get her?" Michael wanted to know.

"She's coming tomorrow," Henry replied.

The next morning, Michael and Terry waited expectantly, watching the long narrow track, which ran from their cottage to the main road. Their wait was in vain.

"Why didn't the cow come?" Judy enquired of Henry that evening.

"She apparently escaped on the way here," Henry answered. "They're going to bring her tomorrow."

The following day, as the sun reached its zenith, a tractor

appeared, chugging slowly from the direction of the homestead, several miles from their house. Tethered by a short rope to the draw bar, an angry bovine trotted protesting behind the huge wheels of the leviathan, tossing its head in protest at the indignity forced upon her. Releasing the irascible creature into the paddock alongside the house, the tractor driver silently mounted his transport and returned along the track, obviously relieved at completing the task.

"That's our cow?" Terry looked doubtfully at the sharp horns and the belligerent stare directed at them from their four legged milk supply.

"It's your turn to milk her first," Michael suggested. The thought of catching this obviously bad-tempered animal and persuading her to part with milk, was one neither boy relished.

"Perhaps we can make friends with her." Terry climbed over the fence to where the cow stood facing them, snorting. A long stalactite of snot and saliva hung from its reddish brown muzzle.

"Here cow. Come on, there's a good girl." He extended his hand proffering a fistful of long dry grass picked from the edge of the driveway.

Michael joined the younger boy in the paddock and they edged their way hesitantly toward the beast, which stood silently, watching this vain attempt to foster better relationships between the species.

Thrown together by the fickle hand of fate, two unwilling parties sized each other up. The two species were light years apart and unable to communicate. Clearly, the cow was not going to grasp the olive branch of friendship. The boy's most sincere attempts at diplomacy were from the outset, destined for failure.

As they approached, the cow lifted a front hoof and like Nikita Khrushchev hammering his shoe on the table at the United Nations, she stamped a warning on the sun-baked ground.

"Go on. She's more frightened of you, than you are of her," Michael urged Terry forward glancing over his shoulder to map out his escape route.

Suddenly, lowering her head, the beast charged. With the agility of trained toreadors, the two boys fled to the fence, vaulting to safety. The cow skidded to a halt and angrily glared at them, snorting her frustration from flared nostrils.

"I think Paul should have the first turn at milking her," Michael offered generously.

"Perhaps she'll settle down after she's been here a couple of days," Terry replied doubtfully.

They need not have worried. The next morning, there was no sign of the huffy heifer. Her mothering instincts inducing a fit of desperation, she had once again demonstrated her abilities as an escapologist, extricating herself from the paddock to return to her calf. The matadors in the making did not protest when Henry announced that henceforth, their milk supply would come from a tin. There was obviously more to having your own personal cow than they had all realised.

Every school day, a large, battered, blue, bus transported the two boys the thirty miles to the Forbes High School. A fat, cheerful, middle-aged bus driver known simply as Bill, somehow kept his boisterous load under control. The trip along the dusty country road invariably brought its' share of exciting moments. Sometimes, gawky, dull, grey emus raced alongside. Long spindly legs flying, they kept pace with the ageing vehicle as it charged over the corrugated road, raising a cloud of thick choking dust in its wake.

Occasionally, Bill would stamp on the brake peddle, skidding to a halt. Jumping from the seat with surprising agility for his size, he would use the jack handle to pound a large tiger snake to death on the road. "I hate the bastards!" The remark directed to everyone and no-one at the same time.

When the Lachlan River flooded, the wide-open plains transformed into lakes. At times, the bus would struggle to get through the swirling brown floodwaters, turning back to the children's delight.

"Sorry kids," Bill would grin. "Looks as if you're going have a holiday today."

"Yaaaaaay." screamed the children in delight.

Floods brought an abundance of easily caught yabbies. Yabby races held in the playground provided a uniquely Australian form of entertainment. Mischievous boys delighted in sending the girls running, screaming in a bid to escape from the sharp pincers of the little freshwater crustaceans.

As the summer rolled on, the mercury often registered in excess of forty degrees, for day after long tiring day. Lying listlessly on the linoleum floor, they searched for a cooler patch under the table, pressing themselves against the hard floor to gain whatever relief they could from the oppressive heat.

Paul learned to work as a tractor driver. With the skills of ploughing and harvesting mastered, Henry wasted no time in securing employment for him on a remote farming property.

"We can't have you lying around doing nothing. It's time you stood on your own two feet," he ordered unsympathetically. "I can't feed you forever."

Paul was unhappy at the prospect of living a lonely and hard life, labouring at something for which he was clearly unsuited. He was given no say in the decision and his mother's attempts to intercede on his behalf were met by a stubborn insistence from Henry that, "It'll make a man of him!"

Henry won the day and they travelled into Forbes to purchase the basic items necessary for the teenage boy to fend for himself in single men's quarters.

As he was too young to hold a drivers licence, the devastated boy had no means of returning home, unless some kindly person gave him a ride. As there appeared to be a shortage of benevolent souls exhibiting compassion for the lad's plight, Paul's only means of contact was via an irregular mail service. Father and son shared the same dislike of letter writing and as Henry considered visiting his son was far too much trouble, the lonely and distraught boy simply disappeared from their lives. Judy lamented the enforced exile of her eldest child and the chilly draught of heartbreak threatened to extinguish the already flickering candle of her love for Henry.

Paul's absence, brought respite from the constant tormenting Terry had endured at his hands since their departure from Willow Flats. Torn between empathy for his older brother's plight and relief at the departure of his tormentor, Terry settled on feeling relieved. Life had been insufferable at the hands of his two elder siblings. On one occasion, Michael had goaded the smaller boy until he could no longer bear the situation.

"I'm telling you to leave me alone. I've had enough of you always picking on me!" Terry paused from splitting kindling for the fuel stove. He rested the axe on the chopping block and looked warningly at his brother. The argument as usual, was over something trivial but needling the youngest member of the family provided ready entertainment for the older boys.

"What are you going to do about it? You're too dumb to even know how to chop wood properly," Michael goaded.

Terry clenched his teeth and tried to ignore the harassment. Aware that the barbed remarks were beginning to have the desired affect, Michael continued with the invective for several moments more. Finally, unable to contain his rage, Terry charged with the raised axe, murder in his heart.

Seeing his brother's blind fury and fearing the consequences, Michael paled and as adrenaline pumped into his veins, he took flight. With his legs pounding, he scrambled for the safety of the house, Terry hot on his heels.

"I'll kill you!" Terry screamed murderously. Judging he was close enough to administer the blow, he slashed downward with all the strength he could muster. With all judgment and common-sense lost in his hatred and desire for revenge for the years of torment, he did not consider the terrible consequences. With millimetres between him and the descending blade, Michael darted inside and closed the door just as the axe blade slammed into the wood. Terry stood shaking with rage, intensely disappointed at his brother's escape. Slowly, composure returned, and although he realised the enormity of the act he had almost committed, he did not yet understand the genetic perpetuation of his father's violent streak.

Paul's absence had created a vacuum in Michael's life. Realising that there was nothing to gain from tormenting his younger brother and in need of a friend after the axe episode, he treated Terry with a new respect. Terry was glad of the attention and ready to make amends for his murderous proclivity. He readily accepted the truce. He had relived the axe incident many times, realising how closely he had come to the murder of his own brother. The knowledge that he was capable of such hatred and blinding rage scared him and he vowed never to lose control again. However, he also knew that he would no longer tolerate bullying and intimidation, no matter what the source.

The family's stay at Jiggalong came to an abrupt end, when less than a year later Henry decided suddenly to hand in his notice without warning. This time they had no escape plan! Henry had no job prospects and nowhere to go. Leaving their furniture in the little cottage, they loaded their ever-dwindling possessions into their Vauxhall utility and headed for the township of Yass. Here Henry pitched a canvas tent in the local camping ground and they led a miserable existence, parents sleeping on the ground and kids in the back of the utility, as he searched for employment.

The family had little money and was ill-equipped for a life under canvas. Somehow, Judy managed to cook basic hot meals for them all, on a single burner primus stove. At night, the boys huddled under inadequate blankets, sleeping fitfully on the cold unyielding metal floor of the small truck. When it rained, the tent leaked. Muddy water flowed under the limp canvas walls, soaking their spare clothing and bedding. Their misery was complete and absolute.

Despairing as the money ran out and with Henry no closer to finding work, Judy fronted him. "We can't go on like this any longer. We've got to go back to the City where the work is. The kid's are going to catch a death of a cold and we've got no money left."

"I'm trying my best woman. What do you want me to do?" Henry shook his head in frustration.

"We'll have to go to your mother's and ask her if she'll put us up for a while."

Henry relented begrudgingly, knowing she was right. Humiliated and defeated, they drove to Ingleburn on the outskirts of Sydney where Grandma Flatley now lived in a fibre cement clad shed, behind a cottage which Henry's brother Jeffrey was building for her. The cottage was unlined and not yet ready for habitation.

The old woman met their unexpected arrival with stern disapproval. "Ooh eh by gum. I suppose you can move in for a while. You've made a mess of things this time, haven't you, my lad?"

It was more of a statement of fact than a question and her son did not reply.

With no furniture or mattresses, they spread their blankets and sheets on the wooden floor amid the dust from the asbestos cement sheeting, the off-cuts of timber, and bags of cement and other detritus of the construction site. There was nowhere to wash but in a concrete trough placed against the dunny wall in the back yard. They carted water from the garden tap in plastic buckets and cooked on a two-burner kerosene stove. Lest the local council learn of their plight and eject them for living in unsanitary conditions, Grandma refused to order an extra toilet pan to handle the additional sewerage. She insisted that they hike a mile to the local railway station each time they wanted to use the toilet.

The old crone was cantankerous, her meanness and eccentric habits caused considerable friction but they dare not incur her displeasure. With no laundry facilities and Grandma's insistence that they conserve water, they used the same sheets for weeks and washed in cold water poured into an enamel basin.

Terry decided, *it was better than living in a tent, but not much better!*

After several weeks, his uncle who was building the cottage in his spare time lined the interior with Masonite sheeting. Grandma couldn't wait to vacate the garage where she had lived for the past year.

"I'm going to move into the house now. You lot can all have the garage," the old woman advised.

"But, the house isn't ready yet. Jeff hasn't painted the walls and the plumbing's not connected," Henry protested.

Grandma was resolute. "Beggars can't be choosers. I'll manage."

They had no choice but to squeeze into the tiny unlined garage with its cold, grey concrete floor. Purloining planks of wood from the building site, they placed them between tea chests and covered the splintery wood with a cloth to form a makeshift table. Using drums as chairs and sleeping on the bare concrete floor, the destitute family had no choice but to embrace their new home.

Henry's search for work eventually paid off. Landing employment as a foreman-mechanic for McCullough Chainsaws, he soon regained his lost self-esteem with the security of a regular income. Michael, who had reached fifteen, discovered it was his turn for ejection from the nest. Managing to find employment as a clerical assistant with an accountancy firm, he left the family to live in private board, freeing Henry from the financial burden.

Terry, who was not yet legally old enough to suffer the same fate, enrolled at the Campbelltown High School. Having missed nearly six weeks schooling while they lived in the tent and later, on the floor of the shed, Terry discovered he was lagging considerably behind his peers. His new school did not offer the same syllabus as Forbes High School, forcing him to adopt unfamiliar subjects with examinations pending. Determined to pass exams, he obtained the relevant textbooks, which he devoured in every available moment, cramming five months of lessons into the few remaining weeks. His mother helped him, testing his knowledge and encouraging her youngest boy's efforts.

Much to his delight and pride, Terry's perseverance paid dividends. Although he didn't top his class, he obtained respectable pass marks in all subjects. Encouraged by success, he began to make further inroads into the learning difficulties created by their almost nomadic existence.

For some unknown reason, Terry once again found he was the focus of attention from the school bully. Remembering his earlier promise, he stood his ground when confronted by the other boy. By this stage, he had grown considerably and although gangly and thin, he was only a few inches short of six feet tall. Colin Greave who was a few inches shorter, was a more solid boy and considerably stronger than his classmates. He had a square flattish face, brown eyes, broad nose and ears that stood out like the open doors of an FJ Holden. His prickly brown hair, cut in a crew cut, completed the caricature of the classic pugilist.

As they crossed the playground at lunchtime, Greave pretended Terry had deliberately walked in front of him. Bumping into the lighter boy, he shouldered Terry away.

"Watch out pretty boy!"

Terry continued walking, ignoring the other boy who followed him, angry at the rebuff.

"Hey you. Don't walk away from me!" Greave pushed Terry in the back, sending him stumbling forward.

Here we go again, Terry thought, sighing resignedly. *I had better sort this one out now, before he becomes a real problem.* "Come on then, have a go!" He turned around to face Greave's challenge. The news of a playground fight somehow always travelled at lightening speed. Other boys soon surrounded the pair, ever ready for a good punch up.

Greave raised his fists adopting a boxer's stance. Terry stood quietly with his hands loosely by his side, waiting for the other boy to make the first move. Colin moved in jabbing his right fist toward his opponent's face. Terry ducked under the blow and twisted to one side. Before his opponent could recover, he leapt up, reaching with his right arm across the other boy's neck. Crooking his arm and stepping behind Greave, Terry completed the manoeuvre, pulling the other boy backward under his armpit in a headlock. The fight was over almost before it had begun. Powerless in the choking hold, his face turning blue as Terry increased the pressure, Greave croaked, "Okay. You win. Let me go."

"Are you sure you've had enough?" Terry squeezed a little harder to emphasise his superiority.

"Yeah. Yeah, I promise."

"Are you gunna leave me alone in future?"

"Yes. Yes. I'm sorry."

"Right. Make sure that's the end of it or next time I'll break your neck," Terry vowed.

"Okay. Okay. I didn't mean anything. I was just mucking around."

"Alright. Nick off before the teachers come and we're both in trouble."

Although Terry had won this battle, he was not entirely convinced that he would win the war. He did not want a repeat performance. However, Colin may have been the kingpin and a bully but he was no fool. Wisely, he opted to recruit Terry to his circle of friends, knowing it was better to be one rung below the top of the pecking order rather than languish as the isolated and fallen leader, subjected to regular derision from his former cohorts. The following day, he greeted Terry with a wide grin.

"How ya goin' Terry? Howdya like to show me that hold you used yesterday. You sure beat me fair and square."

"As long as you promise there'll be no more funny business Colin. I don't like fighting much, but I'm not going to let anybody push me around either."

"Nah, mate. You and me should be friends. I reckon you're not a bad bloke after all."

From that day on, the two boys became the best of friends. Terry's newly found reputation as the kid who licked the school bully, ensured he was not troubled again.

With regular income and fewer mouths to feed, Henry managed to save a few pounds. Despite Judy's hopes, he had no plans to provide a home for them. Instead, he purchased a new

Holden EH utility and a twelve foot six inch long Millard aluminium caravan. Moving to a caravan park on the Hume Highway near Cabramatta, Henry parked the tiny van beneath a shady tree on one of the cheaper un-powered sites. They used battery power, changing the twelve-volt car battery over from the van to the utility each day to keep it charged. Judy cooked on the two-burner methylated spirit stove in the caravan and they trudged fifty metres to the ablution block each time they needed to use the toilet, wash their clothes or have a daily shower.

Once again, Terry found himself at a new school, Cabramatta High. To get there, he walked nearly two miles in the morning and home again in the afternoon, lugging a heavy case filled with schoolbooks. Yet again, he found he was the focus of attention from the inevitable bully, surrounded by his pack of cowardly supporters. Numerous fights ensued and although Terry could not beat the odds, he refused to be cowed, often trudging home with his clothes in disarray and ears hot from blows rained on him from all sides. Eventually gathering his own circle of friends about him, their united stance reduced the attacks to those occasions when the bully could ambush Terry from a side street as he walked home alone.

Judy, bored with living in the tiny caravan all day, sought something to occupy her time and supplement her small housekeeping allowance. The affluent local Browning family employed her to clean their house and take care of the children. Ill with cancer, Mrs Browning could not manage to care for her four teenage children.

Judy appeared to enjoy her new source of interest and the independence provided by a small wage, working uncomplainingly for nearly eighteen months.

One morning as usual, Terry trudged to the caravan park's ablution block for his morning shower. As he stood at the urinal to relieve himself, a severe knife like pain pierced his right side. In agony, his legs buckled beneath him. Falling to the grubby concrete floor, he lay for several minutes until the pain subsided. Scared of the possible prognosis, he did not mention the incident to his mother. However, within days, pains wracked his body from every joint and muscle. His strength waned and his mother, realising something was seriously wrong, took him to the family Doctor. After X-rays and tests, the Doctor referred him to Mr

Stuckey, a prominent urologist in Sydney's prestigious Macquarie Street.

Mr Stuckey occupied plush consulting rooms lined with mahogany wood panelling and carpeted with deep red Berber carpet. A tall thin, middle-aged gentleman, with a long youthful face, brown hair greying at the temples and a kindly smile, he sat behind a monstrous mahogany desk inlaid with green leather. Framed medical certificates and an assortment of degrees completely filled the space above the wooden dado running around the room.

Stuckey finished examining X-Rays and a pathology report. Pushing his chair back from the desk, he surveyed them over a pair of steel rimmed, bi-focal glasses, perched on the bridge of his bony nose.

"Your son has severe nephritis and his left kidney does not function. I would advise an operation for its removal."

Mystified, Terry wondered silently, *how can it be my left kidney when the pains are in my right side?*

"I've had my appendix removed. That wasn't much to worry about. I guess this will be just like that won't it?" he asked naively.

The specialist smiled, "We'll do the operation at Liverpool Hospital. That's the closest hospital for you. I'll arrange to get him in immediately."

"What will it mean for him in the future, Doctor?" Judy's brow was creased with concern .

"Oh, he'll be fine. The right kidney will enlarge itself to take over the work normally done by the other kidney. The only thing he'll need to be careful about, is ensuring that he doesn't suffer a blow to the right side and damage that kidney. I would advise that he give up rugby and never ride motorcycles."

Terry laughed inwardly at the Surgeon's assumption that he played rugby like most boys his age. *Great,* he thought. *Now I have a really good excuse to get out of playing.*

In his ignorance, Terry underwent the pre-operation procedures stoically. "Make sure you don't take the wrong kidney out," he joked with the medical staff, as they wheeled him to the operating theatre.

A face partially covered with a surgical mask leant over him as he lay on the operating table. "We're just going to give you an injection son. There'll be a small prick like a mosquito bite and then I want you to count down from ten."

I wonder if I can resist the anaesthetic if I try really hard? Terry wondered counting down. "Ten, nine, eight........"

He came to as they wheeled the trolley down the long cold sterile corridors. Through the blur of drugs, he was immediately aware of an intense nagging pain in his left side. Reaching the ward, the orderlies lifted him from the trolley to transfer him to his bed. Suddenly one of the orderlies slipped and they dropped him. He landed on the edge of the bed, his legs falling to the floor. A sharp tearing sensation seared his side.

"Aaag.. My stitches. You've ripped my bloody stitches open!" he screamed.

"It's alright son. You'll be alright! Lie back and go to sleep," the culprit murmured, anxious to conceal his clumsiness.

Terry sank back on the bed weakly, immediately falling into a state of semiconsciousness. Later, when the nurses changed his dressing, he discovered that one of his stitches had indeed ripped through the flesh in his side.

The recovery process was long and slow. During his stay in hospital, his mother visited him every day, bringing him treats and comics. There was no sign of his father.

"Dad can't stand hospitals. They upset him." Judy explained.

It's more likely that he can't be bothered, Terry thought. Still, he did not question his father's absence. "How long will I be in here, mum? I'm worried that I'll fall too far behind in my schoolwork. I simply must pass my Intermediate Certificate this year!"

"Hush, you'll be alright. You've caught up before. You can do it again."

On his eventual return to the caravan, his father's greeting was less than warm. "Have a good holiday?" he asked sarcastically.

Terry turned to his mother. When can I go back to school, Mum? I'm worried about the exams."

Before his mother could reply, Henry interjected, "You can forget about school. You're fifteen now and it's time you got out and got a job!"

Terry's jaw dropped in amazement. *He's joking, surely?* One look at his father's face dispelled any doubts. Henry's jaw was set firmly. His thin lips were pressed into a tight line and his pale blue eyes burned fiercely.

Terry refused to recoil in fear as he had so often done in the past. "How do you expect me to get any sort of a job without at least obtaining my Intermediate Certificate? About the only job I'll get will be on the rubbish truck!" He challenged defiantly, anticipating a wild haymaker aimed at his head.

The blow did not come. Instead, his father's voice dropped to a low rumble of stubborn determination. "You'll find something. You can get out there and knock on doors every day until you do. I'm not keeping you any longer!" He turned away, indicating the subject closed.

Terry knew it was no good pursuing the matter for the time being. However, with each day that he missed school, he was aware that time was running out. He raised the question on several occasions over the next few days, pressing the issue with new arguments. Henry remained steadfast. The more Terry argued the more resolute his father became. To Terry's chagrin, his mother failed to rally to his defence.

"It's alright son. There are plenty of good jobs out there. Look at your father. He's done alright for himself without paper qualifications."

Has he? Terry wasn't so sure. "The world is different now Mum. Every employer is asking for at least the basic qualifications. "I want to do more than just dig ditches."

"You aren't going back to school and that's final. You made the decision to repeat a year at Primary School without asking us!" Henry roared.

It was as if a light bulb had flashed on in Terry's head. *So, that's it! He's paying me back because I had fallen behind through being dragged around the countryside. I didn't feel confident to tackle High School. I had needed another year to catch up at that point.*

Terry turned imploringly to his mother. She averted her gaze. "Your father has made up his mind and that's the end of the matter," she stated resignedly.

Terry knew he was beaten. To him, the decision was the pinnacle of his father's meanness. Eclipsing all previous acts of selfishness, unreasonable discipline, physical abuse, deprivation and lack of affection, the denial of the basic right to a reasonable education was the final straw. *You rotten old bastard*, he thought despairingly. A feeling of betrayal overwhelmed him as he realised without his mother's support, he was fighting a lost cause.

"You can start looking for work tomorrow. Get the paper and look at the jobs. If there's nothing there for you, you can knock on the door of every factory in the area until you get a job." His father commanded.

Rising at 5.00 am to be first in line at the gates of the biggest factory in the area, Terry began what was to become a daily routine. Coincidently, a downturn in the economic climate accompanied his father's decision. Each day, long queues of men waited at factory gates, all looking in vain for employment.

Day after day, Terry repeated the same question many times. "Are there any vacancies today?"

It was always the same answer. "Sorry son. Come back tomorrow"

Sometimes, a sympathetic Personnel Manager suggested he complete an application form, thinking this would provide the eager well-dressed boy with some hope and encouragement in his search for work.

Weeks passed fruitlessly. Terry spent his days trudging the streets, never giving up hope. *I've just got to be in the right place at the right time. Somebody will give me a job eventually*, he told himself

The Sydney Morning Herald advertised few vacancies. Those that did appear were mostly for experienced persons or those with the educational qualifications he lacked. By the end of the day, his feet ached and his shoes, which had commenced the day with a high sheen, were scuffed and dusty. With no money for bus or train fares, his face became a familiar sight in the industrial suburbs, within comfortable walking distance. His confidence never waned. Heeding his mother's advice, he squared his shoulders, looked prospective employers in the eye, and forcing a friendly smile to his tired face, asked politely, "I am looking for work. I am willing to do anything. Please, are there any vacancies?"

Late one afternoon, on his way home, he decided to inquire again at a joinery factory a short distance from the Cabramatta Caravan Park. The whine and clatter of wood turning machines and the odour of sawdust pervaded the summer heat as he entered the dusty yard. Expecting the inevitable reply, he rapped his fingers on the factory manager's door.

"Yes, son?" The balding executive looked up from a dishevelled desk where he had been examining blueprints.

"I'm sorry to bother you again sir. Do you have any vacancies?"

A smile displaced the look of annoyance at the unwelcome interruption. "You're persistent aren't you?"

"Well, I've got to keep looking sir. I'm sorry to have bothered you." Terry turned to walk away.

"Wait! As a matter of fact, we are looking for a couple of lads. Do you think you'd be interested in a trainee glazier's position?"

"Oh, yes please! I'd be happy to do anything." Terry could scarcely believe his ears.

"Be here at seven thirty tomorrow morning and we'll give you a try."

Terry ran the mile back to the caravan park, bursting with happiness. "I've got a job at Stegbar. I'm going to be a trainee glazier and work with Mr D'Autorio, one of the glaziers. They're going to pay me six pound a week!"

Judy's relief that her son's stoic efforts had borne fruit equalled Terry's enthusiasm and excitement. She hugged him. "There, I knew you'd do it. This could lead to big things for you." Always a dreamer, she already imagined him as the manager of the factory before he had even started.

Henry, was less enthusiastic. "About time. Six quid, eh? You can pay us five pound for board. With the other quid, you can buy your own clothes, soap and toothpaste. If you don't like it, you can get out and get private board. You'll find they won't feed you as well as we do and it'll cost you that much."

Umberto D'Autorio took Terry under his wing. Treating him as a son, he imparted the skills of glazing. His new trainee learnt to swiftly roll putty up the wooden window frames, creating a bed for the sheets of glass, which Umberto cut on a special platform built across the back of his utility vehicle.

Terry enjoyed the work and especially enjoyed the company of the tall Italian glazier.

"Umberto D'Autorio is my name, but you can call me Bert. I come from the north of Italy. That's why I'm tall and fair. Not like the little dark blokes that come from the South. They're all mafia down there. Those little Sicilians would stab you in the back!" Umberto spoke with a heavy Italian accent punctuated by much hand waving.

Of indeterminate age, perhaps thirty, the glazier stood nearly six feet in height. With a face, reminding Terry of a hatchet, he had straight, light brown hair and an athletic frame. He also possessed a quick temper and brooked no nonsense. Noelinelly cheerful, he enjoyed joking with Terry. Working hard and fast, they sometimes finished early, stopping at a handy pub, where Umberto treated Terry to an icy schooner of frothy Millers Lager.

Living on the outskirts of Cabramatta, he was in the process of building a brick cottage for his wife and brood of young lively children. Umberto's bricklaying skills were rudimentary and the house crudely constructed from an assortment of different coloured bricks. Terry was soon to learn the reason behind the various colours used in its construction. Every day, Umberto would stack rows of stolen bricks into the back of his ute from each construction site where they worked.

"Everything in my house has come from building sites. I don't pay for nothing!" Umberto announced proudly.

Terry was horrified. This went against everything he had been taught. However, he was fond of Umberto and hoped his new friend wouldn't be caught. *I wonder what they will do with his house if they catch him.* he mused, imagining the police ripping the house down to retrieve the stolen bricks, window frames and roofing iron, while Umberto's wife and children stood weeping on the road verge.

Terry worked happily with Umberto for nearly nine months. During this time, Stegbar offered him a carpentry apprenticeship but as an apprentice's wages were less than he currently received, he declined, knowing his father would never accept less board money.

One day Umberto looked rather sad, "I don't have enough work for you. I sorry. Perhaps when things get better, we work together again, eh?"

"What am I going to do?" Terry asked, aghast at the prospect of losing his job.

"Mister Overand, he say you work in factory. I sorry but there just not enough new houses to keep us both busy."

A further economic downturn had been the cause for the slump in the building industry. With fewer orders for windows, the factory began scaling down its operations, resulting in the sacking of many of the workers. Terry went to see the Factory Manager, fearing for his job.

"It's a shame lad but things'll pick up. They always do. In the mean time I can keep you busy but it means sweeping the floor and helping out wherever we need you."

Knowing the alternative, Terry reluctantly agreed. Pushing a broom around the factory was better than dismissal with the other less fortunate workers. He hated the demotion, finding his new role encompassed all the unpleasant jobs nobody else would do.

"Hey lad." The factory foreman called one hot summer morning. "The sawdust hopper's blocked. Grab a ladder and get up there and clear it!"

With the production halted temporarily, Terry hurried to erect a long wooden ladder against the huge hopper looming over the building like some predatory prehistoric monster. With legs shaking, he climbed to the trapdoor on one side of the bin.

"You've got to get right inside and break up the blockage." The foreman stood watching from below.

Thick choking wood dust rained over the reluctant boy as he pulled the door open. He was soon covered in fine sawdust, which invaded his nose, mouth and eyes, and sticking to his sweat in a filthy itchy coating. Holding a handkerchief over his mouth, Terry pounded the offending blockage. A small avalanche of shavings, dust and wood chips buried him. "Bugger this," he swore, fighting his way to the manhole.

On other occasions, he worked as 'a tailer out' on the huge wood machines. Without the benefit of hearing protection or goggles, he stood for up to ten hours a day, iron-hard woodchips bombarding his face as he guided heavy lengths of tallow wood from the machine and stacked them.

Staggering home at the end of each day, eyes watering and ears ringing from the incessant roar, Terry longed for the peace and quite, the freedom of outdoor work and Umberto's cheerful, good-humoured banter. However, that era had gone. His thoughts turned to country life and the happiness he had known at Willow Flats. *I know*, he thought, *I'll get a job on a farm*. The idea was appealing. Without considering the practicalities, he began scanning the "positions vacant" columns once again. In his laborious untidy scrawl, he penned several letters for farm help and was overjoyed to receive a positive response.

"Dear Terry," he read the letter aloud to his mother, "We were happy to receive your application for a position on a farm. We run a sheep property near Coonabarabran and need someone to take over from our present employee who is leaving us to join the army." Terry paused to inquire, "Where's Coonabarabran?"

His mother retrieved the tattered Golden Fleece road map from the glove box compartment of the utility. "There it is." She stabbed a finger, wrinkled from years of housework at the map.

Terry checked the distance against the scale. "Hmmm. It's about four hundred miles north west of Sydney. How would I get there from here?"

There's a train line running there, see." Judy showed him the black crosshatched line denoting the railway. "Are you sure you want to do this?" Concern for her son created deep furrows in her brow.

"Sure mum. I'll be okay."

Terry's lanky, curly haired figure presented an incongruous site as he boarded the ancient wooden carriages at Sydney's Central Railway Station. The little black steam locomotive sat quietly, hissing secrets to the electric trains waiting on adjacent lines. Clutching a suitcase in one hand, an old .22 calibre rifle bought from a pawnshop slung over his shoulder, and a pet budgerigar in its cage in the other hand, Terry took his place on one of the hard wooden seats. He'd always loved the noisy, intelligent little parrots, having kept one as a pet for years. Although pets had been against his father's orders, Judy had gone to bat for him, insisting, "it's good for the child to have something to love." For once, she had won the day. There was no way Terry was going anywhere without his little feathered companion.

With romantic notions of shooting rabbits and exploring rolling green hills in his spare time, he imagined an idyllic life as an adopted member of a kind farming family providing the home he had never known.

As the train rattled away from the city, the drab squalor of the suburbs fell behind. Terry turned, hoping to survey his sole travelling companion surreptitiously. A petite young woman, with long auburn hair, a cute snub nose and freckles was watching him, a quizzical smile playing around the corners of strawberry red lips. A hot flush crept up Terry's neck and turned his face a cherry red.

"Where are you going?" the goddess enquired, surveying with interest the birdcage resting on the seat beside him.

"I've got a job on a farm," he answered proudly, fighting to control the embarrassment at having to speak to such a beautiful creature. "This is Charlie! He's my budgie. He can say lots of amazing words and things and he sits on my shoulder."

The girl smiled amusedly. "You didn't say where you were going."

"Coonabarabran. Do you know it?"

"Of course. I live there."

The two chatted happily, the girl quizzing him, amusement at his awkwardness showing in her bright green eyes. The shadows lengthened and the train rattled slowly across the barren plains. As darkness fell, his companion stretched her lithe body on a coat placed over the slats of the uncomfortable bench seat opposite him. She slumbered quietly, managing to look even more beautiful asleep, leaving Terry alone with his thoughts.

The antediluvian engine found a reason to stop at every town during the long weary journey into the desolate interior of the vast continent. Terry watched as fence posts and poles slipped slowly by, thinking, *I could almost run faster than this.* The iron wheels seemed to be chanting the same message repeatedly as the train swayed in a sickening rhythm, "Better go back. Better go back. Better go back." A feeling of loneliness and dread threatened to overpower the boy as the knowledge of what he had done dawned. *Don't be a baby*, he admonished himself silently. *It'll be okay. You're just tired.* He was unable to shake off the dreadful feeling as the sun rose over the flat dry paddocks stretching to the distant horizon. Although home had been a mere caravan, he longed for it desperately.

A thickset youth with sandy hair and a baby face met Terry at the tiny Coonabarabran station. As they parted, Terry's attractive travelling companion called, "Good luck." He realised with dismay that he hadn't had the presence of mind to ask her name or learn anything about her. He had been too busy talking about himself.

After shaking hands and introducing himself as Colin, the

youth led the exhausted, homesick boy to a dusty pickup truck parked nearby. Terry had been travelling for over twenty-five hours without sleep. The sandwiches his mother had lovingly thrust in his hand before departure lay in his stomach like concrete. The youth he was replacing prattled incessantly, telling Terry about his new position and responsibilities.

"Yeah. He's really crazy about those chooks. He has hundreds and hundreds of all sorts of hens that I bet you've never seen before. They're prize hens and he's got so many ribbons, cups and certificates from all the shows. Your job is to look after the chooks and the dogs."

Terry knew suddenly that he had no inkling of his duties prior to accepting the position. He had assumed that he would be something akin to a jackeroo, learning real farm work. *Looking after chooks? You've got to be joking! That's not what I came here for.* He didn't voice his dismay however, preferring instead to conceal his stupidity at accepting such a job.

After driving for what seemed like hours, they swung off the dirt road, juddering over a cattle grid, then along a dusty, rutted track to a lonely looking weatherboard cottage surrounded by a motley collection of corrugated iron sheds. Colin parked his souped up Morris Minor in a corrugated lean to. Grabbing Terry's suitcase he led him to the back verandah where one end had been enclosed, forming a sleep out. "This is your room," he said, slinging the suitcase on the bed. At once, four small noisy children spewed from the back door, bursting into the bedroom, they surrounded Terry, babbling excitedly to each other. The new farmhand was an exciting curiosity and they were eager to inspect him.

"Come on you lot. Leave him alone." A tall thin woman with round shoulders and long straight mousy hair appeared on the back verandah, wiping house worn hands on a floral apron. She smiled at Terry, offering a damp warm hand for him to shake. "Hello, Terry. I'm Mrs Cummings. It's lovely to see you. You're not what I imagined from your letter, but never mind, welcome to your new home."

Terry wondered what impression he had conveyed from his correspondence but did not inquire. The children ran off into the house where he could hear them squabbling noisily. "Thank you. It's nice to be here," he lied taking the proffered hand, shyly.

"You must be tired, but Colin's got to leave for the Army tomorrow, so leave your things here and he'll show you around and tell you what your duties are."

Too exhausted and homesick to feign enthusiasm, Terry followed Colin to the farm sheds a short distance from the house. The older boy proudly showed him a most amazing assortment of poultry he had ever seen. Cages and cages of birds of all sizes and colours, some with plumage sprouting from the tops of their heads looking like Hottentot warriors, others with brilliant plumage of all colours and hues, filled several sheds. Their owner's obsession with the show birds was obvious from the care taken to ensure the best possible conditions for their housing. Colin demonstrated how to feed the noisy cackling birds and clean their cages daily to prevent infestations from mites and disease.

He led Terry to a tiny fibro privy sitting alone some twenty metres from the homestead. "It's your job to make sure the can doesn't overflow. It has to be emptied regularly," he instructed, dragging the stinking toilet can from beneath its wooden seat.

The stench from the putrid contents festering in the summer heat caused Terry's stomach to churn. Fat yellow maggots wriggled luxuriously in their faecal heaven.

Looking after chooks and feeding dogs were bad enough, but having to empty the dunny can? That was the final straw!

The flat arid isolated landscape, the prospect of the unpleasant menial nature of the work, his fatigue and overpowering homesickness, was at once too much for him to bear. He was fully reliant on the Cummings generosity and unlike Colin, he had no vehicle and could not escape to town for respite and relaxation. Realising he had made the biggest mistake of his life, Terry immediately felt physically sick.

At lunchtime, it was apparent that the Cummings family did not intend to adopt him as one of their members when his dinner was brought to him on the verandah. "You'll take your meals out here," Mrs Cummings told him.

I'm just the farm help he thought. I'm not good enough to eat inside with them. He looked at the tiny portions of uninteresting food on his plate. Still hungry after the meal, he knocked on the back door.

"What is it?" Mrs Cummings answered.

"I am very sorry. I think I've made an enormous mistake. I am not the right sort of person for this job. Can you take me to town please?"

Homesickness and despair far outweighed the feelings of guilt he harboured for leaving the Cummings's in the lurch. Without ever having met Mr Cummings, Colin immediately drove Terry to the Coonabarabran airport in a stony silence. Fortunately for Terry, he had just enough money saved to purchase a one-way ticket on the one daily flight to Sydney.

Judy showed no surprise at Terry's return. His parents knew him better than he knew himself and had decided that he should learn a hard lesson rather than try to dissuade him from his decision to accept the farm job. To Terry's relief, they made no mention of the incident and he offered no explanation.

Within days of his return, Terry answered an advertisement placed in the Sydney Morning Herald by Peacock Brothers Pty Ltd. The company was located in Martin Place, Sydney and serviced office equipment. The interview went well and he began a new career as a Comptometer Serviceman.[4]

Although Terry knew little about the workings of these noisy mechanical contraptions, and was not permitted to attempt repairs, he felt important strutting proudly into offices with his little brown case and tool roll containing an oil can and a rudimentary collection of tools. The female operators were unaware of his ignorance of the machines. Rather than suffer the embarrassment of admitting his lack of expertise, he would pretend to solve various mechanical defects reported to him in the course of his routine. Usually, the problem was simple, such as the build up of dirt or sticking components from a careless operator spilling a cup of tea into the cogs, levers and springs.

Each day Terry grabbed a handful of cards listing the firms requiring his services. After collecting money for public transport,

---

[4] Comptometers were the forerunners to modern day calculators. Mostly mechanical contraptions, rows of numbered keys when depressed registered on numbered wheels behind small windows below the keys. Operators were known as Comptometrists and were responsible for the arithmetical calculations associated with invoicing and accounts.

he ran between each appointment or rode the electric trains, hiding in railway station toilets until the ticket collectors left their turnstiles. The extra few shillings he saved by not buying a ticket augmented his low pay. By working quickly, he was able to finish his calls long before the scheduled time for "knock off," allowing time to attend an afternoon session at one of Sydney's many picture theatres or stroll in Hyde Park, taking pleasure from the tranquil surroundings.

Evenings spent in the confines of the tiny caravan with his parents failed to meet the needs of an energetic teenage boy. His father still insisted that he be in bed by 7.00 pm despite Terry's sixteen years. Unable to accept this Draconian rule, Terry rebelled leaving the van to spend time with close friends, Laurie and Peter who also lived in the caravan park.

"Where do you think you're off to? I've told you, you're not to go out after tea!" Henry blocked his path as Terry stepped out the door of the van.

"I'm going to see Laurie and Peter," he replied, looking unabashedly at his father.

"No you're not. Get back in there!" Henry began clenching a fist, anger boiling.

Terry stood his ground. Looking his father in the eye, at six foot three inches he was at least a head taller. "I pay my board. I earn my own living and I am not a kid anymore."

Henry raised his arm but stopped as something in his youngest son's eye warned him that any violence would meet with physical retaliation.

In keeping with the popular saying, "the worm had turned." Although Terry continued to treat his father with respect, he would no longer be cowed or subdued, demanding and receiving respect in return.

A flimsy cotton curtain separated his bunk at the front of the van from his parent's bed a few feet away at the rear. After Judy and Henry had retired for the night, arguments became commonplace. By design, the cryptic and monosyllabic nature of their conversation failed to enlighten him as to the cause of this tremendous discontent. Whatever the arguing was about, he knew it was something very serious indeed but in respect for their privacy, he sought to escape in the music from the earplug of his tiny transistor radio.

Sometimes, his father would get up from the bed and rush outside where Terry could hear him puking and retching as his stomach convulsed in paroxysms of vomiting. For as long as he could remember, his father had suffered from chronic peptic and duodenal ulcers. When Henry ate something that didn't agree with him, or when he was extremely upset, his fickle stomach rebelled, violently ejecting its' contents. Terry's heart went out to his father at the terrible agony of his condition.

During the arguments, his father often uncharacteristically pleaded with his mother. "No, Judy. Please. I need you!" When the pleading failed to yield the desired result, the arguments often degenerated, becoming nasty, as Judy could not be placated.

Terry became increasingly apprehensive. *Surely, they know this is tearing me apart? It's like they've forgotten I exist.* Finally, he was unable to stand their sniping any longer. "For goodness sake! Stop it you two and go to sleep." he called.

Silence followed.

After his reprimand, the nightly squabbling ceased, although both parents continued to appear strained and introspective.

Two years had gone by since they made the caravan their home. One evening Henry arrived home from work and after his customary glass of beer, he sat brooding.

"We're going bush. You better hand in your notice if you want to come with us," he announced unexpectedly.

Stunned, Terry turned to look at his mother. She continued working unfalteringly at the little methylated spirit stove as she prepared their dinner. *She already knows about this,* he thought. *Why didn't she say something to me?* "I've nowhere else to go. Of course, I'm coming with you. Why are we leaving?"

"Your father has had enough of the city."

Terry knew there were other reasons behind the decision. "What am I going to do in the country?"

"You'll be alright," his father murmured. "We'll head south and find work for one of the Shires."

Terry's faith in his parents had taken a battering but the alternative was to find private board. He balked at the thought. His father had created such a grim picture of starvation and mistreatment at the hands of greedy landlords that he decided, life in a caravan would be better.

The next day Terry asked to see his boss.

"I'm sorry sir. I really like this job but my parents have decided that they want to go to the country and I must go with them, as I can't afford to live on my own."

Old Mr Peacock rocked back on his chair; his rotund figure causing the springs to squeak their protest. "I am sorry to hear that lad." He peered benignly over the rim of his spectacles. "I'll write you a good reference and I hope things work out for you."

Terry sadly bid farewell to his friends and small team of co-workers whom he had grown to know and trust. After the debacle of his trip to Coonabarabran, he had lost his yearning for 'a life on the land.' The Aussie outback now seemed a harsh, cruel place and very different from his childhood memories. His newfound aspirations of learning a trade servicing and repairing office machines evaporated with his farewells. *I suppose I'll end up working on a rubbish cart or digging roads somewhere in the back blocks*, he thought miserably. *There won't be many opportunities for me without my Intermediate Certificate.*

They lowered the little van off the bricks on which it had stood immobile since making the caravan park home. They set off along the Hume Highway, heading south toward the country Terry loved and thought he would never see again. Sitting alone in the rear of the ute, he was oblivious to his mother's melancholy. Occasionally, he glanced through the rear window to where his parents sat in apparent silence. As usual, his father's poker face and brooding silence gave little away.

They reached the delightfully pretty, Snowy Mountains town of Tumut where they pitched camp in the local caravan park. Terry explored the gin clear, snow fed waters of the Tumut River while his father enquired with the Snowy Mountains Hydro Electric Authority and the local Shire as to their employment prospects.

"Nothing doing here," Henry muttered on his return. "We'll have to keep looking."

Unperturbed with the negative answer, they moved on the following day. *Why are we heading north again?* Terry wondered. *I suppose I'll find out when we get there.* He was annoyed to think that his parents had not included him in the decision making process. However, Judy and Henry were too preoccupied with their own thoughts to worry about their son.

"Goulburn." Terry read the wooden sign above the entrance

to the rambling town's railway station. *We're in Goulburn. What are we doing here?*

The answer came in the form of one of the most unexpected and traumatic events of his life.

CHAPTER THREE
THE MAKING OF A MAN

Judy alighted from the cab of the ute, her eyes red and cheeks puffy from crying. Walking past Terry to the caravan; she unlocked the door and entered. He could hear her rummaging in cupboards and drawers. Henry remained seated behind the steering wheel staring silently ahead. Sensing that something dramatic was unfolding, Terry waited under the tonneau cover at the back of the ute where he rode during their travels. A few moments elapsed before his mother appeared carrying a cardboard box. She leant this on the side of the vehicle and addressed him, "I'm leaving your father. You have to make a choice whether you are coming with me or staying with him."

Terry reeled in a state of complete shock. "But, where will you go?"

Not privy to the discourse between his parents over the preceding three days they had been on the road, he was unaware of the earnest discussions ensuing in the cabin of the Holden. Suddenly, like the final pieces of a jigsaw puzzle falling into place, it all made sense. The nocturnal arguing, his father's pleas and horrible vomiting, the stony silence, which had descended between his parents and the sudden decision to leave Sydney, all these things fitted neatly together. *How could he have been so stupid not to see what was going on?*

"I'm going to live with Mr Browning. There's a place there for you if you want to come. He'll make you very welcome."

Terry's mind was in turmoil. *Go and live with a man whom I have never met? The suggestion is unthinkable. He's got kids of his own. How am I going to fit in with them? Mum's been having an affair with this bloke she's been working for all this time. His wife's only just died recently. How could she?*

That his mother had sacrificed the best part of her life enduring privations and cruelty while always putting the needs of her children foremost did not occur to Terry's immature mind. Neither did it occur to him that she had persevered in an unhappy marriage for many years until her sons could fend for themselves. That his mother was entitled to love and happiness was the furthest thought from his mind. In his selfish misery, Terry instantly condemned his mother's desertion. He condemned her for her decision to live with someone who was a stranger to him. *How long had she pursued this clandestine affair?* His stomach churned with nausea and a newly born hatred he had previously never known.

"I'll stay with dad," he muttered.

Judy moved to kiss her youngest son goodbye. Terry pulled back, turning his face away, not wanting to look at her. Picking up the cardboard box containing her few possessions, she strode in the direction of the railway station.

"Wait, Judy! You can't go like that. At least let me get you a suitcase." Henry called after her, great anguish evident on his pale lined face.

Judy had made up her mind and did not want to delay any longer. Tears streaming down her face, she called back over her shoulder, "I can manage."

The pitiful sight of his mother carrying the result of twenty-one years of marriage in a cardboard box as she left his life forever was like a dagger piercing Terry's heart. He climbed from the back of the ute and sat next to his father as a strange new feeling of pity overwhelmed him. Silently, his father turned the ignition key and they moved off. Terry didn't ask where they were going but he guessed from the direction that their country adventure was over.

Returning to Grandma Flatley's house, Grandma met the news without comment. They pushed the caravan into the backyard and Terry quickly discovered that his father expected him to take over the domestic chores previously handled by his mother. With no work and still reeling from shock and an awful aching emptiness in his chest, he was happy to comply. Cooking meals, cleaning the caravan and attending to their washing distracted him from the dreadful empty ache of grief.

Henry soon found work. Terry had no money and his father offered him none.

Leaving Terry alone with his grandmother each day without a thought as to his son's employment prospects or emotional welfare, he settled into a daily routine.

Each evening Henry returned, taking it for granted that Terry would have his dinner waiting. Although there was a new closeness between father and son, Terry quickly tired of the situation. Scrounging the occasional sixpence from Grandma

Flatley to purchase a newspaper, he commenced his search for employment.

It was not long before his efforts bore fruit. When his father returned home one evening, Terry greeted him. "Dad, I've got a job in Sefton as a Storeman."

His father looked crestfallen. "How are you going to look after me?"

"Dad, I can't stay here in this caravan every day playing housewife. I've got to find work and have a life of my own."

Henry did not reply. His disappointment was obvious. Without his wife he was emotionally lost and a broken man. Although Terry felt tremendous pity for his father, he knew with certainty that he had to leave.

"I've found private board with a Mrs Fenn, in Sefton, just down the road from Dulmisons where I'll be working. I'll come and visit you on the weekend. Don't worry dad, it'll be alright!"

Terry's new life and independence proved a welcome relief from the emotional trauma of recent events. As the sole boarder with the widowed Mrs Fenn, he was at first treated kindly. Assigned his own thickly carpeted room with a comfortable bed and nice furniture, he liked the novelty of being able to come and go as he chose and happily parted with the major portion of his wages each week. *This isn't as bad as the old man made out*, he said to himself. *I wish I'd had the guts to leave sooner."*

The world of entrepreneurship was new to Mrs Fenn but she grasped the principles of profitability quickly. Realising that she could profit handsomely if she had more boarders, she soon filled the house with single men. Terry lost his privacy when a young Dutchman moved into his room. The quiet congeniality ceased to exist with the inevitable personality clashes between the various boarders. Terry's relationship with Mrs Fenn deteriorated in direct proportion to the little widow's increasing greed.

He managed to save a few shillings from his pay each week and he used the money to purchase a tiny underpowered Puch moped from the Dutchman. True to his word, Terry putted out to Ingleburn, battling strong headwinds on the underpowered velocipede to visit his father each weekend. Sometimes Michael and Paul would be there too. Having left his job as a tractor driver Paul embarked upon a career in commerce working for a large Insurance Brokerage. Michael had also chosen a career in the insurance industry and seemed reasonably happy boarding with a family in Bankstown.

All three boys felt so betrayed by their mother's desertion and infidelity that they never discussed her, choosing instead to sever all ties with her. In the nineteen sixties, it was unforgivable for women to desert their husbands or have sexual liaisons outside their marriage. Needless to say, life and morals would change drastically in the ensuing decades.

Terry had maintained his friendship with his childhood mates from the caravan park, Laurie Daly and Peter Shepherd. The three boys were almost inseparable, spending every available moment together. On occasions they travelled by train to Kings Cross visiting nightspots and inevitably getting into their share of fights with other youths. On one occasion after attending a rock concert in Sydney's famous Hyde Park, they caught the last train home. The deserted carriages rocked crazily as the old electric train raced between stations. It was probable the driver was keen to finish his shift, as he seemed to abandon any safety considerations. At Granville Station, they screeched to a halt to uplift a scruffy group of youths waiting on the platform.

The six young men appeared belligerent from the outset, shouting and cursing loudly as they boarded the carriages. As the train gathered speed, they moved along the carriages, no doubt seeking other passengers to harass.

Peter, Laurie and Terry sat quietly, watching as the young men approached. "Here comes trouble." Laurie remarked unnecessarily.

"What can we do?" Peter squeaked, frightened by the pending confrontation.

"There's nothing much we can do. We're outnumbered. Perhaps they'll just walk through to the other carriage." Terry knew this was unlikely but hoped by avoiding eye contact they'd be left alone."

The first youth to reach their carriage, a lanky aboriginal boy of about sixteen shouted, "Hey, we've got some surfies here!"

"We're not surfies," Terry replied quietly. It was no good. In the era of the early nineteen sixties one was either a "surfie" or a "bodgie." Bodgies hated surfies with a passion and welcomed any excuse for a good stoush.

"Well, you look like bloody surfies to me," the youth replied looking meaningfully at Peter's bleached hair.

The remaining youths crowded into the compartment jeering. "Chuck 'em off the train!" "Lousy, bloody surfies." "Where's ya surfboards?" "Left at the beach, did ya?" "Come on, show us how tough you are!"

Laurie stood up, towering over the nearest youth, his face red with anger. "Just leave us alone, mate. We don't want any problems."

"Nah, you're piss weak. Couldn't fight ya way out of a wet paper bag," sneered a pasty-faced thickset teenager. He ran his fingers through his greasy black hair, combed back from his forehead in the classic bodgie style.

One of the group shoved Laurie in the chest, simultaneously hooking a leg behind Laurie's leg in an attempt to drop him to the floor. Terry sprang to his friend's defence, shouldering the offender to one side. Shouting and punching the remaining youths joined the melee. Struggling to stay on their feet against the rocking motion of the train, Laurie, Peter and Terry fought bravely, swinging fists wildly as a hail of blows hammered them from all sides. The doors of the old carriage stood open throughout the struggle and the rushing air and noise of the train added to the commotion. Telegraph poles rushing past and the likelihood of another train approaching from the opposite direction guaranteed the death of anyone falling from the carriage.

The train slowed as it approached the next station. Terry received a massive push in the middle of his back, sending him through the open carriage door. With no time to feel fear, he began running in mid flight to lessen the impact as he hit the sloping railway embankment nearly six feet below. He landed on the sharp blue metal ballast of the train tracks, the momentum hurling him forward. As the ground rushed up to meet him, Terry curled into a ball, tumbling over and over in pace with the still moving train. At last, his body ceased rolling. Ineffable fear took hold. *Oh my God! What if there's another train coming?* He scrambled to his feet, amazed that no bones had been broken. Looking around, he saw that he had fallen into a "no man's" land between the tracks.

Hobbling toward the nearby railway station, he took stock of his injuries. Apart from bruises and grazing to his knees and elbows, he was remarkably unscathed.

"Are you okay?" Laurie called concernedly from the platform.

Peter stood with him, ashen faced and dishevelled. Now disappearing in the distance, the train raced away with the victorious hoodlums, whooping and shouting with glee.

"Yeah. Christ, I thought all my birthdays had come at once then." Terry re-joined his mates on the yellow gravel surface of the deserted station.

"What are we gunna do now?" Peter wondered. "Should we go to the cops?"

Laurie looked at him scornfully. "Don't be bloody stupid. We'll probably just get ourselves in more trouble."

Their lack of faith and fear of the New South Wales Police Force was not without justification. The majority of the Force's hard-bitten men had no time for teenagers, particularly those out late at night. In particular, the notorious twenty-first division's reputation for administering beatings to extract false confessions played upon their minds.

"Well, there's no more trains now until about five o' clock. We had better start walking," Terry suggested.

Several weeks after the incident on the train, the three friends were strolling along Cabramatta Road when a grey Holden sedan slowed and pulled alongside. Terry looked to see why the vehicle had stopped. He paled and panicked at the site of his mother and the male driver whom he knew must be Tom Browning, her new partner. Judy began opening the door to speak to him. The unwelcome confrontation with his mother and the man whom he blamed for his parents separation, filled Terry with a mixture of horror, fear and loathing. Turning away quickly, he took flight, racing with all the speed he could muster from his long legs and leaving his friends standing open mouthed. Without pausing to look back and in fear of pursuit, he continued running, dodging and weaving through the side streets, until he was sure he wouldn't be caught. At the back of his mind was the fear that somehow his mother would seek a custody order from the Courts, forcing him to live with the family he had never met but hated with all the passion his young brain could muster. The prospect of losing his new found freedom and living with a family who, in his mind he assumed to be monsters and home wreckers was akin to the worst fate he could imagine.

He waited for over half an hour, watching both ends of the

street in case Tom's car should appear as they searched for him. Finally, judging it safe to do so, he made his way to the railway station, taking the train back to his boarding house.

After that, he avoided Cabramatta, and in the process, severed contact with Laurie and Peter, so great was his fear that he would cross his mother's path again.

Eventually, the acrimonious nature of his relationship with Mrs Fenn forced Terry to leave. Knowing she would create a scene if he confronted her with the news of his intended departure, he quietly packed his belongings and crept from the house under cover of darkness. Having recently moved into a large boarding house in Strathfield, his good friend Peter had suggested Terry move there also. The proposition appeared attractive as the two friends could knock about together again without fear of Terry stumbling across his mother's path.

If Terry thought things were bad with Mrs Fenn, he was unprepared for the life in the once majestic two-storey mansion, housing fifty men.

Some rooms held as many as six beds. Due to the large scale of the purely commercial operation, the owners dished out meals in a regimented fashion. Forced to join a long food queue, they found helpings were barely adequate with the cuisine falling far short of a desirable standard. Allocated a room shared by two other men, both much older than him, Terry felt very uneasy.

"Better watch out for old Tom," one of the boarders warned him.

"Why?" Terry asked innocently.

"He's only just been released from Callan Park."

Oh no! Terry felt sick. Callan Park was Sydney's most infamous mental hospital. He had been raised in a society which, in its ignorance believed that persons suffering from mental illness were all homicidal maniacs and mental illness was contagious.

Unbeknown to Terry, his other roommate in the tiny cell-like space was a huge, muscular homosexual who took an instant liking to the fresh faced, curly haired youth.

In his naivety, Terry was completely unaware of Warren's perverted intentions, as he cautiously watched "old Tom." He felt extremely uncomfortable in the presence of the older, ugly, former mental patient, misinterpreting the attentions of the homosexual Warren as being merely friendly.

In his forties, with a large, hooked nose, lantern jaw, perpetual leering grin and an infestation of warts on his face, the mental patient presented a repulsive site. Warren on the other hand, was a massive man in his early twenties. Weighing approximately 170 kilograms and with a fetish for leather clothing, he had black, straight hair, combed back from his forehead and slicked down with Brylecream, the universally popular hairdressing of the era. With oval features, ready smile and a softly spoken manner, he immediately set out to lull Terry into a false sense of security.

Warren was notorious amongst the other boarders for his penchant for young boys but none of the other boarders had sufficient sense of responsibility to warn the unsuspecting youth, choosing instead to await developments with malicious glee.

One Sunday morning, as Terry lay in his top bunk above Warren's bed, the big deviate produced a length of sash cord. "Let me show you a rope trick Terry," he suggested. Standing erect, Warren's head and shoulders towered over the teenager in the bunk, which was itself nearly six feet above floor level. "Put your hands together in front of you," he instructed.

Obediently, Terry complied, curious to know the nature of the rope trick. Almost before he knew what was happening, his hands had been bound tightly together, Warren hauled him from the bunk onto the floor where he pinned down the defenceless boy with his huge bulk. Soft, flabby, yet amazingly strong hands began to molest him, feeling every inch of Terry's crutch to the accompaniment of delighted guffaws from the lunatic on the other side of the room.

Rage and terror leant Terry almost superhuman strength. Bellowing at the top of his lungs, he kicked and struggled with all his might, even butting at the face of his molester with his forehead. Warren had clearly underestimated his victim's ability to resist. Lest the unholy din created by the less powerful boy bring someone to his rescue, Warren released Terry from his groping hands and sat back disappointedly. Leaping to his feet, Terry wrenched the bedroom door open and tore outside somehow undoing the knotted sash cord with his teeth. His headed for the boarding house manager's office, his heart racing and head pounding from the terror of the attack.

"What's the matter son?" The middle aged boarding house

proprietor resented the intrusion to his office where he was engrossed in watching "The Beverley Hillbillies on his black and white television set. With silver hair combed back in a futile attempt to conceal his bald pate, a long, thin, pale face, watery blue eyes and thin lips, the owner favoured a white shirt and light grey trousers as his usual uniform. The lack of colour leant him a cadaverous appearance and it always came as something of a surprise to Terry when he actually moved.

"That big, fat, bloody slob that you've put me in with has just tried to rape me!"

"Calm down son. I'm sure you're exaggerating."

"I'm not bloody well exaggerating. Go and ask the lunatic. He was there. He saw the whole thing. That bastard should be shot!" Terry went on to explain in detail how Warren had tricked him with the rope and had fondled him while he'd been held down.

"I'll put you in the front room," the walking corpse offered. "You won't be going to the police will you?" The question seemed to carry an element of implied threat. "We don't want the cops coming around here!"

"Just keep that bastard away from me. He makes my skin crawl. He's bloody sick in the head!"

Terry had no intention of relaying events to the police. Not only did he distrust them, but also the idea of being the complainant in a sexual assault somehow made him feel dirty. No, it was far better to put the incident down to experience and become wiser for the future.

Despite his escape from the indecent assault, Warren continued to harass him, making unwelcome advances and indecent suggestions at every opportunity. It mattered not to Warren whether or not the advances were public. "Jee, you've got beautiful eyes," or "What lovely curly hair you've got," he remarked loudly across the expanse of the packed dining room, smirking lewdly.

Much to Terry's disgust, the other heterosexual young men who also shared the establishment thought the comments hilarious. "Oooh Terry, you've got lovely eyes," they mocked.

"Piss off, you bastards!" he retorted.

Terry developed a deep-seated hatred for sexual deviates resulting from this and previous incidents from his schooldays. Unable to bear the unpleasant atmosphere of the old mansion any longer, he sought and found homely accommodation with an elderly couple in the southern Sydney suburb of Jannali. His friend Peter joined the navy and Terry lost touch with both he and Laurie.

About this time, Terry changed jobs again and began to plan a new life away from Sydney. To the lonely troubled teenager, the overcrowded and unfriendly city seemed to epitomise misery, poverty and depravity.

On Saturday 30th June 1964, an Air New Zealand Lockheed Electra aircraft took off from Sydney's Kingsford Smith Airport. Seated in an economy class seat, Terry looked down on the smog-shrouded metropolis. "Good riddance," he muttered angrily.

"That's how I feel about cities too." The comment came from the balding middle-aged male passenger occupying the aisle seat next to him. "Hello, my name is Terry Flatley." The man offered Terry his hand, smiling warmly.

"What? Are you having me on, or what?" Terry thought he'd misheard.

"What do you mean?"

"Saying your name is Terry Flatley. How can it be? That's my name!" Terry pulled the airline ticket from his shirt pocket, pointing to the typed name on the document.

"No! You've got to be joking. What an amazing coincidence. We must be related. Where do you come from?"

"Sydney, of course but my father was born in Bury, near Manchester."

"That's where I come from. Bury is my home town. What was your father's first name?"

"Henry. My Grandma is Lois Edge Flatley."

"No. I don't know either of them. Flatley is a very common name in the north of England, but what an amazing coincidence that we should be on the same flight today."

Apart from the similarity of their names, the older man and the youth had nothing in common. They quickly exhausted topics for conversation and just like his father, the older Flatley was a man of few words. As the aircraft touched down at Whenuapai Airport, they went their separate ways.

Catching the airport bus to Auckland, Terry arrived at the Star Hotel where he had pre-booked a room. He set his suitcase down before the counter and requested the key to his room.

"Mr Flatley has already taken the key to the room sir."

Oh, no! Not only was he sitting next to me on the 'plane, now he's pinched my room. Terry's felt awful dismay. "Do you realise that you have two T. Flatleys booked into your hotel? My name is Terry Flatley and I booked a room weeks ago."

The clerk looked perplexed, "I'm sorry sir, but the hotel is full. Surely, there can't be *two* people with such an uncommon name?"

Terry shoved his airline ticket under the nose of the clerk. "I'm afraid there is. Now, I don't know how you're going to do it, but I want the room I booked in advance."

The next morning he left the hotel and walked to the pretty harbour city's Queen Street, where he stood with his suitcase and his entire savings of five pound.[5]

Okay, what do we do now? he asked himself. With no job and nowhere to go, he wandered around, eventually passing an old tenement house on Symonds Street. A wooden sign laconically announcing, "Vacancy" hung above the entrance. Enquiring within, he learnt that it was a boarding establishment, offering bed and two meals per day for one pound. He scribbled his name in the register, glad to find a cheaper base from which to operate.

The landlady, a dowdy woman in her forties, with a scarf concealing curlers in her lank brown hair, showed him to a dingy basement room which smelt of dampness and neglect. A single window looked straight out onto a brick wall of a similar dwelling approximately 1 metre away.

"Here's my board money for the week." Terry offered the necessary currency, eager to meet his financial commitment before his small cash reserve evaporated.

The woman waved his money aside. "We're in the process of changing hands Luv. Pay the new owners. Oh, and I'm sorry but there won't be any meals this weekend. You'll have to fend for yourself."

Terry watched her apron clad figure stomp backup the stairs. "Thanks for nothing," he muttered. "Welcome to Auckland!"

Not long after moving in, heavy unrelenting rain commenced. The decaying roof guttering of both dwellings directed a waterfall between the two buildings. Terry shivered in the unheated room

---

[5] $10.00

and pulled a frayed, grey, war surplus blanket around his shoulders while he considered his position. His mood matched the weather.

When dinnertime came, he left the chilly bleak room in search of the dining room. The rain continued unrelenting, discouraging him from any further exploration of the city. He was hungry and eager for some companionship. Unable to locate anyone within the unlit building, he noticed a handwritten sign on the door to the meal area advising, "Due to the establishment changing hands, there will be no meals served." Although the landlady had pre-warned him, he hoped some kind soul would permit him to scrounge something from the kitchen. However, the cold stove, empty refrigerator and the smell of rancid, congealing fat caused a change of heart.

Donning a raincoat, he went in search of food, purchasing fish and chips from a small suburban shop. Amazed at the low prices, he also bought a bottle of beer and a packet of cigarettes, each costing two shillings and sixpence.[6] Reluctantly returning to the loneliness of his basement room, he spied another establishment offering rooms for three pound and ten shillings per week. An inspection revealed a clean, warm attic room, which he immediately accepted.

Instantly glad at his first landlady's refusal to accept his money, Terry returned to the basement and retrieved his bag. Although there was still no sign of life, he climbed out the basement window lest someone accost him and request payment for the room he no longer wanted or needed.

When Monday came, he approached the Government labour exchange. A scruffy bunch of no-hopers lounged around the doorway, waiting for dole cheques. Approaching the desk, he advised the clerk that he was looking for work. The white shirt clad public servant, a man twenty years Terry's senior, laughed uproariously, "What do you think you're doing coming in here? If you want a job, all you have to do is go and ask for one!"

From this response, it was obvious the unemployment situation was much different compared with Sydney. Terry purchased a copy of the New Zealand Herald and upon discovering six jobs where he thought it was worth expending the

---

[6] $0.25 cents

effort, he located a telephone box and made the appropriate calls. Granted immediate interviews to all six vacancies, he went from one appointment to the next, presenting his references and expressing great willingness to work.

Unconvinced that he would be successful, he set off along Queen Street, deciding to ask for employment in the larger shops. The first of these, Woolworths, hired him immediately.

Of the six interviews Terry attended earlier, four companies offered him immediate employment, although he decided to stay with Woolworths.

Elated with his success, he answered a newspaper advertisement placed by someone in Mount Eden seeking, "a quiet clean, gentleman boarder." Having enjoyed living with the couple in Jannali, he sought to replicate the warmth and homeliness in preference to the impersonal atmosphere of the inner city B and B. To conserve his rapidly dwindling supply of cash, he walked several miles from the city centre to Grange Road in the shadow of the extinct volcano after which the suburb derived its name. A plump woman in her forties with a homely face and a mop of bushy grey hair answered his knock. "Yes love? Oh, you must be the gent who rang up." she exclaimed in a cockney accent. "I'm Ivy Hall."

Terry took an immediate liking to this cheerful, friendly and unassuming woman. Shown through the neat, whitewashed stone bungalow, he felt instantly at home. Ivy obviously felt comfortable with him, quickly acknowledging his politeness and domestication.

"How old are you, Luv?" she enquired, studying his fresh youthful features carefully.

Not wanting to be treated as a child, Terry lied, "I'm twenty one, Mrs Hall. Why?"

"Nothing Luv. It's just that you look very young to be away from home."

"I don't have a home. My parents separated years ago. I've been looking after myself since I was fifteen."

"Oh, you poor darling. I hope you'll be very happy with us. We've got two children. There's our Ian who's a little older than you and Elizabeth who's thirteen. Ian doesn't live at home any more. He's moved away from home and joined the Air Force.

You can have his room. Bob will be very pleased to meet you. He's my hubby, you know."

While settling into the Hall household, a dreadful emptiness and unfathomable feeling of longing consumed Terry. Letters to his father had been unanswered. Although he maintained a tenuous link to the past by writing frequent letters to his brother Michael, he had no friends in this unfamiliar city. All ties with his mother whom he still regarded with a deep-seated resentment, remained irrevocably severed. The childhood torture sessions were painfully fresh in his mind and he felt sure writing to Paul, whom he felt resented him, would elicit no response. Filled with self-pity, he decided that were he to die, few people would know or care. The self-pity degenerated into depression as the miserable adolescent regularly turned to the gin bottle for comfort, secretly drinking himself into a stupor, hoping to quell the terrible ache emanating somewhere deep within his being.

One Friday, the Hall's went away for a few days holiday, leaving Terry alone in the stone bungalow. It was a long weekend and he had three days to fill in. With nobody to talk to, the cold emptiness of the house matched his depression.

He occupied his time on the Saturday, wandering the city streets and watching the boats on the harbour. The shops did not open on Saturdays and he returned home to cook himself a small meal, eating alone in front of the television set. Bored with the lack of choice on the two available government run channels, he retired to bed early, falling into an alcohol induced sleep.

The next morning, the silent house seemed to be closing in on him. Outside the streets were deserted. The emptiness reminded him of the song, 'Everyone's Gone to The Moon!"

Terry often found himself wandering up Mt. Eden when he wanted to think. This time he headed there consciously, climbing the steep slopes to the summit where he flopped on the grassy hillside, surveying the city from his perch four hundred feet above the surrounding suburbs. The day was clear and with a three hundred and sixty degree view, he could see Waitemata Harbour, sparkling like a million blue diamonds to the east, Manakau Harbour to the west and the other extinct volcanoes for which Auckland is renowned, dotting the landscape. It was a uniquely beautiful site and he wished he had someone with whom he could share the experience. Suddenly, he felt deeply alone and grieved for the stable and supportive family life he had never known. He lay back, staring at the fluffy, mash potato like clouds floating across the azure blue sky, tears streamed down his cheeks. That familiar dreadful emptiness descended upon him, engulfing and overwhelming him. Clambering to his feet, he slid down the mountainside on his haunches, bouncing over sheep tracks and tussocks to the bottom. *Where will I go?* He wondered, delaying his return to the morgue like silence of his room.

Hours passed, as the desperately lonely boy walked aimlessly, mile after empty mile, until near exhaustion, he made his way back home through the quiet streets to the darkness of the waiting bungalow.

Unable to bear the dreadful despair, he broke open a packet of headache tablets. Filling a glass with gin, he washed the entire contents of the packet down his throat, desperately hoping that a rapid oblivion would end the terrible grief from which he could see no escape. He lay back on the bed and as the tablets dissolved and the gin took affect, the room began to spin. His vision blurred. The room spun faster and faster, until he felt that he was disappearing into a black vortex of horror. Terror gripped him as he confronted dreadful finality of death. Forcing himself to roll over, he inserted his middle finger in his mouth, reaching far into the back of his throat, tickling his epiglottis in the hope that he could vomit enough of the deadly mixture to prevent his demise. His stomach convulsed, vomiting the grey sludge of pills and gin from his nearly empty stomach. Retching so hard he felt his very entrails would appear before him, he vomited on the bare linoleum, until only green sour bile filled his mouth.

The Halls returned that evening, blissfully unaware of the tragedy and the horror that they may have discovered. Terry welcomed them warmly, as if he had known them all his life.

The young man's relationship with Ivy and Bob proved to be long lasting and symbiotic. Terry happily tended their garden, mowing lawns, weeding and pitching in with domestic chores. He often brought home small gifts for his unofficial surrogate parents, enjoying their unsophisticated companionship.

A lanky and likeable Welshman with a singsong voice, shiny baldhead, blue eyes and a gapped tooth smile, Bob possessed a wonderful sense of humour and an infectious laugh endearing him to the young man whom he treated as a son. The couple's thirteen-year old daughter, Elizabeth, was smitten by the new lodger. Terry, who had never had a sister, was uneducated in feminine wiles, and felt no physical attraction for the budding teenager. However, he liked her immensely, shyly fending off the advances stemming from her pre-pubescent crush. For their part, the Halls took Terry with them on picnics and excursions. He felt very happy in the newly discovered, comfortable family environment.

Despite enjoying the warm hospitality, the dreadful emptiness that even his surrogate family could not fill, sometimes returned to haunt him.

In an effort to distract himself from pain, he readily accepted part time work as an attendant at the Museum of Transport and Technology at Western Springs. The position came to his attention through Stan White, a fellow employee at Woolworth's. Stan was a confirmed bachelor from Townsville, Queensland, which he described as, "a morgue with neon lights." Terry had never been there and accepted Stan's description with alacrity.

Stan was somewhat similar in appearance and age to Les Hall. At six foot, his thinning hair was combed carefully over his bald dome. With sharp features, a hooked nose and a pencil thin moustache, his generous mouth smiled readily and often. Slightly effeminate in manner and gesture, Stan was meticulous in his appearance and with the care he lavished on his pride and joy, a little Honda 50 c.c. step through motorcycle. He loved ballroom dancing and Terry suspected the older man might have homosexual tendencies. Although Terry was ever watchful, his older friend never displayed other evidence to support this theory. Most importantly, he made no advances toward Terry of a sexual nature. Over time, the two became close, albeit unlikely friends.

With no friends of his age, filling every available moment with work seemed like a panacea for Terry's loneliness in the beautiful but strange city, which he was quickly learning to love. Unfortunately, the decision to work long hours was a two edged sword, for by working every day of the week, he was even less likely to make new friends. Somehow, in between his jobs as a Storeman during the week and as a Museum Attendant on the weekend, Terry decided to join the Auckland Rowing Club to continue a fledgling interest he had pursued while living in Jannali.

Despite having only rudimentary skills learnt from The Cook's River Rowing Club, the aspiring athlete presented himself for membership. It seemed that the New Zealand coach had misinterpreted the boy's lean physique for athleticism and wrongly assumed he possessed the physical coordination of his contemporaries.

On his first day at the club, he arrived for training at 5.00 am as instructed. Whereupon he immediately embarked upon a five mile run over the hilly terrain of St. Heliers Bay, puffing along at the tail of a group of perhaps thirty extremely athletic young men. It was to Terry's credit that despite never having run that far in his life, he completed the run in a creditable time. However, the run was just a warm up. Immediately upon returning to the clubhouse, the group then went through a strenuous routine of callisthenics and weight training lasting nearly half an hour.

Exhausted from the unaccustomed exercise, Terry assisted in carrying one of the flimsy rowing shells to the water's edge. On instructions from the coach, he took his place in the rowing eight as stroke, the position normally allocated to the fittest and most able rowers.

1964 was an Olympic year and at that time The Auckland Rowing Club was the proud holder of a gold medal for the men's rowing eights. Terry was with seven of the world's best rowers!

They pushed away from the launching ramp, the coach calling the pace as the craft knifed through the mirror smooth surface of Waitemata Harbour. It was like rowing on a huge black pool of oil. The sun's rays had not yet touched the peak of nearby Mount Rangitoto. The distinctive outline of the extinct volcano little more than a black shadow to the north. Lights from the man made structures of Auckland Harbour Bridge and the city buildings cast distorted, almost ghostly reflections in the languid waters.

Terry set the pace in time to the coxswain's count. Pulling smoothly back on his oar, he used the big muscles in his legs to power the blade through the water. His seat slid noiselessly backwards and forwards on its rails in harmony with the rowing action, as he lifted the blade from the water and pushed forward for the next stroke. Each time the highly varnished blade completed the full length of its travel, he pushed down on the oar, lifting it from the water smoothly, while simultaneously turning the blade so that the back skimmed lightly and across the surface before biting down for the next stroke.

They covered a hundred metres without incident, Terry settling into the familiar rhythm learnt in Sydney. Then, the coxswain called for the pace to quicken. Terry increased his stroke, concentrating hard on the stentorian voice dictating the cadence.

Sweat beginning to pour into his eyes, his chest heaving from the exertion, and with co-ordination slipping, he could see in his peripheral vision, the other rowers' blades effortlessly keeping pace with his. Again, the coach called for the pace to increase. The highly glossed skin of the boat slid through the water with arrow like speed. Suddenly, Terry was unable to maintain the rhythm with the other rowers. Unable to lift his blade from the water in time, the momentum of the craft caught the blade, thrusting the opposite end back into his stomach. The oar knocked him backward, driving the wind from his lungs. The coach called them to a halt as the other members of the crew roared with laughter. "Did ya catch a crab[7], sport?" He asked sarcastically, satisfied that his newest recruit had learnt that his rowing prowess left much to be desired.

Terry's reasons for joining the club had been for fun and companionship. Unfortunately for him, he had chosen the most competitive club in the country. Rowing was the highest priority among all the members, who thought nothing of resigning from careers to pursue the sport. After a few weeks, he decided that he lacked the necessary dedication and fell by the wayside.

The Museum continued to offer the young man sufficient interest. He enjoyed showing visitors around the exhibits and assisting with minor restoration projects. The collection boasted a Lancaster Bomber, a Vampire jet and a Harvard trainer aircraft. Terry found the most fascinating exhibit was a weird looking contraption, with a jumble of mechanical junk beneath a single wing. This machine only vaguely resembled an aeroplane and according to documented eyewitness accounts, its inventor Richard Pearce, a New Zealand farmer, had flown it shortly before the Wright Brothers. However, with popular opinion

---

[7] A rowing term to describe the consequences of not syncronising one's rowing action.

crediting Wilbur and Orville Wright with this claim to fame, there seemed little likelihood that the history books would ever acknowledge the substantial evidence of Pearce's amazing feat.

One Saturday afternoon, Terry was dusting the showcases in the telecommunications hall when Stan bustled in excitedly. "Hey, there's a couple of young Sheilas up at the pump house. They're not bad looking sorts. If you're quick, you might do alright for yourself!" Stan was well aware of the shy teenager's loneliness. "Go on. Get up there and ask one of them out. They can't bite."

Summoning up courage, Terry thought, *He's right. It doesn't matter if I get a knock back, I'll never see them again.* He strode to the old pumping station, slowing his pace at the last moment in an attempt to appear as if he was simply wandering in during the course of his duties. There were few visitors and the two girls were easy to spot. In the early days of white settlement, the huge steam powered beam engine had pumped fresh water to the city from the springs. The girls were examining the giant cast iron flywheel in fascination.

"Good afternoon, ladies. The engine you're looking at was once used to supply the entire city of Auckland with freshwater." He launched into a well-rehearsed spiel, relating the reciprocating engine's impressive statistics and history. The two girls listened politely, not comprehending the arcane mechanical intricacies of the ancient marvel.

Terry completed his narrative and showed them other small engines and mechanical marvels, one of which was a small engine powered by hot air. He was proud of this contraption, having rigged it so that the heat from an electric light globe powered the motor, providing a working exhibit.

While the girls inspected the little engine, he stood to one side inspecting them. Both girls were in their early twenties, he guessed. One, a petite blond with creamy smooth skin, blue eyes and dainty features was to him, one of the most gorgeous creatures he had ever seen. Her companion, a slim girl with brown short wavy hair and hazel eyes, had an attractive figure and although not exactly pretty, her smile encouraged him to continue. She returned Terry's gaze, looking directly into his eyes.

"There's some good exhibits upstairs if you'd like to see them. We haven't the room to display them yet but they're well worth a walk up the stairs. By the way, I'm Terry," he said, offering his hand politely.

"I'm Jane. This is Margaret," the dark haired girl replied, shaking his hand. Her grip was warm and firm. "That'd be nice. We'd like to see those."

Terry led them up the narrow wooden staircase to the loft above the heavy beam of the engine. Here all manner of weird inventions had been stacked against the old brick walls gathering dust as they waited for the cash strapped museum to find display space. They rummaged through the heaps, examining curios such as old phonographs, hand operated vacuum cleaners, machines for peeling and coring apples and other strange paraphernalia.

"Ooh look. An old church organ!" Jane exclaimed in delight.

Unabashed, the young woman pulled an ancient wooden Captain's chair over to the instrument and sitting down, began to pedal the bellows, which emitted an asthmatic wheezing. Lifting the heavily embossed wooden lid, she exposed the ivory keyboard and pulled out several of the wooden stops. As she began playing, music wafted hauntingly down into the chamber of the pump house, filling the old building with the strains of "Abide with me." Peering down to the floor below, Terry could see visitors instantly stop in their tracks as they looked up to see where the music was coming from. The moment was reminiscent of a scene from "Phantom of the Opera."

Jane stopped playing and they laughed in unison at the macabre atmosphere the music had created in the historic building. As Terry escorted the girls to the next exhibits, he broached the question, directing his words toward Margaret, "Would you like to go out somewhere with me?"

Margaret shook her head, "I'm sorry. I'm engaged but I'm sure Jane would like to."

Terry looked inquiringly at Jane, quietly disappointed that Margaret had rejected his advance. "I'd love to," Jane replied, enthusiastically.

By any measure, their courtship was stormy. Jane, a girl from a devout catholic family, had harboured aspirations to become a nun. Entering the convent during her tender years, she was determined to pursue a religious career, enthusiastically taking vows of chastity, poverty and obedience. However, after several years as a novice, she was due to take her final vows when without warning, The Mother Superior called her to her study.

"Your bags have been packed for you. You are leaving here tomorrow!" The edict devastated the young girl, destroying her life's ambition in an instant.

"But, please Mother, what have I done?"

"You just don't have what it takes to be a Bride of Christ!"

Bitterly disappointed she travelled to Auckland, hoping to bury herself in work and forget the shame and pain of her rejection. In a state of severe grief, she accepted the bumbling attentions of the desperately lonely youth.

The unlikely union between the unhappy pair was only Terry's second serious experience with the opposite sex. The first, a whirlwind romance with Patricia Sullivan, a fellow employee at Woolworths was over almost before it began. His blind infatuation with the dumpy little brunette had been too intense for her liking. Despite showering her with expensive gifts, Patricia left Auckland to return to her parent's home in Christchurch. Terry decided to follow her not understanding that she had run away to escape his attention. When he knocked on her door hoping to surprise her, she rebuffed him soundly and finally. Thoroughly embarrassed and shattered he caught an Air New Zealand flight to Melbourne with the intention of heading to Perth to start afresh. However, after walking disconsolately around the city he could not face the five-day train journey across the vast continent, and instead returned to Sydney. One look at the bustling, smoggy metropolis was sufficient. All the old ghosts and bitter memories flooded back. Hailing a passing taxi and using his last few pounds, he managed to grab a seat on a flight to Auckland where he once more picked up the threads of his life.

Fearing her rebuff, he clung to the relationship with Jane with all the tenacity of a barnacle clinging to the hull of a doomed ship, even forsaking a career as a fireman when she threatened to dissolve the engagement.

"I'm not going to marry a fireman," Jane had announced upon learning of his career plans. "It's far too dangerous an occupation." Ironically, Terry's later career path was to be equally perilous and her dictatorial pronouncement should have signalled stormy times ahead.

Another hurdle to holy wedlock was Terry's lack of religious upbringing and Jane's insistence for his baptism into the Catholic faith. So terrified was he, that he would not find another prospective partner and the chance for a normal happy home life, he readily agreed to undertake religious instruction, concealing his true age, lest Jane sever the relationship.

On 11 April 1966, the pair married in St. Matthews Church, Bryndwr, Stan fulfilling the honour of Terry's best man. Jane's family sat both sides of the aisle to compensate for lack of relatives on Terry's side. Apart from his brother Michael, there was no-one he wanted to invite as he feared they would spoil his special day.

After the wedding ceremony, Terry and Jane returned to Auckland, settling into a tiny, rented, austere, basement flat at Takapuna. Jane obtained work as a police typist, preparing reports and prosecution files for the Auckland C.I.B. By this time, Terry was working as a retail supervisor in the Para Rubber Company's Queen Street store, which was situated directly across the road from Woolworths where Stan worked.

Tragedy struck during the spring of 1966.

One Monday morning Terry was bringing stock from the basement storeroom to replenish counter displays. His former boss, whom he knew only as Mr Beale, crossed the road from Woolworths. His ruddy, oval face creased with the lines of concern, Terry knew at once that he was the bearer of bad news. Mr Beale wouldn't leave his post at Woolworths and cross the main street to speak with Terry unless it was something of major significance.

"Hello Terry. I'm afraid I have some very bad news. I thought I should come and tell you personally, because I know how much of a shock it will be to you."

Terry put down the boxes he was carrying, dread enveloping him in its chilling embrace.

"Stan has been involved in an accident. He's in the intensive care unit at Auckland Hospital. I'm afraid it doesn't look too good!"

"What happened?" Terry knew Stan often drank heavily, sometimes riding his little motorcycle without regard for the risks.

He imagined Stan colliding with a pole or another vehicle while riding in an alcoholic fug.

"We don't know but he apparently fell off the back of his motorcycle and fractured his skull. There was nobody else involved. He was found on the road in Ponsonby, his crash helmet was still in place but it didn't save him."

"Had he been drinking?"

"Apparently not. I'm really sorry, Terry. I know how close you were to him."

The use of the past tense did not escape Terry. He turned away, dazedly. He had never experienced the pain associated with someone close being involved in a sudden and serious accident. Mr Beale's words sounded ominous and tears welled in his eyes.

The stark sterility of the I.C.U. ward and cloying antiseptic hospital smells brought memories flooding back as Terry and Jane approached the cot. With his head heavily bandaged, Stan lay on his back, covered only by a starched white sheet. An array of tubes fed lost blood and other fluids into his body and an oxygen mask covered his mouth and nose. Stan's eyes remained closed, his face ghostly white and his chest motionless, as if he had ceased to breath. Suddenly, with an horrendous deep sucking sound, his chest expanded and oxygen rushed noisily into his lungs. Slowly, beneath the sheet, his ribcage contracted as the expired oxygen whispered quietly from his mouth and nose. An eternity followed before Stan took the next breath in the same frightening, shuddering, sucking sound. So protracted was the space between each breath, that Terry feared it was Stan's last.

They maintained a bedside vigil for what seemed like hours, hoping in vain the Grim Reaper's call would go unheeded. At last, Jane drew Terry away, knowing there was no likelihood the dying man would ever open his eyes again. Terry silently said goodbye to the cheerful kindly man with whom he had often joked and shared so much, hoping that by his prayers he could save Stan and so diminish the grief and pain tearing at his heart.

Stan lingered in his deep coma for two more days before his damaged brain finally shut down. Sadly, only a small contingent flew from Toowoomba to attend the cremation. The mourners were mainly comprised of the affable bachelor's workmates and New Zealand friends and Terry felt a strange sense of alienation from proceedings when approached by Stan's sister. It dawned on Terry that he knew little if anything at all about Stan's past life and family ties. That Stan was known and loved by others he had never met, somehow seemed unfair.

"I believe you were a close friend of Stan's?" a matriarchal woman interrupted his reflections, her lined face almost completely concealed by a black muslin veil.

*How could she not know that I was his **best** friend?* Terry thought unreasonably, as if she had cheated him of that status.

"You might like some of Stan's things. He didn't have much, but if you would like to select anything, you are welcome."

"No thank you." Terry replied, realising that she did understand his pain after all. "I don't know if I could do that." His grief was too real and too painful. The thought of rummaging through the little room Stan rented seemed like a betrayal of his friend's trust.

After living for a few months in Auckland, Terry and Jane decided to move to Christchurch to be closer to Jane's parents and family. Transfers organised through the New Zealand Government and the Para Rubber Company, they rented a flat in Aikman's Road, Merivale. Jane resumed working for the C.I.B. and Terry accepted demotion to a shop assistant's position in Para's Cashel Street store.

As Christmas loomed, the shops brimmed with merchandise and shoppers filled the tidy streets of the garden city as they bustled, busily gathering gifts.

An original member of the Skjellerup family, the tall, thin, grey-haired and elderly Arthur Skellerup, presided over staff at the Cashel Street store. His family had founded the Skellerup Empire, which included the chain of Para Rubber Stores. A strict disciplinarian, Arthur was nonetheless a fair man and well liked by his employees.

In the week leading up to Christmas, the little city's shops opened for late night trading on the Tuesday and again on Thursday, which was Christmas Eve. Already tired from the Christmas rush and one late night, staff took periodic breaks in a small tearoom at the back of the shop. A mezzanine floor packed with stock, encircled the perimeter of the building. Empty, discarded cardboard boxes filled a light well at the rear of the premises. Overlooked by windows from the adjoining

Ambassador Hotel, the light well had no street access and reached five storeys, creating a giant chimney just waiting ignition.

During afternoon smoko, Terry drank a welcome cup of tea with other staff members. An extractor fan whirring soundlessly, removed tobacco smoke, blowing it into the light well outside. It was during this time that a staff member carelessly flicked a cigarette butt into the extractor fan, amused by the shower of sparks created by the spinning blades.

Smoko over, Terry returned to his post behind one of the counters, serving customers alongside another staff member.

At approximately 5.00 pm, Arthur Skellerup opened a ground floor door providing access to the light well. "Great Jesus Christ!" he blasphemed, immediately slamming the door shut.

Grabbing a fire hose from a nearby wall, the old man opened the door with the intention of extinguishing the flames leaping from the cardboard and packing materials. Fed by an inrush of oxygen, the light well became an instant furnace. Flames roared upward and the jet of water from the small rubber hose was as ineffectual as a dog urinating on a bushfire.

"Out! Everybody out. Fire! Fire! Fire!" Arthur bellowed and slammed the door as the heat forced him back.

Customers and staff streamed from the shop to stand on the other side of Cashel Street. The wail of sirens reverberated off the shop fronts as the fire trucks screamed to the emergency. Fire-fighters rushed to and fro, uncoiling hoses in organised chaos. Hydrants rapidly engorged the flat canvas ribbons, swelling them into a dozen white boa constrictors, crisscrossing both Cashel and Manchester Street. Water gushed along gutters and smoke billowed thickly into the evening sky. As the fire broke through the thin wooden and glass partitioning adjoining the light well, a fireball suddenly erupted. Racing the entire length of the mezzanine floor with lightening speed, it engulfed three sides of the building in a matter of seconds. The extremely inflammable gumboots, garden hoses and wet weather clothing, spontaneously combusting in the intense heat.

The heat from the blaze was enormous; the speed with which the entire building became a blazing inferno, frightening. A fire truck hoisted an incredibly long ladder high into the air, playing hoses onto the roof and into the light well. Despite the huge torrents of water, the heat was too enormous, turning the jets to steam before they could reach the fire's seat.

The fire raged like some monster out of control, threatening to engulf nearby buildings and the beautiful old Hotel. Realising that an entire city block was in danger of destruction, the firemen concentrated their efforts on preventing a major calamity.

With a gigantic whoosh and a shower of sparks, rising high in the air, the roof collapsed, completing the Para Rubber Company's destruction.

It was several hours before the brigade announced that the fire was under control. By this time, a blackened shell was all that remained of the prosperous store.

Fortunately for Terry, Para accommodated its staff at their High Street, Bishopdale and Riccarton stores.

After the Insurance Assessors finished their work, the company set about salvaging what stock it could from the wet stinking aftermath of the inferno. Remarkably, some items remained useable, although smoke damaged. Arthur Skellerup arranged the transfer of these to a disused warehouse where the company hoped to recuperate some of its losses by holding a fire sale.

The High Street fire had been a major event in the lives of Christchurch's citizens and the fire sale required little publicity. People camped overnight in the street, eager to be first into the building when the doors opened. On the day of the sale, hundreds packed the street, excitedly waiting to gain entry. The size of the crowd and their eagerness to get a bargain resulted in mob hysteria.

Inside the building, Para employees waited to serve the mob. A shrill hubbub of voices penetrated the heavy wooden entry doors, which strained under the press of tightly packed bodies.

At 9.00 am, Arthur Skellerup approached the doors, his normally erect frame stooped from fatigue and the ageing effect the fire had had upon him. An impatient hammering and the anguished cries of the unfortunate individuals crushed against the doors, reached those inside.

"Somebody's going to be killed out there. For God's sake open the doors and let them in," cried Agnes, an ageing female employee who had worked for the company most of her life.

Arthur reached above his head and withdrew the bolts securing the doors. Before he could turn the door handle, the sheer weight of the mob forced the doors open, knocking the old man to one side. The maniacal mob burst into the building with the violence of tons of water breaching a shattered dam wall.

"Back! Get back you bastards!" Arthur bellowed, attempting to instil some semblance of sanity into the deranged shoppers. His face red from anger and fear, he waved his arms and shouted for order but his voice was lost in the din of yelling, screaming people.

The human tide spread through the building, grabbing madly at anything they could get their hands on. They cared little whether they actually had a need for the things they seized. Like sharks in a feeding frenzy, they pushed and jostled, snatching from each other, squabbling over whom grabbed something first and when unable to carry anything more, they screamed for service. Any shred of decorum, good manners or decency had evaporated long before the bargain crazed fools entered the building. The din was tremendous and the raw emotion of the mob, frightening. Miraculously, there were no deaths or serious injuries. Within an hour, the warehouse was almost bare as if a hoard of rats had laid waste to a grain store.

Terry could see little future for him as an employee of the Para Rubber Company. By transferring to Christchurch, he had forsaken a promising retail career. In Auckland, he'd managed suburban stores at the tender age of eighteen. However, by moving to Christchurch where nepotism was rife among the powerful Skellerup family, he had slipped irretrievably off the ladder of promotion.

One evening, there came a knock on the door of their rented Merivale flat. Jane answered the door to find the baggy suited figure of Detective Sergeant Trevor Joy on the doorstep.

"We need you back at the office for an urgent job that's just come up," the burly ruddy faced detective explained.

"Oh. I won't be a moment. Just give me time to change. Come in and meet my husband."

Trevor stepped inside the tiny lounge room while Jane was readying herself for the unexpected overtime. His generous mouth spread in a wide smile beneath an overly large hooked nose. His blue eyes sparkled as he thrust out a meaty paw. "How come a big

117

tall bloke like you isn't in the police service?"

Terry shook the big detective's hand, instantly warming to the rumpled, cheerful senior policeman. "Well, I did try, both in Sydney and in Auckland but as soon as they found out I've only got one kidney, they told me I was wasting their time."

"Well, apply again. Only this time don't tell them until you have to. You might just end up being lucky."

Jane appeared from the bedroom and giving Terry a goodbye peck on the cheek, she disappeared with the policeman.

Taking advice from Trevor Joy, Terry couldn't wait to see Bill Stock, the stern but fatherly recruiting sergeant. He sat the pre-entry test and having passed, attended the local medical examiner's office. He made no mention of his missing kidney, leaving the doctor to discover the three hundred-millimetre scar on his left side.

"Hello, what's this?" Stuart Dunn, the portly police Doctor enquired, peering over his spectacles as he examined Terry's scar.

"Oh, that's nothing to worry about Doctor. I had a kidney removed when I was fourteen years old but I am as fit as a horse now."

"Mmmm. Yes, well you seem perfectly fine in every other respect and I'll recommend you but it will depend upon the Chief Medical Examiner in Wellington. It will depend whether the application hits his desk on a good day whether you get in or not."

"I'll just have to cross my fingers then Doc."

The C.M.O must have been in a good mood the day he read Terry's report, for on 15 May 1967, at Christchurch district police office, Constable Terry James Flatley and a dozen other young men and women took an oath of allegiance to the Queen before Chief Superintendent George Austing. That same night Terry sailed on the Lyttelton to Wellington ferry to commence three months training at the New Zealand Police Training School, Trentham. He was one of approximately sixty recruits comprising the 37th recruit wing.

Terry could not believe that his wife had raised no objection to a police career after objecting so strenuously to his earlier decision to become a fireman. Assuming her intimate knowledge of police life had convinced her that this was the correct path for her husband, Terry did not pursue the matter.

Terry found the old Trentham Military Camp with its World War I corrugated iron Nissan Huts, a bleak and depressing place. The entire site appeared reminiscent of scores of long, grey, pipes, lying half-buried in a wasteland of black bitumen. With a low mountain range as a backdrop, the camp sprawled over a sizeable area of flat terrain adjacent to the Trentham Racecourse.

Much of the camp being superfluous to the needs of the Army, now housed a migrant hostel, where dingy washing flapped desultorily on rusty, squeaking, clothes hoists protruding from neglected and weedy lawns. The remaining area provided makeshift training facilities for an eclectic array of cash-strapped government agencies, including the police. Although the New Zealand Army retained a small percentage of the huts, the Army's area was out of bounds to police recruits and cadets and lay on the other side of a no-man's land bearing the scars of condemned, but long-since demolished barracks.

Despite the police taking considerable pride in their allocated area, the police school was deliberately Spartan. Vast macadam parade grounds separated the ancient structures and there had been no attempt to give the camp any pretence of home comforts. The ageing electrical system was easily overtaxed, resulting in frequent blackouts. With New Zealand winters bitingly cold, the Hutt Valley area was notoriously bleak. Low cloud often hung over the miserable place for days or weeks at a time and when a door at one end of a tube-like hut opened, the long hallway became a very effective wind tunnel. Icy blasts of moisture-laden air whistled through a myriad of cracks in the sagging wooden joinery, testing inadequate heating systems provided by penny-pinching administrators as an after-thought.

The meals were ineffably disgusting. A typical dinner fare consisted of rubbery rissoles swimming in green fat, lumpy mashed potato and stringy beans doused in an equally disgusting concoction masquerading as gravy. Former police recruits claimed that the unkempt, dirty looking creatures, who prepared the meals, were the only cooks who had the ability to ruin cornflakes!

With no choice but to eat the revolting mess, Terry who was already thin at the time of recruitment, quickly lost six kilograms.

His bony frame and winter pallor, earned him the unflattering nickname, "Sudden Death."

Extremely rigid discipline prevailed, with a recruit's day commencing at 5.30 am and concluding with lights out at 10.00 pm. Daily hut inspections, marching drill and punishment details were the order of the day with recruits even having to muster and march to the mess hut for breakfast!

Modelled on an environment reminiscent of army boot camp with the express purpose of either making or breaking trainees, Trentham attracted societal misfits who, finding themselves in a police uniform gravitated to an area where they could feed their own inadequacies. Terry, who had never experienced anything like it before, immediately resolved to endure without complaint anything the most sadistic of instructors could mete out.

In his early thirties and holding the rank of senior sergeant, Terry's instructor Peter Victor Costello, nicknamed "the plastic policeman" because of his initials, was an academically inclined individual with a determination to rise through the ranks to the highest possible level. A sour-faced man who rarely smiled, Costello was Terry's equal in height. With straight, straw coloured hair, pale, watery-blue eyes and a piercing stare, he possessed the capacity to unsettle everyone who became the focus of his attention. A humourless individual, the instructor loved to humiliate his pupils. Although others may have held differing opinions of the man, Terry immediately branded him in the same ilk as the school bullies, he had so often encountered in his childhood. It was no surprise to him that this man should choose the training school, as it was the perfect environment in which to perpetuate his desire for control. Costello delighted in mercilessly culling any hapless individual who exhibited any form of weakness.

For a while, Terry thought that despite his best endeavours, he would become just another of the sanguine instructor's conquests. Unused to studying and being considerably behind his peers academically, he found the going extremely hard but consoled himself with the fact that he was far from the worst when Costello published the weekly exam results. He learnt never to query the plastic policeman's pronouncements or seek clarification on some point during class, for his reply was always, "You find out and come back and tell the class the answer!"

Terry was used to the police carrying firearms in Australia and during one early class innocently questioned his dour instructor as to why New Zealand Police went unarmed. Ordered to research the topic, he discovered his adopted country's law enforcement body emulated those of the United Kingdom. He also learnt that unlike the United Kingdom where police relied heavily upon Common Law, their New Zealand counterparts had the benefit of Statute law, which largely eliminated grey areas. Nevertheless, with policing methods very similar, the New Zealand police was also a very passive service.

The rationale behind having an unarmed service was based upon the belief that, "if you arm the police, you also arm the criminals." For a country where ownership of firearms was a privilege and not a right, there seemed to be much common sense in this line of thinking.

Terry discovered that, regardless of how well an unarmed police service managed to perform its role, among the legal and illegal gun owners of the Nation there were always malcontents who, whether in the heat of the moment or through careful premeditation, saw guns as a quick resolution for their particular grievance. Such incidents fell within the bailiwick of the police Armed Offenders Squad, a specially trained body using the tactics of negotiation and patience as the principle weapon in their arsenal.

The Armed Offenders Squad (A.O.S.) was comprised of officers from both the Criminal Investigation Branch and uniformed sections who, in the event of a firearm incident, could mobilise quickly. However, regardless of the expediency or efficiency of specialists, front-line officers were always the ones required to handle the extremely perilous initial moments of any incident with his or her immediate response proving vital in determining a tragic or peaceable resolution.

A.O.S. members usually enjoyed an esprit de corps found in very few other bodies or organisations. By necessity, they needed to be able to rely upon fellow officers and were therefore, carefully selected, highly trained and extremely well motivated.[8] Terry felt in

---

[8] Until the scourge of drugs created an exponential growth in armed robberies and organised crime, the strategy worked well. Later, when the criminals routinely carried weapons regardless of the best efforts of the country's

awe of his black-uniformed police brothers, never dreaming that one day he might join their ranks.

After the first four weeks of training, Terry's rusty brain slowly began assimilating the huge volume of legal information and procedural detail without the need to learn by rote. To his amazement, he acquired the skill of photographic recall. Reading a lesson note several times, he formed a mental picture of the document, its headings and layout. When the time came to answer questions, he was often able to call up the relevant paper in his imagination and read the printed word from that picture. However, although his marks steadily improved, dogged persistence and extremely hard work were still the main factors in his academic success.

Some of Terry's contemporaries were not so fortunate. One such individual was an athletic man with an impressive physique excelling in all the physical aspects of the training. Monty McGoogan stood six feet four inches in his socks, his bullet shaped head, with wedged features above huge shoulders, biceps and chest, give him a Neanderthal like appearance. Luckily, he was as gentle as a lamb with a likeable disposition and a willingness to help others.

In order to pass examinations, most recruits studied during every available moment, learning legal definitions, case law and criminal statutes word perfectly, as nothing less would satisfy the examiners. Poor Monty, try as he might, he was unable to get the information into his brain.

One evening, the struggling giant's roommate called to Terry, "Hey, come and have a look at this."

Although Terry hated interruptions, or anything causing him to lose concentration, he lay his lesson notes down and went to Monty's room. The incredible sight that confronted him caused him to double up in laughter.

After dragging a chest of drawers to the centre of the room, Monty had climbed on top of the cabinet. Tied around his head were half a dozen lesson notes. The affable athlete had his head close to a bare light globe, which lit the cell-like room with as much efficiency as a monastery candle.

---

leaders, police officers found it necessary to have firearms more readily available.

"What the heck are you doing, Monty?" Terry asked when he had his laughter under control.

"What the f... does it look like? I'm trying to X-ray this bloody stuff onto my brain!" Monty replied indignantly while showing a marked reluctance to leave his pedestal.

"Come on, mate. If that worked, we'd all be bloody geniuses," Terry coaxed.

Monty refused to budge. With his skull inches from the hot bulb, he insisted the wisdom espoused on the typewritten sheets could be radiated through the denseness of bone to the reluctant grey matter hidden somewhere in his cranial cavity. After much, cajoling Terry and several of the other occupants of the hut managed to persuade the frustrated man that his theory would not work. He climbed down from the cabinet, sighing in frustration. "I just can't get the hang of this," he said hanging his head in despair.

Although Monty's friends tried coaching him, it was no use. He failed the next Saturday morning exam and received his marching orders, much to the disappointment and sadness of his fellow students who felt that despite his slow-wittedness the giant deserved better.

Marching and drill practice formed an important part of the recruit's training. The instructor for these sessions was a former sergeant major from the British Marines. An expert at hand to hand combat, Jimmy McVay stood no taller than five feet five inches in height. As he was well below the height requirement for the New Zealand Police at that time, the police hierarchy had decided to make an exception in Jimmy's case due to his impeccable credentials. The diminutive Liverpudlian possessed the patience of a two-year old child, the temper of an angry bull, the viciousness of a piranha and the voice of a foghorn. His deep bellow often reverberated over the entire camp, inspiring fear and dread amongst his unfortunate victims.

Inevitably, Terry's poor coordination destroyed any chance of anonymity.

"Mr Flatley!" The deep-throated roar a few feet behind him caused Terry to jump. As his section marched around the parade ground, he struggled to keep in step. Jimmy's ruddy complexion was almost flashing with rage. "Where did you learn to march?" It was more of a statement than a question and Terry felt sure that in this case silence was golden. "Squaaaaaad! Halt! Squaaad. Stand at heeeees!" The orders bounced off the surrounding buildings and nearly a hundred pairs of booted feet slammed down in unison on the hard surface. "Mr Flatley. Step forward!"

Terry came to attention and stepped two paces forward of his cringing co-students, each one tremendously relieved that they hadn't been chosen.

"Mr Flatley. Give us a demonstration of how you march. Quick march."

Terry stepped forward in what he thought was the best marching style he could muster, imitating the way he had been taught as a schoolboy. Unfortunately, New Zealand military had a very different style to his recollection of marching.

"Haaaalt!" The little man shouted. His voice rose an octave as his incredulity showed through. "What are you doing? You march like you're bringing a herd of cows through a swamp." Jimmy mimicked Terry's stride, exaggerating so much that the entire assemblage burst out laughing.

When the laughter subsided, the little Fuhrer advised quietly, "Marching is just a formal way of walking son. Now, get back in line."

Suitably chastened and extremely embarrassed, Terry returned to his section. The incident served to provide him with sufficient motivation to practise marching and following various drill commands secretly, until satisfied he would never again face such humiliation.

Jimmy's sadistic streak prevailed during self-defence and baton training. "You need to be on the receiving end and feel the pain. Otherwise, you have no idea how effective you are," was his fond saying. To prove the point he always selected the tallest and most conspicuous of students, or threw out a challenge to anyone who harboured misconceptions as to their fighting ability.

Laurie Colebrook was one such individual. A quietly spoken man of dark countenance and thin features, he stood six feet four inches in height and possessed a lean but athletic frame, towering over the irascible instructor. Although Laurie wasn't sufficiently naïve as to challenge Jimmy, his height made him a conspicuous target. What better way was there to make a point, than for a diminutive man to bring down someone twice his size?

"Mr Colebrook. Step out here!" Jimmy barked.

Assembled in a loose circle before a number of padded canvas mats thrown on the wooden Gymnasium floor, Jimmy decided it was time to impart some basic skills in the art of subduing uncooperative or potentially violent offenders. Reluctantly, Laurie complied.

"Now son, I want you to attack me," the Liverpudlian invited, like a spider beckoning an insect into its web.

Laurie moved toward the little man and half-heartedly threw a straight right towards his head. Jimmy avoided the blow easily. "Not like that! Come on I want you to really give it all you've got," he sneered. "You're like a blinkin' sheila swatting a fly."

This time the lanky recruit raised both fists in a boxer's stance and dancing around the smaller man, jabbed quickly with each fist, attempting to make contact. The master of martial arts deflected the blows and with lightning speed retaliated. The sharp edge of a calloused right hand chopped into Laurie's Adam's apple. Laurie reeled backward, clutching his throat and choking for breath in obvious pain.

Laurie took no further part in the class. Unable to speak, he sat watching proceedings miserably from the sidelines. Although the incident had clearly demonstrated that size and boxing ability counted for little before a skilled exponent of the martial arts, it also inflicted serious albeit temporary damage to Laurie's vocal cords, ensuring for the remainder of the course he could speak in little more than a whisper. Jimmy who was known to have overstepped the mark on previous occasions, once again earned the displeasure of his superiors who temporarily demoted him from senior sergeant to sergeant. The demotion only served to render him even more ill-tempered. Although he managed to curb his penchant for inflicting actual harm, the recruits from the thirty seventh-recruit wing would never forget the little man and cringed when called upon to "volunteer."

On 18 August 1967, fifty-four recruits remained from an initial contingent of eager and unsuspecting individuals who had entered the bleak, Spartan confines of the training school. Although pre-selection tests weeded out the majority of unsuitable candidates, six failed to make the grade, either as a result of illness, lack of academic or physical ability, or because their integrity and honesty had been tested and found wanting. Fifty- four men and woman with varying backgrounds and characters, each with their own personal aspirations and motives, brought together and moulded into disciplined but autonomous individuals, able to wear the police uniform with confident pride.

Along with the recruits, sixty or so cadets reached the culmination of their two years of training. Although healthy rivalry would always exist between ex-recruits and former police cadets, on this day they were one body, united in their sense of achievement.

Like a butterfly emerging from its chrysalis, the pressure-cooker environment of the training school had transformed Terry from a shy introverted boy with poor self-esteem, into a disciplined individual with a sense of purpose and direction.

Standing on the black macadam surface of the parade ground, surrounded by his peers, the experience had a surreal quality. He could scarcely believe that he was now a trained police officer, wearing the navy blue serge and bobby's helmet of The New Zealand Police. He had done it! All those long days and evenings of tedious study, the rigours of the boot-camp, the tests of his mental and physical endurance, the marching, physical training, self-defence, mock incident situations and the endless round of tests and examinations, it had all been worth it.

"Squaaad! 'Tenshun!" Jimmy McVay's unmistakable bark seemed to echo off the surrounding hills. In perfect unison, one hundred and ten pair of black shod feet slammed together.

"Squaad. Squaad, left turn! By the left. Quiiick march."

The four sections of uniformed clad, soon- to- be enforcers of the law, paraded before the podium bearing the Minister of police, the commissioner and other dignitaries.

"Squad. Eyes right!"

Heads snapped so sharply in obedience to the command it seemed as if necks would almost break.

"Eeeeyes front! "

Police Commissioner Colin Urquhart, took the salute, his uniform bedecked with medals and service ribbons, the crossed baton emblem of his high office prominent on the lapels of his tunic. On command, the new constables halted and turned to face the dais. Formal speeches ensued, designed to inspire the graduates to promotion and high standards of ethical conduct.

Peter Costello rose from his seat on the stage and strode to the microphone clasping a sheet of paper in his gloved right hand. At last, it was time for the awarding of prizes. The top male and female officers stepped forward to shake the Commissioner's hand and accept various awards as the lanky instructor called their names. Terry observed his fellow graduates achievements admiringly.

"Constable Flatley!"

Terry was almost unable to believe he had heard his own name called. Recovering from his astonishment with the aid of a slight nudge from the policeman on his right, he came smartly to attention. "Sir!" he responded and stepping forward, turned on his heel and marched to the end of his section, then again turning smartly to his right, he marched forward to the waiting Commissioner. Coming crisply to attention, he snapped a salute. *Up, two, three, down,* he counted silently.

"Constable Flatley is the recipient of the Commandant's Progress Prize for Number One Section," Peter Costello read.

Although he had achieved a placing of only sixteenth in the final examinations, Terry's tenacity and hard work during the preceding months were recognised. He accepted the indecorous certificate in its unprepossessing black frame with proud embarrassment.

***

CHAPTER FOUR
"NOW FORGET ALL THEY'VE TOLD YOU!"

"**J**ust because you've spent three months at Trentham, doesn't mean you're a policeman. Forget everything they've told you. Now we'll show you how it's really done!" The words came from Neville Gilchrist, Terry's sectional sergeant.

A stocky man of medium height, a sardonic grin seemed to play almost perpetually around the corners of his straight mouth. Neville's strong chin, square face, sparkling blue piercing eyes and a somewhat bow-legged swaying walk, gave him the appearance of a redundant boxer turned police sergeant. When exasperated or worried, which he frequently seemed to be, he habitually ran his fingers through a thick mop of wavy hair, combed back from a broad forehead. He had little patience with recent graduates of the less than illustrious seat of police learning.

Terry had presented himself for his first day of duty, butterflies holding rehearsals for the Olympic Gymnastics finals in his stomach. Introducing himself to the other members of his shift, he lined up in the muster room for inspection.

Neville had bustled in announcing loudly, "Right. Produce your appointments."

Each member of the crew demonstrated that he was carrying the required baton, handcuffs and notebook. The sergeant had run an appraising glance over each officer. "Turnbull, your boots could do with a polish! Kenworthy, it's time you got a haircut! Make sure you attend to it. Have you all got the list of missing vehicles and persons?"

"Yes, sergeant," the group intoned.

After the briefing session, Neville had taken Terry to one side to administer the oft-repeated homily. Then he said, "John Cruickshank will show you the ropes. You'll be on Number One Beat."

Terry guessed Cruickshank was a few years older than he was. A receding hairline accentuated a surprisingly round face and florid complexion. His manner was attentive and the role of mentor adopted with a serious diligence. "Neville's okay. He's a good copper and sergeant but he doesn't take any nonsense," he explained.

Together, they walked along Hereford Street, away from the greying sandstone buildings of the old Christchurch Police Station. Cathedral Square, the hub of the little South Island city, comprised the greater part of their beat. Terry was uncomfortably conspicuous in his police uniform. With the peak of the white day shift helmet placed the regulation two finger's distance above the bridge of his nose, he felt certain the awkward appendage would surely topple embarrassingly from his head and be run over by the nearest bus.

It was slightly after 3.00 pm and the winter's sun barely warmed the busy streets thronged with shoppers. Terry knew his inexperience was evident and felt as if people were watching his every move. Which of course they were, the police uniform guaranteed that!

"Excuse me constable?"

Terry stopped to face the small boy who had addressed him. "Yes son?"

The freckled face of the urchin split into a cheeky grin, "Does your head go all the way up to the top of your helmet?" He skipped off laughing as the butt of his joke blushed hotly.

Cruickshank smiled. "Keep in step with me," he instructed. "We don't want to look like a gaggle of geese. It's important that you always walk at the regulation two and a half miles per hour and always keep in step."

They stopped on the corner of Colombo Street and "The Square," surveying activity in the surrounding streets. "No. Don't fold your arms. Neville'll tell you off if he sees you standing with your arms folded, and never put your hands in your pockets!" Terry mimicked the other officer's stance, clasping his hands behind his back in the, "at ease" position. This wasn't going to be as easy as he thought.

After standing for a few moments with John's shrewd eyes taking in every detail of the scene before them, they moved off again in the slow measured tread of the beat policeman, carefully watching the clock to ensure they arrived exactly on time at each quarter hour and half hour point. "If you're late for your point, you better have a good reason.[9] It's the only way the sergeant knows how to find you. If you're not on your point, he'll have to search for you, to make sure you're okay. Look out, if you don't keep to your points!"

They continued around the beat, Cruickshank showing Terry various points of professional interest. "You need to learn each beat like the back of your hand, the location of every shop, telephone box, alleyway, fire escape, taxi rank and bus stop. It's called local knowledge and it's invaluable."

Terry soon learnt the boundaries of Number One Beat and on their second circuit, they discovered a small group of indolent youths loitering outside the Christchurch Central Post Office. Although the gathering was well behaved, the youths were obstructing the flow of pedestrian traffic.

"Look at those shit-kickers. If we let them hang around, there'll be trouble later." The senior policeman continued walking, shouldering his way between the lay-a-bouts. "Move on you lot. You're obstructing the footpath!"

A skinny teenager of about nineteen stepped to one side. His overly long, lank, brown hair, framed thin features that bore a derisive sneer. Amateurish tattoos covered the backs of both hands and a small blue tattooed dot was distinguishable on his right cheek. Known as a "Boob Dot" the tattoo was the proud insignia worn by ex-convicts. Their antagonist was wearing dirty blue denim jeans and a black T-shirt covered by a denim jacket. As he turned, they could see a patch on his back proclaiming, "R.I.F.P." above a skull and cross bones and the name," Epitaph Riders[10]."

"Stinkin' Fuzz. Why don't ya leave us alone?" the yob snarled.

Cruickshank stopped in his tracks. Turning to face the youth, his blue eyes narrowed in a penetrating stare. With a very quiet menacing voice, he replied, "Michael Patrick Murphy, thief, liar and gaolbird, just back from Borstal and already looking for trouble." Raising his voice slightly, he continued ominously, "I won't tell you again. Get out of The Square. If I see you in here again today, I'll lock you up!"

---

[9] Portable radios were not issued to beat constables of the N.Z. police until the 1970's.

[10] A notorious N.Z. "bikie" gang.

"Yeah? And what will that be for?"

"Idle and disorderly, with insufficient means of support, will do for starters. Now, piss off!"

Reluctantly, Murphy sauntered away. Casting an insolent backward glance over his shoulder, he fired a parting shot in an attempt to save face with his companions, "You'll keep Copper. You'll keep!"

"Bloody shit-heads. That one is a nasty piece of work. Watch him when he's been on the piss, he'll have a go. He's got a list[11] as long as your arm for assault on police, resisting arrest, fighting, you name it, he's done it."

"But they hadn't really done anything. Why couldn't you just tell them to move to one side?"

"Listen. You can't give these bastards an inch. The first thing you've got to learn is, that you have to show them whose boss. As soon as these louts start to congregate in the Square, kick 'em out, or you've got trouble on your hands. They can pick a new cop and will be eager to try you out to see how far they can go. I advise you to establish a reputation as soon as you can for being tough, or they'll walk all over you and you'll have no respect! You can't pussyfoot around out here Terry."

On several occasions, youths drove into the Square, their old Ford Zephyrs and Vauxhalls leaning heavily to one side as they circumnavigated the busy city centre, gunning their engines noisily. Each time a testosterone-laden lout attempted a second circuit, Cruickshank stepped into the roadway and flagged him down. "Leave the Square and don't come back," he ordered.

One youth decided to challenge the legality of the constable's command. "I haven't done anything wrong. You can't make me leave. I know my rights!"

"Okay, mate pull over to the side. We'll see how roadworthy this heap of junk is."

A detailed mechanical inspection of the rusting hulk revealed several defects providing sufficient justification to deem the car not roadworthy. After conducting a thorough search of the vehicle and verifying the youth's personal details, the constable produced a typed form from the back of his notebook. "Okay mate. I've written this vehicle off the road under the Traffic

---

[11] Prior criminal convictions.

Regulations. This order allows you to drive the vehicle to your home by the shortest possible route for the purpose of mechanical repairs. You are not to exceed 30 miles per hour. You are not permitted to drive this vehicle on the road again until those repairs have been affected and you have renewed you warrant of fitness. If you do so, I will arrest you for failing to obey a lawful order. Now, if you want to give me any further cheek, I'll make you surrender the keys and have the vehicle towed away at your expense. Do you have anything more you want to say?"

Cowed and beaten, the young man climbed back into his car and drove off muttering to himself. He had learnt a valuable lesson. Never argue with a policeman!

They completed remainder of their shift without major incident. Terry's initiation into the realities of policing had been a very rapid learning curve and vastly different from his expectations.

As the end of their tour of duty drew near, they stood in a darkened doorway, looking toward the distant police station. "You don't leave your beat until the next shift comes on duty." John explained.

At precisely 11.00 pm, a small contingent of uniformed constables appeared, wearing heavy black greatcoats, black helmets and carrying torches. Led by a uniformed sergeant, they marched toward the waiting officers. Almost miraculously, the figures of other constables materialised from adjacent doorways where they had been waiting for the oncoming shift. Hurrying toward the station, they exchanged brief greetings with the new arrivals.

"Good evening sarge. How ya goin' Bert. Hi, Norm? Hope you have a good night fellas."

"G'day John. Been quiet?" Sherman Woodman, the night duty sergeant was young and fresh-faced, a member of new, well-educated breed of police officers currently emerging. Regarded with scorn by the old guard for their rapid rise through the ranks, they were changing the face of the service for the better.

"Yeah. Just the usual shitheads. Murphy's out. You might run into him."

"Okay. He had better not show his face on my patch. I'll bin him if he gives me the chance."

In the ensuing days, Terry was to become acquainted with each of the four main beats. Although there were eight city beats in all, staffing was never sufficient to cover them all, leaving at least four of the beats unattended. Each duty section of nine or ten constables had to provide a two-person incident car crew, (usually the more experienced members of the team) a driver for the "paddy wagon," known as the station beat vehicle and staff for the Watch-house and Operations Room. The officer assigned to station beat duty usually ran errands, ferried the sectional sergeant around when required and backed-up beat constables.

On Terry's first night shift, Neville assigned the raw officer to the most hated beat, number three. Avoided by cinema and partygoers, this part of the city had an air of menace and was a maze of darkened alleys, old warehouses and seedy hotels. Nothing much seemed to happen on three beat making it the least popular and most boring of all the beats. Despite this, procedures dictated that the security of every door and window be checked at least twice during the night.

Terry, who had yet to conquer a secret childhood phobia, decided that the time was ripe to conquer his fear of the dark. As the streets grew quiet, he steeled himself to enter the darkest alley lined with rubbish tins and high brick walls. The sole source of illumination emanated from a dim street light some distance from the entrance. Resisting an almost overpowering urge to turn on his torch, he stood quietly in the gloom while waiting for his eyes to adjust. As he felt his way along the cold brick walls, the childhood dread swamped him, causing his imagination to work overtime. He knew his fear was irrational but he expected any moment to feel the vice like grip of a hand grasp his throat from behind or hear the footsteps of someone shadowing him. Goose bumps broke out on his arms and the hairs on the back of his neck stood erect like a thousand soldiers on parade. Subconsciously, he placed the thumb of his right hand into the leather thong of his wooden baton, ready to draw it immediately from the concealed pocket in his trousers, should the need arise.

Reaching the first door, Terry tried the handle gently. Finding it locked, he moved along the alley, checking each door and window as he went, listening for any foreign sound or movement. He began to relax, continuing the routine task with greater confidence. Coming to a small, blackened alcove, he reached in to feel for the door handle. Suddenly, a hand closed around his wrist pulling him sharply into the black hole. Striking out at the unseen attacker with his torch, he fumbled for his baton. Attempting to growl with rage, all he could manage was a strangled high-pitched squawk.

Torchlight suddenly illuminated the face of Lyn Kenworthy, the station beat constable. "Ha ha ha!" he roared with laughter. "Welcome to the night shift."

"You bastard!" Terry swore. "You scared the shit out of me!"

"It's just a little joke we always play on the new cops." Lyn cackled, "Boy, you should see your face!"

Terry relaxed and seeing the funny side, he returned the laughter. "Just remember, two can play at this game," he warned.

The incident was one of the many "rights of passage" Terry was to undergo during his initiation and acceptance into the role of a law enforcement officer. Despite almost being frightened out of his wits, he felt satisfied that he had at least responded with aggression. Thereafter, the young policeman practiced greater prudence when reaching into dark niches.

The determination to overcome the paralysing phobia paid-off. Although he always experienced some disquiet before entering darkened alleys and buildings, he learnt to use the cover of night as his ally. There was something quietly satisfying in slinking silently behind buildings, his ears and senses attuned to the sounds of the night. Occasionally he would emerge unseen and unheard, surprising the city's few nocturnal inhabitants, such as, street sweepers, milkmen, delivery persons and the occasional drunks or cinema patrons making their way home.

Shortly after Terry graduated from the police Training School, Jane and he moved into a new house built for them in the rapidly expanding suburb of Hornby. Terry's annual police salary was a meagre $1,800 and although the cost of living was comparatively low at that time, the young couple struggled to meet mortgage repayments and purchase food. With Christchurch winters being notoriously cold and accompanied by heavy frosts and occasional snow, the cruel chill seemed to find its way through the bare floorboards of the uncarpeted house.

After purchasing necessities there was nothing left over to buy firewood or coal for heating and they struggled to scrounge enough fallen branches and pinecones from beneath the trees of a nearby park to light a smoky flickering fire. They possessed little furniture and no carpets. The acquisition of a motor car was beyond question. Shopping trips necessitated picking their way along a potholed bitumen footpath to the shopping centre nearly two kilometres away. After loading groceries into the pram around baby Liam, they trudged home again.

If necessity is the mother of invention, then she was alive and well in the struggling couple's tiny brick home. Unable to afford curtains, Terry purchased spring-loaded blind rollers for a few dollars and using cheap furnishing fabric, Jane put her sewing skills to the test, fashioning blinds for the windows. Relatively cheap sheepskin pieces were plentiful and by gluing these to a backing of old Hessian bags, Terry created a large hearthrug where Liam could roll around and kick in the feeble warmth of the later winter sun as it filtered through the glass door.

Terry loved his newly born son with a passion. He'd lie beside Liam for hours on the rug, fascinated by the baby's every move and sound. Despite the paucity of his and Jane's financial circumstances, being a father made Terry feel as if he was the most fortunate man alive.

The New Zealand police worked a five weekly roster, with three of the five weeks entailing the physically taxing and much hated, 'Late/Early' shifts. After commencing duty at 1.00 pm officers worked until 9.00 pm before 'knock off.' At 5.00 am the following morning they reported again for duty, having only eight hours to get home, go to bed, rise, shower, eat breakfast and return to work. In the event of an arrest near the 9.00 pm knock off, the service demanded they submit the arrest file before finishing duty, while still reporting for their allotted shift at 5.00 am the following morning.

Arrests invariably meant being in an emotion charged state for several hours after, making sleep impossible. Shift work was demanding enough, placing tremendous strain on marriages, health and the ability to follow a normal life style. Being a policeman or woman working shift work eventually meant ones circle of civilian friends gradually diminished, as people who led normal life styles tired of 'rainchecks' and cancellations in relation to social engagements. For the uninitiated, the five weekly rosters were an unfathomable conundrum.

During Terry's first cycle through the roster he became so accustomed to the seemingly endless 'Late/Early" shifts, that one Saturday, when he was supposed to commence work at 5.00 am, he slept in, mistakenly believing he was due to commence his shift at 1.00 pm. The Duty Station Senior Sergeant, Aden Stuartson, was a particularly short-tempered individual, who had for some unknown reason, taken an intense dislike to the young policeman. When Neville advised him of Terry's absence, Aden dispatched a patrol to Terry's home to check on his whereabouts.

At approximately 7.00 am, a loud knocking on the bedroom window roused Terry from a heavy slumber. Peering bleary-eyed through the curtains, he was surprised to see Bert Armstrong, the thin, dark-haired police driver from his shift looking back at him.

Stumbling to the door, Terry asked, "What's going on?" In his sleepy state, it had not yet dawned on Terry that the driver wouldn't be at his home unless he too was supposed to be on duty.

"You better get dressed and get into work quickly. The boss's not too happy with you!"

"But, I'm on afternoon shift." Terry replied, mentally scratching his head.

"Afraid not. You've stuffed up. There's two earlies in a row."

At that precise moment, the telephone rang. Jane went to answer it in the kitchen.

"Jane. It's Michael. I am sorry to have to tell you over the 'phone but dad had a heart attack last night. I'm afraid he didn't make it!"

Stunned, she put the receiver down and approached Terry, her face ashen. "You can't go to work, Terry. That was Michael. Dad died last night. I've got to be with mum as soon as possible."

Terry turned to Bert. "You heard that. I can't possibly come in. Can you let the boss know?"

Bert shook his head, a look of deep concern on his dark features. "You'd better speak to the senior sergeant."

Leaning into the patrol car, Terry lifted the microphone. "Operations senior sergeant from Constable Flatley, over?"

Aden's gruff voice replied tersely, "Receiving!"

"Senior sergeant, I have just received news from my brother in law that my wife's father died last night. I know I am supposed to be on duty but I need to be with my wife."

"Your wife's brother can stay with her. Get yourself in here. Out!"

Terry was incredulous at the unsympathetic response to the sudden and tragic news. Seething with anger, he hurriedly donned his uniform. "I'm not going to stand for this. I'll have it out with that mongrel when I get to work but you'll just have to cope on your own for the moment," he told his distraught wife. Bidding her goodbye, he jumped in the front seat of the police vehicle, which then sped off.

Upon reaching the station, Terry confronted the stocky senior sergeant, who stood glaring at him as he tried to explain why he had over slept. Aden listened for a moment to Terry's explanation. "I don't care what your reasons are. I expect you to report on time for duty," he grumbled.

Livid with rage at the older man's insensitivity, Terry raised his voice with scant regard for the possible consequences. "So it doesn't matter to you that my wife's father has just died? Don't you think you're being bloody unreasonable?"

Aden's face grew dark at the challenge to his authority. It was unheard of for a junior constable to speak back to a senior sergeant. "Come with me," he glowered, stomping from the office.

The watch house keeper and the operations room staff had listened with interest to the entire exchange. Reaching the medical room, Aden led Terry inside and slammed the door. Pivoting on one heel to face his errant subordinate, he glowered, "You don't speak to me like that. Just remember who you're speaking to. I can make life very unpleasant for you, young fella. Now get out on the beat where you should be."

Terry wasn't to be cowed, "When the duty inspector comes on, I want to see him immediately. We'll see if he's as unreasonable as you!"

Matt Lawrence was the inspector rostered for day shift over the weekend. At 9.15 am, Bert Armstrong's patrol car pulled alongside as Terry plodded dejectedly around Cathedral Square, still smarting from the injustice. "Hop in. You've stirred up a hornet's nest. Jesus, I wouldn't like to be in your shoes from now on."

Unafraid and certain that he held the high moral ground, Terry climbed the stairs to the duty inspector's office. The highly polished linoleum of the corridor softened his tread as he located the relevant room. He could see Lawrence through the open door, his be-spectacled countenance, large nose and bald head, reminded Terry of an absent-minded professor. Placing his helmet under his left arm, Terry knocked lightly on the doorframe and waited in the doorway. He stood to attention as Matt looked up from his desk.

"Come in, constable. Now what's all this I hear from the senior sergeant?"

Terry explained how he had misunderstood the roster and how the news of Les Trafford's death had only just reached him that morning. "Under the circumstances sir," he continued, "I think Senior Sergeant Stuartson was more than a little unreasonable by not allowing me compassionate leave."

Matt nodded. "I have to agree. You are excused from duty to be with your wife. I am very sorry to hear of your loss."

"Thank you, sir."

As Bert predicted, Aden now bore a grudge and a pressing need to save face. Terry's hostile run-in with the senior Non-commissioned officer filtered down the line to Neville. The irascible sergeant already resented Terry's inclusion on his closely-knit team, and the news further vindicated his dislike for his newest recruit.

More than ever, Neville offered no guidance to the young policeman, choosing instead to admonish him gruffly for the smallest perceived infraction. The preparation of reports and prosecution files, although executed to the standard shown by his training school instructors, failed to meet the NCO's exasperating requirements.

"It's not right. Do it again," he'd say laconically, throwing the tendered document back at the frustrated junior officer.

"But, what's wrong with it?" Terry queried.

Time after time, he received the same reply, "It's just not right."

Returning to the battered old Imperial 66 typewriter, Terry puzzled over the wording and format of his files. At last, he turned to the one member of the team who seemed to spare him any time.

"Lyn, what's wrong with this?"

Lyn Kenworthy shook his jet black hair, a frown creasing his smooth brow. "It beats me. He's just got it in for you. Tell you what. Have a look at this and copy from what I've done."

Gratefully, Terry adopted the proven style of the other officer. He re-typed the Statement of Facts and dropped it on the cranky sergeant's desk. This time the file did not return. Terry concluded that Neville was just playing games.

One night, Terry was trudging the number three beat again. His sergeant's trust in him was insufficient to put him anywhere other than the quiet beat, judging him to be out of harm's way. Despite Police General Instructions dictating that beat constables receive at least two visits per shift, an entire night often passed without sighting the N.C.O. Terry soon learnt not to expect a meal break during his entire shift and often wondered what would happen if someone whacked him over the head in an alleyway. *Bugger him*, he thought. *I'll show him! We'll see who wears who down in the long run!*

It was almost as if Neville had read his thoughts. As he rounded a corner, a black Holden sedan pulled alongside. Terry recognised the unmarked vehicle Neville favoured above all others in the fleet. The sergeant wound down the window, glaring at the young constable. "Get in. I've got a job for you," he growled.

Terry slid into the rear seat nursing his clumsy police helmet on his knees. Lyn Kenworthy who was driving, shot a quick sympathetic glance over his shoulder but remained silent, his youthful face serious.

They sped away from the kerb toward an old and dingy part of the city. Terry subconsciously noted from a street sign that they had turned into Chester Street. Almost immediately, the car slowed and it was obvious that something extraordinary had taken place.

A number of C.I.B. vehicles occupied the parking spaces immediately outside a small rundown, weatherboard cottage, where lights blazed brightly. Spotlights mounted on special stands bathed the entire front of the house in a white glare, illuminating the number 109 on a wooden verandah post. forensic officers were laboriously dusting the walls and door frame for traces of fingerprints. The front door was ajar and additional plainclothes officers were visible inside.

As they pulled up, Neville turned his head to address Terry with something akin to malicious glee. "There's been a murder here. You're job is to guard the scene until you're relieved."

Neville sat staring straight ahead. It was apparent that he did not intend to alight from the vehicle, so Terry got out and approached the front door. Neville sped off as if glad to be rid of his most junior officer.

A burly detective strode to meet Terry before he had entered the gate. Terry recognised Detective Sergeant Patrick Donaldson.

"Follow me. Walk exactly where I walk and don't touch anything," he instructed needlessly.

Terry had already thrust his hands into his pockets. He knew that it was very important not to contaminate the crime scene. He glanced around as they took the short walk to the front door. Situated in close proximity to the city centre, the suburb was a mixture of various commercial premises and small cottages of similar vintage to Number 109. Curious, Terry guessed the majority of homes were rented to the city's underclass. Bounded by the high brick wall of a factory on one side, shrubs and trees partially concealed an unkempt front yard. His escort led Terry through the narrow entrance into a tiny, carpeted, lounge room. A white telephone stood on a small coffee table beside an ashtray brimming with cigarette butts. A beige and dirty, three-piece Chesterfield lounge suite and a television set almost filled the available space. Blood splattered the walls and formed a trail toward the rear of the house.

"From what we can tell, the victim Miss Jesty, occupied the house with one other girl. They were both employed as nurses. It appears that Miss Jesty answered the front door in her dressing-gown sometime this morning only to be attacked and stabbed up to sixteen times. She has run through here toward the bathroom, in an attempt to get away from her attacker." The detective gestured toward the bloody floor. "We haven't cleared the crime scene yet, so it's important that you keep to this path. This is where she died," he stated, standing to one side to give Terry a clear view of the bathroom.

The scene was horrendous. A large pool of congealing blood covered the bottom of the white porcelain bath. Bloody hands had streaked the walls and the sides of the tub. It was obvious that the unfortunate victim had fallen into the bath and bled to death from multiple stab wounds. A cold blast of air entered the room through the broken pane of a small window. Shards of glass littered the floor. The charnel house smell was amazingly reminiscent of a butcher's shop.

Donaldson led Terry back to the lounge room and motioned toward a hard, wooden, kitchen chair placed inside the door. "You can sit here to guard the scene. We're about to knock off for the night but we'll be back in the morning to continue the examination of the scene. The murder weapon hasn't been found yet and we don't have any suspects at this stage. The other occupant of the house is staying with relatives. If you need to contact anyone in an emergency, you can use the telephone but don't touch it unless you need to."

As Terry watched, the Homicide Squad turned off their spotlights, gathered their crime scene paraphernalia and departed carrying a portable radio he had spied on his arrival. *Bugger*, he thought. *Why can't they leave that behind for me?* A single globe lit the room where he stood, surrounded by the grisly reminders of the shocking crime perpetrated only hours before. He realised with a sinking feeling that he was alone with no backup and no means of communication, other than the telephone he'd been virtually forbidden to use. He surveyed the murder scene for a third time. Looking from the dimly lit room, he was unable to make out any detail outside the house. The only source of exterior illumination came from the hazy yellow glow of a single, ineffectual, incandescent street light nearly fifty metres away.

Feeling like a gold fish in a bowl, he picked up the uncomfortable wooden chair and moved outside away from the grim and grisly scene. Placing the chair beneath a large forsythia shrub, he settled down to wait out the night, confident in the knowledge that his back was protected by the brick wall and his vantage point in the darkness enabled him to watch the street, the front of the house and part of the rear yard. Instinctively, he stretched his left arm causing the sleeve of his heavy greatcoat to ride up. It was only then he remembered that his wristwatch had chosen that day to break down. He had no means of knowing the time. *This is going to be a long night*, he thought.

Desperate for some way to keep track of the passing minutes, he unbuttoned the pocket of his heavy cotton uniform shirt for the nearly full packet of cigarettes. *It takes me about ten minutes to smoke a cigarette. If I chain smoke, they should last me three hours and twenty minutes. It's nearly midnight now, so by the time I run out, the sergeant will surely come for a visit. Maybe I'll get a relief then and can either get some more fags or borrow a watch.* He lit his first cigarette, taking care to conceal the flare of the match and the glow of the butt.

He estimated nearly two hours had passed when the breeze freshened, causing the branches above his head to thrash noisily. It began to rain. Large icy blobs splattered against the black cloth covering of his fibreglass helmet, dribbling coldly down his exposed face. *Damn! I'm not going to sit out here and catch my death*, he decided. Picking up the chair, he retreated inside the inhospitable cottage to sit by the front door. The rain drummed on the iron roof, tree branches beat against each other, swishing menacingly as the old house creaked in protest at the sudden change in the weather.

Terry did not know how long he had been sitting there but his imagination was working overtime. Every creak and sound played havoc with his nerves. *What if the murderer comes back? What if he decides to destroy evidence?* The "what ifs" and a dozen different scenarios invaded his mind seizing control of his thought processes.

CRASH. The noise came from the bathroom. *The open window! My God, he's come back and climbed in the window!* Visions of a maniacal intruder wielding a huge bloody knife flashed before him. Galvanised into action, he leapt to his feet, knocking over his chair in the process. Whipping his baton from its special pocket, he bounded toward the bathroom with a blood curdling bellow. "Right you bastard!" The adrenaline surged through his veins as every drop of blood retreated from minute surface capillaries, causing the hair to stand up on the back of his neck and goose bumps to break out all over his body. He was ready to fight for his life and prepared to kill if necessary.

Reaching the gory bathroom, the wind whistled eerily through the broken window. The sound was like the ghostly voice of the murder victim crying to him from another dimension. Woooooo! Woooooo! Terry braced himself expecting attack, his feet apart, left arm raised to protect his face and baton drawn back to strike.

142

The breath gushed from his lungs in a huge sigh of relief and he dropped his arms. "You f...ing little bastard!" he swore.

A large black cat looked at him alarmed, its yellow eyes wide and glaring like those of some evil demon. Startled by the baton wielding lunatic standing in the doorway, it ceased licking at the congealed human blood and leapt through the window.

Not surprisingly, in that dreadful traumatic moment, Terry lost and never regained any affection for furry four legged felines.

[12]He spent three long nights guarding the crime scene. Not once did Neville visit him or check on his welfare.

Neville's reluctance to trust his probationary constable endured for months. Occasionally the taciturn sergeant relented and placed his youngest charge on Number Two beat but stubbornly refused to entrust him with the busy Cathedral Square. Once every five weeks the cycle of the rosters dictated that Terry spend one week on the twilight shift (5.00 pm until 1.00 am). On such occasions, he fell under the supervision of another sectional sergeant. He looked forward to this spell eagerly for it was a change and provided a chance to prove himself.

During the first few years of Terry's police career, The New Zealand Police was undergoing a transformation. It was in effect the end of one era and the beginning of another. The organisation had suffered from a poor self-image, an undesirable culture of hooliganism and a prevalence of arrogance among some of its officers. Public confidence in the service was at an all time low and a popular saying at the time was, "if you can't get a job anywhere else, you can always join the police!"

In an attempt to change the public's perception, the New Zealand Government dropped the word 'Force' and adopted the more user-friendly, 'Service' instead. The decision makers rationalized that, "force" implied heavy-handed tactics, whereas

---

[12] Homicide Detectives located the murder weapon under a mattress in the master bedroom the day after the murder. It transpired that the offender was one of the victim's former lovers. A diminutive and quietly spoken Englishman by the name of Cross. After Jesty broke off the affair, Cross purchased a large hunting knife from a city sports store for the sole purpose of killing her. Although he denied the crime, a sheet of brown paper found in a rubbish bin at his home provided damming evidence. The shop assistant who sold the knife to Cross had wrapped it in brown paper. The wrapping clearly showed the outline of a knife, which matched the murder weapon.

service, conveyed the impression of a body on which the public could readily call for assistance. Considerable effort and expenditure on training increased service quality and overall performance. The hierarchy then focused its attention on stamping out rampant abuse of power and position and the arrogant bullying tactics, which until that time had been prevalent. Unfortunately, many of the "old guard" remained in positions from constable through to the commissioned ranks.

One particular sergeant from the 'old guard' was in charge of Terry's twilight shift. A heavy-set man in his mid to late thirties, Charlie Hughes[13] stood around six feet in height. With a large square face, dark eyes and a head of thick, black hair, he possessed a loud, brusque manner. Hughes was a notorious larrikin who took short cuts and expected those in his charge to follow his example. He wasn't against bending the truth and frequently 'verballed' his unsuspecting victims or obtained confessions by dubious means. He was a disgrace to his uniform and the organisation he purported to serve. Unfortunately, through the power of his position and his authoritarian manner, Charlie often led junior officers astray. Life could become very uncomfortable for any subordinate brave or silly enough to go against Charlie's style and instructions.

It was a quiet Wednesday night in late spring. The weather was warm and for some unusual reason, Cathedral Square was without the omnipresent hooligans tearing around in battered old wrecks. Local youth regarded the famous town square as an unofficial drag strip. There were few pedestrians, as the evening sessions of the movies hadn't yet spilt patrons onto the street. The day before the traditional payday, hotels were quiet and only a sprinkling of orderly youths congregated around the centre cenotaph and post office corner. Terry had been around Number One beat several times and satisfied everything was in order, he adopted a vantage point on the post office corner, surveying the major part of his "patch" as he liked to call it.

The hooligan sergeant swaggered onto the scene, regarding the harmless, lounging youths with leering contempt. "How's it

---

[13] For obvious reasons, wherever this story refers to an individual in uncomplimentary or unflattering terms, names referred to are fictitious names. References to any person, living or dead are purely co-incidental.

going. Had any arrests yet.?" The question was pointless. Terry knew the N.C.O. would have checked the watch-house Charge Book before embarking on his rounds and already knew what Terry's response would be.

"No sarge. It's pretty quiet. I've only been out here for about half an hour. Everyone's behaving themselves for a change."

"That's not good enough. Can't you make someone swear?"

Terry glanced at the sergeant, convinced he was joking. He was not.

"I don't know what's wrong with you young fellas. I'll show you how it's done!"

With that, Charlie stealthily withdrew his baton, sliding it into the sleeve of his tunic so that the 'business end' protruded unseen into the palm of his hand. Adopting an air of nonchalance, he sauntered toward the nearest group of teenage males who were quietly chatting among themselves. Selecting a likely victim from the group, Charlie walked right up to the unsuspecting fellow and stood almost touching him. The youth recoiled from the stench of Charlie's breath as the N.C.O. belligerently invaded the young man's personal space. Bringing the heel of his heavy boot down on an unprotected toe, he simultaneously jabbed the hidden baton into the unfortunate boy's solar plexus.

"Oof. F...! What's that for?" The expletive slipped involuntarily from the poor fellow's lips.

Charlie smirked in satisfaction. "You don't use that sort of language around here young fellow. You're under arrest for using obscene language in a public place!"

Struck dumb, Terry wondered, *how could he do such a thing? It was unspeakable!* He had heard stories how one of the same sergeant's team favoured the practice of carrying a piece of paper with an obscene phrase written on it. Presenting this to his victims, he'd instruct them to read the phrase aloud and when they complied, arrest them. Terry now knew the stories to be true. The poor unfortunate 'offenders' rarely had the presence of mind to plead not guilty and when they did, their version of events sounded so improbable, the Magistrate chose to believe the word of law, which was invariably corroborated by one of Charlie's minions. It was even more fun if he could somehow engineer the alleged phrase to refer to the presiding Magistrate in an uncomplimentary fashion.

'The Hagley 500' was another favourite past-time of the thuggish policeman. The beautiful garden city proudly boasts one of the world's most impressive public parks in the inner city precinct, bounded by the four main avenues of, Bearley, Hagley, Moorhouse and Fitzgerald. In the early hours of the morning, Charlie Hughes and his willing team of racers used marked police cars to charge around the outskirts of the city, attempting to clock the fastest time possible. To lend greater excitement to the event, they climbed from one car into the other, while tearing along, or moved from the front seat into the back seat via the car windows. It was even more challenging to race the engines, changing into a higher gear while ignoring the clutch pedal as the protesting engine's valves bounced in protest.

Surprisingly, there were no complaints from members of the public. However, in the event of a complaint, Charlie and his uniformed idiots had a string of fictitious emergencies ready to justify their behaviour.

Fortunately, such antics were not indicative of the vast majority of police officers but such incidents did little to enhance the reputation and respect of the service as an entity. Although a few brave and concerned members of the constabulary privately dissented against hooliganism and thuggery, the policeman's unwritten code of silence prohibited officers from "grassing" on their colleagues. When the subsequent expanding tide of more professional conduct rendered men of Charlie's ilk dinosaurs, they opted for more responsible behaviour, were caught and sacked, or chose to leave the system.

Eventually, staff shortages left Neville with no choice. Terry was the only constable available for beat duty and the need to have a policeman in Cathedral Square forced Neville to move Terry to Number One Beat. It wasn't long before Terry vindicated that decision.

One warm summer's evening, after walking out alone to commence his Saturday, night-shift vigil, Terry found The Square abuzz with activity. The weather encouraged pedestrians to linger after spilling onto the pavement from cinemas and hotels at closing time. With no police available on the previous afternoon shift to control the unruly louts, a steady stream of noisy wrecks screamed around, chasing each other, their occupants yelling abuse and foul language at all and sundry.

Indolent groups congregated here and there, obstructing the orderly flow of law-abiding citizens attempting to reach late night buses. Terry counted three separate fights in progress. The young combatants, primed with the demon drink, had removed shirts and were slugging it out to the noisy encouragement of their intoxicated seconds.

Terry approached the nearest fight. In his deepest authoritarian voice, he ordered the young men to cease fighting under threat of arrest. Amazingly, they complied. Unwilling to risk arrest, they also did not appreciate that the lone constable would have to walk them several hundred metres to the police station. Should they choose to resist, his chance of accomplishing this unaided was to say the least, remote!

Under the stern threat of arrest for non-compliance, they departed the scene, each going his separate way. Terry turned to deal with the next fracas, only to find that this had already broken up. An ancient rattling hulk of a vehicle careened around the traffic island on which Terry stood. With its occupants hanging from the windows, the obviously un-roadworthy Ford Zephyr threatened to sideswipe a pole. The rear of the vehicle slewed, fishtailing as the driver gunned the smoking engine. Waiting for the wreck to complete a second circuit, Terry stepped into its path and shining his torch into the face of the driver, signalled for him to stop.

Terry knew he had to restore order swiftly on his beat, as any likelihood of gaining control of the situation was decreasing with each passing moment. If he affected an arrest, he would be out of circulation while he processed the offender and the louts would be free to run amuck in his absence. Fortunately, the disorderly larrikins were unaware of the unavailability of backup. A firm hand and liberal threats might just work.

"If I write this heap off the road, it's going to cost you a lot of money to make it road worthy. Not only that, if I arrest you for dangerous driving, you'll spend the night in the cells and cop a hefty fine. You've got thirty seconds to get out of The Square. If I see you in here again tonight, I won't hesitate to lock you up. Get moving!" Terry's tone left the youth with no doubt that he would make good with the threat. He obeyed, meekly driving from the precinct to Terry's relief.

Terry maintained his post. As each offending vehicle approached he issued the same instructions to the occupants until finally, order prevailed. With confidence built upon the minor victory, he adopted his favourite vantage point on the Post Office corner. Six members of the inimical Epitaph Riders motorcycle gang lounged nearby, their gleaming, black and chrome machines backed into the kerb to expedite their hasty departure. They watched the lone, young lawman with interest, swigging from half-gallon jars of draught beer. A palpable atmosphere of trouble prevailed.

Adrenaline pumping, Terry feigned disinterest while surreptitiously observing their every move from his peripheral vision. One young thug guzzled the dregs of his jar and swaggered along the footpath in front of his friends. The empty jar swung from the middle finger of his right hand, which he had inserted in to the neck of the flagon. The affects of alcohol had glazed the youth's eyes and his long greasy hair fell across his thin, pallid features. The ubiquitous, dirty, denim jacket and blue jeans covered his unwashed body and the highly polished steel caps of his boots shone brightly where the leather had been cut away from the toes and polished. His attitude was clearly hostile.

Terry knew it was only a matter of time before the situation erupted. His very presence challenged the gang and the site of the uniform was an affront to these renegades from a lawful society.

Bugger them! He knew if he walked away or avoided them, they would win a moral victory, claiming the Square as theirs to behave as they chose. *I'm not moving. I'm going to stay right here. I'll deal with the first thing they do wrong,* he promised himself.

He was not disappointed. The youth with the flagon called a loud expletive to one of his cohorts.

Terry moved casually toward the offender. "I am placing you under arrest for using obscene language in a public place!"

The words had scarcely slipped from his lips before the lout recoiled. Drawing his arm back, he hurled the empty glass jar at the young policeman's head. Terry ducked. The flagon sailed overhead to crash on the concrete footpath, showering passers-by with glass fragments. Seizing the youth by the arm, Terry began to drag him away.

A second youth leapt from his motorcycle. "Let my mate go, or I'll do you!" he shouted. Holding another empty flagon by its neck, he threatened to hurl it at Terry's head.

"Keep out of it, or I'll arrest you as well, for threatening behaviour," Terry replied. Drawing his baton, while simultaneously winding its leather thong around his fist to prevent it being taken from him, he backed away, dragging his prisoner with him.

The second youth replied by hurling the flagon at the young policeman. Terry ducked. The lethal missile sailed over his head, smashing on the concrete pavement as his prisoner struggled to escape. The flagon throwing youth ran to free his mate, swinging punches as he tried to pull his friend away. Terry hung on to his prisoner determined that his arrest would not be thwarted. Before he could turn his back to the wall and protect himself from attack, an unseen arm went around his neck from the rear, dragging him to the pavement. His clumsy police helmet fell off and rolled away but his grip on the first offender did not break. As he fell, he dragged the youth to the ground with him, landing with his prisoner on top. The second youth pounced and while raining punches, attempted to break Terry's grip. Beneath two denim clad gang members, Terry swung the baton striking at the heads of his attackers. He felt the hard wood make contact and rolling free, leapt to his feet. One youth gripped the end of his baton, attempting to pull it from his grasp. Terry swung his free fist at the youth.

"Let go! he demanded his chest heaving from the exertion

"No. You'll hit me again," the youth replied.

"You bloody well bet I will!"

As if from nowhere, a huge crowd had gathered to encircle the combatants. Despite his anger and excitement, Terry observed that the fight had progressed some thirty metres along the footpath. His uniform was torn and blood covered his shirt. A quick inventory of his own condition reassured him that the blood wasn't his. As he tried to wrest the baton from the youth, a long-haired, scruffy male suddenly broke from the crowd and ran into the circle. Covered in tattoos, and with a fearsome appearance, Terry was in no doubt the man was no stranger to confrontation with the law. Turning to meet this new threat, he was surprised to see the man fell one of the gang members with a single blow. A moment before the youth had been fighting Terry, now he lay motionless on the ground.

"Thanks mate," Terry gasped, enormously relieved that the man had chosen on this occasion to be on the right side of the law.

Alerted by radio calls from nearby taxi drivers, the station Beat van screeched to a halt. Within minutes other police patrol vehicles converged on the scene. Leaping from patrol cars, the reinforcements dispersed the mob. Lyn seized Terry's prisoners one by one and unceremoniously threw them into the back of the paddy wagon. He grinned at Terry. "Having a bit of fun are we?"

Terry smiled. He had just witnessed the policeman's unspoken creed in action. No matter how urgent a task may be, when one of their own is in trouble, police officers drop everything and rush to help.

The incident served to establish Terry's reputation, not only on the streets, but also with Neville and his fellow officers. The local louts now knew better than to call his bluff and his previously untrusting sergeant seemed to consider that he had at last served his apprenticeship, allocating him with a wider range of duties.

Although Terry kept in touch with his brother Michael through intermittent, albeit lengthy letters, he still smarted from his parent's separation and found it impossible to forgive his mother for shattering their lives so dramatically. Able to view the situation objectively, Jane knew she had to somehow persuade her young husband to make contact. Her initial suggestions that Terry write to his mother evoked a blunt, "No way!"

Although Terry thought the subject closed, he had much to learn about the ways of women. Jane had only just begun her campaign to reunite mother and son. As water will eventually wear away stone, so too will the gentle but determined cajoling of women work to sway men, if for no other reason than to obtain peace and quiet. And so, in the spring of 1968, Judy and Tom Browning flew to Christchurch in what was to be one of three visits to Terry and his growing family.

It was a tense time for Terry as a baby-faced, gangly young policeman and proud husband and father pacing nervously outside the Customs Hall at Christchurch International Airport. Stopping to scan the faces as each passenger entered the hall he agonized over the pending visit. *What will this man be like? Will I be able to get along with him? What does mum look like now? What will they think of me, married so young and with a baby son?* A hundred similar anxious thoughts tumbled through his brain and his stomach churned sickeningly.

Can that be them? he wondered amazed as a slightly-built, greying man with thinning hair combed back from sharp features came into view leading a teenage youth and a plump, curly-haired woman in her fifties. Not expecting a threesome, Terry's gaze had initially swept past the trio.

A broad smile of recognition lit up the woman's face. "Terry!" she cried, tears immediately welling in her eyes.

Forgetting the prohibition on visitors in the secure area, Terry dodged through the barricade only to be stopped by a uniformed customs officer.

"Where are you going, son?"

Terry's hand dived into his pocket. Producing his police identification card, he flashed it at the customs officer, not caring that he was abusing his official status. The man glanced at the card and shrewdly summing up the situation withdrew. Terry barely had time to cross the carpeted "no mans land" and hug his mother before the stout figure of the middle-aged airport constable appeared, striding purposefully toward him.

"Come on lad! You shouldn't be in here." Malcolm Haussman ordered sternly.

Red faced and ashamed at his faux pas, Terry retreated to wait with the other passengers. What a start to the reunification of mother and son and first meeting with his stepfather!

If Tom or Judy noticed his indiscretion, they made no mention of it. With the turbulent mixture of emotions, the event quickly assumed minor significance. Noticing Terry's puzzled stare directed toward the teenage youth standing awkwardly to one side, Judy explained, "Terry, this is Michael. Michael is Tom's youngest son and we've brought him along to see New Zealand and to meet you."

"Hello, Mike." Terry offered a hand to his stepbrother. "Welcome to New Zealand," he said jovially, wondering where they were going to find room in their tiny house for everyone to sleep.

Acutely short of money and unable to afford a motor vehicle, Terry and Jane could offer their Australian guests few creature comforts. Their newly built tiny home in the battler's suburb of Hornby had only sparse furnishings, bare wooden floors and inadequate heating. Spring temperatures rarely rose above 19 degrees and with heavy frosts each night, Judy, Tom and Michael must have shivered. However, they never complained.

Tom seized upon the window of opportunity presented by their obvious poverty to demonstrate his generosity, lavishing them with presents, quietly paying for everything he could and surreptitiously stocking up their meagre food supplies. His obvious honesty, friendliness, diplomacy and non-judgmental attitude toward his new son in law, quickly dismantled any prejudices held by Terry who soon warmed to the older man who treated him as an equal. The two men quickly discovered a common love for a game of darts and over a quiet beer, Tom, Michael and Terry escaped the clutches of the women whenever possible.

They toured the South Island in a hired and very conspicuous fire engine red Holden sedan. With New Zealand roads mostly occupied by small and antiquated vehicles during the 1960's, the late model Holden attracted considerable attention. The famous scenery had them all spellbound and they marvelled at the majesty of Mount Cook's snow capped peak, the sparkling alpine jewel of Queenstown, The Remarkable Mountains, the strangely pulsating waters of Lake Wakatipu[14], Arrowtown with its quaint historic buildings and the snow-fed beauty of lakes Tekapo and Pukaki.

They hiked along bush trails to stand agog at Franz Joseph and Fox glaciers before continuing along through the temperate rainforests of The West Coast to the dull, grey mining towns of Hokitika and Greymouth.

Although they spent many happy hours together, the bitter events of the past were never far from Terry's mind. In the desire to prolong the joy of the present moment and for the sake of diplomacy, he put aside the answers for which he longed. It was for him, a time of unprecedented love and a new feeling of

---

[14] Maori legend says a sleeping giant lies at the bottom of the lake. The waters rise and fall with each breath.

belonging. Paradoxically, as time passed and he observed his mother's obvious happiness, he found those answers and in the process gained a new maturity.

Sadly, the holiday was over far too quickly. Judy, Tom and Michael flew out of Christchurch and as they waved goodbye, Terry felt grateful that Jane's gentle nagging had resulted in a bridge across the previously impassable divide between mother and son.

* * *

In the final week before Christmas of 1968, the entire complement of the Christchurch Police Armed Offenders Squad gathered for their traditional end of year celebration at the police Wet Canteen. policeman love a party and celebrations were well underway when a petty criminal, Stephen John Burrows[15] chose that very same evening to break into a sporting goods store at Church Corner, a well-known Western Suburbs Shopping precinct.

Burrows had been courting the same young woman, as a certain Christchurch policeman. Finding the policeman more attractive, the young woman severed her relationship with Burrows, leaving him heartbroken and angry. In an irrational act of revenge, Burrows decided to break into the store, steal firearms and shoot police as they responded.

Fortunately the officers answering the shop's intruder alarm, ducked for cover as a volleys of shots blasted through the rear door of the shop. Racing to their patrol car, both constables called frantically for backup and help from the Armed Offenders Squad.

As the officer in charge (O.I.C.) of the elite response unit, Trevor Joy faced a quandary. Many of his men were too inebriated but this was without doubt, a life and death situation. Leaving frontline officers to deal with the situation, for at least the first half hour, frantic telephone calls rallied a skeleton response team of former A.O.S. personnel. Although he had consumed his share of celebratory drinks, the wily detective adjudged himself sufficiently sober to head the team.

---

[15] A fictitious name for obvious reasons.

As with his fellow officers, Terry had received minimal firearms training, which due to tight cost constraints, had been limited to rudimentary instruction in the use of 1914-18 war-surplus, fully wooded .303 calibre rifles and the universal friend of policeman, the trusty, .38 calibre, six shot, Smith and Wesson revolver. Although he had not fired a weapon, either in anger or for practice for nearly two years, limited manpower and the unavailability of the A.O.S. Squad, meant proficiency in the use of firearms and Terry's distaste for them was not an issue. The situation was desperate and he responded with alacrity.

The duty inspector at that time was an arrogant man whose ability to avoid disciplinary action for numerous past transgressions, had earned him the undignified nickname of Slippery. Despite the most regular members holding him in contempt, the tall brusque commissioned officer possessed excellent organisational ability. Issuing curt orders, he rapidly mobilised an initial response team from the few police on duty.

With standard police practice dictating the placement of two cordons around incidents involving armed offenders, unarmed general duties personnel normally formed the outer cordon, with the inner cordon comprised of the superior equipped and skilled A.O.S. With both measures in place, the next step was for a police Negotiator to make voice contact with the offender by telephone or loud hailer. With the primary aim of police being to negotiate a peaceful resolution to the situation, the best strategy was usually to outlast the offender in a waiting game, which the police were able to play indefinitely.

With the paucity of A.O.S personnel, Slippery ordered the issue of rifles and revolvers to every available member. Those first on the scene were to assume the role normally played by the A.O.S.

Police General Orders and Instructions leave no doubt that on every occasion a commander issues firearms, he must also disseminate verbal fire orders, reminding police of their legal obligations and the circumstances under which they may discharge a weapon. Briefly speaking, fire orders dictate that shooting an offender is only lawful when the life of the officer or a third person is in imminent danger and there is no other means available to prevent death or serious injury.

Slippery's fire orders left much to the imagination.

Mustering for the emergency with other on duty personnel, Terry was one of the first to arrive at the car park of the Bush Inn Tavern, across the road from the siege. Handing Terry an ancient .303 rifle and a full magazine, the highly-stressed inspector barked, "Get up to that corner and watch the front of the shop. If he comes out, shoot him!"

With Burrows firing numerous shots wildly through both front and rear doors of the small premises, one unlucky patron in the front bar of the hotel had sustained a gunshot wound. While Terry was aware of that fact, he was also young, inexperienced and as yet, not fully indoctrinated in General Orders and Instructions. He accepted Slippery's order quite literally. *Who was he as a junior policeman, to query the command of someone of such exalted status?*

With the outer cordon in place, traffic was unable to enter the scene and hotel customers now knew to lay low. Despite these precautions, there was a likelihood of further injury, as hundreds of shots peppered the surrounding buildings.

In a half-crouching position, Terry ran to take up the designated vantage point. His only protection being, a slim brick pillar beside a plate glass window. Sprawling on his stomach, he squinted through the sights of the old weapon. Training the barrel on the front door of the shop, he held his finger ready to squeeze the trigger. Adrenaline coursed through his veins as another volley slammed into the hotel wall a few yards away. He had no doubt that should the armed offender walk onto the street; he would not hesitate to kill him.

Slippery stood a few feet behind him, protected by the brick wall of the bottle shop. His face flushed with excitement, he snapped orders into the microphone of his portable radio. "Who let that man through the cordon?" he asked abruptly.

Glancing to his left along the brightly lit empty street, Terry saw an elderly man come into view. Blissfully unaware of the drama unfolding before him, he led a small dog on a late night stroll. *Surely, he must have noticed that the streets were unusually deserted?* Terry wondered.

"Get back, you silly old bastard!"

The urgent call from the concealed policeman went unheeded. The old man continued walking blithely into the centre of the siege.

"Get out! Go back! Shit. He's gunna get shot!"

Revealing himself from the shadows, the uniformed officer jumped up and down, waving his arms frantically in an attempt to attract the pedestrian's attention. Still the old man took no notice. He continued walking toward the shattered, glass front of sports shop.

BANG! BANG! The sound of shots echoed loudly down the empty street.

As Terry watched the scene, it was as if the frame of a motion picture had stopped for a split second. Both the old man and the dog became immediately motionless. Then, as their predicament dawned, they turned and bolted. The poor fellow's ageing legs amazingly finding the agility of his former years; he disappeared around the nearest corner.

Pow! Pow! Pow! Pow! Another burst of random gunfire pelleted a thin, paling fence across the road from the sports store.

"Shit. Let's get out of here!" Several armed A.O.S. personnel quickly reassessed their position, scampering for protection behind the more solid walls of a nearby building. Miraculously, they remained unscathed while learning the basic lesson of those trained in combat: concealment from view does not necessarily mean the same thing as cover from fire! Burrow's stolen semi-automatic rifle had easily penetrated the palings above their heads.

For what seemed an eternity, Terry and his fellow officers kept watch on the shop as volley after volley of shots rang out in the still air. Burrows had a seemingly inexhaustible supply of ammunition, firing at will through the remnants of the plate glass display window at the shop front.

Over thirty minutes had elapsed before Slippery's radio crackled into life. "O.I.C. Scene, this is Detective Senior Sergeant Joy. We are en route to the scene. Where is our safe arrival point please and can I have a SITREP,[16] please. Over."

Slippery visibly relaxed. "A.O.S., this is O.I.C. Scene. the safe arrival point (SAP) is the car park of the Bush Inn Tavern. The offender is holed-up in the sports shop directly across the road from the hotel. He has fired hundreds of rounds from the building with a semi-automatic rifle. One person in the hotel has

---

[16] Situation report.

been struck by a round and injured. We have an armed cordon in place and the offender is contained. Do not approach the scene from Riccarton Road. I repeat. Do not approach the scene from Riccarton Road. Over."

"Roger, O.I.C. Scene. Our E.T.A. is 10 minutes. Over."

The sound of police vehicles skidding to a halt in the car park reached Terry's position. Spilling from the vehicles with telescopic sighted, .222 rifles, the black clad figures of the Armed Offenders Squad dispersed, taking up pre-designated positions around the offender's position. The ruddy faced senior detective wasted no time entering a rear door of the hotel to commandeer an office with a telephone as his scene headquarters.

Within a few moments, each of the A.O.S. officers acknowledged Joy's check that they were in position. At that stage, the detective sergeant lifted the telephone handset and stabbing at the dial with a thick finger, spun off the sports store's telephone number. The sound of a telephone ringing emanated clearly from the bullet-riddled glass, sounding strangely shrill in the eerie silence of the night.

Agitatedly pacing back and forth within the shop, Burrows shifted the rifle to his left hand and placed the receiver to his ear. The deep authoritarian voice of the detective boomed, "My name is Detective Senior Sergeant Joy of the New Zealand Police Armed Offenders Squad. Who am I speaking to?"

"Steve Burrows. What do you want?"

Joy's voice became quietly soothing, "Steve, you are obviously extremely upset at something. Before we discuss what has upset you, I want you to know that we have armed officers all around the shop. Please don't do anything silly as we don't want you to get hurt. At this stage there hasn't been too much harm done. Tell me what's bothering you and we'll see if we can help you."

As Trevor Joy talked, using years of skill and experience as a negotiator and trained interrogator, he gradually soothed the young man, guiding him with reason and calm compassion toward the inevitable path of surrender. After several moments discourse, Burrows eventually replaced the telephone and lying the rifle down, opened the door and walked into the street.

Never taking his eyes from the shop, Terry heard Trevor Joy's amplified voice carry plainly through the night air, as he continued an almost hypnotic and unbroken commentary, with a loud hailer.

"That's right, Stephen. Come into the street. You're doing well. There's nothing to be afraid of. Just keep your hands where we can see them. Now walk into the street. That's right. Come right out into the middle of the road where we can see you. Now, kneel down with your hands on your head. Don't move."

Burrows did as instructed. Walking slowly into the middle of the floodlit street, he glanced nervously around for the unseen officers he knew were aiming weapons at him. Unable to detect their positions, he knelt looking down at the bitumen, waiting.

A police dog handler with his German Shepherd and two A.O.S. members ran into the roadway. With efficiency borne from well rehearsed practise, they handcuffed Burrow's hands behind his back while the dog handler stood guard.

After Burrows left the scene in police custody, Terry approached the sports shop. Although the heavy plate glass remained intact, innumerable bullet holes marred the glass. He counted over two hundred and fifty bullet holes in the front of the shop and the wooden back door resembled Swiss Cheese.

After that incident, Terry had just begun to break the ice with Neville when new rosters resulted in a staff reshuffle. Neville moved on to other duties and a new NCO took his place. Bob Morgan was much closer to Terry's age. Of similar height and build, his brown eyes, dark straight hair and olive skin placed Bob in the tall dark and handsome category so sought after by women. His ready smile and good humour quickly endeared him to his charges. Although he brooked no nonsense or disrespect, Bob enjoyed a good time and interacting well with his troops. He was decisive and courageous in the face of impending danger and somehow, things always seemed to work out well. His team trusted his judgment, following his instructions implicitly.

A new bunch of recruits arrived at the Christchurch Police Headquarters and the cycle of promotions and transfers now meant despite having less than two years service, Terry was one of the more senior members on his team. A former cadet who had graduated at the same time as Terry joined the group and with his skill for man management, the young sergeant matched Terry with Barry Thompson, judging the two as compatible Incident Patrol members.

Terry and Barry hit it off immediately, working closely as a team and socialising when off duty. Barry, an exceptionally tall young man, with a big open face, a deep throaty voice, wide blue eyes and a generous mouth also enjoyed a laugh and was an inveterate practical joker. This latter predilection sometimes incurred the displeasure of the hierarchy, including Inspector 'Slippery,' who Barry openly despised.

During the early 1960's Slippery had been a junior constable on inquiry duties. As his mealtime approached, he purchased hot fish and chips but deciding they may grow cold before he could return to the police station, the young officer activated the vehicle's siren, rushing through the traffic with it blaring loudly to clear his path. The resultant public outcry at such irresponsible use of the device did nothing to enhance the reputation of the already beleaguered service. In a knee jerk reaction, politicians of the day ordered the police Force to remove all sirens from police cars, depriving future officers of this essential traffic-clearing device. From that day, every time Slippery's successors had cause to rush to an emergency, they cursed the stupidity of his actions.

Slippery enjoyed golf and more than one or two drinks in his leisure time. He somehow managed to ingratiate himself with the hierarchy and was seemingly untouchable. Rumour had it that he possessed inside knowledge as to his senior officer's past misdemeanours, using this knowledge to blackmail his way out of trouble.

On two occasions, Slippery managed to involve police vehicles in motor "accidents." In one of these, he was returning along the Main South Road from his golf club, when an errant pole leapt in front of his unmarked car. With destruction of his late model Holden complete, Slippery called for an on duty patrol to transport him from the scene, thus avoiding routine breath tests.

The stern faced authoritarian inspector was himself; a notorious disciplinarian and unhesitatingly charged junior officers for minor infractions, which often resulted from inexperience or innocent errors of judgment. His unseemly behaviour and double standards engendered no respect or liking amongst the ranks. When the unmistakable sound of his voice wafted over the radio, derisive comments and a barrage of animal noises invariably followed. Fuming with rage, he stupidly demanded that the offenders make themselves known. Secure in the knowledge of guaranteed anonymity, his requests provoked further guffaws of laughter, infuriating the commissioned officer to the point where his normally pale face could have replaced the red flashing light on a police car.

Barry Thompson owned a small battery powered gadget he'd found in a shop specialising in fun toys for practical jokers. Whenever Slippery logged onto the air, or transmitted from his vehicle, Barry activated his toy, emitting a maniacal laughter over the airwaves. Without doubt, the behaviour was childish, unprofessional, and breached radio procedure, but it served to demonstrate junior ranks low opinion of the Teflon-coated commissioned officer.

Sometimes when the freezing cold winters kept even the criminals at home in bed, the long nights of patrolling could become a little monotonous. At such times, Barry enjoyed playing pranks on his fellow officers.

It was good police practice for Patrol officers to refuel vehicles toward the end of their shift, ensuring that the next shift could respond immediately to any emergency. Refuelling entailed leaving their designated patrol zone to attend the Central Police Station where the police maintained its own fuel supply.

One evening Barry and Terry pulled into the yard to find a suburban patrol vehicle parked beside the fuel pump, which was engorging the tank of the unattended vehicle. The driver anticipated that the automatic shut off mechanism would activate when the tank reached capacity. The opportunity was too good for the sanguine joker. Extracting the jack from the boot compartment of the unlocked vehicle, he raised the wheels from the ground. Then, concealing his patrol car, he entered the police Station control room. With a knowing wink at the operations constable, he called the officers from the suburban patrol. "Eastern I, from Operations, over?"

The officers from the New Brighton Police Station answered using their portable hand held radio. "Eastern I receiving. Over."

"Eastern I, we have a report of a prowler at 160 Ferry Road. Please make your way to the scene. Further details will follow."

Rushing back to their vehicle, the two constables quickly pulled the nozzle from the filler pipe and replaced it on the bowser. Jumping into the vehicle, the engine fired as they slammed the doors, preparing to rush to the scene of the prowler complaint. The engine screamed, the wheels spun but the vehicle did not move. Barry's huge guffaws of laughter reverberated from the station's brick walls as the two officers alighted from the vehicle to investigate why they remained stationary.

Despite his larrikinism, the big fellow was a dedicated and competent policeman. Between them, Terry and Barry successfully handled a plethora of incidents, ranging from the dangerous uncertainty of dealing with domestic situations, through to the apprehension of burglars, car thieves and armed robbers.

Domestic situations are perhaps the most disliked of all incidents requiring police attention. There is always an element of uncertainty and danger when dealing with emotional individuals. The inclusion of drugs or alcohol into the equation is almost certain to create an explosive mix. Despite the precautions taken by competent and trained control room officers, it is not always possible to ascertain whether weapons have added further danger to the situation.

Few things inflame the emotions with such severity as those of a cuckolded husband. The normal standards of civilised behaviour often vanish, along with all reason and the fear of the consequences for violent behaviour. One such domestic situation attended by Terry and Barry may easily have ended in tragedy but for luck and quick thinking.

It was a busy Saturday night. The usual calls to street offences, pub brawls, noisy parties, assaults and drunks amongst the city's two hundred thousand inhabitants, kept six patrol cars and two vans busy. After Terry and Barry deposited a prisoner at the watch-house they were in the process of returning to their designated area, when above the usual bedlam of the two-way radio, they heard their call sign, "City I from Operations. Over"

Terry who was the observer, reached for the microphone. "City I receiving."

"City I. We have just received a telephone call from an unknown male. He states that he has found his wife in bed with another man and is going to kill them both. The caller has given an address in Spreydon. From his demeanour, I would say he means to carry out the threat. Please proceed immediately to 133 Summerfield Street.[17] Are there any other cars free to respond?

Over"

From the lack of response, it was obvious all other patrols were committed to other incidents. Barry pressed the accelerator to the floor and switched on the red flashing light. In the absence of a siren, Terry seized the spotlight to shine into the rear view mirror of vehicles barring their path. He had discovered this was an excellent way of alerting drivers to the presence of the speeding police car, giving them ample time to move over. Occasionally, he used the amplification of his voice through the loud hailer to imitate a siren. Although on this occasion, it was clearly a life and death situation and he did not want to alert the suspect to their approach.

Slowing only for the red traffic lights, they sped to the scene. The Traffic Regulations did not permit them to drive through an intersection against the lights, unless they displayed a red flashing light and used a siren. Once again, they cursed the errant inspector for his foolish behaviour. Knowing time may be of the essence, Barry crept through each intersection, watching both ways for inattentive motorists. Without the siren, they risked disciplinary action and their own lives but placed the victim's life ahead of their own and their careers.

As they approached Summerfield Street, Barry turned off the headlights and eased his foot off the accelerator, placing the gear shift in neutral. The momentum of the speeding vehicle carried them along as Terry counted out the street numbers and unbuckled his seatbelt. Judging that they had reached the correct address, Terry threw the car door open and bailed out. The sound of breaking glass reached him as he ran to the front door of 133. A huge man with the shoulders of a heavyweight wrestler wielded a spade with immense strength, striking the glass panel in the front door. The door disintegrated before the onslaught as he smashed his way into the house.

Terry had already burst through the door in pursuit of the spade-swinging giant when Barry who was a few seconds behind, caught up with him in the bedroom. A terrified man and woman huddled under the blankets as the giant raised the spade above his head, preparing to chop downward with the sharp edge of his weapon. Hearing the commotion behind him, the attacker turned

---

[17] The actual address has not been used for obvious reasons.

to aim the blow at Terry's uniformed figure coming through the doorway. Without considering the disparity in size, Terry leapt onto the man's broad back. Grabbing frantically at the spade handle, he rode the enraged maniac like a rodeo rider on a bucking bull, trying to wrest the spade from his grasp. The man's immense strength was too great. It was all Terry could do to retain his grip on the spade handle.

Summing up the situation in a fleeting glance, Barry raised Terry's 5-cell torch, which he'd grabbed from the car, and smashed the offender repeatedly about the head. Red Eveready batteries flew in all directions as the torch broke apart. The giant shook his head dazedly providing the two constables with just enough time to lock the offender's thick wrists behind his back. "Okay, sport. That's enough. You're under arrest for assault with intent to cause grievous bodily harm!" Terry gasped.

Throughout the struggle, the hapless couple showed no gratitude to their rescuers. Instead, they spat insults and invective from the double bed at the rude interruption to coitus. Rather than lead their attempted murderer to the patrol car, it was tempting to let him lose to complete his grisly task.

Terry and Jane's new house, sat unfenced, without paths or gardens among the wild grasses of a former sheep paddock. Other young couples, who were equally penniless, surrounded Terry and Jane. Keen to transform the grounds into something resembling an established home, Terry moonlighted in his spare time, putting aside a few dollars each week for the purchase of fencing materials, cement, sand and gravel. The hire of a cement mixer was unaffordable. Nailing planks together to form a mixing board, the young father hand mixed cement, and laboriously laid all the garden paths and the driveway.

On 16 July 1969, he had his head in a posthole scraping gravel from the bottom with a jam tin when Jane advised him that Neil Armstrong had stepped on the surface of the moon. A few months later, on 3 December 1969, their second child, Veronica came into the world.

For Terry, Veronica was a beautiful bundle of snowy haired enchantment. She completely captivated him with her smile and gentle nature. With a boy and girl, his life should have been complete. However, Jane's growing discontentment marred the happiness he felt. Attempts to fathom the cause failed. Unable to break through her increasing coldness toward him, Terry surmised that the several miscarriages preceding Veronica's arrival were the probable cause and hoped in time her indifference toward him would thaw.

The mid to late 1960's were the era of the Vietnam War. As with Australia, there was a division of public opinion in New Zealand as to whether the country should be involved in the conflict. The country's leading newspapers reported almost weekly demonstrations and student protests and with anti-American sentiment running high, these often turned violent.

During January 1970, American Vice President Agnew visited Auckland, necessitating police reinforcements be flown from the South Island to maintain public order. Terry was among the police contingent bussed to the New Zealand Air Force base at Wigram for the uncomfortably bumpy and tortuously slow flight to Auckland.

The ancient propeller driven Bristol Freighter squatted on the tarmac, the cowlings of each of its two engines stained with oil leaks. *My God,* he thought. *Is that thing safe?*

"Forty thousand rivets flying in formation! That's how the Air Force describes them." Bob Mather, a young former cadet and son of Bill Mather, the Christchurch Police Station Property officer, seemed to read Terry's thoughts. His square face pensive, he continued, "They're old, but they're reliable workhorses. Don't worry; it won't fall out of the sky!"

Terry wasn't so sure.

Dressed in overalls, the Air Force Loadmaster dished out headphones as they found their places in the hastily installed hard, troop seats of the cargo deck. "Put these on. The engines make a frightful din," he grinned.

With the last of the policeman on board, the door closed and the flight crew climbed a short ladder into the flight deck above the human cargo. Hearing the whine of a starter motor, Terry looked out a tiny starboard window and watched as one of the ancient propellers turned reluctantly, as its' engine emitted a chuffing sound. As each of the pistons in the radial engine compressed the mixture of fuel and air, the engine fired, caught and stopped again. The propeller turned a second time. This time the engine fired and roared into life, accompanied by a cloud of thick black oil smoke.

Although he couldn't see the second engine on the other side of the aircraft, through the dubious protection of his earmuffs, he heard the same noise emanating from the port side. He lifted the corner of his ear protection, instantly acknowledging the necessity for the earmuffs. The clattering roar reaching him through the thin fuselage was akin to the hand of a giant violently shaking marbles in a tin can. The entire frame of the ancient Museum exhibit shook in consort with the bellowing engines.

With a mighty roar, the Bristol Freighter moved slowly down the runway. Gathering speed after a seemingly endless, lumbering run, taking the entire length of the airfield, the contraption lifted sluggishly from the ground. There was a slight thump as the undercarriage retracted. They lifted above the flat terrain of the Canterbury Plains and as they climbed into the low clouds, the pilot levelled the nose of the aircraft, maintaining the same altitude for the entire flight. Occasionally, through the cotton wool enveloping them, they glimpsed the white caps of waves, which seemed to be but a short dive beneath the wing tips.

After what seemed an interminable flight during which the racket from the engines precluded any conversation, they felt one wing dip as they turned to make their approach to the Whenuapai Air Force Base. The farm paddocks lay beneath them, the contrasting chequer board effect of the green fields punctuated by grazing sheep and cattle. Waiting buses from the New Zealand Navy transported them to the harbour side suburb of Devonport and the Navy Training Base, H.M.N.Z.S. Philomel.

The following morning, after a very substantial breakfast feast, they travelled into the city centre where the Auckland police had already formed a human barrier between several hundred demonstrators threatening to storm the plush, Inter-Continental Hotel, which housed the American Vice President.

Three hundred uniformed officers stood before the demonstrators enduring intolerable conditions, silently suffering insults, missiles and spittle, hurled at them by angry students and rabble-rousers. Instructed not to act in the face of extreme provocation, they received no refreshments or relief, standing all day in the oppressive humidity of the Auckland summer.

Being one of the tallest constables, Terry found himself in the front line, facing verbal abuse from various demonstrators, who saw the police as a symbol of a compliant Government acceding to the demands of the U.S.A.'s war mongering regime. One particular demonstrator thrust a bearded and pimply countenance into Terry's face, shouting invective unrelentingly. Despite the man's foul breath and the sputum striking his cheek, Terry remained poker-faced while inwardly noting every detail of the offender's features should his superiors sanction an arrest.

Bob Mather, unable to contain his dislike for the unkempt mob, engaged in debate with a demonstrator, calmly countering every rehearsed cliché with logic and reason. To the young constable's amusement, this only served to infuriate the debater further. Terry could see no point in responding to the taunts and abuse. After listening to the argument for several minutes, he turned his head to address his fellow officer. "What's the point of arguing with him, Bob? You won't get anywhere."

"He's just a bloody idiot and doesn't know what he's talking about," Bob replied.

Terry gave up, understanding that the other policeman was merely amusing himself by inflaming the protester.

Finally, a smoke bomb thrown into the police ranks, provoked retaliation from a constable a few feet to Terry's right. The officer attempted unsuccessfully to seize the culprit, who escaped back into the crowd. Terry spotted him running from the scene at the back of the assembled mob. As the offender neared his position, he looked inquiringly at Jack Wheeler, his sergeant, for permission to give chase. Jack's nod was barely perceptible but it was all Terry needed. Removing his helmet, he sprinted after the miscreant, who by this time had covered some fifty metres.

Despite the weight of his baton, handcuffs and helmet Terry gained ground, his heavily booted feet pounding against the bitumen surface of the roadway. Several buses used to transport the police lined the street some distance from the demonstration. As he tired of the chase, Terry understood he would have to pursue the fleeing offender for several hundred metres before he had gained sufficient ground to execute a tackle. Then, if the man was fitter than he was, he might not have enough wind left from the chase to overpower him.

Glancing over his shoulder as he drew level with the buses, he judged that he was out of site of the demonstrators, who were yelling encouragement to the escapee. Terry raised his right arm.

Holding the police helmet by its peak, he lined up the back of the offender's head and flicked the helmet. The fibreglass headpiece proved to be remarkably aerodynamic when thrown in this manner. The knob caught the man on the back of his head, causing him to stumble and fall. As the watching mob roared angrily, Terry discovered that he wasn't quite out of sight.

Before the unfortunate felon could recover, Terry was on top of him. Placing him in a headlock, he dragged him back toward the jeering crowd. The police arrest squad rushed from their hiding-place in the basement car park of the hotel and relieved Terry of his prisoner.

The size and mood of the demonstration was unprecedented. Although The New Zealand Police had dealt with other violent demonstrations, such as the riots accompanying the infamous waterfront strikes of the 1950's, it had no recent experience of mob mentality. The service had forgotten valuable lessons of former years and formal procedures for dealing with major demonstrations did not exist. There was no training for police officers in the specialised techniques essential for dealing with mass demonstrations and no guidance available for commanding officers.

The decision to subject uniformed, law enforcement personnel, who were used to acting autonomously, to such degrading and hostile behaviour without respite, was ill-advised. After many hours of abuse, every one of the three hundred policeman forming the human shield, inwardly and silently seethed with rage and the desire for revenge. All the ingredients existed for a major calamity.

Toward evening, Senior Sergeant Mick Huggett, the officer in charge of the police party, received instructions from his superiors to disperse the demonstrators. With a loud hailer in his hand, he attempted to address the hostile, yelling mob. As the amplified voice of authority reached them, the demonstrators shouted even louder, drowning out his pleas for their calm dispersal.

Huggett lost his temper. Striding forward, the burly policeman picked up one of the demonstration organisers in his massive hands. Holding the man at arms length, Mick shouted the instructions to disperse into the demonstrator's face. There was no doubt the man heard the order for dispersal, but as the senior policeman set him down he remained defiant. Returning to his cohorts, he continued shouting while awaiting the prescribed deadline.

It was obvious to all assembled, that the mob was intent on remaining outside the Vice President's Hotel. Along with other politicians, The Minister of police appeared on the hotel balcony, watching the commotion below. From their presence, it was clear that they expected a conclusion to events. Glancing at the Minister, Mick Huggett beckoned with his right arm and stepped toward the demonstrators.

What the senior sergeant's gesture intended to convey, later became the subject of much conjecture. Some said he merely wanted a small group to begin arresting the demonstrators, some hypothesized that the entire front line of policeman was supposed to disperse the crowd, but whatever his intention, the consequences of that simple gesture were far beyond the wildest imaginings of those present. As if of a single mind, three hundred, navy blue serge clad figures flooded forward with alarming speed, intent on seeking revenge for ten hours of pent up rage and frustration.

Nearly every-one of the policeman had a specific target in mind. Some had the same target. They presented a fearsome sight to the unruly mob. There was no thought of taking prisoners or abiding by any of the usual niceties of the law. Fists flew and panicked by so much unleashed hatred, the demonstrators fled for their lives.

When Terry saw his fellow policemen move in response to the command, he noticed a uniformed sergeant grappling with a very fearful young man. The man had wrapped his arms and legs around a wooden telegraph pole as he hung on for his life. He looked like a monkey trying to climb a slippery tree. As the angry N.C.O. tugged unsuccessfully to free him, Terry concluded that the sergeant intended to place the man under arrest for some perceived offence. Reaching forward, he grasped the individual's shirt collar and with his other hand, reached between the man's legs. Seizing a large handful of crotch, and anything else unfortunate enough to be included in his grasp, promptly caused the unfortunate fellow to let go of the pole. Terry carried him across the road as the arrest squad rushed forward to receive the first prisoner.

The arrest squad O.I.C. a young Auckland sergeant enquired, "What's he been arrested for?"

Terry turned, expecting to find the non-commissioned officer behind him to explain. There was no sign of the arresting officer. Faced with the dilemma of having used considerable force on a prisoner and unaware of the reason for the sergeant's actions, he tossed the man headlong at the arrest squad. He landed like a bag of wheat.

"Buggered if I know. I didn't arrest him!"

Not waiting to explain, he turned and ran back to the melee. Just like the aftermath of a cavalry charge, bodies lined the footpath and roadway. Men and women fled in all directions, hotly pursued by avenging policeman. Wounded demonstrators leaned against power poles, moaning. Glancing up the road toward Auckland's famous Albert Park, Terry could clearly see figures running and diving through the shrubbery as they attempted to escape. A policeman picked up one unlucky fellow. Throwing him head first into some bushes, the man landed at the feet of uniformed officers on the other side. Like and undersized fish, he was promptly picked up and thrown back again.

There had been no arrests but the demonstrators had suffered a plethora of injuries. Noelinelly disciplined veterans of the service eventually made their way back to the buses after the commotion died down, laughing hugely. Jock McSkimming, a giant of a man from Christchurch, sat in the bus, his ample belly wobbling with mirth as tears ran down his big moon face. Removing his black rimmed glasses to wipe away the moisture, he exclaimed in a broad brogue, "Och, laddie! I've ne'r had so much fun in me life!"

It was sometime before the last of the stragglers returned. After explaining that they had chased many of the demonstrators as far as Queen Street, a distance of nearly two and a half kilometres, they boarded the police buses for the return trip to their billets.

That evening, the Auckland Star bore a large front-page picture of Terry carrying the demonstrator across the road. He cringed and with his fellow officers, waited for the repercussions that must certainly follow the unconventional police action.

Amazingly, there was no inquiry. The violent and panicked dispersal of the demonstrators and the ensuing assaults by police, were clearly the fault of hierarchical bungling by the police and the Government of the day.

With the benefit of hindsight, the result of subjecting policemen and women who are after all, human beings, to prolonged violence and abuse was not surprising. It was no coincidence that later amendments to police General Orders and Instructions carried detailed procedures for the selection of staff and the correct handling of demonstrations.

* * *

Terry's return to Christchurch coincided with the announcement that the body of an Australian hitchhiker, Jennifer Mary Beard, had been discovered under The Gates of the Haast Bridge. A witness described seeing the unfortunate girl before her death, with a stout, middle-aged man who drove a cream 1954 Vauxhall Velox.

Enlisting New Zealand Army support, police launched a massive search for the killer and the suspect motor vehicle. Officers returning from the anti-Vietnam protests had little time to pack their bags and say goodbye to wives and families, before heading for the swamps and dense rainforest country of Haast Pass. The police Service initially confined the selection of search teams to those officers skilled in bush craft, or, who were members of the esteemed police search and rescue squad.

At that time, the Beard murder inquiry under the direction of Detective Senior Sergeant Trevor Joy, was the largest manhunt ever mounted by the New Zealand Police. Teams contact-searched[18] the vast and inhospitable West Coast terrain, wading through the oozing gelatinous mud of a myriad of swamps, beating their way through creepers and thorns, plagued by ravenous mosquitoes and stinging sand flies, drenched to the bone by the relentless torrential rain, their task was seemingly impossible. After ten days of painstaking work, search teams were exhausted. With huge areas to left search and a mountain of reported sightings to process, Trevor Joy called for

---

[18] A contact search is a highly concentrated method of searching where the searchers are able to maintain at least visual contact with the searchers either side, thus ensuring every square centimeter of the ground is covered.

reinforcements.

Terry volunteered along with Leo Manford, a former tourist guide from Fox Joseph Glacier turned policeman and Rodger Millard, a six foot seven inch, seventeen stone champion basketball player. They travelled by overnight train to Greymouth, situated on the West Coast of New Zealand's South Island. An army Landrover met them for the long drive to the Deep South. After an exhausting trip, the three men arrived at the search base, to learn that a change of orders meant that apart from them, all teams were to be withdrawn from the search area. As the senior member of the small team, Terry was in placed charge. His orders were to investigate and report by radio all suspicious sightings to the search headquarters in Wanaka.

Fortunately for Terry and his team, the weather, which had until that time been exceedingly wet, cleared. Brilliant sunshine leant a holiday atmosphere to the task despite the hardships of existing on ration packs, sleeping in the open and being eaten alive by a myriad of insects that would have had an entomologist salivating with delight. During the day, they combed bush tracks and clearings, ably assisted by Leo who possessed a detailed knowledge of the local area.

Rodger (better known as, Stretch) Millard, a man of immense strength and possessing excellent bush skills, revelled in the task. They took the Landrover to places where no motor vehicle had been before, confident in Stretch's faith in the rugged four-wheel drive.

When confronted with seemingly impassable country, Millard would exclaim, "Put the bastards in the right gear and they will climb trees!"

They stripped the canvas canopy off the vehicle and mounted the skull of a steer on the bull-bar. Apart from the tell-tale army number plates, the vehicle could have passed for one owned by a team of feral deer hunters. Terry laughed inwardly when thinking how horrified the New Zealand Army would have been at the sight of their trusty and formerly pristine vehicle.

At night, the team spotlighted for deer, managing to shoot two of the beautiful but unfortunate animals as they grazed in small clearings at the edge of the deserted gravel road. Leo was an inveterate storyteller and hailing from the under populated West Coast, appeared to have an intricate knowledge of its local inhabitants and their life stories. He regaled them incessantly with anecdotes, in his inimitable slow drawl, punctuated liberally with obscenities. It became apparent that Leo had enjoyed numerous sexual liaisons and was unselective in his choice of bed partners, earning him the nickname 'Mounter.'

Although they were far from civilisation and the close supervision of senior officers, Terry took the task seriously, allowing his team sufficient latitude to build close bonds and enjoy the demanding work, but insisting thoroughness in their search. The majority of sightings turned out to be a wild goose-chase. The victim, Jennifer Beard had hitchhiked around New Zealand wearing a green canvas backpack and carrying a Kodak Instamatic Camera. The camera and backpack were not with the body when found and were therefore crucial to the investigation. Although there had been numerous sightings of the suspect vehicle, or one similar, all leads had so far drawn a blank.

After a week of fruitless searching, Terry's team received a promising report from Homicide Headquarters. A witness had telephoned to say that shortly after the last sighting of the victim; he had seen a middle-aged, portly male on the side of a remote bush road. The man appeared to be burning a green canvas pack and a camera.

Terry and his team rushed to the area and sure enough, on the side of the road they found the charred remains of green canvas and rolls of film.

The sighting was extremely significant. It appeared that this discovery might be the much sought after key to solving the crime. Due to the remoteness of the area, they were beyond radio range. It was impractical to post a guard over the seemingly vital evidence and due to its remoteness; Terry adjudged it safe to leave things as they were.

They travelled for two hours before they were within radio range and reported their discovery, expecting a flurry of interest to result. H.Q. received their report with apparent disinterest, failing to issue any instructions to Terry and his search crew.

"Obviously, this information is not important after all," he remarked dejectedly. "We're only small cogs in a very big wheel. Let's move on and keep searching."

Despite maintaining their vigil and continuing the exhausting search, they received no further information of interest. Search

Headquarters failed to contact them or provide updates on the inquiry and the silence led them to the conclusion that they had almost been forgotten.

After ten days with no contact, someone remembered them, instructing Terry to scale down efforts and withdraw.

Although a prime suspect lived in the small township of Timaru, inquiries failed to find sufficient evidence to build a prima facie case against him. Despite almost dismantling his Vauxhall car and extensive interrogation, the man maintained his innocence. Eventually, with all leads exhausted, there was no alternative but to close the case.

Several months elapsed and Terry had resumed normal duties. The Beard murder Investigation had faded from the news and in the need to carry on with other police matters, had almost from his mind.

"Hey, Terry? Have you seen the paper today?" The query came from Gary Doyle, a stocky red-haired member of the Hornby Constabulary where Terry had been transferred.

"No. What's new?" Terry answered, as he changed into his police tunic to commence his shift.

Gary tossed a copy of the Christchurch Star on the desk. "It seems someone's got tired of waiting for the wheels of justice and taken the law into their own hands!"

Terry picked up the paper. "Murder suspect dies in hit and run," the headlines announced. He continued reading aloud. "Timaru Police are investigating possible links between the death of a Timaru man in a hit and run accident and his alleged involvement in the murder of Tasmanian hitchhiker, Jennifer Beard." He finished reading the article. Dumfounded, he lay the paper down. "Well, I bet they don't look too hard to find out who killed that bastard," he concluded.

Several years later, with memories of the burnt back pack and film still vividly in his mind, Terry had a chance meeting with former Detective Senior Sergeant Joy. Trevor was by then heading the New Zealand Aviation Security Service. When Terry broached the subject of the charred evidence, the detective claimed to be unaware of the find!

It seemed that there had been a terrible break down in communication.

CHAPTER FIVE
"EVERYTHING'S ALRIGHT.
IT'S JUST YOUR IMAGINATION!"

When Terry returned from Haast, Staff Senior Sergeant Bill Prentice, a quietly spoken and well-mannered man, ordered the young constable to become on of the team in the Christchurch police operations room. Terry was extremely upset at this decision, interpreting it as a slight on his ability to handle frontline policing. He requested an interview with the staff sergeant.

Bill rocked back on his chair and smiled, "That's not the case at all. It's because of your experience and excellent radio skills that I have decided to put you on to operations. It won't be forever and you'll be a better policeman for it."

Terry looked doubtful. *He's just buttering me up*, he decided. Reluctantly, he reported to Aden Stuartson, who was to be his direct supervisor.

"You'll be taking Sergeant Brown's slot on the roster." Aden advised him, the corner of his mouth pulled down in a tight grimace. Aden still smarted from Terry's earlier challenge to his authority. He did not relish having to work with someone so rebellious. "Merv's on six weeks annual leave," he continued.

"Okay, Senior. I am looking forward to working with you," Terry lied.

Maybe I'll get higher duties allowance, he thought, brightening at the prospect of the extra much needed remuneration as an Acting Sergeant. However, upon further examination of the rosters, he discovered he was one day short of the twenty-eight days necessary to qualify for the extra payment. The wily senior sergeant had pre-empted his application for higher duties allowance by switching Terry to another line on the roster after twenty-seven days.

That'd be right, he thought. *I get the responsibility but don't get paid for it.*

The watch-house keeper also fell under Aden's direct control. Mark Penn was a good-natured lanky constable with fair straight hair, blue eyes and a face badly pock-marked from a chronic

175

infection of teenage acne. Possessing an infectious hyena like laugh, and quick wit, Terry soon warmed to Mark and the two men quickly developed a firm friendship.

As Terry's competence in the Operations Room became apparent, Aden relaxed, revising his previous opinion of the younger man. For his part, Terry gave his senior sergeant the benefit of the doubt.

I guess it was just a misunderstanding, he mused. *I must have caught him on a bad day, or Neville Gilchrist had influenced his opinion of me.*

It normally took two officers to run the Operations Room. On the busier nights or, when there happened to be 'a flap,' a third officer usually occupied a space at the long glass desktop, helping to answer an array of different coloured telephones each with a different purpose. The police used two radio channels. The main channel handled normal traffic and the second was reserved for special operations and emergencies. A bank of red lights and switches nearly covered an entire wall, linking the police directly with the Reserve Bank and the intruder alarm systems of other important sites. Closed circuit television monitors provided close up views of the Government Bank's vaults and passageways. Contingency plans for various civil emergencies filled a cabinet below the desk and a small aperture at one end of the room gave access to the teleprinter operator whose machines connected Christchurch with every major police station in the country.

Being an Operations Controller was an extremely stressful task, necessitating an unflappable personality, an intricate knowledge of the city and policing procedures and excellent judgment. The job entailed making rapid-fire decisions in the deployment of police resources and co-ordinating the police response to a plethora of incidents. The heady feeling of power and the adrenaline rush, which accompanied major incidents, filled Terry with excitement. He felt at home and began looking forward eagerly to the uncertainty and challenges of each new shift.

One of the most challenging situations of Terry's police career occurred one quiet weekday, when by chance, Mark Penn found a scrap of paper on the front counter. He had not heard or seen anyone enter the front doors of the old police station and might easily have thrown the paper in the rubbish bin without

176

reading its contents. Opening the note, he smoothed the paper and read the pencilled scrawl. Mark's eyebrows shot up in surprise and he hurried through to Aden's Stuartson's office.

"Senior, I've just found this note on the watch-house desk." Mark handed the crumpled missive to Aden, his scarred brow wrinkled with deep concern. The threat read;

"To the police,

There is no justice in our Court system. The women get everything and the men get shafted. Following the end of my marriage, my wife got the house, the kids and all my money. Not content with that, she's denied me access to my children. The Courts don't care. It's been two years now since I applied for access and I am still waiting.

I will not wait any longer. I have nothing to live for and nothing to lose. Unless my application to see my kids is dealt with immediately, I intend to blow myself up in the middle of this city today.

Take this seriously!"[19]

Stuartson reached for the telephone. "I had better notify, the C.I.B. to check this out. There's a name and signature at the bottom. The Courts will be able to tell us if this fellow has a case pending."

"Okay, Senior." Mark returned to the watch-house leaving Terry and Aden to deal with the pending crisis.

Inquiries with the Christchurch Magistrates Court revealed that one Jonathon Robertson was the subject of divorce and custody proceedings. The Court had found against him, awarding his estranged wife custody of the couple's children, filing a crippling maintenance order and granting his wife possession of the family home.

What was more alarming was Robertson's former occupation in the mining industry. There was little doubt he possessed the knowledge and skills to construct an explosive device.

Trevor Joy mobilised the A.O.S. and a team of detectives to track down the suspect. They learnt Robertson was the owner of

---

[19] This is not the exact wording used but the note was along similar lines.

a Volkswagen mini bus, which was missing from his home. Robertson's workmates told how he had become extremely agitated, failing to report for work that morning. Aden and Terry broadcast a general alert for the Robertson and the missing vehicle, while plainclothes officers mounted a watch on Robertson's home and that of his estranged wife. There was little more to do but await developments.

In the Operations Room, Terry commenced a log of events, carefully recording all radio transmissions and developments in relation to the search on the Operations Room typewriter. This standard police practice for major operations would later provide valuable information during de-briefing procedures. Anticipating the usual quiet Tuesday afternoon shift, Bill Prentice had given Terry's off-sider a day off in lieu of previous overtime. With the telephones and both radio channels running hot with the extra traffic, Terry was almost overwhelmed. Aden gave him no assistance and failed to appreciate his predicament. Terry struggled on alone.

As evening drew near, the city streets filled with normal peak hour traffic. It was the worse possible time for the news, which reached Terry in the narrow confines of the busy room.

"Operations from City I. Ten Ten.[20] Over!"

Grabbing the microphone, Terry responded immediately. "Operations receiving."

"Operations, we have just discovered the suspect's vehicle. It's parked on the fourth floor of the Manchester Street car park building. There is a middle-aged male fitting the description of the suspect Robertson seated in the front of the vehicle. We can also see oxyacetylene cylinders with wires protruding from them in the rear of the vehicle."

Aden Stuartson leapt from his chair in the adjoining office. Seizing the radio microphone he responded, "City I from operations senior sergeant. Do not approach the vehicle. Maintain surveillance. Switch immediately to channel six. Do you read, over?"

"City I, Roger."

---

[20] The highest priority radio call, denoting a dire emergency.

Within seconds, Slippery who had been preparing to finish duty, stormed into the Operations Room. He'd been monitoring developments from the radio in his upstairs office. With customary officiousness, he assumed command of the operation while Terry continued struggling to maintain the vital typewritten log of every communication, respond to Slippery's demands and answer routine radio and telephone calls.

"Constable, begin calling out every available staff member!"

"Yes sir!"

"Constable, answer that telephone!"

Terry placed a second handset to his free ear as the radio squawked for attention.

"Constable, has a criminal history check been done on Robertson?"

"Excuse me," Terry diverted his attention from the telephones. "Yes sir."

"Constable, contact the Traffic Department and have them cordon off all the streets surrounding the car park building."

"Yes sir. I'll attend to it in just a moment."

"Constable, have you contacted all off duty staff yet?"

"Not yet sir. I'll do it when I've answered these 'phones, sir."

"Constable, why aren't you keeping the log up to date?"

"I am a little busy sir. I'll get to it in a moment. I am keeping notes to type in when I can get a moment sir."

"Why is that radio not being answered? Get on with it man!"

On and on it went until Terry felt like screaming, "For Christ sake, get me some help in here!"

At last, realising Terry's predicament, Aden slipped into the vacant chair, relieving some of the burden from his overworked subordinate.

Suburban patrols joined the chaos, clearing pedestrians from the car park and throwing a wide cordon around the building. The mammoth task of evacuating commercial premises within the danger zone commenced as the A.O.S. scurried to the scene.

According to those who knew him, Robertson was extremely desperate and quite prepared to execute his threat. With his vehicle apparently loaded with explosive packed cylinders, the stakes were extremely high. In the event of an explosion, there was every chance the pre-stressed concrete car park would collapse. Anyone or anything on the decks of the building would become the fillings of a giant sandwich. In addition, there would be extensive damage to surrounding buildings and the loss of many lives.

There was without doubt; the potential for the worst man caused disaster in the city's history. The fact that Robertson did not immediately detonate his mobile bomb at the first sight of the City I patrol, gave police some cause for hope. At the scene, Trevor Joy and his men discussed their options.

"I don't think we should use the loud hailer this time." Trevor told his second in command, Detective Sergeant Bruce Scott, a dapper, quietly spoken man in his late twenties. "It's too risky."

"I agree," Bruce replied. "The sudden amplified bellow of the electronic bullhorn might just frighten or provoke him into detonating his bomb."

"The offender's depression and instability makes the decision to approach him extremely dangerous but we have no choice." Trevor continued. "I'm going to see if I can talk him out."

The situation called for excellent negotiation skills, courage and a cool head. Although there were other officers just as competent, Trevor's success in negotiating peaceful resolution to numerous past incidents spoke for itself. Apart from that, he wasn't going to ask one of his team to do something he wasn't prepared to do himself.

"You'll need backup. I'll come with you." Bruce volunteered. "Shouldn't we advise Operations of our decision?"

"No, I don't want that bloody Slippery sticking his oar in with what he thinks is a better idea. Let's just do it!"

The radios had gone silent. Unaware of the drama unfolding at the scene, the three police officers waited tensely in the Operations Room, expecting at any moment to hear the sound of a mammoth explosion and the rumble of collapsing buildings.

"What the hell's going on," Slippery demanded to no-one in particular. Fidgeting nervously for a few minutes, he couldn't tolerate being kept in the dark any longer.

"O.I.C. Scene from Operation Commander. SITREP please."

There was no response. On the upper level of the car park building Trevor Joy cautiously approached the old mini bus, having first divested himself of his sidearm. He didn't want to

180

spook Robertson and the sight of his armed, black uniform and bereted figure, may do just that.

Bruce Scott sidled around the concrete pillars and abandoned vehicles, approaching unseen from a different direction. His telescopic sighted rifle held tightly against his body to present the smallest possible outline, he was conscious of the five reasons which enable the identification of objects by the human eye; Shape, shadow, silhouette, shine and movement. By watching the direction of the setting sun, he made sure his body did not cast a tell-tale shadow and by remaining concealed, he discounted the other four factors.

Trevor lifted his hand in a passive gesture and smiled as he made eye contact with the distraught would-be bomber. He indicated for Robertson to wind down his window.

Although the agitated man held his thumb on the switch of his explosive charge, he complied. "Don't come any closer copper!"

"Okay. Relax Mr Robertson. My name is Trevor Joy. We got your note and I want to talk to you and see how we can help. Is it okay if I call you Jon?" Trevor's enquiries had already established that Robertson preferred the diminutive version of his name.

"What makes you think you can do anything?" Robertson replied suspiciously.

Joy smiled, relieved. He'd already opened the door slightly for discussion. "I've got a lot of contacts," he replied, wedging a foot firmly in the afore-mentioned figurative door. All he had to do now was gain the distraught man's confidence and give him hope and a reason to abandon his plans for self destruction.

It is doubtful if after the event, either Trevor Joy or Robertson remembered the actual conversation, for under such extreme stress, the brain goes into overdrive and the situation assumes an ethereal quality. Using all the psychological skills acquired through intensive training, maturity and past operational experience, the likeable detective quietly placated the distraught suspect, restoring the man's hopes for a brighter future. Eventually Robertson began to appreciate the distress his children would suffer if he pressed the switch. Providing assurances that he would do what he could to expedite the man's Court case, Trevor eventually persuaded him to lay down the switching device and abandon the vehicle.

The successful resolution to this incident, resulted in both Trevor Joy and Bruce Scott receiving the Queen's Police Medal for bravery.

* * *

Terry completed his two years probationary period and keeping abreast of the law through continuing study, achieved fourth place in the final examinations. He had settled happily into his chosen career, enjoying the vital and fulfilling role law enforcement officers play in every community. However, there was one down side; shift work.

Although shift work provided Terry with the opportunity to be with his family when other fathers were at work, there were many disadvantages. More often than not, whenever a family occasion or social event arose, he was working. It was also impossible to keep young children quiet when he was sleeping during the day, resulting in severe sleep deprivation and frayed tempers.

Terry knew shift work was jeopardising his marriage, but his only chance of leading a more normal life was to follow the hard road to promotion in the hope of securing one of the daytime positions enjoyed by senior ranks. He immediately set out to study for his sergeant's exams. Unfortunately, the burden of two small children meant Jane expected him to spend every moment of his free time with the family.

Terry found the task of dividing his time between family, shift work and study impossible. Jane resented every moment he spent with his nose in a book, constantly interrupting his study periods. She was unable to accept his need to be disciplined and focused to achieve his goal, which would ultimately provide a better life for them all.

"I seem to be caught between a rock and a hard place!" he muttered to himself. "Whatever time I allocate to the family is never enough!"

Arguments ensued.

"I can't seem to win. You are always claiming that we don't have enough money to buy all the things you want and you know shift work is wrecking our marriage but you won't let me study to get a higher income and a day job," he lamented.

"I'm stuck with the kids all the time while you shut yourself in the spare room."

"I bet you'll soon put your hand out for the extra dollars when I'm promoted," he retorted, frustrated and angry.

Although Terry appreciated that his wife craved attention, he could not understand why she couldn't comprehend that the studying was only for a limited period. He did not know how to get ahead and keep her happy at the same time. He took to parking the family car in the countryside where he could concentrate without the constant interruptions.

Unfortunately, his latest ploy caused immense resentment.

Eventually, after many requests, Terry had managed to obtain a transfer to the Hornby Police Station, a short distance from their home. Being stationed close by meant he could drop in often to see his family and to share meals with them while on duty. He decided to try the strategy of leaving early for work so he could shut himself in an office to study for an hour or so before commencing duty. Even that made Jane extremely hostile.

"Bugger it! I give up," he swore, tossing his study material aside. "It looks like I'm destined to stay at this rank forever."

As examination time drew near, Terry thought he might as well sit the tests to see what would happen.

"I've got nothing to lose. I may just jag a pass," he told Aub Geary his fatherly old sergeant.

"You'll do alright, son. Let me talk to your wife and see if I can get her to understand."

"No, Aub. You'll only make things worse. Thanks for your concern though."

In addition to three literary subjects, Terry sat four additional subjects, Evidence, Statutes, Administration and Practical Police Duties. He arrived at the examination room feeling decidedly unconfident. He answered the question papers as well as he could and if he didn't know an answer, fudged the written response hoping common-sense might win a few additional marks.

"How do you think you went?" Geary enquired, his thin, lined face creased with concern. Aubrey had taken Terry under his wing, treating the young man as his son. Terry liked the veteran policeman but thought he was sometimes like an old mother duck fussing over its chickens.

"I don't think I've got a snowball's chance in hell," he retorted.

Aubrey smiled. "You never know. Keep plugging away. You'll get there."

"Aub, it just isn't worth it."

"It's pretty hard on the women you know." Terry knew Aubrey was referring to the exigencies of police service.

"I know but as well as the law subjects, I still have to get through my literary exams.[21]"

It was not until February 1972, that the examination results appeared in the Police Gazette and notices were posted to each candidate. Resigned to the fact that he would fail, Terry opened his envelope from the examiner dispiritedly. He couldn't believe his eyes. He'd scraped through in Evidence and Statutes and received pass marks above 80% in Geography and English. Unfortunately although not unexpectedly, he'd failed Mathematics.

"Oh well. At least I can concentrate on getting a pass next time," he told himself.

That same year, Jane decided they should sell their tiny house in Hornby. "We need a bigger place and I think I can find a better house within our price range," she stated.

"I don't mind. But if you want to sell, you can make the arrangements with the agent. I've got enough on my plate," Terry told her.

As a constable on shift at Hornby, he carried a heavy workload of inquiry files. As well as dealing with these, he also attended to whatever incidents occurred within the immediate precinct. Although the staff complement comprised a senior sergeant, sergeant, watch-house keeper and twelve constables, shift officers operated solo, often meaning exposure to considerable danger, as seemingly innocuous situations could quickly turn nasty. Terry had experienced his share of these, being

---

[21] Because Terry did not possess basic educational qualifications, the police Department required that he attain the equivalent qualification through correspondence. In order to be promoted to Sergeant, he required pass marks above 60% and to achieve commissioned level pass marks above 75%.

bailed up with a knife wielding man at a domestic confrontation and on one occasion stumbling into an incident where an angry husband threatened to shoot his spouse and children. With no means of contacting backup, he'd had to do some very fast talking to save his own hide.

Jane went house hunting, tracking down a large weatherboard dwelling in the small outlying country town of Tai Tapu.

"It's beautiful. The rooms are so big and there's a separate shower, large garage and room for a good vegetable garden." Jane knew Terry loved gardening. Although it was priced beyond their budget, she hoped to persuade Terry to buy the spacious weatherboard cottage.

"Okay, let's go and have a look at it. It seems a long way out though. What about when you have to get to the hospital?" Terry was concerned that his very pregnant wife would be too far from medical assistance as her time drew near.

"It's alright. I've already timed how long it will take to get to the Lincoln Hospital. I can have the baby there. It's only about seven minutes away."

Terry immediately fell in love with the house and the little country village. They wasted no time in putting the Hornby house on the market and within a week received a favourable offer. With the sale almost assured, they negotiated a deal on the rambling Tai Tapu cottage.

The township's local inhabitants were overjoyed to have a resident policeman. Trying to explain that he merely lived there, Terry found some chose to believe they could call on him at any time to deal with their problems. Even the local Publican, Norm Fisher, became embarrassingly hospitable, refusing to accept payment for any purchases Terry made at the quaint hotel. Rather than have Norm think he had a policeman in his pocket, Terry refused to patronize the establishment. He needed to be impartial, knowing that the opportunity might arise when he would have to prosecute the amicable publican should he fall foul of the archaic liquor licensing laws.

Liam and Veronica attended the extremely friendly local Government School. The Flatley family settled quickly into the tiny community, making friends with neighbours and participating in community and church activities.

Nine months after a temporary thaw in their relationship,

Terry and Jane's third child, Michael Thomas Flatley arrived on 2nd October 1971, squalling healthily in the tiny theatre of the nearby Lincoln Hospital. With no resident doctor, Jane gave birth assisted by a midwife and Terry who was unprepared for the graphically messy, painful and exhilarating birthing process. Holding the naked, bloody, noisy, protesting, and wet infant, the twenty five-year old father of three marvelled at the new addition to his family.

Shortly after Michael's birth, Terry received a promotion to the Hornby Enquiry Office. No longer working night shifts, he found life much more pleasant. Apart from the icy wall between husband and wife, which Terry hoped soon to melt, he thought his life was, at last, complete. He had achieved his much longed-for dream and life seemed sweet. Alas, it would not remain so for long!

After the Baird murder inquiry Terry decided, that he thoroughly enjoyed being out in the remote and beautifully challenging New Zealand countryside. He successfully applied to join the Christchurch Police Search and Rescue Squad (S.A.R.) and attended a gruelling ten-day search and rescue training course in the Tauarua Ranges of New Zealand's North Island where the renowned mountaineer, Bill (W.E.) Bridge taught bushcraft and the various techniques for mountain search and rescue.

On his return to Christchurch, he participated in many search operations throughout the South Island. As a natural extension to the demands of mountain rescue, he assisted in forming the Christchurch Police Tramping Club to further enhance his knowledge of the Southern Alps and gain greater proficiency as a member of the elite and closely knit S.A.R. community.

The Police S.A.R. squad comprised an eclectic group of policemen headed by the erstwhile Sergeant Robert ('Twelve Gauge') Grierson. 12 Gauge was a tall, well-built baby faced N.C.O. in his mid forties, possessing a reputation for unconventional police tactics and spectacular errors of judgment in his early police career. With the policeman's penchant for embellishing stories, legend said he had once lined up a squad of constables to deal with a rioting mob in Cathedral Square.

186

Instructing his officers to draw their batons and shouting, "Take no prisoners!" he led a non-selective charge on the disorderly mob, beating them into submission regardless of their guilt or innocence.

Although he attended to his duties as the officer in charge of the S.A.R. Squad conscientiously, "Twelve Gauge" rarely ventured into the field, possessing little practical expertise and even less sense of direction. Fortunately, the remainder of the squad was highly skilled and respected by the mountaineering community and Robert, knowing his limitations, confined himself to matters of logistics.

With any one of the factors of; severity and unpredictability of weather, harshness of terrain, lack of knowledge or experience, poor physical fitness or unsuitability of equipment being sufficient to cause one's demise, the Southern Alps had claimed many lives. Even the most experienced, well equipped, extremely fit and highly skilled being at the mercy of nature and the terrain, with avalanches and violent snowstorms taking their grim toll annually. Terry was to learn this last lesson through a bitter and almost tragic experience during the spring of 1973.

"We need two volunteers from the squad to act as missing shooters for the annual Search and Rescue exercise. I wondered whether you and Roger Millard might like to do the honours?" Twelve Gauge enquired.

"Where is the exercise this year?" Terry was keen to play a pivotal roll in the forthcoming training exercise but remembering the old soldier's maxim of "never volunteer," he did not want to show his eagerness before learning more.

"It will be in the Lake Sumner area. As usual, all the civilian search and rescue units will be involved and the exercise will run for three days. I want you and Constable Millard to go into the area on the Friday and make your way to this grid reference." Grierson's finger traced a path over the Department of Lands topographical map of the Lake Sumner area. "You should be able to reach the reference point if you drive up to Lake Sumner early Friday afternoon. You'll park your vehicle at the road and walk in. When you get to your destination, you'll radio back here to me. You'll take two radios with you. One will be for contact with me and the other will be to monitor the search team's progress. I want the teams to take most of Saturday searching for you and by late Saturday afternoon, when they are getting close, you are to light a smoky fire to guide them to your location. One of you is to play the part of an injured shooter who needs to be carried out of the area or to a suitable point where a helicopter can lift the injured person out."

Terry studied the map carefully. The faint wiggly lines denoted the steepness of the terrain, suggested an altitude of over six thousand feet at the grid reference point. "Jees, where going to be pushing things to get to that spot by nightfall!"

"That's why I've chosen you and Millard. You're probably the fittest and fastest men for the job."

Terry noted that Grierson had already taken it for granted that he would agree to the task. "How are we going to get to Lake Sumner. Will we take one of our own vehicles?"

"No. You will use the police Landrover."

"Are you coming out into the field for this exercise?"

"No. I'll have my base at Christchurch Central Police Station where I will be the liaison officer. Field search headquarters will be on the flats beside Lake Sumner."

"What is the weather forecast for the weekend?" As usual, weather conditions would play an important role in the operation's success.

"The forecast looks good at this point. The Bureau is saying that it will be fine all weekend."

Shortly after his briefing session, Terry telephoned Constable Roger Millard, arranging to meet the super fit athlete and basketball player at lunch time on the coming Friday. Having worked closely with Millard during the Beard murder inquiry, he felt confident of playing the role indicated by the script for the search exercise. With usual laconic manner and dry humour, the big man assured Terry he would be suitably equipped for the rigours of the allocated task.

"We've got a lot of equipment to carry, Stretch," Terry told him. "Twelve Gauge wants us to carry two portable radios. With the batteries for these, our rifles and a two man tent on top of our usual gear we'll be pretty well loaded down."

As arranged, the two men left the Christchurch Police Station shortly after lunch on the Friday. Terry's pack had been stuffed to overflowing with all the warm woollen clothing necessary for survival at high altitude, his sleeping bag, waterproof sleeping bag cover, groundsheet, tent, radios, cooking gear, sundry equipment and food. He struggled to lift the police issue pack into the rear of the police Landrover and placed his .303 calibre rifle alongside.

"Have you got everything you need, Stretch?" he asked his companion. "Your pack seems a bit light-on."

"Yeah, 'course I have!" Millard tossed his half empty pack alongside Terry's.

Travelling for nearly two hours in the ponderous long wheel base police Landrover, they turned off the Lewis Pass Road near the Hurunui River and bounced along a rutted track toward Lake Sumner. Unable to move more than a fast walking pace, their progress to the foot of the distant mountain range was slow.

"Looks like we'll have to walk from here," Stretch remarked as a large swamp confronted them, barring further progress.

Terry looked at his watch and directing his gaze to the distant mountain peaks exclaimed, "I think old Twelve Gauge's been a bit optimistic if he thinks we can climb that lot and reach his grid reference before dark!"

"No bloody problem." Millard had already hoisted his pack effortlessly onto his muscular back and with rifle slung over one shoulder, started on his charge through the swamp.

Sinking thigh deep in the thick mud, they were unable to move at more than a snail's pace. The physical effort of lifting boots from the cloying mire and pushing through thick Manuka scrub was taxing Terry's energy before he had even begun the steep climb to the mountain top. At six feet seven inches in height, his companion's enormous stride and physical strength was far beyond that of the average man. Roger Millard seemed not to notice the difficulty of moving through the mud, quickly leaving Terry behind.

It took perhaps an hour of hard wading before the already exhausted Terry made his way from the swamp to harder ground. Millard sat on a rock, impatiently waiting for him, shaking his head.

"Not very fit, eh?"

Annoyed, Terry could only wonder how his companion had been able to move so fast. *I can't be that unfit*, he thought. *There's something wrong here.* "You need to remember the cardinal rule," he replied.

"What's that?"

"Always move at the pace of the slowest man. I should be setting the pace as it seems that I have a heavier pack than you."

Roger did not reply. Leaping to his feet before Terry had time to catch his breath he set off up the slope like a man possessed.

With thigh muscles burning from the effort, Terry followed his companion, attempting to keep the big man in sight. The ground before him seemed almost perpendicular and each time he made it to the top of a ridge, there was another long climb ahead of him.

Millard offered no quarter. With no regard for the basic rule of which Terry had reminded him earlier, he'd wait only until the slower man reached his position, resting and observing the valley vista far below as if he was on a Sunday afternoon jaunt. When Terry staggered to a halt, the rangy giant would immediately lope away up the slope again, giving Terry no chance for respite.

"You big bastard," Terry swore at his retreating figure. "For Christ's sake slow down and stay with me!"

After climbing for over two hours without rest, Terry finally reached the jagged mountain ridge. Shale and broken rocks littered the ground. A few stunted tussocks struggled for survival on the barren and often snow covered peaks. Several hundred metres below him a thick beech forest carpeted the hillside, its dark green wall marking the winter snow line. Black clouds gathering over nearby peaks signalled an imminent change in the weather. The temperature had dropped sharply and an icy wind snatched at Terry's parka, whipping around his exposed legs and face. Suddenly a white mist enveloped him and stinging sleet beat against his face. There was no sign of Roger Millard.

Where has that stupid idiot gone? Terry asked himself, as his strength waned and heavy fatigue swamped him. He plodded on along the ridge, hoping to find his companion's footprints but the ground was far too rocky. The heavy pack and rifle seemed an intolerable burden and he could barely lift his aching legs as his muscles began cramping. The thought that he could be in serious trouble unless he found shelter quickly, slowly dawned on his exhausted brain. *I've got to get rid of this bloody rifle. It's a burden I can't afford to carry any more,* he thought. *If I put it down here and mark the spot, I can come back and get it later. Without its weight, I'll be able to move faster.*

Standing on a shingle slide[22] which disappeared down into the

190

mist, he lay the rifle carefully on the lose rock and trudged upward. He realised that an almost overpowering urge to lie down and sleep, despite the stinging cold, was a message from the Grim Reaper. Hypothermia had seized his body in its pernicious grip.

"Bloody Millard! I'll kill you! Why would you bugger off and leave me? You should know better," he shouted angrily into the enveloping gloom and sleet.

Fighting to stay awake, Terry began to drop down off the ridge toward the beech forest, hoping the wind would lessen under its canopy. Crack! Crack! The rifle shots carried to him. Realising the big policeman was signalling his position, Terry followed the sound, finding renewed energy to keep moving. The retorts had come from the beech trees to his right and approximately two hundred feet below. As he descended, the mist cleared and his foolhardy companion materialised at the edge of the shadowy forest. Millard waved and Terry lifted his hand in acknowledgement. All the pent up frustration and anger at the big man vanished instantly as relief took over.

"We've got to make camp here and get a fire going. We can't possibly reach Twelve Gauge's grid reference!" Millard seemed annoyed that Terry had been unable to match his pace.

"Well, it was bloody well unrealistic to start with," Terry retorted as he flopped to the ground and slid his arms out of the pack straps. "Where's your parka, Roger?"

Despite the cold and sleet, his companion had not donned the obligatory parka any person venturing into the mountains was expected to carry.

"I didn't bring one," Millard replied. "I thought I'd keep the weight down. Have you got the tent?"

"Yeah, and the radio and all the other bloody gear."

Together, they gathered fuel for a fire, breaking dead twigs and leaves from the nearby trees[23]. Despite the driving rain and

---

[22] New Zealand's Southern Alps are frequently scarred with rivers of broken shale. Extending from the top of mountains to the valley floor, the shingle slides are often the site of old avalanches and are notoriously unstable. Terry often used the tendency of the shale to almost flow downward as a convenient and rapid means of descent.

[23] No matter how heavy the rain might be, it is always possible to find dry wood from standing trees rather than attempting to gather fuel from fallen

howling wind, they soon had a fire burning fiercely and stacked larger logs around its perimeter to dry. On a slope of almost forty five degrees, pitching the tent proved difficult and standing upright an effort. However, by clearing fallen wood from a niche on the hillside they were able to create a perch.

"You better get in your sleeping bag in the tent and warm up," Millard advised Terry. "Can I borrow you sleeping bag cover? You shouldn't need it in the tent."

"Sure, but where's yours?"

"I didn't bring it."

"Where's your groundsheet?"

"I didn't bring one."

"What!" Terry could feel his anger rising. "We need to get some food into ourselves. Get your billy and plate and I'll cook up a stew. "Have you got your camp stove?"

"No."

"Okay, I'll use mine. Where's your billy and frypan?"

"I didn't bring a plate or a billy. Can I borrow yours when you finish with it?"

"What *did* you bring Roger? No bloody wonder you were able to charge up the bloody hills so fast. You've got no gear, no sleeping bag, no parka, and on top of that, I've been carrying the tent, the radios, spare batteries, and all the correct gear. Shit, man. I should bloody well let you freeze and go hungry. Don't ever expect me to go out in the bloody hills with you again. You've almost killed me with the cracking pace you set and you wonder why I couldn't keep up!"

Looking sheepish, Roger huddled under Terry's sleeping bag cover to protect himself from the driving rain. Together, they stoked the fire and cut ferns and other greenery to cushion the tent floor for sleeping. After a hearty feed of dehydrated stew and rice, Terry felt much more cheerful. They crawled into the tent. Terry didn't feel like talking to his companion and still could not believe that Roger had obviously planned to borrow anything he needed for the exercise, leaving Terry to lug all the heavy equipment to an altitude of six thousand five hundred feet above sea level. He had expected much more from the man with whom

timber and debris.

he'd spent so much time during the hunt for the killer of Jennifer Beard. With nothing else to do and totally exhausted, Terry soon fell into a dreamless sleep.

The following morning as they peered out through the tent flap, incessant drizzle and thick fog greeted them. "I'll go and see if I can find my rifle. I'll be back soon," Terry advised.

Retracing his steps from the previous almost disastrous day, he followed the ridge line to the dark grey shingle slide. There was no sign of his rifle. Thinking that perhaps he'd missed it in the gloom, Terry crisscrossed the steeply sloping shale. Each footstep created a mini avalanche of flat rocks, which slid with a shooshing sound down the mountain. *Well it's goody bye rifle*, he told himself silently, presuming that during the night his prized firearm had slid down the mountain.

Returning to the campsite, he unpacked the heavy, yellow-metal Search and Rescue radio and strung its aerial wires between the trees to monitor the search exercise. Using the second radio, they reported their position to Roger Grierson at the Central Police Station, deliberately omitting details of the previous day's debacle.

During Saturday, both men amused themselves listening to the search teams battling the elements in their task, empathising with their exhausting work. Late in the afternoon, one of the teams detailed to search the square of country in which they waited, drew close. Judging that the smoke from their campfire should be visible, they piled dank green branches on top of the blaze sending thick smoke skyward. Within half an hour, the first of the search party materialised from the dripping gloom of the forest.

"Hurray! We found you at last," they cried, staggering forward to greet Roger and Terry.

"You poor buggers," Terry replied. "We've been feeling very sorry for you and wanting to radio in and give you a lead as to where we are."

"Well, we won't be descending the mountain tonight." The leader of the search team, a stocky man with a head of bushy grey hair exclaimed. Noelinelly a farmer, the man loved the bush and mountains and believed passionately in serving his community through search and rescue. "Let's find a place where we can all camp and make ourselves comfortable for the night. I think the weather is going to get nasty."

Gathering Terry and Roger's tent and gear together, the small group descended the ridge-line until they found a tiny plateau large enough to accommodate all their tents. The temperature had plummeted throughout the afternoon and although the wind had dropped, steady rain continued falling. Despite the appalling conditions, an almost festive air prevailed as the men swapped stories around their campfire. Neither Roger nor Terry mentioned Roger's lack of equipment or his failure to adhere to the basic rules of mountain safety.

Sunday dawned deathly quiet. There was no pit pat of raindrops on the nylon roofs of the tents, no swishing of branches or birdsong, just an eerie silence. Lifting tent flaps, they discovered a thick white blanket covering the trees and ground. Huge feathery flakes of snow floated down and the temperature must have been well below zero.

Their first consideration was making contact with Search Headquarters, provide a SITREP and receive instructions. Turning on the radio, they could hear nothing. Repeated calls elicited no response.

"We've got a total white out," the team leader reported. "Okay, now it's a case of survival. We've got to get down off this mountain as quickly and safely as possible. The exercise is over!"

Snatching a quick breakfast, they broke camp and stomped down through the cloud in the direction of the Lake Sumner Valley. Throughout their ascent, they'd seen no creeks. Now, the countryside appeared vastly different. Torrents of water cascaded everywhere off the sheer cliff faces into gullies and ravines, forming rushing rivers and waterfalls, which must be crossed. Any one of a myriad of streams had the capacity to sweep a man's feet from beneath him, carrying his body in the gushing, gurgling cascades to the valley far below.

The descent took far longer than their ascent and they had to call upon all their skills and teamwork to reach the valley in safety.

As the team leader predicted, the exercise had been abandoned and the exercise transformed into a very real operation, concerned only with the safety of extracting parties without mishap. Fortunately, all teams returned unscathed. At the subsequent search de-brief, Terry remained silent on the folly of Roger's actions, for he guessed the lanky giant had realised his stupidity. Terry felt there was nothing to gain by embarrassing his companion but resolved never to venture into the mountains with anyone in future, unless he felt confident as to their ability.

As much as he enjoyed search and rescue activities, Terry had no desire to be involved in the more demanding high altitude or cliff face rescue. This field being extremely specialised, required certain fearlessness and an intimate knowledge of climbing techniques possessed by an elite few. The Christchurch Squad was extremely fortunate in having Constable Tony Cunningham as their representative on the acclaimed Mountain Face Rescue Team. It was the task of this dedicated fraternity of skilled mountaineering volunteers, to execute the perilous rescues when climbers get into difficulty, as they frequently did in the rugged New Zealand Southern Alps.

At six feet six inches tall, Tony was an extremely powerful and rugged individual, possessing a calm unprepossessing nature. His quietly spoken voice, modesty, mountaineering skills and dark good looks endeared him to all and sundry. Always very willing to share his knowledge and experience with team members, Cunningham patiently instructed each in the skills of rock climbing, abseiling, belaying, rope techniques and general bushcraft. The Port Hills behind Christchurch provided a convenient venue for such training, with the various rock faces and quarries offering variety for both the novice and veteran climbers.

"When you're climbing, you must always ensure that you have three points of contact with the rock face," Tony instructed Terry and his fellow squad members, one warm summer afternoon. Although at an altitude of only fifteen hundred feet, they could look down on the Canterbury Plains and the neat grid pattern of the streets of the beautiful garden city of Christchurch. "Only move one hand or one foot at a time. Never overstretch. As you climb, plan your next move. Look where you are going to place the next foot or the next hand. The tiniest crevice can provide a hold for a finger or sometimes you can jamb a fist into a fissure if there's nothing else to hang onto. I know it is against your natural instincts, but if you lean outward from the rock face, your weight is transferred down through your feet, making you much less likely to fall."

Moving about the sheer cliff with the synchronised ease of a huge cat, the big man seemed at home in the alien environment. "If you lean in and hug the rocks, your feet are much more likely to shoot from beneath you." He jumped down to join them. "Now you have a go."

Awkwardly at first, the squad members tried to emulate the experienced climber, each making his way up the 'nursery slope', as Tony called it. Where he had located holds with ease, they struggled, their knees knocking and legs quivering from fright and unaccustomed exertion. Watching impassively, Tony urged them on encouragingly. "That's it. Now look for your next hold before you move. It gets easier with practice."

"To think people do this for fun." Terry remarked as halfway up the rock face the sweat began running down his face and the muscles in his arms and legs began cramping. Looking down, a sick knot of fear gripped his guts and his head swam from the effects of vertigo. He pressed his face against the hot grittiness of the rock, hugging the cliff face as he tried to gain control over the panic threatening to overwhelm him.

"No. Don't look down. Remember what I said about leaning outward." Tony called up to him.

Fighting against the little voices inside him calling for him to climb back down, Terry pushed away from the rock, his mouth dry and his stomach churning with nausea.

"Where's my next hand hold? Ah, that little knob of rock looks okay. Now, I need to move my right foot. Where can I get a foothold?" Terry muttered to himself. In comparison to Tony's effortless progression about the cliff face, he moved with the speed of a snail and the grace of a pig.

Eventually, he reached the top, a small thrill of triumph lost amid the relief of finding safer ground. Looking around, he was surprised to see Tony had already climbed to the top, having passed him with the speed and agility of a mountain goat.

"Come along here," the affable man-mountain called to the squad members from further along the ridge. Joining him, they peered down. They were on the edge of a quarry and there was nothing between them and the broken shale, some thirty metres below.

Tony tied a braided climbing rope to the trunk of a substantial tree, and tossed the remaining coils out into space. Knotting a second rope to another anchor point, he produced a small blue nylon harness and a karibina from a rucksack. Stepping into the nylon harness, he undid the karabiner and looped the braided rope around the D- shaped device. With the dangling end of the rope in a gloved right hand, he leant backwards over the edge of the cliff, pausing momentarily before leaping into space, his powerful legs spread wide. They watched as his lanky frame sailed halfway down before slowing smoothly and stopping. Taking another leap, Tony repelled to the quarry floor, the speed of his descent controlled by the friction of the rope through the karabiner.

Within a few minutes, he scurried up the rock face to rejoin them. "Okay. Now each of you can have a go. Only this time I will attach a safety rope, just in case," he smiled. He showed them how to make a harness from a short length of rope and dished out a karabiner to each squad member.

"Ted, you've already got plenty of experience and know what you're doing, so you can belay."

Ted Robinson, a carpenter before he joined the police, had been a member of the same recruit wing as Terry. Nicknamed 'Edward G' after the famous actor Edward G Robinson, the stocky, curly haired man was an experienced climber in his own right. The New Zealand Police had been quick to recognise his skills, seconding him to the Search and Rescue Team immediately upon his graduation.

Taking the nylon lifeline behind his back, Ted brought the rope together in calloused hands. Sitting with his booted feet braced against a convenient boulder, 'Edward G' prepared himself to belay each novice climber, acting as a human brake in the event of mishap. For the new chum walking backward over a cliff, while trusting one's life to another human being, is foreign to logic and natural instinct.

"You don't have to do it if you don't want to." Tony called to Terry as he teetered on the lip of the cliff, his face pale and legs shaking.

Terry knew if he didn't conquer his fear he would be little use as a member of the S.A.R. Squad. He opened his mouth to reply, but all that came out was a strangled squeak. *It's now or never*, he told himself and stepped out backward into the void. Looking over his shoulder, he could see the figures of his fellow students made diminutive by the height. *Its okay, you silly bugger*, he told reminded himself. *You've got a life line. You can't fall.*

Things became easier. Letting the rope slip through his gloved hand, Terry experimented with the speed of his descent, stopping to jump spider like about the cliff face. "Let's do that again. Only this time, I want to do it from somewhere really high," he called back to Tony, having conquered his fear of heights.

Tony had successfully applied for a posting to Takaka in the remote north of New Zealand's South Island. Although the posting created a vacancy on the Face Rescue Team, none of the S.A.R. Squad wanted to assume that role. They each enjoyed the mountains and were extremely proficient in bush craft and search techniques, but their reluctance was understandable. High altitude rescuers cannot reasonably expect longevity.

Regular training ensured squad members honed skills and maintained fitness for the rigours of search and rescue call-outs. Being extremely mountainous with high rainfall, the South Island has many major rivers and crossing these safely is a vital part of search and rescue and tramping.

One such river is the Waimakariri. Flowing into the Pacific Ocean near Christchurch and fed by the melting snows of the Southern Alps, it weaves a wide and tortuous path through the Canterbury Plains, feeding the artesian system from which Christchurch draws much of its drinking water. The subject of many rescues and known colloquially as 'The Waimak' the mighty watercourse provides an excellent training venue for river crossing.

On one cool and cloudy October day, the S.A.R. team assembled at the edge of the fast flowing river, with packs and fully kitted in boots and woollen clothing. The training day was supposed to focus on various methods of crossing rivers and streams.

The 'Waimak' is notorious for its numerous fast flowing channels, which often make it difficult to determine the main water flow. With the depth of the water and the rate of flow determined by the seasons, October presented the best opportunity to view the river in its fully engorged and icy glory. Tiny particles of rock, eroded from the mountains, tinged the water with a cloudy light blue hue, concealing the treachery of potholes and submerged obstacles.

The team successfully practiced various river crossing techniques, crossing individually, in pairs and as a team. They linked arms, used poles, floated on laden packs and swam across with ropes tied to their bodies. Although they treated the session seriously, there was also an element of fun as their confidence increased in direct proportion to their proficiency.

Moving along the river to a particularly deep hole, Tony Cunningham instructed half a dozen team members to don packs and lift a stout poplar pole cut from a river sapling. Linking arms while simultaneously gripping the pole, Terry and his fellow squad members waded into the fast and normally impassable water, trusting their lives to their instructor's impeccable judgment.

Being the tallest person in the group, Terry took position upstream, where his height provided greater stability for the remainder of the team. As they crossed, using the stout pole their linked arms provided tremendous support against the power of the rushing torrent. The water rose high around their bodies until they were waist deep. Still they resisted the current, making their way steadily toward the opposite bank. Suddenly the bottom dropped away beneath them. Weighted down by their packs, boots and the waterlogged timber, the shortest members of the group suddenly disappeared below the surface leaving their hats to floated downstream. Concentrating on the challenging task, Terry, whose head was still above the surface, was unaware that everyone except he was submerged. Suddenly, he too went under. Each policeman let go the pole in his quest for air, floating to the surface and bobbing along with the flow like so much flotsam. Sitting on the riverbank watching, Tony and the remaining team members rolled about laughing at the success of their prank.

Each year New Zealand rivers exact a terrible toll, taking the lives of unsuspecting, inexperienced, foolhardy, or just plainly unfortunate individuals. The tiniest tinkling and innocent mountain stream, quietly trickling gin clear water over the mossy rocks, can change in a moment to a raging liquid monster. Many a hunter or tramper has lost his life, by misjudging the potential of running water to sweep away one's feet. Even ankle deep water is deadly, when flowing fast enough.

During the Spring of 1973, the relatives of two fit and experienced shooters hunting in the headwaters of the notorious Rangitata River, reported them overdue. A search was mounted and one team tracked upstream from their abandoned vehicle, finding the bodies of both men lying in the almost dry creek bed. The gravel and stones throughout their clothing and packs and their many bruises and cuts left little to the imagination.

Tasked with transporting the grim discovery to the Christchurch mortuary, Terry and his fellow S.A.R. member, Hugh Webb, loaded the two body bags and the men's possessions into the rear of a police Landrover for the long drive.

Night had fallen and being tired and hungry, both Hugh and Terry weren't looking forward to the evening ahead. They knew that on their return, they would have to strip the bodies, prepare inventories of the clothing and contents of the packs, contact relatives, conduct identifications and prepare sudden death files for the Coroner. It promised to be a long and unpleasant night.

With a shock of straight black hair that always fell into his eyes, Hugh Webb possessed a slow drawling voice, a macabre sense of humour and a quick wit. Although only in his early twenties, the young constable had already established a reputation as one of the police Service's more memorable characters. He and Terry were firm friends, having been closely associated through their exploits with Search and Rescue and on several hunting trips. Hugh often regaled Terry with his extensive repertoire of risqué jokes, limericks and songs.

As they rattled silently along through the darkness with their grim cargo, each occupied with his private thoughts, Hugh broke the silence, proclaiming dryly, "Jees, they don't say much, do they?"

"I'd be a bit worried if they did." Terry replied, immediately envisaging their silent companions sitting up unexpectedly to enquire, "Are we there yet?"

A dull glow in the distance alerted them to approaching civilisation. As the reached the brightly lit Rangitata Hotel, Hugh announced, "I'm as dry as an Arab's fart and I could eat his jock strap if it had salt on it!"

Terry beckoned to the shapeless mounds behind their seat, "What about them?"

"They can come too, but only if they shout the drinks," Hugh answered with a straight face.

"No, I meant, we can't leave two bodies in the back of a police vehicle while we go into the pub."

"Why not? They're not going to pinch the bloody car."

Terry considered the situation. He was concerned that some inquisitive member of the public might peer into the rear of the Landrover and discover the dreadful and unattended cargo. Although shrouded in heavy plastic, the outline of the bags left little doubt as to their contents. As it was a cold night and the crowded car park was unlit, he decided leaving the vehicle was worth the risk.

They parked the Landrover away from other vehicles in a dark corner of the car park and made their way to the country pub for well-earned refreshments. Dressed in woollen bush shirts, shorts and boots, they were indistinguishable from the other patrons comprised mainly of local farmers.

"I wonder what they would think, if they knew what was outside in the back of the Landrover?" Terry mused quietly.

"She'll be right," Hugh brushed Terry's concerns aside.

As they opened the door to the bar, the cold draught of air accompanying them caused patrons to turn and examine the new arrivals. The hubbub ceased as if someone had turned a switch. Feeling suddenly conspicuous, they shouldered their way to the bar through the silent throng of drinkers.

"Evening. How ya goin?" Hugh nodded to the patrons.

Somehow, he seemed to blend in with the country yokels, who recognising one of their own, transferred their attention to Terry as he followed his younger companion. They found a place at the bar and ordered beers. As the unintelligible din resumed Terry felt conscious of a pair of eyes studying him intently. He turned to find a bearded man of indeterminate age, dressed in the ubiquitous stained moleskin trousers and checked bush shirt holding a pool cue while he waited for his shot at the table.

"You're a cop!" The simple statement came like a punch to the solar-plexus.

"What makes you say that?" Terry queried, amazed at the speedy loss of his anonymity.

The pool player simply smiled and turned away. *Surely, I'm not that obvious?* Terry wondered but then realised it took more than inconspicuous clothing to hide the authoritative stamp and mannerisms of a policeman.

Terry and Hugh finished their drinks hastily and left before their presence attracted undesirable questions and further attention.

Terry's membership of the Christchurch Police Tramping Club meant he was able to share a mutual love of the mountains with other like-minded people. Two such individuals were Senior Sergeant Mack Simmonds and Mark Penn.

One week day, the trio met at the Hornby Police Station to plan an ambitious tramping expedition into the Southern Alps. Having worked closely with Penn, he was comfortable with the idea of tackling the demanding hike from the foot of New Zealand's highest mountain, Mount Cook, to the West Coast of the South Island. They planned to take the trail leading over the famous Copeland Pass, necessitating a steep climb and then a gradual descent to the township of Franz Joseph. While the hike was potentially dangerous, he trusted Mark's judgment as to the senior sergeant's tramping prowess.

As they sat around the kitchen table in the station's small mess drinking instant coffee, Mack mentioned that it was his teenage son Stephen's wish to accompany them.

"We've done quite a few trips together and he's very fit," the amicable N.C.O. announced. "We'll need to take ropes, ice axes and crampons. Sometimes there's ice near the top of the Pass, although it shouldn't be a problem at this time of the year."

Terry studied the older man. At around forty years of age, of solid build and with dark straight brown hair and a square open face that broke easily into a grin, Mack appeared very fit. He carried no excess weight that Terry could see and through general conversation, Terry deduced the senior sergeant was no stranger to the challenges of the New Zealand wilds.

Spreading a detailed topographical map of the Mount Cook area on the table they poured over the route they proposed to follow.

"We'll drive into the Hermitage on the Friday evening. There's a tramping hut just up the valley where we'll spend Friday night. We'll set off to the Copeland Pass at sparrow fart on Saturday morning," Mark advised, tracing his finger over the wavy, narrowly spaced lines on the map.

The closeness of the markings depicted the steepness of the terrain over which they would travel. Terry noticed that at seven thousand five hundred feet[24], the Copeland Pass was considerably lower than nearby Mount Cook. Never the less, it was going to be quite a climb.

"The Forest Service has airlifted a hut to the top of the Pass. If we get caught by the weather, we can stay there," Mack added.

"How long will the trip take?" Terry asked, wondering at the length of time he would be away from his family. Understandably, Jane did not like the idea of looking after the children alone, but this trip offered the chance for a once in a lifetime achievement.

"About four days to reach the West Coast. I've arranged with a pilot friend of mine to pick us up at the Franz Joseph Glacier airstrip and fly us back to Christchurch," Mack answered.

"It sounds great." Terry was excited at the prospect of crossing on foot from the barren snow capped mountains of the East Coast, to the lush rainforests of New Zealand's West Coast.

After ensuring that each was adequately equipped with sufficient warm woollen clothing, highly nutritious food, down sleeping bags, strong hiking boots, ice axes and crampons, they travelled by coach to the Mount Cook National Park. As they spilled from the luxurious interior of their transport, they cast lascivious glances at the plush Hermitage tourist resort, offering five star comforts.

"Take a long last look, boys. It's the hard ground or wire bunks and de-hydrated stew for us from now on," Mark announced.

Shrouded in clouds despite the warm sunny day, the familiar jagged tooth shape of Mount Cook stood head and shoulders above the surrounding peaks. As they watched, the clouds parted, revealing the tantalising snowy cap for a brief moment as if teasing them. "The mountain is so high, it makes its own weather.

---

[24] Approximately 2,286 metres

It can be calm and sunny down here and a raging storm up there," Mack explained.

The walk to the hut where they would spend the night, took nearly an hour. A dozen trampers occupied the large rambling wooden and corrugated iron structure. Equipped with numerous bunks spread through several rooms, the hut was a frequent haunt of hikers. The camaraderie between the tramping fraternities enabled them to share the wood-fired fuel stove and other facilities without friction. During the evening, they swapped yarns and gleaned valuable information as to the condition of the track through the Pass. Knowing they had a long march in front of them, the four men retired early. Terry found sleep difficult. This was to be his most challenging trip yet.

After an early breakfast, Mack, Mark, Terry and Mack's son Stephen, donned their heavy packs to set off up the valley. The first weak rays of the sun had only just tinged the snowy peaks with a strange orange light, when in Indian file, they picked their way over the lose shale and grey stones worn smooth by prehistoric glacial action. The sky was leaden and Mount Cook no longer visible. A strong breeze blowing down the valley heralded an unfavourable change to the weather.

As they turned to their left, joining the faint trail toward the distant high altitude Copeland Pass, they met a small group of trampers heading back down the valley. Stopping briefly to exchange greetings, the man in the lead enquired, "Are you doing the Copeland?"

"We hope to," Terry replied.

"Well, we've just come down from there. We turned back when we got to the top. The wind was blowing so hard, it was not safe to continue. I'd advise you not to attempt it today."

"Thanks, but we'll go and have a look anyway," Mack replied cheerfully.

"Please yourself," the man sniffed, shrugging at his heavy pack, clearly miffed by their refusal to accept his advice.

"They must have stayed in the Copeland Hut overnight. There is no way they could have climbed up there and come down again this morning," Terry observed.

The trail became steeper as they trudged upward, leaning heavily on ice axes for support. The straps of their laden packs bit deeply into aching shoulders. Terry was glad of the fitness built through previous trips and regular jogging, without which he could never have kept up with Mack's loping stride. Obviously superbly fit, the other three did not stop at all to rest. Despite the gloomy weather, the spectacular view made the effort worthwhile. It seemed as if they were alone on the very top of the world. Like hundreds of broken white fangs, the rugged peaks stretched before them in a magnificent panorama of icy desolation.

The climb toward the pass had been virtually uneventful. Reaching the snow line, they saw the barrel shaped hut clearly, its windows glinting in the reflected glare of the snowy white surroundings. Thick wire stays running from each end and anchored firmly into the rock were a precaution against the cyclonic winds, which would otherwise sweep the structure away. Blue ice, never melting and eons old, covered the mountainside, rock hard and as slippery as wet glass. Fortunately, the path to the hut led them through powdery snow, easily traversed without resorting to the sharp spikes of their crampons strapped to the outside of the packs for easy access. Terry was glad. Previous experience negotiating hard ice had taught him that it could be very tiring work.

Pausing only for photographs and quick refreshments, they pushed on toward the summit, keen to reach the shelter of the more hospitable, thickly wooded terrain of the West Coast.

As they climbed higher, the wind increased in intensity. Forced to lean heavily into the gale, they struggled to move forward against the hidden forces threatening to bowl them over. Small stones and other lose debris, picked up and carried by the wind, stung their faces.

Wearing a heavy grey vinyl hooded parka against the cold, Terry shouted, only to find his voice blown away by the wind. "This is getting a bit hairy!"

Ahead lay a razor sharp ridge. An almost sheer drop either side meant one slip or wrong footing and they would plummet thousands of feet, bouncing off sharp rocks to their death. They had two choices. Traverse the ridge, or retreat.

"We'll go one at a time. Wait until there's a lull in the wind and then make a run for it!" Mack's stubborn refusal to yield to the elements would surface repeatedly during future trips.

Sheltering behind a large boulder, they waited for the wind to lessen.

"Okay, here I go!" Mark cried.

Bending almost double to lessen wind resistance, he bolted across the exposed ridge, a distance of some fifty metres. Although the wind buffeted his stooped figure, causing him to stagger like a drunken sailor, he reached the far side without mishap.

Mack and Stephen followed uneventfully. It was Terry's turn. Impatient to join the others, he judged what he thought to be a momentary lessening of the howling wind. Rising to his feet, he gripped the lower end of the straps on his pack, pulling tightly against his body to prevent it bouncing as he ran. He was halfway across the ridge, when a sudden wind gust filled his parka causing it to balloon. The ground beneath his feet seemed to be falling away. Realising that he was almost airborne, Terry let go the pack straps. Emulating an All Black rugby forward diving for a try, he threw himself forward to land spread-eagled on the ridge. On hands and knees, with his heart almost in his mouth, he scurried the remaining few yards to safety.

The four men stood marvelling at the difference in terrain over a few short metres. They could almost stand with one foot in the rain forests of the west and the other in the much drier and very barren east.

"How weird," Stephen remarked.

"Yes. It's a very unique phenomenon," Mack replied. "When the prevailing westerly winds bring rain-bearing clouds in from the Tasman Sea, they are virtually blocked by the Southern Alps causing heavy precipitation on the western side. By the time the winds reach the eastern side of the Alps, they have shed their moisture."

The temperature differential was also quite remarkable, with the western side being much warmer than the east.

Dropping into dense beach forests, festooned with lichens and moss, they discovered a forest floor carpeted thickly with the rotting detritus of fallen vegetation. Forced to push their way through vines, stinging nettle and giant tree ferns, they found the going became more difficult. It was not long before they were wringing wet as their sweat combined with moisture from the dripping vegetation.

The trail was difficult to follow, as the fast growing vegetation almost seemed to conspire with mosses to hide the occasional round red trail markers placed by the Forest Service. Terry consoled himself with the knowledge that his clothing, sleeping bag and foodstuffs would remain dry in the tough plastic bags he'd used to protect them against the inevitable moisture encountered when tramping.

"I seem to recall from the map that we have a long hike to the first hut," Terry remarked. "I hope we can make it before nightfall."

They were almost running now, at the unpleasant possibility of spending a night in the open.

"At least it's all downhill from here." Mark responded his face scratched from numerous encounters with the scrub. "There's hot pools at the hut. Boy, they're going to feel good! When I get there, I'm just going to walk right in, pack and all, and collapse." It was the first time he'd given any indication of the fatigue they all felt after the long climb.

On the way through the forest, they disturbed a large stag as it fed in a small clearing, the creature's magnificent antlers silhouetted by the afternoon sunlight flooding through the emerald green canopy. With the wind in their faces and their footsteps muffled by the thick moss, the animal failed to detect their immediate presence. Lifting its beautiful head in startled surprise, it turned to crash through the undergrowth showing the white flash of the underside of its tail. In a fleeting moment, it was gone.

"Wow! What a beauty. I bet he would have been a twelve-pointer," Mack cried. "I wish I had my rifle."

Terry felt shocked. "I know they're an introduced pest, but these days when I see one, I just want to photograph it. They seem too beautiful to kill," he said whimsically.

Unfortunately, the gentle animals did not belong in New Zealand. Early settlers had introduced them for sport. Along with thar[25], chamois, wild pig, opossum, rabbits and feral goats, deer were noxious animals with a bounty on their heads. The sharp hooves of introduced species were responsible for serious erosion, while possums spread bovine tuberculosis.

---

[25] Himalayan mountain goats.

As the shadows lengthened Mark's nose twitched like a police dog discovering a criminal's scent. He exclaimed, "I can smell smoke. We must be near the hut!"

Sure enough, the tiny one room hut constructed from native birch and iron, came into view. Blending with its surroundings, it would have been easily missed but for the smell of wood smoke curling from the corrugated iron fireplace at one end. They pushed open the crude door to find several packs littering the floor. Sleeping bags thrown carelessly on bunks constructed from stout saplings and dainty nylon panties drying by the stove, advertised female presence. However, there was no sign of the occupants. Guessing that they would not be far away, the four men made their way to the nearby hot springs, where steam hung lazily a few feet above the languid surface.

The three women were unaware of male presence. Stripped naked, they frolicked in the steaming sulphurous waters like forest nymphs.

"Good afternoon ladies!" Unabashed, Mark plodded fully clothed into the pools closely followed by Terry, Mack and Stephen.

The girls didn't even blink in surprise. Making no effort whatsoever to cover themselves, they merely smiled in response, naked white breasts with pink nipples bobbing on the surface like albino puppies paddling against the stream's current while getting nowhere. Near exhaustion, the four men had looked forward to the soothing mineral waters and false modesty was not going to spoil that enjoyment. This unexpected and delightful surprise was merely an added bonus at the end of a long tiring day!

The remainder of the hike to Franz Joseph was an anti-climax. Heavy clouds blanketed the mountains resulting in the cancellation of their plans to fly home to Christchurch. With the poor visibility, Mack's pilot friend would have difficulty bringing his light aircraft into the tiny airstrip.

Although Terry participated in other major trips during his love affair with the mountains, even a mid winter traverse of the Southern Alps from Lewis Pass to Arthur's Pass, could not equal the feeling of accomplishment from the Copeland Pass trip.

Jane resented his involvement with Search and Rescue and his love of the Alps. After flooded rivers held up his return from one five-day exploit, she remarked in all seriousness, "I was really worried when you were overdue, because I couldn't find your life insurance policy." That he might have perished, leaving the children fatherless was of only minor significance. With the utterance of those few words, Terry knew he was nothing more than a meal ticket in her eyes.

During the mid 1970's, New Zealand suffered from the lawless scourge of gangs. Although the North Island was home to some of the worst and most violent racist underclass societies, such as, the notorious Mongrel Mob, Black Power and The Storm Troopers, the South Island also harboured organised criminal 'bikie' gangs.

Adopting such names as 'The Epitaph Riders,' 'The Lost Breed' and 'Hell's Angels,' the societal outcasts, who made up the membership of such anti-social groups, indulged in ingeniously disgusting and degrading initiation ceremonies. Funding their activities by trafficking in drugs and assuming control of illicit brothels, gang members built elaborate fortifications around otherwise normal suburban dwellings. These security measures were supposed to protect them against unannounced police raids and attacks from rival gangs as they fought to control illicit markets.

There had been several violent murders and tensions between gangs were at an all time high. Affiliated with similar groups from other towns, various gangs would, on occasions visit each other, sometimes massing in their hundreds to terrorise the innocent populace. Such rallies called for extraordinary police tactics to handle the resultant violence and disorder.

One such tactic consisted of police Shadow Patrols, comprising four officers specially selected for their size and ability to handle themselves. It was the task of patrol to accompany the bikies in an escorting patrol vehicle, carefully noting and recording unlawful activity. Out numbered sometimes by as many as a hundred to one, it was common-sense to wait until sufficient reinforcements enabled the safe arrest or prosecution of offenders. Often when bikie gangs set off on such excursions, the police would meet and corral gangs at a suitable location on the outskirts of the home town. Each member's name and personal details recorded in a dossier and any weapons confiscated, the mob could then continue. These Draconian and very successful measures were unpopular and incurred the gang's hatred and contempt.

As successful as the police tactics were, they could not entirely curb the terror and criminal activities associated with such large numbers of organised and intractable individuals.

Although a low level of intelligence among such gangs might be expected, this was often not the case. Qualified professionals, such as lawyers, accountants and even doctors seemed to attain some sort of satisfaction by shunning the laws of society and donning dirty leather and denims to ride Indian, Triumph and Harley Davidson motorcycles and engage in pursuits beyond normal societal conventions.

During the summer of 1973/74, The Epitaph Riders played host to gangs from outside Christchurch, cramming numerous scruffy, longhaired, leather-jacketed outlaws into their rented suburban Headquarters. Gleaming black and chrome motorcycles covered what once passed for the front lawn, leaning drunkenly as a mechanical reflection of their owner's sobriety. Thundering, unsilenced engines, all night boozing, fist-fights, shouted obscenities, beer bottles intentionally discarded in neighbouring gardens, drunks pissing wherever they chose, orgies with half-clad sluts on trampled lawns and general mayhem ensued, terrorising the unfortunate inhabitants of nearby, quiet, working-class streets. Understandably, residents telephoned the police, pleading for action and restoration of order. Although the police arrested several members for minor street offences, the disorderly conduct continued unabated.

New Year's Eve was fast approaching. Traditional celebrations normally required the cancellation of all police leave to deal with unruly revellers. If the police waited until then to bring the bikies under control, the added potential burden of a hundred rioting gang members would stretch resources beyond their limit. Chief Superintendent Gideon Tate, the popular and uncompromising Christchurch police district commander, decided to take action under the yet-to-be tested unlawful assembly provisions of the Crimes Act.

Placing gang headquarters under surveillance, Gideon requested the presence of every available police officer at the Christchurch police headquarters for a briefing. Packed to capacity with uniformed officers the assembly area was abuzz with anticipation.

The slightly built, bald headed Commander, strode onto the stage to address the officers involved in the operation. All the top brass occupied the platform, including the unpopular, blond haired and slightly effeminate looking Superintendent George

Twentyman. As Second in Command, Twentyman actively opposed his boss's unconventional tactics.

"This is the situation. We have approximately one hundred bikies at the Epitaph Riders Headquarters in Woolston. For the past few days, the numbers have been building and we are expecting extra gang members to arrive before New Years Eve. The gang has been drinking, fighting and terrorising the local residents by throwing bottles, swearing and urinating on front lawns and in the street. We have statements from nearby residents who are prepared to say in court, that they fear for their safety. If we wait until New Year's Eve, the bikie numbers will swell further and in their drunken state and disregard for the law, we anticipate that they will be uncontrollable. I plan to take action under the unlawful assembly provisions of the Crimes Act 1961 and arrest all the gang members. We need to get them off the street as soon as possible."

The room was hushed. The proposal to invoke the unlawful assembly provisions was unprecedented. Every police officer knew the invocation of that particular recently amended section of The Crimes Act, carried a heavy burden of proof. There had not yet been a successful prosecution.

As if reading their collective minds, Gideon removed his glasses to peer at the uniformed assembly. "I believe we have the necessary proof. Even if we do not, we can at least get the gang off the street for New Year's Eve. Our mission is to arrest every one of the gang and seize their motorcycles. In order to execute this mission, we will surround the headquarters and contain the gang. Senior Sergeant Warwick Nichol will head the arrest squad. senior sergeant, your squad will enter the house and bring the gang members out onto the front lawn where you will keep them under guard until they can be processed individually by the processing squad under mass arrest procedures. Every gang member is to be handcuffed, searched and photographed. They will be loaded into the prison van and shuttled to the cells. I don't expect that they will go quietly. If there is any hint of armed resistance, the Armed Offenders Squad will take over and contain the situation."

The senior policeman continued reading the carefully prepared Operation Orders, assigning command of the various sub-groups to be involved in the cordon, the custody of offenders and the compilation of arrest files. It was unusual for an Operation Commander to involve every member in such a detailed briefing for a major operation. Noelinelly, he would restrict briefings to his lieutenants, who would each brief their respective members. However, the wily policeman knew by including every single officer, he would obtain optimum co-operation and input, increasing the chances for a successful operation.

One of the reasons the Chief Superintendent was so popular, was because he respected the opinions of even the least experienced officer.

"Are there any questions?" Gideon looked expectantly at his audience. Apart from a few minor clarifications, everyone knew the role expected of them. "Right, move out and take up positions as instructed!"

Assigned to the cordon, Terry arrived on the scene as night fell. The interior of the bikie house was ablaze with lights. Situated on the corner of the street, paling fences enclosed three sides of the old weatherboard structure. The bikies quickly became aware of their presence, retreating inside the fence line to hurl a barrage of missiles including, bottles, bricks, stones, rubbish and any available lose object at the police.

Grabbing the lid from a conveniently placed rubbish tin, Terry used it as a shield, fending off the dangerous projectiles raining down from the darkness. So unrelenting was the attack, it appeared that gang members knew of the pending police action and had prepared themselves for the siege.

The arrest squad mustered in front of the house. Led by the powerfully built senior sergeant, who was coincidentally a Commonwealth Shot Put champion, they assembled into a tight formation and marched along the concrete path toward the front door. The bikies retreated inside, bombarding the police anew from the front doorway and windows, forcing their retreat. A large rock narrowly missed Warwick's head. Stooping to retrieve the missile in a huge fist, the N.C.O. quickly adopted an athletic stance preparatory to putting a shot. Wasting no time, he hurled the rock through the open front door, striking its owner squarely in the face. The bikie reeled back, blood pouring from his smashed nose. The front door slammed and the gang members began barricading the entrance.

Terry ran to the rear of the house to foil any escape plans as an A.O.S. member knelt in the roadway, putting the butt of a C.S. gas rifle to his shoulder. With a puff of blue smoke, the long aluminium rocket canister burst from the huge bore of the launcher, its retractable wings unfolding to provide aerodynamic stability. It crashed through the front window, striking an overturned sofa, beneath which some gang members huddled, using it as a shield to throw various objects at the police. A stinging gas cloud poured from the projectile, filling the house in seconds. The red hot capsule ignited the couch.

In panic, the dirty outlaws poured from almost every aperture of the old building, desperately seeking escape from the choking fumes. No sooner had they reached fresh air, when excited police dogs straining on short leashes menaced them, barking and snarling savagely. Herded together in the front yard the cowed ruffians sat with hands on their heads to await processing.

A slight breeze carried the tear gas to Terry's position at the back of the dwelling. Without the benefit of a gas mask, he abandoned his vigil, returning upwind to the front of the cottage where he assisted in gathering the gang's motorcycles. One by one, police searched and photographed the scruffy and subdued miscreants, handcuffing them with nylon electrical ties for transportation to the cellblock.

A large flat bed tow truck arrived and the operator commenced loading the bikies pride and joy, stacking each motorcycle side by side across the deck like so many pieces of bread in a toast rack. With the deck filled to capacity, the operator who was obviously no fan of motorcycle gangs, loaded one more motorcycle at the rear of the tray. Then lifting the boom of the hoist, he crushed the entire load together. The sound of crumpling metal and popping headlights was like rubbing salt into a wound for the prisoners who watched the performance in dismay.

A count of prisoners revealed over one hundred persons in custody. Safely crammed into the cells of the Christchurch Police Station and denied bail, the mob was out of circulation, defusing the potential for a violent and riotous New Year's Eve. As expected, each of the bikies entered a plea of 'not guilty' in the Magistrates Court. By the time trials eventuated, the residents who had initially been sufficiently terrified by the mob to lodge written complaints, had second thoughts about testifying. Fearing reprisals from the hoodlums, their resolve evaporated and they withdrew their statements, without which the police had no case. The Court had no choice but to dismiss all charges of unlawful assembly. Despite the acquittals, the police deemed the operation a resounding success.

Legislators later plugged the loopholes in the unlawful assembly section of the Crimes Act, enhancing the chance of success in future prosecutions. Gideon Tate had endeared himself to all frontline policemen with his no nonsense methods, however, the incident marked the end of an era of tough police tactics. As a new generation of young people conditioned to question everything and challenge all the traditional bulwarks of society emerged on the scene clamouring 'I know my rights,' resultant fears of litigation heralded a new age of weakness and soaring crime rates fuelled by the need to satisfy rampant drug addiction. Many from the old school of policing would wonder how long it would take society to cry, enough to sexual permissiveness, drug abuse, foul language, violence and other humanity-diminishing behaviour.

* * *

Another short-lived thawing of Jane's frigidity resulted in the birth of Helen, Terry and Jane's fourth child on 27 September 1973. Alas, the melting ice soon re-froze again and Terry now understood that, along with his role as the financial provider, he was merely convenient for siring Jane's children when her two-yearly urges for motherhood overwhelmed her. Fooled twice into believing that she had overcome her abhorrence of physical contact with him and wanted a normal marital relationship, he subjected himself to a vasectomy, thus ensuring there were no more pregnancies without his consent. He dearly loved all his children but he knew, unless he took this irrevocable step, she would trick him again.

It was about this time that Terry became interested in scuba diving. Coincidentally, a vacancy existed on the Christchurch

Police Diving Squad and Hugh McLachlan, one of Terry's fellow constables at the Hornby Police Station and a member of the squad, spent considerable time teaching Terry skills acquired on the New Zealand Navy's diving course.

Hugh was a slightly built young fellow in his early twenties. With a shock of dark brown straight hair and slightly crossed eyes, he was congenial and patient, but a hard taskmaster when it came to diving instruction. He accepted only the highest standards, rigorously putting Terry through the same syllabus he had endured with the Navy. Although deserted for the winter, the local diving pool provided an excellent, if icy venue for practice sessions. Throwing Terry's gear into the bottom of the pool and making him swim down and put it on without surfacing was one of Hugh's favourite ploys. Mask clearing, rescue drills and swimming underwater with the facemask blacked out, instilled great confidence in Hugh's pupil.

As usual, with mortgage repayments and five mouths to feed, Terry was short of money. New scuba gear was beyond his means. However, on learning that another member of the constabulary possessed an old twin hose regulator and a set of oxygen cylinders, he acquired these for a few dollars.

Examination of the cylinders and the regulator revealed the equipment to be nearly twenty years old. There had been many technological advances in regulators since the manufacture of Terry's equipment in Germany during the mid 1950's. With no replacements available for perished rubber seals, hoses and valves, he set out to restore the regulator. Obtaining a sheet of pliable rubber, he painstakingly fashioned new valves. The convoluted rubber hoses had perished and their replacement proved difficult and necessitated much search for a suitable substitute material. Each of the tiny forty cubic foot former oxygen cylinders provided only sufficient air for a limited time below the surface. Enlisting the help of his clever Aviation Crash Fireman friend, Bruce Brooks, Terry joined the cylinders together to double their capacity. Although the test dates on both cylinders showed no testing for many years, subsequent hydrostatic tests showed them to be serviceable. With a restored but untried set of ancient scuba gear, Terry was ready for the water.

The ocean surrounding Bank's Peninsula, that the club shaped lump of land on the East Coast Banks of the South Island seemed the best place to test the apparatus. Terry and Bruce drove to Pigeon Bay, a remote indentation in near Akaroa, the picturesque village first established by the French in the early 1800's. The curly haired Fireman proudly boasted the best equipment money could buy. Self taught and possessing a devil-may-care attitude, he exhibited great confidence in Terry's ability to resurrect equipment, which perhaps should have ended its days as a Museum exhibit.

It was a fine warm spring day and a slight swell washed against the barnacle-encrusted rocks. Terry approached the water, walking backwards in his awkward fins, nine kilograms of lead around his waist and the heavy steel cylinders strapped to his back. Bruce joined him and together they swam away from the shore, watching the bottom drop steeply away beneath them. When they judged the depth sufficient to test Terry's equipment, they stopped and trod water.

"As long as you don't go below one atmosphere, you should be okay. If something goes wrong with the regulator, you can ascend from that depth safely using the residual air in your lungs." Bruce advised. Clad in his thick double-lined wetsuit, hood, booties and single hose regulator, he watched as Terry cautiously descended.

Although he had tried the equipment on land, Terry didn't know how it would fare under the pressure of the sea. Sucking a lungful of cold dry compressed air through the rubber mouthpiece, he duck-dived through the thick bull kelp. He exhaled, bubbles gurgling past his face as he sucked again on the mouthpiece. To his surprise, the regulator provided air effortlessly on demand, the homemade rubber valves functioning perfectly. He swam on down escorted by Bruce. Trying the regulator in all positions, he was unable to fault its performance. Together they explored the reefs and subterranean ledges. Shoals of brightly coloured fish followed them, snapping at tid-bits stirred up by the diver's fins. Like undersea cockroaches, crayfish retreated backwards into crevices, waving gnarled feelers as if to say, "Keep out!" Spiny sea urchins clung to boulders and a Moray eel emerged from its lair like a menacing Jack in a Box. Terry stopped swimming. Taking a sea urchin from a nearby rock, he cut the creature open and hand fed huge lazy blue cod that had joined the other marine spectators attracted by the strange spectacle of the rubber-suited divers.

After nearly forty-five minutes in the chilly waters, Bruce pointed toward the surface, signalling his desire to ascend. Keeping pace with the bubbles from their regulators, they ascended, taking care to exhale continuously so they would not suffer air embolism.

The cheap equipment served its purpose, providing Terry with many hours pleasure, diving in a variety of locations until he was able to afford a new regulator and better equipment.

Bruce and his wife Margaret had two children Andrea and Phillip, who were nearly the same ages as Liam and Veronica. Margaret and Jane were close friends with both families spending considerable time together, either at Margaret and Bruce's government house at the Timaru Airport or at Jane and Terry's Tai Tapu house. A tall woman in her early thirties, Margaret had a rather large nose, straight dark brown hair and an infectious giggle.

Neither couple enjoyed sound relationships. Sadly, Bruce enjoyed baiting his wife, who, to his sadistic amusement, never failed to take the bait. Often commiserating on the shortcomings of their respective spouses, the men and women were quite happy to be away from each other.

With a three day holiday weekend imminent, Bruce telephoned from his home in Timaru, to invite Terry on a diving expedition.

"I've found a great spot for crayfish, just out from Oamaru. How about we go for a dive?"

"Sure. You know me. I'll dive anywhere. How far out is it from the coast?" Terry enquired, knowing that Bruce owned a very tiny inflatable dinghy.

"Not far," he replied unhelpfully.

Jane welcomed the respite from suburban drudgery and agreed to drive to Timaru on the Friday evening, knowing she would enjoy Margaret's company while the men dived during the three-day holiday. On their arrival, Terry quizzed Bruce again about the dive but failed to elicit any further information.

"Just wait and see," the bushy haired man smiled as he refilled Terry's beer glass. "You won't be disappointed."

The following morning they set off at daybreak, driving southward in Bruce's Commer van to the nearby township of Oamaru. Although Terry continued to quiz his companion on the exact location of the reef, Bruce's laconic, "It's not far," was singularly unhelpful. Reaching a small sandy beach near the township, Terry scanned the ocean for the elusive reef. It was a cloudless day. A moderate breeze ruffled the deep blue ocean creating small white caps. Although Terry strained his eyes searching, he was unable to see the tell-tale sign of white water as waves broke of an offshore reef.

"Where *is* this reef?" He asked again.

"Oh, just around the point, out of sight."

"How long does it take to get there?"

"Not long."

It was obvious Bruce wished the exact location of the reef to remain secret. Terry decided he would have to be satisfied with his companion's exasperating response.

Fitting the tiny two and a half horsepower Evinrude outboard motor to the transom of the diminutive boat, they loaded on board catch bags and air cylinders. After donning their wetsuits for protection against the frigid waters, they shoved off the beach out into the waves. The motor fired and started with the first pull of the cord. Bobbing like a cork in the choppy seas, they headed straight out to sea. The further from the coast they went, the higher the waves became. Climbing slowly up huge watery mountains, they teetered on the top before rushing down the other side into deep troughs, which obscured any view of the horizon. Fortunately, Terry did not suffer from seasickness, although he became increasingly apprehensive as Bruce refused to elaborate on their intended destination.

They were perhaps four kilometres from the coast when a commercial fishing boat appeared, throwing great plumes of spray from its bow as it ploughed through the rolling swell. They seemed to be making little headway, as their craft, which was little more than an inflatable mattress, bobbed and rolled its way through the swell. The fishing boat wallowed past, its skipper gawking incredulously at the incongruous sight of two black rubber clad figures so far from land. Bruce merely waved cheerfully, as relaxed as if he were enjoying punting on Christchurch's placid little Avon River.

Becoming impatient and increasingly concerned for their safety, Terry enquired once more, "Where is this bloody reef?"

He again received the same response, "Not far."

As Terry strained his eyes toward the horizon, he noticed Bruce was grinning stupidly at him. As they rode to the top of a swell, he could just see waves breaking at least another four kilometres further out to sea.

"Don't tell me that's the reef way out there!"

"Yep. That's it."

"You've got to be joking! You must be crazy. If I knew we were going to come this far on a bloody airbed, I would never have come."

"I know. That's why I didn't tell you."

Terry shook his head. Bruce's foolhardiness never failed to amaze him. *Oh well*, he thought. *We're out here now. I may as well make the most of it.*

It took another twenty minutes for them to reach their destination. As they chugged nearer to the reef, dark barnacle encrusted rocks thrust upwards like the back of some giant marine creature hiding just beneath the surface. After a journey of several thousand kilometres, the long, black, rolling Pacific Ocean swell remained almost unchecked. To the deep booming sound of crashing waves and the sickening pneumatic lurch of their absurdly flimsy craft, they threw the small shiny galvanized steel anchor into the inky depths, watching its shimmering disappearance far below.

Terry felt decidedly uncomfortable being so far from land. Apart from the bemused skipper of the fishing boat, nobody knew their whereabouts. There was little doubt that if the outboard failed to restart, or if the weather changed for the worse, they would be in serious trouble. Shaking his head in disbelief, he berated the cavalier attitude of his diving companion.

"You're a mad bastard, Brooks. You won't pull a stunt like this on me again!"

220

Chuckling gleefully like an escaped mental patient, Bruce shrugged the straps of his aluminium, compressed air cylinder into a comfortable position on his neoprene-covered shoulders. So narrow was their tiny boat that their knees touched as they sat either side, pressing their masks tightly against faces tinged faintly blue from the chill salt spray. With thumb and forefinger forming an "O" to signal their readiness, they rolled simultaneous backwards into the sea.

Terry was completely unprepared for the sight, which confronted him. Covered in heavy bull kelp, a rocky outcrop rose nearly thirty metres from the seabed. Shelf like crevices and fissures bulging with crayfish seemed to be everywhere. No matter which way he turned, there were huge, almost prehistoric creatures waving long antlers and claws, watching the divers without fear.

Catching the crustaceans was as easy as picking them from shelves in a Supermarket. So big was their prey, that he had difficulty grasping the hard scaly bodies in one hand. Stuffing catch bags full, they ascended each holding aloft one of the huge prized marine delicacies while grinning like idiots.

"Don't you think it was worth coming out here?" Bruce asked as they pull themselves on board. Terry didn't reply. *Some of the crays must weigh over nine pound,*[26]he thought. *But, it's still not worth risking your life.*

Fortunately, the faithful little motor started again and with a stiff breeze hastening progress, they returned to the bay with their catch. Terry breathed a sigh of immense relief at the feel of sold land beneath his feet. Although he didn't consider he was a coward, venturing so far in a tiny vessel had been almost sheer madness.

Gaining in confidence as a diver, Terry applied to join the police Diving Squad who accepted him immediately. He was now in the enviable position of being a member of two elite police units; Search and Rescue and the Christchurch Police Diving Squad.

Senior Sergeant Alan Adcock headed the diving squad. Mark Penn, Hugh McLachlan, and a Maori constable, Te Rangi Matunuku Kaa (Mat Kaa for short) were its members. The squad

---

[26] 4 kilograms.

had responsibility for all police diving commitments in the South Island[27]. Used for rescues, searches for evidence or bodies, and the recovery of equipment, the squad trained regularly and specialized in searching under conditions of limited or nil visibility. Although there was always an element of fun and a strong spirit of camaraderie, much of the work was unglamorous and at times fraught with danger.

Unfortunately for Terry, his tour of duty lasted only twelve months. Promotion and the resultant transfer to Dunedin terminated a short but exhilarating professional diving career. Tempted to refuse promotion Terry was thankful that he did not when within a few months of moving to Dunedin the police service decided in 1975 to disband the South Island unit. Henceforth the Wellington and Auckland Diving squads assumed responsibility for National operations.

---

[27] Unfortunately, the police Service decided to disband the squad in 1975. Terry maintained his love for recreational diving and in 1976; he was instrumental in forming the Tasman Bay Aquanauts Underwater Club with a close friend and police dog handler, Rod Curtis.

CHAPTER SIX
"BLOODY SHIFT WORK!"

1974 was a year of mixed blessings for Terry. Having passed two of the four subjects' necessary for promotion, he felt obligated to continue with his studies, despite almost unassailable opposition from Jane. His persistence created immense friction between them.

Fearing the prospect of transfer and the uncertainty as to where the police service might post them, the young mother felt comfortable in their new surroundings at Tai Tapu where she was close to her family and childhood friends. The prospect of moving to a strange town away from these things filled her with dread. With Terry working shift work and studying, she felt neglected and considered he should spend his study time with her and the children. In addition, she feared the changes in their lives if her husband climbed the promotional ladder.

The publication of examination results early in the New Year showed Terry was now almost qualified for promotion. The single hurdle to the sergeant's chevrons was an Arithmetic exam, which to his annoyance and embarrassment he had previously failed. The lack of this qualification did not prevent the police hierarchy deciding to transfer him from Hornby back to district headquarters, where he was to perform acting sergeant's duties for twelve months. Terry didn't resent the move. He knew he would soon pass the last examination and receive promotion. The experience would be welcome, as would the increase in pay. There was one downside in the change of duties. Once again, he would be required to work night shifts.

In charge of a shift of sixteen very inexperienced constables, Terry re-acquainted himself with handling street offences, hotel raids, and a new generation of street hoodlums. Being away from that particular scene for the past few years on uniform investigation work, his knowledge was somewhat rusty. However, it wasn't long before he formed close bonds with his young subordinates, delighting in the new role of on-the-job trainer and mentor. In fact, this period of his career proved to be particularly rewarding. Knowing so many looked to him for guidance and held him in high esteem, brought tremendous responsibility. He vowed not to let them down, doing his utmost to build a cohesive unit, loyal to the Service and each other.

Part of Terry's duties as an acting N.C.O. meant taking responsibility for ensuring patrols handled every incident expeditiously and correctly. As the designated Incident (I) Car Supervisor for a shift, he tried to be first on the scene wherever possible, taking initial action until the appropriate patrol arrived to take over. Until he was satisfied, the attending constables could take over and continue with the correct responses, he remained on the scene, assisting as necessary with witnesses or the distribution of resources. Later, he would check their reports, the appropriateness of action taken and address the question of ongoing inquiries if warranted.

The role of I Car Supervisor was intensely demanding and often very exciting. With uniformed officers called to attend many incidents, including armed robberies, of which there had been a dramatic increase, Terry took to carrying a firearm as a matter of routine. More often than not, he was first on the scene when the likelihood of confrontation with an armed offender was very high.

The 1970's was a period when the Irish Republican Army was most active and airline high-jacking at its height. Bombings in Northern Ireland received much publicity in the New Zealand Press, provoking a spate of hoax bomb threats around the country. Pranksters knew the police were unaccustomed to dealing with this type of situation and nearly always evacuated the threatened building. Fortunately, it was not long before the police realised that this was not necessarily the correct way to deal with such situations, but in the mean time, making such a threat was a sure way to create disruption and chaos. The frequency of hoax threats was such that nearly everyone became blasé, creating the potential for real disaster.

It was approximately 10.00 am on a routinely quiet Wednesday-early shift and Terry was patrolling the central city area as I Car Supervisor. Feeling somewhat drowsy from lack of sleep and only half listening to the two-way radio, the drone of voices related mainly to requests for suburban patrols to attend overnight burglaries, car thefts and the occasional motor accident.

Halfway through an uneventful shift, he looked forward to knocking off at 1.00 pm and his usual six or seven mile run. Exercise was an effective way to eliminate the mental fug and sluggish feeling, which always accompanied 5.00 am starts.

"I car Supervisor, this is Operations. Over!"

Instantly awake at the mention of his call sign, Terry responded, "I Car Supervisor, ten three."[28].

"I Car Supervisor, we have a call from an amusement parlour operator at 209 Manchester Street. He reports finding a suspicious package in his premises. Please attend and report. Over."

"Roger, Operations. E.T.A. five minutes. Over."

Terry double-parked outside the small amusement parlour, the single roof-mounted red light on his patrol vehicle flashing to warn approaching vehicles. He found the proprietor waiting anxiously outside his shop, the little man's black Brylecreamed hair slicked back from a flabby face flushed with concern. His jowls wobbled as he danced nervously from one foot to the other, wringing sausage like fingers in agitation. "What took you so long?" he squeaked in a high-pitched effeminate voice.

Aware that a minute can seem like an eternity to someone in a panic, Terry ignored the question. "What exactly is the problem?" he asked.

"It's in there underneath the pinball machine. It's addressed to me." The proprietor pointed to the interior of the shop. An assortment of game machines and electronic gadgets stood unattended, bright lights flashing in the otherwise dim interior of the building.

"What makes you think it's suspicious?"

The fat man looked at Terry incredulously. "Are you joking? Who would leave a package there like that, unless they were up to no good?"

"Do you have any idea, who might want to threaten you?"

"I guess it's my opposition. I'm taking most of their business these days."

"Okay, we'll come back to that later. Show me this package."

Terry noted their surroundings while they were talking. Pedestrians busily hurried along the street, cars occupied every

---

[28] 10/3, police radio code for, "I am free."

one of the metered bays and traffic moved slowly past. He was going to need plenty of help to cordon and clear the area if this was a genuine emergency. As they entered the building, he inquired, "Where are all your customers?"

"There was only a couple at this time of the morning and I cleared them out."

"Do you know who they were? He was thinking, *maybe one of the patrons had seen something or was responsible for planting the package.*

"I know them by sight but they reckoned they hadn't seen anything."

"Okay. I'll get their descriptions later and you'll need to let us know when you see them again."

The object of interest was a small cardboard box tied with string. It appeared to be completely innocuous with no outward sign as to its contents until he saw that letters cut from magazines and stuck to the brown paper wrapping spelt out the proprietor's name. There was no address. Whoever had deposited the package had shoved it beneath one of the pinball machines in the darkest corner of the shop. "What time did you close yesterday?" Terry was wondering if the package had been there for some time.

"About 11.00 pm. Why?"

"Do you know if it was there when you closed last night?"

"It may have been. I found it when I was cleaning this morning."

"How often do you clean under that machine?"

"What are you worrying about my housekeeping for? That thing could go off any moment!"

"Just answer the question please."

I clean the floor every day."

"Did you move the box at all?

"No, of course I didn't. Do you think I'm bloody stupid? When I first saw it, I thought at first somebody had left it behind. Then I saw my name on it. As soon as I saw that, I panicked and cleared the customers from the shop and rang you."

"Is there any way that the box could have been placed this morning without you noticing?"

"No. I was in the shop cleaning all the time?"

226

"Was either of the customers who came into the shop this morning carrying a bag or anything?"

"No."

"So it looks as if it was placed sometime yesterday?"

"I suppose so. Why?"

"It's important. The fact that it was placed yesterday means we can almost certainly rule out a timing device if it is a bomb. It would have gone off within a twelve-hour period. We can't rule out any sort of movement switch, such as, a mercury tilt switch but I would say somebody is just trying to scare you. Nevertheless, we'll have to treat it as genuine."

Terry radioed Operations, explaining what the proprietor had told him. "Under the circumstances, I think we had better cordon off the area and call the Department of Labour[29] to deal with the package," he continued. "In the mean time I'll keep customers out of the shop and get a statement from the owner."

Terry expected his situation report to throw the Operations room into full emergency mode. To his surprise, they chose to play down the incident, refusing to dispatch additional manpower for cordons and evacuation. He tried again, "Operations, I view this package as highly suspicious. It may well be an improvised explosive device. As a precaution, I request someone bring the bomb blanket[30]."

Still, Operations did not take the matter seriously. Although a suburban patrol vehicle delivered the bomb blanket almost immediately, they departed, leaving Terry to handle the situation alone. It seemed as if last night's burglaries were a higher priority than a probable bomb with potentially devastating consequences. He was unable to comprehend their cavalier attitude and amazed that a high-ranking officer hadn't heard the communications and questioned the lack of response. There was nothing else to do, but muddle through as well as he could.

Fortunately, the Department of Labour viewed the request seriously, responding with all haste. A baby faced, slightly built

---

[29] The N.Z. Police did not have trained explosive experts at that time. Army Ordnance officers dealt with military explosives and The Department of Labour supervised civilian explosives.

[30] A heavy anti fragmentation shield lined with Kevlar and designed to minimize the explosive impact of devices such as letter and parcel bombs. These devices had only recently been issued to the police.

young man with fair hair and fine features parked his Government vehicle behind the patrol car and approached Terry. "What have we got sergeant? I'm Dave Skinner."

Terry shook the man's hand. Although he wondered how anyone so young could have the requisite knowledge and experience. Nevertheless, he was relieved. At last, someone who presumably possessed knowledge of explosives was on the scene to deal with the package. He briefed the man quickly and instructed the fat proprietor to keep out of the way while they examined the item in question.

"I've arranged for the bomb blanket, if it's any use?" Terry said.

It was obvious that the explosives man had never seen a bomb blanket, let alone knew anything concerning its uses or limitations. "I think we'll try and tie it up as a shield," he said, feigning expertise in bomb demolition.

Terry looked dubiously at the bomb man. *I guess he knows what he's doing,* he thought. *I thought the idea was to cover the item with the blanket and contain any explosion. Oh well. Who am I to question him? He's the expert, or at least, I hope he is!*

Tying ropes to the corner of the heavy Kevlar device and a roof beam, they hoisted it in position between the package and the front of the shop. Terry could not help wondering just how much force a package of that size could contain. *Surely, it would hold enough explosive to blow the entire building apart, bomb blanket or no bomb blanket.* Feeling decidedly unsettled and concerned for the safety of passers by, Terry worried about Operations refusal to cordon and evacuate the immediate area. *Perhaps I'm being too melodramatic,* he consoled himself. *If the Government fellow thinks its okay to proceed like this, it must be safe.*

Standing by to render assistance if called upon, he watched nervously as the young fellow inspected the package. To his amazement, the man tied a string to the box, and retreating behind the blanket, yanked the string. The box tumbled over, but there was no explosion.

This bloke's absolutely nuts! He thought. *If that thing blew up, the bloody blanket's not going to save us. We'll be blown to bits!*

Satisfied that movement would not activate any device within the box; Dave Skinner picked up the box and weighed it in his hands. "Well, there's something in there. Let's see what it is."

This was too much for Terry. "Blow you Joe!" He muttered to himself, convinced the man had taken leave of his senses. He bolted out through the front door and stood to one side away from the likelihood of flying debris to stop pedestrians walking past the shop front.

A few moments elapsed. There was no explosion and another moment passed before the so-called expert stuck his head out the door and called, "Come and have a look at this."

The package lay open on top of a pinball machine, revealing a small electric detonator, batteries and wires. A wooden clothes peg formed an improvised switch connected to a shotgun cartridge.

Skinner poked the electronic components with a pencil. "Someone wanted this to look like a bomb. However, the wire from the battery to the switch isn't connected, so it's harmless. If they'd connected it up correctly, the clothes peg switch would have activated when it was opened. It would have made a nasty noise, but that's all!"

"I guess we don't know if that was deliberate, or a mistake, but I'm bloody glad the shotgun cartridge wasn't a stick of gelignite! Thank you for your help. I'll hand this over to the C.I.B. They'll want to conduct the investigation from here. I think our little fat friend might have some explaining to do." Terry's gut feeling told him that the owner of the Amusement Parlour knew far more than he was letting on.

Gathering the makeshift device under his arm, he loaded it into the boot of his patrol car and returned to the police station, feeling tremendous relief. The outcome could have been so very different.

Terry worked on after the conclusion of his shift, submitting a detailed report fully outlining events and his concerns as to the off-hand manner adopted by the Operations staff. He could not believe their casual attitude and indifference to what may well resulted in disaster. He submitted his report expecting his superiors to re-act almost tumultuously. Days went by and Terry received no feedback. He could only hope, the C.I.B. would follow up on the investigation, but like so many inquiries initiated by uniformed members, he didn't expect to learn of the outcome and this proved to be the case. His report had seemingly disappeared into a hierarchical vacuum.

When his shifts permitted, Terry tried to spend as much time as he could with the family. With only one weekend off in five, that time was precious. Night shifts were particularly dreadful. Arriving home shortly after 5.00 am, he would try and catch some sleep before the family awoke, for once the children were up and about, sleep was almost impossible. Toward the end of the week, severe sleep deprivation meant frayed nerves and no matter how hard he tried, invariably his temper snapped, resulting in Jane and him arguing heatedly.

Terry's experience was no different to that of most police officers. Apart from the stresses of shift work, dealing with horrendous motor accidents, sudden deaths, the aftermath of vicious assaults, burglaries, high-speed car chases, domestic disputes and a plethora of other incidents on a daily basis, exacted a high price on emotional stability. It was extremely difficult for him to leave the job on the front door mat and switch immediately from the role of enforcer of the law, to that of family man. With his head still spinning from some extremely exciting, worrying or tragic event, or with adrenaline still coursing through his veins, it was only natural, that no matter how hard he might try, police life invariably intruded upon the entire family. Perhaps the worst part for any policeman is that he may not share his burden with his partner owing to the pledge of secrecy.

However, being a policeman's family wasn't easy for any of them. Nevertheless, family picnics, drives into the country, visiting relatives and friends and just doing things with the children assumed great significance.

With only his father's bad example to follow as a parent, Terry struggled with the role of parenthood. He loved his children dearly and vowed to be involved in their upbringing as much as possible, playing with them and taking an active interest in their education. Struggling to find the right balance, he tended toward being a strict disciplinarian, believing his children needed to know their boundaries. He knew he was sometimes too hard and frequently regretted having to be the main one administering punishment.

The marriage continued to deteriorate and try as he might; Terry had been unable to find the reason why his young wife rebuffed him. Attempts to communicate elicited her infuriating and indifferent response, "It's all your imagination. Everything is all right!"

Terry knew things were not right. However, he could do little until Jane was ready to reveal the problem and give him the chance to make amends. In the mean time, the rift between them became an impassable chasm, culminating in a very unpleasant surprise, with almost tragic consequences.

Arriving home from an early shift one afternoon, Terry was not surprised to see the Parish Priest, Father Miles' car parked outside their home. The amiable tall young priest was well liked and respected in the parish. He possessed the gift of being able to bridge the generation gap, often calling for children from the congregation to sit around the Alter while he took Mass. Although not a devout Catholic, for he always wanted to question the Church's teachings, Terry liked Father Miles, whom they sometimes invited to dinner.

Expecting a jovial greeting from the bald headed young priest, he found Jane sobbing uncontrollably on Father Miles' shoulder. Terry's stomach immediately churned in shock and despair. "What's happened?" he enquired.

The Priest stood up, gently disentangling himself from the distraught young woman. "I'll go now and leave you two alone. Jane has something to tell you." Miles face was grave as he studied Terry. "If you need me, I'll be there for you both."

"What on Earth's going on?" Terry asked again, as the clergyman departed.

It took some time before Jane was able to control her anguished sobbing. Eventually, she stammered the news of her affair with one of the neighbours. Racked with guilt, she had tried unsuccessfully that morning to take her life, overdosing on tranquillisers. "Do you want me to leave?" she asked.

"I just want to know why. What have I done, or not done that would drive you to do that?" Terry blamed himself, presuming his shortcomings had driven her to seek the solace he had been unable to provide.

"You never seem to be here. You're either away with Search and Rescue, or the diving squad, or working. Whenever anything comes up that I would like to go to, we can't go. My life is so boring with nobody to talk to but the kids. I guess when Ian showed me some affection I felt flattered."

So, that's who she was playing up with! He found it hard to believe that his neighbour, whom he had always looked up to and regarded as a pillar of the community, had taken advantage of his wife. His mind was in turmoil. Torn between desires for revenge and self-blame, the calm inner voice of reason prevailed, telling him that there was nothing to be gained from violence.

Stunned by events he accepted her assurances that it would never happen again, castigating himself for having failed her. Whatever the cause, their relationship had reached crisis point. Suddenly, Tai Tapu and the house he loved so much seemed soiled, and life there had become untenable. For the next week, it was as if his brain had been switched to auto-pilot.

Several weeks later, when the promotional postings appeared in the police gazette, Terry accepted his transfer to Dunedin with alacrity. Turning down promotion and remaining in Christchurch was not an option worthy of consideration. Dunedin presented a welcome opportunity to rebuild his marriage. Amazingly, Jane had other ideas.

"I'm not going there," she complained. "There are other policemen who are senior to you and who have been in Christchurch all their service. Why do they have to move you? It's not fair."

After recent events, Terry was in no mood to discuss the matter. He issued his ultimatum. "I've worked hard to be promoted. I am not going to turn this down. It's your place to go where my career takes me. Either you come with me, or you stay here alone. I'm going and that's it!"

For the first time in their turbulent relationship, Jane acquiesced to a major demand, begrudgingly accepting the transfer.

Situated on the forty-fifth parallel with majestic old grey stone buildings, Dunedin's inhabitants are predominantly dour Scots. The old city straddles the steep hills of the Otago Peninsula, cautiously dabbling arthritic toes in the icy waters of the Pacific Ocean. Like a frigid Scottish spinster, she can be both beautiful and hostile, her fickle moods determined by the weather. For,

232

when the pale southern sun smiles from cloudless blue skies, the Otago Peninsula's rolling green fields and sparkling sapphire blue ocean captivates the most callous heart. However, when black clouds stream in from the sea, filling shadowy valleys with dirty cotton wool fog, when stinging rains freeze upon the bleak frosty streets and its inhabitants retreat behind closed doors, she is as inhospitable as a morgue.

Having obtained a more than fair price for their Tai Tapu house, Terry and Jane decided to purchase the best home they could afford. After visiting numerous sunless and chilly homes with a Real Estate Agent, they settled on a double storey white painted brick bungalow in the hillside suburb of Opaho.

Sunny Opaho, the locals called it and while it was true that the former doctor's residence sat above the often cloud filled valleys it also caught the icy winds blowing in from the southern ocean. When the young family took up residence on 1 June, the city was already in the numbingly cold grip of winter.

Suffering badly from asthma, Dunedin was the wrong place for little Liam whose attacks became more frequent. Required to descend the steep streets to the Catholic school in the permanently frosty North East Valley, Veronica suddenly developed bronchitis. When Jane ventured outside to hang washing on the line, she developed painful chilblains on her fingers. The washing refused to dry, simply freezing solid on the clothesline. Heavy frosts in Dunedin often had no chance to melt before rain fell, covering the streets with a dangerous coating of slippery ice. With most of its inhabitants in virtual hibernation, Jane found the city unfriendly and longed for the more hospitable Christchurch, where she at least knew frosty mornings heralded sunny days.

Determined to make the most of the winter posting, Terry went on a reconnaissance of the unfamiliar city, learning its layout and places of interest. With local knowledge playing an important role in determining the effectiveness of policeman, he felt like a fish out of water, having to rely upon guidance from his subordinate officers.

Lacking in experienced volunteers, the Dunedin Police Search and Rescue Team was almost defunct. Terry now knew why the police hierarchy had chosen to transfer him ahead of other seemingly more appropriate candidates. They expected him to rebuild its reputation by training suitable police volunteers and liaising closely with the civilian tramping and climbing fraternity. With a wife who was unhappy and unsettled, sick children, strange surroundings, and a new team of constables with who he needed to become acquainted; this additional task foisted upon him so quickly placed him under a great strain.

Striving to help Jane settle in Dunedin, Terry took the family on outings, visiting the local sights, such as Larnach's Castle and sightseeing along the beautiful but now bleak Otago Peninsula. The most positive aspect of their move was their house. Warm and comfortable, it enjoyed a spectacular view across the valley and the city. They often watched fascinated as the grey cotton wool of the clouds floated lazily across the hills, before pouring down into the valleys concealing the entire city. They could then look over the grey fluffy carpet from the big picture windows of their lounge room.

Unfortunately, the view and the luxury of the house offered little consolation to Jane, who was extremely miserable.

In New Zealand, August is traditionally the coldest month of winter, with night-time temperatures falling well below zero and daytime temperatures struggling to get above freezing. Dunedin is not renowned for hot summers, so it was extremely unusual for the thermometer to register thirty-six degrees in August 1975. Obviously, Mother Nature had something exceedingly unpleasant in store.

Terry had no sooner left for work in his capacity as Dunedin Central Police Station's Night Station Sergeant, than Cyclone Allison struck with incredible ferocity. As he pulled into the tiny cramped station yard, the north-westerly winds buffeted his old Morris Oxford sedan. Leaning heavily into the gale, he ran toward the Watch house door and shelter. Before he reached the door, it opened as a uniformed officer exited. Instantly, the wind snatched the door from the man's hand, throwing it back against a nearby brick wall, shattering the glass and snapping the pneumatic door closer. A heavy drumming sound attracted Terry's attention to the street. To his amazement, a large steel waste bin, which would normally, only be lifted with the aid of a hydraulic hoist, careened down the roadway like an out-of control army tank.

After normal routine hand over procedures, Terry settled into his chair next to the police operations room where he could supervise the activities of the two constables handling calls. All over the city, burglar alarms set off by the wind screeched for attention. The station's telephones ran hot with emergency calls as roofs lifted and trees snapped like twigs. To venture outside was akin to madness. Walking upright became impossible and flying debris made driving extremely hazardous.

Amid the confusion, the radio crackled noisily as the sole constable in the tiny Otago town of Roxburgh called, "Dunedin Operations. This is Roxburgh. Over."

Wendy Hughes, the Operations Controller responded, "Receiving Roxburgh. Your signal is strength three[31]. Over."

"Roger, Dunedin Operations. We have a major bushfire encircling the township. Every available person is fighting the fire, but we are losing the battle and I don't know whether we can save the town. Over."

Terry grabbed the microphone, "Roger, Roxburgh. We have a major emergency situation here also but please advise how we can assist."

"I don't think you can get through to us. The roads are impassable ......" The policeman's voice ceased abruptly.

"Roxburgh. Roxburgh. This is Dunedin operations. Come in please, over." Terry called, desperately worried.

Despite several further calls, the Roxburgh Station did not respond. Not knowing whether bushfires had already encroached upon the town and with cyclonic winds negating any rescue attempt, there was little Terry and his team could do but hope and pray. He ordered the commencement of a log of events, as it became apparent that they were in the grip of a major civil emergency.

From Cook's Straight, that narrow and notorious stretch of storm tossed sea between the North and South Island, the eye of the cyclone moved slowly and destructively southward. Passing through the jagged snow capped peaks of the Kaikoura Ranges, it moved relentlessly into the exposed Canterbury Plains, wreaking havoc and snapping mature trees in its path as if they were

---

[31] Radio signal strength is measured on a scale of one to five, with one being the weakest possible signal that is unreadable.

matchsticks. Whole pine plantations snapped and fell as if a giant scythe had swept through them. Wind speeds measured in excess of one hundred and sixty kilometres per hour. Power poles collapsed, electricity transformers exploded and fireballs raced along transmission lines like maniacal Catherine wheels, starting innumerable wildfires fanned to intensity by the howling winds.

Fifty-five kilometres north of Dunedin, bushfires charged relentlessly toward the major coastal settlement of Palmerston, threatening to wipe the town from the map. Helped by every able-bodied resident, fire fighters struggling to save the township pleaded desperately for assistance. However, Dunedin had its own problems and only a brave man or a fool would venture outside to face the fury. Nevertheless, Terry could not sit idly by as the town's beleaguered residents faced disaster.

"Shift sergeant from night station sergeant, over."

"Sergeant Holmes receiving."

As the sergeant in charge of the Night Shift General Duties Section, Holmes was in his early thirties. A well-built, cheerful man with squarish, clean-shaven features and straight black hair, he knew Dunedin well, having spent most of his police service in the coastal city. Accompanied by a junior officer, Holmes patrolled the city streets in a Holden sedan, attending calls for assistance as they arose. Fortunately, the town's criminals seemed to have taken a night off, no doubt huddling in their homes like the rest of the populace.

"Sergeant Holmes, I have received a call for assistance from Palmerston. The township is in grave danger from bushfires. Please proceed en route to provide what ever assistance you can in evacuating the town."

Wayne Holmes responded, "Roger. It will take us some time to get there as we will be battling headwinds and will not be able to get the police car out of second gear. There are power lines and trees down all over the place and debris flying through the air. It's extremely hazardous to be out in this. Over"

"Roger that. I know you will do your best. Take care and good luck."

Things are getting too hot for me, he decided. Turning to Wendy Hughes, he voiced his concerns. "Things are getting beyond the control of a lowly sergeant. I am going to call out the duty inspector."

Fortunately, the telephones still worked. As the cyclonic wind beat against the solid, old, grey, stone police station, threatening to tear the shingles from the roof, Terry dialled the duty inspector's home number and quickly briefed him on the gravity of events. After listening thoughtfully for a moment, the man decided to handball the responsibility for the emergency to the district commander. Within minutes, both commissioned officers arrived, taking over command from their very relieved junior sergeant.

Cyclone Allison raged all night, leaving a country wide swathe of devastation throughout the South Island as it tore off roofs, smashed buildings, flipped over 'planes and sank boats at their moorings. As she drew close to Palmerston, the fickle maelstrom miraculously veered away from the township at the last moment, averting almost-certain fiery obliteration of the township. In Dunedin, Civil Defence volunteers, firemen and police officers risked falling power lines and flying debris their lives to answer dozens of calls from desperate embattled residents. Somehow, Allison spared human life and equally surprisingly, as daylight tinged the gorse-covered hills with a peculiar yellowish light, the wind ceased abruptly, replaced instead by steady, silent, drenching rain. It was as if the city wept in its relief.

As the day shift arrived to take over, Terry briefed them as to events before hurrying home, anxiously wondering how his family had fared. Amazingly, the storm had completely spared their house. Jane recounted how the glass in the large picture windows had bowed dangerously inward, threatening to break under the tremendous strain of nature's fury. Terry was grateful that the storm had not been even slightly more powerful as few buildings could have withstood such fury.

Although he was relieved that his family was unscathed, there was to be no sleep for Terry after such a horrendous night. Blown away by the wind, the roof of his immediate neighbour's house sat halfway up the hillside as the rain drenched exposed furniture and household effects. He hurried to assist, carrying various items to the safety of nearby garages and rigging tarpaulins over the skeleton of the once palatial home. As the lunchtime siren of the rock quarry across the valley from their home sounded, he at last sank exhausted into his bed.

Liam's worsening asthma, Veronica's bronchitis and Jane's deep depression caused Terry to conclude that to remain in Dunedin was to invite tragedy. Although the police service often appeared heartless, somewhere along the line the police Union had managed to persuade the hierarchy to appoint welfare officers to look after member's interests. Having never availed himself of this service, Terry felt an understandable reluctance to bare his soul. *Would the welfare officer respect sensitivity and confidentiality? There was only one way to find out.*

The appointee to the position in Dunedin, Ralph McPherson was a thin, balding, middle-aged senior sergeant. Terry arranged an appointment, to see the welfare officer in his dingy office at Dunedin police Headquarters. Behind closed doors the man listened quietly to the anguished young N.C.O. "I'll see what I can do," he replied sympathetically. "Where would you like to go?"

A few days earlier, police Daily Notices had carried a vacancy for a sergeant in Nelson, a delightful holiday town considered by the service to be a "plumb" posting. *Dare he hope that someone as junior as he could land such a position?* Mentally crossing his fingers, he boldly suggested the reputedly warmer and pretty town although he had never visited the place.

Without hesitation, McPherson lifted the telephone handset and rang straight through to the officer responsible for determining postings at police headquarters in Wellington. "I've got a young sergeant here whose family has health problems. His marriage is on the rocks unless we move him out of Dunedin. I'd like him to get the Nelson job." There was barely a moment's delay before he replaced the telephone on its cradle. He looked directly at Terry and smiled. "Done. Congratulations, sergeant. Start packing."

Terry couldn't believe it had been that easy and wanted to go straight home and break the news. McPherson seemed to read the young sergeant's thoughts. "Go on. Off you go home. The world won't collapse while you're away."

Jane brightened at the prospect, although clearly, a return to Christchurch would have been her first choice.

"I could hardly tell old Mac that the kids needed warmer climes and then ask for Christchurch darling," he told her. "We'll

238

have to put the house on the market and hope it sells quickly. In the mean time, we'll be allocated a police house. I understand we'll be living in the Old Port police station."

"Thank God we're getting out of this depressingly bleak town. Everybody hibernates here and it's impossible to make any friends in the winter," Jane replied. "I just wish we could have stayed in Christchurch."

Terry bit back the angry retort before it reached his lips. Recent events were still too painful and for him Christchurch was the last place on earth he wanted to be.

Nelson's reputation as a sunny holiday town formed the sole basis of Terry's decision to transfer there. In his opinion, any town north of Dunedin had to be better than the bleak Scottish city. While Jane and the children stayed in Christchurch for a few days, Terry went on ahead to ready the police house for their arrival. Although the holiday city lived up to its reputation as a pretty place with a mild climate, had Terry known where they would be living for the next thirteen months, he may well have re-considered his decision.

All the parking bays outside Nelson police station were full. Terry drove into the rear yard with a newly purchased cabin runabout in tow and parked to one side of the compound, a few steps from the door to the cellblock. . He marched in the back door and introduced himself to Senior Sergeant Pat Baker, one of two N.C.O.'s in charge of the Nelson Station. A greying, curly haired man of few words, Pat was in his mid-fifties. His shrewd grey eyes appraised the new sergeant from square, flattish features as he shook hands warmly. "It's not a palace, but if Arthur Chippendale could live there for thirteen years, it can't be too bad," he remarked as he handed Terry the keys to his new abode. "Chips, was a real identity in the Port and you might still get a few of the old diehards knocking on the door now and then."

Terry didn't mind if the locals still thought they had a resident policeman but he knew Jane wouldn't be so keen. "I'm sure we'll soon educate them," he replied. He was to learn that the burly, elderly Arthur 'Chips' Chippendale, a policeman from the "old school" was nearing retirement. Until recently, Chips had been the sole policeman at the Nelson Port police station. He despised paperwork and rarely arrested or charged anyone with minor offences, choosing rather to administer justice with the well-placed toe of a large boot to a backside, or a hefty cuff about the ears. Well liked and respected as a tough but fair man, he now occupied the remaining days of his long career grumpily shuffling paper in the Nelson police district office, an ignominious end to a long and successful career. Unfortunately, time had passed Chips by and his style of policing was no longer acceptable.

Well, Pat was surely not joking when he said it's not a palace, Terry mused silently as he swung into the narrow concrete driveway. Situated on the extremely busy main road serving the bustling Port area, the old brick dwelling was sandwiched between a Post Office and a fish-processing factory. Directly across the road, the old Tasman Hotel and the T.A.B. were doing a brisk trade from the wharfies, fishermen and truck drivers, while immediately behind the rusty corrugated iron back fence, ships loaded and unloaded various cargo. Heavy trucks thundered by the main gate in a constant stream, ferrying wood chips for export to Japan. The pong of rotting seaweed and fish guts pervaded the salt laden air, while dust, used beer bottles and fast food containers littered the footpath and the front yard of the silently brooding and empty house.

Opening a heavy, green door from a small front verandah, Terry found the dank wall papered interior of the house dim and uninviting. Dust and sand blown under the front door almost concealed the varnished surface of the floorboards. Constructed during the 1920's, heavy wood panelling, high ceilings, thick brick walls and small windows gave the house a formal and sombre appearance. A disused cellblock dominated the cramped backyard where the previous occupant had obviously struggled to grow a vegetable garden in the sandy arid grime. A few spindly weeds and a thin patchy lawn sporting a rusty clothesline struggled valiantly to survive in the polluted, hostile environment.

"Let's hope the Dunedin house sells quickly," Terry muttered, as he swept away the accumulated dust in readiness for the furniture, scheduled to arrive that afternoon. The almost unbearable din from passing traffic made conversation in the front rooms impossible. "I wonder what Jane's going to think of this," he asked himself.

The furniture truck did not arrive until late in the afternoon when the shadows were already lengthening. The driver and his assistant were clearly in a hurry to drop their load and head back to Christchurch. Hurriedly off-loading everything on the front verandah, they left Terry to struggle inside with beds, boxes, wardrobes, a washing machine, a refrigerator, lounge suit, tables, even the piano. It was well beyond 10.00 pm by the time he had it all unpacked and safely stowed everything away. Rolling some lengths of carpet over the cold dark floors, he stood back exhausted, to survey his handiwork. "Well, that's the best I can do to make you look like home," he told the grim old house.

Despite the unpleasant surroundings, Jane and the four children settled quickly into their new home. They seemed oblivious to the contrast between it and their up-market Dunedin house with the hospitality offered by locals, Rod and Noeline Curtis being pivotal in their rapid acclimatisation.

The four Curtis children, Philip, Stephen, Glen and Leanne were roughly the same age as Liam, Veronica, Michael and Helen. Previously stationed in Christchurch, Rod was a police dog handler who shared Terry's love of SCUBA diving and tramping. The two families soon became very close, sharing each other's company whenever shift work permitted. When on duty, Terry and Rod often paired up, patrolling and attending incidents together. The lean dog handler's dry sense of humour and sardonic manner counterbalanced Terry's more analytical and introspective personality.

As a newly appointed dog handler for the entire Nelson police district, Rod needed someone with knowledge and experience of a police dog's capability to assist with training and the indoctrination of police officers unused to working with dogs. Terry happily assumed that role, laying tracks for Pirate, Rod's big, black and very intelligent German Shepherd. The powerful canine loved man work, lunging fiercely at the heavy rubber sleeve Terry sometimes wore during training sessions to give the dog practice in subduing armed offenders. Biting down hard, Pirate would hang on, growling savagely, forty kilograms of muscle and sinew against which only the most foolhardy would struggle.

Rod kept the faithful animal at home, where in a Jekyll and Hyde transformation, Pirate immediately became as gentle as the cuddliest of children's pets, often wanting to climb on Terry's lap and nuzzling into an armpit for attention. As soon as Rod donned his uniform and commanded the loping hound to jump into the rear seat of his Holden, Pirate knew he was on duty, snarling savagely if Terry tried to get into the front seat before his handler.

"Jees, how can the bastard be all affectionate one minute and a monster the next? You'd think he didn't know me," Terry exclaimed.

Rod merely laughed maliciously.

As Nelson's newest sergeant, Terry discovered an expectation from officialdom that he would assume several roles. Among these was the requirement to appear in the local court as a police prosecutor.

A local magistrate, George Kiernan, was known through police ranks as a cantankerous, diminutive, bald-headed man with glasses and a nationwide reputation for an explosive temper. Known behind his back as, 'Crazy George,' the little magistrate did not suffer fools lightly, blasting lawyers, witnesses, criminals and police officers with impunity. Terry had often been a witness in the Christchurch Magistrate's Court, before the ill-tempered distributor of justice and was well acquainted with his red-faced outbursts. Fortunately, he had thus far, been spared Mister Kiernan's verbosity and any accompanying pompous, public humiliation, finding the little man's legal pronouncements well considered and just. Unbeknown to him that situation was about to change.

Lacking knowledge of the finer points of court procedure, which only comes with experience as a prosecutor, Terry was understandably nervous, when, in the sudden absence of the full-time police prosecutor, Senior Sergeant Bert Barber foisted the job on Terry with little notice.

During his first morning in the unwelcome role, Terry managed the routine guilty pleas and a defended case without incident. The luncheon adjournment then offered a welcome respite for him to collect his thoughts and sooth his frayed nerves, before the court resumed at 2.15 pm.

Unbeknown to Terry, while he was sweating over his unaccustomed role, Nelson's detectives had arrested a man on burglary charges. Cognisant of the Criminal Justice Act's requirements for the offender's appearance before the court at the first available opportunity following arrest, and with no time to prepare the relevant paperwork before the Court re-sat, the head of the Nelson C.I.B. Detective Sergeant Ross Tyson approached Terry.

A heavy-set, senior sleuth with a shiny pate, potbelly and a wry smile, Tyson entered the lunchroom where Terry sat munching hungrily on his sandwiches. "I've got this joker in the cells who needs to go before the beak this afternoon," Ross grumbled in his abrupt, no nonsense manner. "I haven't got any paperwork yet, so when his case comes up, you'll have to ad lib."

Terry hastily swallowed a mouthful of chicken and salad. He'd been enjoying the food and psyching himself up to tackle the afternoon list. Until that moment he had felt confident and was almost looking forward to the challenge. Now the sandwich stuck in his throat. "What's he done and what do you want me to say Ross?"

The big man smiled at Terry's distress, "Just ask for a remand in custody for seven days, without plea. Okay?"

Oh no, Terry thought. *I have enough to worry about, without having to proceed unscripted.* "No problem!" he lied. His mind was now in turmoil and his appetite lost. *What can I do? I can hardly show my lack of confidence and experience.* He jotted the defendant's name in his notebook along with the notation; *"Remand in custody without plea."*

Terry had resumed his place at the prosecutor's table well in advance of the court's resumption. Although his back was to them, constables from his shift sat either side of Tyson's prisoner, guarding the man closely.

Butterflies were dancing an Irish jig in Terry's belly and his mouth was dry.

"Silence. All stand!" The Court Registrar bellowed to the assemblage as 'Crazy George' bustled into the court. The dyspeptic-looking magistrate bore the expression of someone who had just lost his house on the last race at Trentham.

The little man flopped into his chair and acknowledged the bowing, black suited, legal fraternity with a barely perceptible nod of his egg-bald head. "What is the first case?" he enquired of the Registrar.

"Rodald Joseph Swift." As the court orderly called the name of the C.I.B.'s prisoner, uniformed officers ushered the alleged miscreant into the dock.

The registrar drawled in his bored monotone, "On the 24th day of February 1976, at Nelson, you did break and enter the premises of Frederick Arthur Sykes with intent to commit a crime therein. How do you plead, guilty or not guilty?"

"Guilty," the prisoner replied.

Terry jumped to his feet, interjecting, "If Your Worship pleases, the prosecution requests a remand in custody for seven days."

Looking up sharply from the documents he had been perusing in an apparently absent-minded manner, the little magistrate's usually sallow face turned instantly bright crimson. He gathered up papers from the highly polished kauri surface of the enormous desk angrily and began squaring them, banging their edges commanding the utmost attention from everyone present.

Terry recognised the danger signs. *Oh, shit! I should not have allowed the prisoner to enter his plea."* It was too late to correct his blunder.

"Sergeant!" With a thunderous voice and an expression to match, the Magistrate's temper exploded. "Never in all the thirty five years that I have been on this bench, have I witnessed such a display of unforgivable ineptitude from a police prosecutor. The basic foundation of British Justice, upon which this country's legal system has been modelled, provides an accused person with the fundamental right for the facts of the matter, for which he has been charged, to be presented immediately upon his plea being entered. These principles go back for hundreds of years and you as an officer of this court should be well acquainted with this rule."

Aware that the courtroom was packed to capacity, 'Crazy George' delighted in the chance to perform before his audience of reporters, lawyers, criminals, police officers, witnesses and curious bystanders. Gathering verbal momentum, the irate Magistrate ranted for a further five minutes, citing relevant sections of the Criminal Justice Act, and legal precedent for the benefit of his unfortunate, cringing victim. Crazy George was on his stage, holding the lead role before his audience and he made the most of every minute to demonstrate his power and intellect.

Although many have said, in recounting situations where they experienced considerable embarrassment, that they had wished the ground had opened beneath their feet and swallowed them, few knew as well as Terry the full implications of that hackneyed saying.

Finally, the tirade came to a climax, "Now, sergeant you *will* present the facts to this court!" Crazy George glared down at the young sergeant, waiting. In the silence that followed his outburst, the sound of a pin dropping would have seemed like an explosion.

With no details of the crime perpetrated by the smirking felon in the dock, Terry could only stammer lamely, "I am sorry sir, but the facts haven't been made available to me as the defendant has only just been arrested and no paperwork prepared."

George Kiernan peered over his rimless spectacles. His voice was stern but quiet and threatening. "Sergeant, this court will take the extraordinary step of granting you a brief adjournment of ten minutes. When I return to this bench, you will present those facts, otherwise you will be held in contempt." With that threat hanging over the novice prosecutor's head, the little despot jumped from his throne and stormed from the courtroom.

Despite there being standing room only, nobody spoke. It is difficult to believe anyone would have felt anything but sympathy for the young policeman's dressing-down. Then, room erupted explosively as the incredulous audience animatedly discussed the incident. Hurriedly gathering his files, Terry rushed red-faced toward the nearby police headquarters.

Bert Barber, smiled sympathetically as his sergeant related events, "Don't worry. It's just a case of small man syndrome. It's been said, that no-one under five-feet-five inches in height should hold a position of authority. Leave it with me, I'll sort it out. Old George's bark is much worse than his bite."

"Christ. I hope so. I have never felt so belittled. I've probably lost all the credibility built up over the past ten years."

The tall senior sergeant set off to the magistrate's chambers to seek an audience. Terry fidgeted nervously while awaiting his return. Ben was back almost immediately. "I'm afraid he refused to see me. I'll take over when court resumes." Picking up the telephone, Ben became engaged in earnest discussion with the portly C.I.B. chief, arming himself with the relevant information.

When Crazy George stomped back and nodded almost imperceptibly to the lawyers before dropping into his padded throne, Ben stood in Terry's place at the Prosecutor's bench, reciting the facts of the case from memory. The Magistrate, who had by then calmed down, showed no surprise at Terry's replacement, remanding the defendant in custody for sentencing. For the remainder of the cases, Kiernan remained subdued, mumbling his pronouncements as if eager to conclude the day's business.

At the conclusion of the day's criminal matters, he consented to an audience with the veteran Senior Sergeant. Ben knocked and at Kiernan's gruff, "Come!" he entered the official's chambers. Almost dwarfed by his paper-strewn desk, the magistrate's wrinkled, egg-bald head nodded toward a vacant chair. "What can I do for you senior sergeant?"

"Sir, I have come about Sergeant Flatley's faux pas today. Sergeant Flatley has not prosecuted before. In his nervousness, he made a simple mistake that, with due respect to you, anyone could easily have made," Ben, explained.

"I know that, Ben," Crazy George addressed the veteran senior sergeant by his first name. However, I am sure he won't make that mistake again, will he?" he smiled knowingly. "It's just rites of passage, part of his initiation into the role so he knows his place. That sort of thing, eh?"

Ben wanted to reply, "There's no need to belittle and humiliate someone before they've even started," but he choked off the words and merely forced a smile. *You bumptious little Hitler. I'd like to chuck you out the door.*

A few weeks later, Terry stood in the witness box facing Kiernan and determined to re-build his credibility. This time it was in relation to a plea of "not guilty" entered by a member of the 'Lost Breed' motorcycle gang to a charge of riding his bike while disqualified. While off duty, Terry had seen Michael Webber, a notorious small-time bikie criminal, riding his noisy gleaming black and chrome machine through the Nelson's city streets. Knowing that the courts had banned Webber from driving, Terry determined to apprehend him when next on duty.

Accompanied by Ike Proctor, a moustached, heavy set, Maori constable of squat stature, Terry tracked the offending gang member to a seedy weatherboard dwelling in the suburb of Worthington Valley. Although divided into several flats, they deduced which one Webber occupied from his distinctive motorcycle, sporting a pair of excessively high handlebars, known colloquially as, 'ape-hangers.'

Kicking a snarling mangy looking cur to one side with his size twelve boots, Terry pounded on the bikie's door. Webber flung the door open, curios to discover the reason for the din created by the barking mongrel, growling its displeasure from a safe distance. Upon sighting the uniformed figures, the unkempt outlaw demanded gruffly, "Yeah, waddya want?" The ape-hanger description appeared very relevant, for, at approximately five feet seven inches in height, Webber was a hirsute individual with swarthy, greasy skin, mud-brown eyes and chimpanzee like features. Attired in the familiar bikie uniform of faded dirty denims, steel-capped boots and sporting the Lost Breed patch and insignia on the back of his filthy jacket, Webber's identity was unmistakable.

"Hello, Michael, nice to see you again. You must be a bloody idiot to ride your motor bike while under disqualification."

"Waddya mean? Who says I have?"

"I am afraid I do, old chap. Last Sunday. About 9.30 am. You rode south along Endeavour Street and turned left into Bridge Street."

"Who says?"

"I do. I was driving south on Endeavour at the same time."

"I didn't see no cop car."

"I wasn't in a police car. Do you admit that you were riding your motorcycle at that time?"

"Nah. Must have been some other joker that looks like me."

"No it wasn't. I recognised your very distinctive features. Michael Webber, I am arresting you for riding your motorcycle while disqualified. You are not obliged to say anything unless you wish to do so, but anything you do say will be taken down in writing and may later be used in evidence. Do you wish to say anything in answer to the charge?"

"You're making a mistake. It wasn't me."

"Okay. Have it your own way. We'll see who the court believes." Expecting resistance from the irate bike, Terry seized an arm and forced it behind the smaller man's back while almost simultaneously snapping handcuffs onto his wrists.

As expected, Webber denied the charge, appointing a prominent local lawyer, Hamish Riddoch to act in his defence. On the day of the hearing, Terry gave his uncorroborated evidence, identifying the bikie as the rider of the motorcycle, which had turned in front of him.

Using the defence of alibi, Webber called half a dozen gang members to testify that he had been attending a club reunion in Mauitipu at the time of the alleged incident.

Scrutinising each of the scruffy tattooed louts as they perjured themselves, George Kiernan was unimpressed. He wasted no time in summarising his verdict.

"Sergeant Flatley has given evidence before me on many occasions over the years. I have always found him to be highly credible and have never had cause to question his accuracy or recollection of events. When this court is placed in the position of having to decide between the uncorroborated evidence of a policeman of the sergeant's calibre, and the evidence of witnesses such as those who have appeared for the defence, it is quality, not quantity that counts! Accordingly, I find the defendant, guilty. Now, I assume there are previous convictions to be taken into account before I sentence the defendant?"

"Yes, your worship." Dave Allen made considerable show of unrolling Webber's conviction list for all to see its extent before passing it to the court registrar."

"Mr Riddoch, do you have anything to say before I sentence the defendant?"

"I would like the court to take into consideration the defendant's concerted attempts to get his life back on track your worship. He has not appeared before you for some time and is now gainfully employed......." Defence counsel rambled on in a vain attempt to forestall the magistrate's proclivity for punishing members of the local bikie gang with time behind bars.

Crazy George listened impatiently to Hamish Riddoch's vain speech. His beady eyes swept over the computer-generated list of convictions. "I don't think the defendant can be said to be a valued member of the community while he associates with persons of the obvious low calibre of the defence witnesses. In addition, he has shown his contempt for this court by ignoring previous disqualification from driving or riding. I am of the opinion that this offence justifies a period of imprisonment. I therefore sentence the defendant to one year in jail." Kiernan banged his gavel loudly.

As the police gaoler, Opie Randall, led Webber from the court, the stocky little bikie glared angrily at the young sergeant while his cohorts left the courtroom, muttering their displeasure at the police victory. In a comparatively small town such as Nelson, almost the entire populace knew the identities of most of its policeman. There could be no escaping the focus of bikie hatred.

Upon his transfer to Nelson, Terry had abandoned any hope of continuing his alliance with search and rescue. Firmly ensconced in his position as sergeant in charge of the dedicated local band of mountaineering experts, Jack Cooper was well liked and respected and unlikely to relinquish leadership in the foreseeable future, leaving Terry to lament the loss of a way of life he loved. However, perhaps sensing Terry's need for the camaraderie elite squads offered, Bert Barber asked his newest N.C.O. to fill a vacancy left by the transfer of the second in command of the local A.O.S.

Terry had never harboured aspirations in that direction and the request came as a complete surprise. With some reluctance, he agreed to accept, hoping he could somehow generate enthusiasm for weapons and military style tactics hitherto foreign and abhorrent to him. *It's worth a re-think to be part of something so elite,* he decided. Although second in command, he would be under the leadership of Robert "Chubby" Whatman. In his opinion, Whatman possessed an arrogance which so often typified ex-cadets lacking worldly experience. Short of stature, and, as his nickname implied, Chubby battled a weight problem. The sandy-haired policeman's primary interests seemed centred on firearms and matters relating to the Armed Offenders Squad. Fancying himself as a master tactician, the portly sergeant loved to lead from the rear, choosing to establish a safe and comfortable command post in any building he had commandeered for the purpose. The abrasive and dictatorial manner of the arrogant N.C.O. reminded Terry of Napoleon Bonaparte as he strutted about, issuing orders and directives, seemingly with scant regard for feedback from the frontline.

There was little doubt Whatman possessed a detailed knowledge of weapons and tactics but his autocratic style of leadership meant he was destined to clash with his new field commander in matters relating to the safety of his troops.

Encompassing an area almost equivalent to one quarter of New Zealand's South Island, the Nelson police district A.O.S. attended more than its share of firearm incidents. After two years as Second in Command, Terry had participated in two residential courses at the police college, training with the Wellington and Auckland squads in weapons and tactics, learning the skills of a negotiator and practising camouflage techniques and various manoeuvres. In addition, the Nelson A.O.S. ran its own training sessions on a monthly basis, practicing various techniques for containment, house clearing, arrest procedures, negotiation, the use of teargas and firearm practice. They invented various scenarios and built a repertoire of ways to deal successfully with them.

The squad's record was impeccable, and as the officer in charge of front line troops, Terry had hard won confidence and respect of his small closely knit team. The primary weapon in the squad's arsenal was the loud hailer, which he had used on several occasions, successfully negotiating the peaceful surrender of various armed miscreants.

During his membership of the A.O.S., the normally serene holiday city's gang problem continued its' escalation, with drug dealing and burglaries increasing exponentially. The Lost Breed gang moved headquarters to take over a suburban Worthington Valley bungalow, installing high corrugated iron fences, barbed wire and sentry posts. Playing host to affiliated criminal gangs from both the North and South Island, who also existed on the proceeds of drug dealing and the control of prostitution, it was now obvious that organised crime had become part of modern New Zealand life.

Unable to crack a safe-breaking team operating in the town, the Nelson C.I.B. seemed bereft of solutions as almost nightly, business premises suffered huge losses with a predictable regularity. Frustrated at the lack of effort expended to catch the hoodlums, Terry devised a plan, which he outlined to Bert Barber in his office at Nelson police headquarters. The big man leant back in his chair, his blue eyes narrowed with interest as he listened without interruption.

"I've looked at the pattern of burglaries and there is one thing that stands out with all of them. Every joint that's been knocked off, has a key-lock safe over thirty years old. These blokes are targeting premises with that type of safe because they are easy to crack. By establishing which places have old safes, we can predict where they're going to strike next. Now, I've got that list. See here, here and here," he stabbed his finger on the street map spread on the senior sergeant's desk. "These businesses are next in line. I reckon if I position my troops on the tops of the buildings in each city block, we can stake out the whole inner city area and respond quickly when they strike. None of the premises is alarmed. With portable detection systems installed in each one and linked back to the police station, we can have any one of the target buildings contained within three to four minutes and catch the gang in the act. Now, my team is on swing shift next week and they have all volunteered to work throughout each night on a stake out. I've prepared an Operation Order which includes Dave Allen's shift who are on night shift. Between us, we should be able to stop this mob making us look like idiots. What do you think?"

Terry had confidence in the quietly spoken Irish duty sergeant with his broad brogue. Dave's knowledge of the Nelson central city area was second to none.

The tall station commander stroked his chin thoughtfully. "It's worth a try. Where will you be?"

"Ike Proctor has a car salesman mate who has lent us a Ford Escort van for undercover work. He knows what it's going to be used for and is quite happy to loan it to us at no charge. I will be dressed rough and carry a portable radio in the van. That way I can be in contact while I am on a roving patrol around the areas we haven't staked out. As soon as Dave Allen's men advise us that an alarm has been activated, I'll head to the target zone along with my troops. Now, it's obvious these fellas are listening in to our frequency, so we'll use codes for each target. All the watch-house has to do when an alarm sounds is to simply call an appropriate one word code and everyone will know which building to hit."

"What about these portable alarms?"

"Detective McMeeking has arranged to install one in each of the target premises. Ben, I reckon we're on to a sure thing here!"

"All right, sergeant. Make sure you brief Dave and his team. You have my permission to put this plan into action for one week."

Being careful to ensure that he released information only on a need to know basis, Terry saved the dissemination of instructions until the Monday night when the cheerful Irish sergeant's team assembled for their customary pre-shift briefing.

"Here is a copy of the plan and the coded call sign for each target premises. It is vitally important that when an alarm goes off, the watch-house keeper uses the appropriate code and gives no other information. My troops who are positioned on the rooftops must get into position first before the uniformed guys and police cars come screaming down the street, otherwise the offenders will get away. Give us five minutes before you respond. That will give us sufficient time to cordon and contain any building in the target area."

Although Dave Allen appeared willing to co-operate with the plan, the body language of some of his team members revealed their resentment. Omnipresent rivalry between uniformed sections meant some interpreted their role in the operation as secondary to that of Terry's men. Terry could almost read their small-minded jealousy. *They think I'm going to steal their thunder,* he realised incredulously.

"Look, this is a team effort. These crooks have been running rings around us for weeks and it's time somebody did something to stop them. I need your co-operation on this, okay?"

Frank Jones[32], an immigrant from the former British Colony of Rhodesia looked darkly at him from beneath bushy eyebrows. "Yes sergeant," he replied sullenly.

Entrusted as watch-house keeper, Terry feared the slightly built policeman would deliberately scuttle the plan if given half a chance. He could do little but hope for co-operation. *"God, save*

---

[32] A fictitious name for obvious reasons.

me from these unprofessional fools," he thought despairingly.

It was the middle of winter and bitingly cold, with a strong wind blowing off the snow capped Nelson ranges to the south. Terry was grateful for the loyalty of his team whom he had assigned to the unenviable task of standing for hours on exposed rooftops while they waited hopefully for something to happen. Rugged up in heavy woollen greatcoats and thick clothing, they were as prepared as they could be for long nights of inactivity and misery. Their uncomplaining willingness to volunteer for the operation was testimony to career dedication and loyalty to their young sergeant. The disparate group comprised Ian Etheridge, a bespectacled, verbose senior constable who had served in Nelson for twelve years, Wayne Fordham a diminutive, self-confident practical joker, Steve Oakland a cocky but likeable young probationer and Ike Proctor, a moustached, cheerful, stocky Maori who was everyone's favourite.

As the operation advanced, the surveillance team was instrumental in the apprehension of youths in a stolen car and in relaying the descriptions of disorderly youths to the night shift, proving the worth of such an operation. Still, they were not satisfied. Their target and justification for the operation seemed to be lying low and they worried that somehow the safe breakers had been tipped-off. Dressed in old, black trousers, navy jumper and a black, woollen balaclava, Terry chose to prowl alone, checking the myriad of untidy yards and deserted industrial premises of the Nelson Port area, hoping to catch burglars unaware.

Having thoroughly checked the entire Port industrial area, he parked the little Escort van in the shadows, convinced that all the premises in that locality were until that moment, secure. From his vantage point, he could watch the only road leading into the industrial subdivision. He settled down to wait, pulling the collar of his heavy, black woollen coat up against the biting cold.

He'd been there for thirty minutes when the local security patrol officer drove past, flashing his spotlight in a cursory inspection of nearby buildings. The guard failed to see Terry, although the white glare illuminated his position.

"Useless bugger!" Terry muttered.

A few moments later, the patrol returned, speeding past and leaving the Port area to Terry's vigilance. A further period of inactivity followed. Despite this, he felt alert and tense, sensing that something must surely happen soon. Despite the thick black woollen gloves and a balaclava pulled down around his ears, the cold seeped through, chilling him to the bone. He shifted uncomfortably in the hard bucket seat, blowing on his hands and hugging himself to conserve body warmth. Suddenly, a pair of headlights flashed, lighting the deserted thoroughfare as a vehicle turned into the street. Sitting up quickly, Terry reached for the ignition key, firing the little four-cylinder engine into life.

It was too early for any of the fishermen to be coming down to their boats and with the port city in the grip of winter, courting couples or normal, respectable people would be home snuggled up warmly in their beds.

A sedan passed, the yellow streetlights briefly illuminating at least four heads. Driving purposefully, the car continued along the road slowing and stopping beside a chandlery store. A rear door opened and a figure slipped into the darkened alley beside the building.

"Nelson watch-house, from alpha golf, over?" Terry called the control centre to alert backup.

"Nelson receiving, alpha golf." Frank Jones sleepy voice carried an edge of impatience. *"I've probably disturbed his forty winks,"* Terry thought before answering, his hand cupped around the microphone to contain his urgent whisper. "Nelson, I have a suspicious vehicle with four occupants in the Port area. They have just dropped one person beside Fifeshire Marine. I have been unable to obtain the rego but the vehicle is a dark coloured 1978 Toyota Corolla. It fits the description of that one knocked off from Mauitipu yesterday." Suddenly, he was shouting, the need for secrecy gone. "Hang on! He's taking off. Get City 'I' heading this way. I'm giving pursuit!"

Terry did not know whether the sound of his two-way radio or the Escort's idling engine alerted the occupants of the Toyota to his presence but the stolen vehicle was about to escape. Gunning the engine, the driver of the Toyota accelerated rapidly, tyres squealing in protest as the vehicle made a desperate U-turn, its occupants anxious lest the police block the only exit from the area.

Terry knew there was little he could do on his own, other than try to follow the other vehicle. Slamming the van into gear, he released the clutch, at the same time stamping the accelerator pedal to the floor. With gravel spurting from the spinning tyres, the little van shot from the darkness to give chase as the Toyota sped past. The faces of the stolen vehicle's occupants showed whitely in the Escort's headlights as they turned to inspect their pursuer.

As he followed the fleeing sedan, Terry frantically steered with one hand while shouting a running commentary into the microphone held in his left hand. The lively little Escort with its manual gearbox proved a good match for the stolen car. The Toyota's headlights went off as the little car dodged and weaved through the narrow streets of Nelson's hillside suburbs.

"The bugger seems to know his way around." Terry cursed. Each time he thought the offenders would be trapped in a cul de sac or dead end street, the driver veered off at the last moment, flooring the accelerator pedal. Throwing the Escort around the bends and squeezing every revolution possible from the protesting engine before changing gears, Terry pitied the future owner of the van who would never know the punishment it had suffered in a police chase.

"It looks like we're heading for Wainui Road. We'll come out somewhere near the hospital. Try and cut him off there!" The sole night shift patrol had responded to Terry's call and following his running commentary, was trying to outguess the driver of the stolen vehicle.

Every policeman loves the adrenalin rush of a good chase. Beat cops enjoying a meal break at the station, left their half-eaten hamburgers and seized the nearest idle patrol car from the police yard in the hope of joining the fun.

Terry's prediction that the stolen car would exit the hilly streets for the more open road where they could outrun the Escort proved correct. What the youths didn't count on was the reception committee waiting for them. As the Toyota threatened to outrun him, the police Holden seemingly appeared from nowhere, its lights flashing as its driver cut off the fleeing vehicle. With their escape blocked, the stolen vehicle's doors flew open as its occupants tumbled out, preparing to scarper. As they did so, Terry and Rod Curtis, the police dog handler, arrived simultaneously, sliding to a halt either side of the stolen Toyota. With the maniacal barking of the agitated police dog resounding through the mausoleum quiet of suburban streets, the three youths surrendered at once, no doubt harbouring vivid mental pictures of canine teeth snapping at their respective buttocks.

During questioning, the three offenders denied off loading an accomplice in the Port area. Knowing they were lying, Terry immediately decided to reconnoitre the area where the chase had commenced in the hope of locating the fourth offender, or discovering evidence of a burglary.

Parking the little Escort, still ticking as its hot metal contracted after the chase, the lanky sergeant crept noiselessly along the alley where he had last seen the fourth youth. In the interest of stealth, he chose to leave his torch switched off, navigating from his intimate knowledge of the area and the faint reflection of the sleeping city's lights reflected off the languid waters of the harbour. He checked the chandlery, and finding no sign of intrusion, ventured further into the bowels of the boat yards. Various marine craft of disparate shape and size littered the area, some propped upright, others sitting in special cradles to facilitate repair or maintenance. Taking great care to avoid the myriad of obstacles, such as, lengths of steel, wood, chains, ropes and other flotsam associated with the business of boat building, Terry picked his way through the maze.

Deciding his quest was fruitless, he turned to make his way back to the van. At that moment, the unmistakable crack of a rifle discharging galvanised him into action. Not knowing where the rifleman was, Terry decided discretion was the better part of valour. Whether the shooter intended to scare him or hit him, he was not going to wait around to find out. Ducking and weaving to ensure he presented the most difficult target possible, he ran among the boats, hoping that he was no longer silhouetted against the backdrop of city lights. Every second seemed eternal and the skin between his shoulder blades cringed in anticipation of the assassin's bullet.

Mercifully, there was no second shot. From the protection of the chandlery building, he quickly surveyed the area from which he had retreated. There was only silence to mock him. *Where had the shot come from?* He waited but there was nothing. Not the crunch of a boot on gravel or the rustle of cloth as his assailant changed position. Just total silence, except for the pounding of his own heart, which he felt certain could be heard fifty feet away. None of the craft showed a tell-tale light and who ever fired the shot was probably watching and waiting for him to show himself. As Terry forced his racing brain to a calmer state, reason prevailed.

"I've probably disturbed some boat owner or fisherman who thought I was up to no good," he decided. It was a reasonable assumption. Clad in black and wearing a balaclava while sneaking among the boats it was a logical conclusion for anyone to draw. Deciding it was best to not to take chances just in case there was an armed assailant loose, he backed the Escort several hundred metres along the road to safety before switching on its' headlights

"Nelson Watch-house from Alpha Golf. Ten Ten!" His voice assumed a higher pitch than usual as he battled for self-control. Although he had previously faced numerous potentially life-threatening situations, being shot at unnerved him more than he liked to admit.

With the young sergeant's use of the priority radio code, Frank Jones voice replied immediately. "Nelson receiving, Alpha Golf. Over!"

Using as few words as possible, Terry related events. "I think it best that the Armed Offenders Section be called out to check this out," he concluded, suddenly feeling foolish. *Why not just ignore it,* a little voice in his head nagged. *No, bugger it. When someone's shooting at you, you can't ignore it,* he argued with himself.

"Roger, sergeant. I'm calling them now." Jones decisive voice carried no hint of derision or mockery, and to some extent seemed to vindicate Terry's instruction.

Chubby Whatman was the first to arrive. Making the decision to go directly to the scene rather than follow the usual procedure of kitting up at the police station, Whatman, although attired in his A.O.S. uniform, was sporting two rifles from his private collection. Thrusting one into Terry's hands, his sneer as Terry failed to conceal a very noticeable tremble was blatantly obvious.

"It's bloody cold!" Terry announced, following the direction of the A.O.S. Commanders gaze.

Chubby merely grinned knowingly. "So what happened?"

Terry relayed events quickly, all the time glancing back to the scene. "It's probably some fisherman who thought I was going to break into one of the boats and took a pot shot to scare me off," he concluded.

"What did the shot sound like? Was it a crack or bang? Did you hear the whine of a projectile before you heard the retort? What sort of weapon do you reckon it was?" Chubby seemed not to believe his fellow sergeant.

"I think it was most probably just a twenty two." Terry answered, referring to the small calibre rifle he guessed the shooter had used.

The rest of the A.O.S. section began arriving. Whatman, in business like fashion, detailed section members to conduct a search of the boatyard. Terry and he waited beside the Escort van. After several minutes, the tall well-built figure of Pat Carson approached, jogging along the road, his curly hair bouncing from beneath his black beret. "We've checked right through the boatyard. Couldn't find anything. What now?" Pat's expression, unlike Whatman's was impassive.

Terry spoke first, embarrassed at having caused such disruption. 'Let's just forget about it. It's probably just as I said. Some fisherman thought I was a burglar and tried to scare me off."

"Well, he certainly succeeded." Chubby laughed mockingly. "Okay, boys. Let's go home to bed."

I wonder how he would have reacted in the same circumstances, Terry thought bitterly. *The little fat shit most probably would have sat in the car and ordered one of his troops to go down the dark alley.*

On the fifth night of the stakeout, the streets were deserted as even the hardiest of souls had sought refuge from the chill winter wind. While parked at his earlier vantage point in the Port area, fatigue had caused Terry to slumber as the radio suddenly crackled rudely into life.

"Nelson 'I' car from Nelson, over?" Frank Jones voice carried an urgency that galvanised Terry into expectant wakefulness.

"Nelson 'I', receiving." The tired voice of Peter Watson suggested he and his companion had been snoozing somewhere.

"Nelson 'I', the alarm at Hardy Spicers has just activated. Please attend."

"Bugger him," Terry swore. The Hardy Street hardware store was one of the robbers' most likely targets on his contingency plans. *Why couldn't Frank follow the procedures he had so carefully devised?* Hissing an exasperated oath, he turned the ignition key, firing the little Ford Escort Van's engine. With the accelerator pedal slammed to the floor, the van shot from the shadows, the rear tyres leaving a black swathe of rubber on the frosty concrete surface. Terry knew his team would already be racing on foot to surround the hardware store. He prayed they would get there in time. Within a few short moments, he skidded to a halt in the gravel car park.

Ian Etheridge emerged from the gloom to meet him. "We're too bloody late. They've already gone."

So close were they behind the robbers, they could almost smell their presence in the room containing the old steel safe. A gaping hole in the ceiling showed rusting corrugated roof sheets torn back, revealing the burglar's entry and escape route. Terry was furious. With the little Rhodesian's pig headed refusal to acquiesce to instructions from any sergeant other than his, they had lost their one chance to catch the burglars, squandering in a mere second the sacrifice his team had made in the pursuit of the good name and reputation of the New Zealand Police Service.

There was nothing more to do but abandon the entire operation. With the bandits tipped off, it seemed unlikely that they would dare to strike again. Indeed, there were no more break-ins with the same modus operandi.

"Look on the bright side." Bert Barber tried to assuage his sergeant's disappointment. "The operation was responsible for some good catches. You've deterred the safe breakers, so it was a great success!"

Terry was far from placated. He felt certain his team could have captured the culprits had his plan been followed. It was a cruel anti-climax to such devoted determination.

Nelson's growing problem with bikie gangs peaked during the summer of 1979. With the annual Nelson summer Mardi Gras in full swing, the local Jaycees had blocked off the main Street through the business district for celebrations. A festive air prevailed as bands played and happy holidaymakers and families gathered for the balmy evening of partying and family fun.

In an effort to raise funds for their diving club, the Tasman Bay Aquanauts, Terry, Rod Curtis and other club members attended the entry gates, collecting admissions fees for the Mardi Gras organising committee. In return, they were to receive a share of the events proceeds. A general bonhomie prevailed and the sordid side of Nelson's criminal underclass could not have been further from everyone's mind.

A pair of uniformed constables patrolled Endeavour Street, their white "Bobby" helmets, sunglasses, short sleeve shirts and relaxed manner blending with the partying holidaymakers. Nobody expected trouble, least of all the beat cops, who laughed and joked with members of the crowd as they sauntered along the pavement, ogling the scantily clad, suntanned bodies of young women who feigned indifference to the constable's attention.

Overriding the music and summer frivolity, the thunder of Harley Davidson motorcycles unexpectedly shattered the happy atmosphere.

Parking their powerful gleaming machines outside the old Nelson Hotel and the steps of the adjacent Cathedral, a group of forty or so unkempt tattooed, hirsute motor cyclists from a North Island gang prepared to invade the popular family event. Their filthy torn denim jackets, shiny steel-capped boots and arrogant swagger leaving little doubt as to their intentions. Within minutes of dismounting, the news of the gang's presence mysteriously reached Lost Breed Headquarters.

Enraged, the Lost Breed swarmed like angry wasps to eject the foreign invaders. With gang headquarters mere minutes from the city centre, they tumbled from a motley collection of available cars, vans and motorbikes, before the visitors had time to infiltrate the mardis gras. Wielding motorcycle chains, baseball bats and other makeshift weapons, the local hoodlums stormed toward the rival gang.

The shrill rattle of a postman's whistle carried clearly above the cacophony of the festivities. Rallying quickly in obedience to the coded whistle blasts from their leader, the visitors responded, each adopting a well-rehearsed position for battle. Almost miraculously, they produced their own hitherto concealed arsenal.

Clashing before the high stone steps of Nelson Cathedral, the two gangs viciously clubbed, stabbed, and punched each other in a maelstrom of frenzied hatred as shocked family groups scattered for shelter.

Caught unaware, Dave Allen and his officers, raced to the scene. With only five uniformed personnel on duty at the time, Allen's men bravely forced a wedge between the combatants, suffering various injuries in the process. Clubbed by a baseball bat, Probationer Steve Oakland fell to the pavement concussed. Miraculously avoiding a depressed fractured skull by the slimmest of margins, he managed to identify his attacker before he fell.

Upon hearing the commotion, Terry and Rod Curtis ran to support their comrades. Unarmed and in casual attire, Terry accepted a baton gratefully from one of Dave Allen's struggling men. Wading into the melee, he wielded the weapon against the bikies. Eventually, they forced a path between the opposing gangs, shoving the angry Lost Breed louts back against a building by desperate brute force. Realising the affray was over for the time; the visiting gang gathered its wounded comrades and hastily departed. With insufficient police numbers to affect arrests among so many enraged gangsters, they released the Lost Breed, ordering their return to gang headquarters forthwith.

Unable to tolerate such outrageous public disorder without retribution, they regrouped at police headquarters. Sergeant Allen called for reinforcements and notified the off duty district commander, "Honest" John McCarthy, who hurried to headquarters after hastily donning his uniform. Despite the urgency, McCarthy had taken time to make sure he was impeccably dressed as usual. A rapid-fire briefing session followed, attended by every available police officer from the station's contingent of sixty five personnel.

They formed a plan for the Armed Offenders Squad to descend upon the bikie lair in an initial assault, containing the Lost Breed and negating any armed resistance. The unarmed uniform members were to then raid the house and apprehend the gang, charging them with unlawful assembly and aggravated assault on police.

As the A.O.S. approached the high corrugated iron ramparts of the bikie fortress, the unmistakable heavy metallic sound of a rifle bolt slammed into the breech of an unseen rifle carried through the now darkened streets. Expecting an assault, either by the rival gang or police, the Lost Breed prepared themselves for battle. Dissolving quickly into the shadows the A.O.S. surrounded the makeshift corrugated iron ramparts, containing the bikies and preventing their escape.

As Terry ran through the darkness to take up position in the vacant block behind the building, the ground unexpectedly collapsed beneath his booted feet. A score of panicked thoughts of the horror that might lie below rushed through his brain as he fell some two metres into a mantrap. He landed heavily, spread-eagled in the bottom of the pit, immediately grateful that the architect of the device had not yet installed nails or spikes to impale him. Clambering over the soft earth of the surrounding embankment, he sprawled flat on the ground with his telescopic sighted .223 Bruno rifle trained on the darkened silhouette of the gang's headquarters. Although he could not see other members of the squad, Terry knew his men would be in position. With a quick radio check, he confirmed the Lost Breed would not escape the cordon.

Within minutes, the main contingent of police assembled in the quiet suburban street at the front of the makeshift fortress directing powerful tripod mounted spotlights into gang headquarters. The electronic squeal of the loud hailer carried clearly through the still night air as Honest John called on the gang to surrender. "Members of the Lost Breed, this is Superintendent McCarthy of the Nelson Police. I have a search warrant to enter and search these premises. I call on you to turn on your lights, open the gates and come peaceably outside in order that we may execute that warrant."

There was no answer or sign of life from inside the old weatherboard house. Although neighbouring homes were in darkness and the streets still, everyone sensed the residents of Worthington Valley would be hanging on every word, watching unobtrusively from curtained windows.

"They'll be thinking it over. Give them another call sir." Bert Barber suggested to his superior.

McCarthy raised the portable amplifier and pressed the trigger again. "We have men from the Nelson Armed Offenders Section positioned around your headquarters. There is also a large contingent of officers stationed outside. I suggest you do not delay or resist. Open the gate and come outside at once." The authoritarian tone of the senior policeman's voice carried with it the threat of force.

Within the darkened wooden building, the Lost Breed held a hurried conference. Unable to see the uniformed police surrounding them, their leaders decided prudently not to resist. The stocky hirsute figure Darby Walsh, shuffled into view as the heavy corrugated iron gates swung open.

"In you go men. Arrest them all!" McCarthy commanded. Without further ado, the police arrest squad swarmed into the yard and through the narrow front door. Bundling the gang outside after some minor protestations and scuffles, they forced each of the bikies to sit on the ground with their hands on their heads. One by one, the arrest squad searched and photographed the entire complement before ordering them into waiting police vans.

Fifty or more Lost Breed bikies stretched the Nelson Police Headquarters tiny cellblock to capacity. There was no room for further arrests and Superintendent McCarthy was in an invidious position. Conferring with his senior sergeants, McCarthy stated, "We have an unhappy quandary here. I would like to accommodate every one of these characters and have them before the Justices in the morning, charged with rioting and assault. However, to cram the rival gang into the same cellblock as the Lost Breed is to court disaster.

"We'd never control them. On the other hand, if I let them go there'll be accusations of persecution of our local thugs. Even though we can bring the others up on summons, the Lost Breed will be convinced we're playing favourites. Do you have any suggestions?" McCarthy asked.

Pat Bickley's sad sack face beneath his curly grey hair was even more pensive than normal. "We'll just have to live with that. We can't afford to do anything else. I suggest we establish the identity of each of the rival gang members and then run them out of town as quickly as possible!"

"I agree sir." Bert Barber stroked his chin thoughtfully. "If we get the Lost Breed convicted, most of them will go away for a long time and we won't have to worry about that problem for some time."

"Right then! We'll send a team down to the back beach where they're camped. Confiscate any weapons, confirm identities and make it clear that charges will follow. Don't bother with interviews. As long as we know who they are we'll charge the lot with unlawful assembly and possession of offensive weapons."

McCarthy's prediction that the Lost Breed would harbour resentment at their incarceration while the rival gang appeared to walk free proved prophetic. Although some heavy prison sentences resulted from lengthy court proceedings, the bulk of the gang received only monetary penalties or short periods of incarceration. The Lost Breed regrouped quickly and whereas a healthy respect had hereto existed between the group and the police, gang members now became openly hostile toward the Nelson constabulary as simmering tensions grew.

The Nelson Armed Offenders Section functioned well until 1979 despite Chubby blustering autocratic leadership style. Terry acknowledged Whatman's superior experience in matters concerning the A.O.S. and readily accepted a subservient role while he increased his knowledge and experience. However, he often silently questioned the logic of his second in command's tactical decisions. As he gained in confidence and experience, conflict with Chubby would become inevitable.

Despite the transfer to Nelson, Terry and Jane's marriage continued to deteriorate with remarkable similarities between the town in which they lived and their relationship. While Nelson sat on a major geological fault line and waited for the inevitable earthquake, Terry and Jane's marital earthquake had already struck and their temple of wedlock teetered on the edge of an abyss. Despite an urgent need of some substantial shoring up of marital foundations, Jane continued to live in denial, maintaining a façade of sweetness and light in the presence of all but their closest friends. Privately her attitude toward Terry was aloof and cold, driving him to the conclusion that she considered him to be nothing more than the financial provider and home handyperson. Despite his frequent attempts to have them attend marriage counselling to work through their problems, she stubbornly refused, maintaining that mediation was merely an attempt by her long-suffering spouse to manipulate her.

Frustrated and miserable, the final straw for Terry came when, without any consultation, Jane agreed to a friend's request to look after her two small children for an extended period. With no say in the matter and his nerves already strained to breaking point from severe sleep deprivation, two more toddlers in an already cramped house was just too much for him to cope with. Packing a few belongings, he left home, having found a tiny flat above an old but graceful inner city mansion, owned by an elderly spinster.

The sudden departure of her spouse came as a shock to Jane, who now had to cope alone with six small children. Never having worked shift work and with an amazing tolerance for chaos, she could not understand why, after working nightshift, Terry would have difficulty sleeping during the day or, why he possessed such a limited capacity to deal with so many noisy and boisterous youngsters.

When his shifts permitted, Terry arranged to have his children visit. Little Helen was too young to understand why the people she loved most could not be together. He attempted unsuccessfully to explain, struggling to put things into context for her innocent five-year old mind.

"But, daddy, why can't you and mummy get along with each other?" she cried plaintively.

I can't bear what's happening to the kids, he thought, feeling as if his heart was being plucked from his chest. *Somehow, I have to try to make things work out.* Often at night, almost overcome with despair, he wandered for hours through the deserted streets searching his soul for a solution.

It was during this period that Terry's close friend, Noel Hanlon discovered his wife Lois's infidelity. After cramming a few possessions in a small suitcase, Noel arrived at Terry's one bedroom flat in an extremely distraught state. A quietly spoken, solidly built man in his early thirties, Noel had once been a boxing champion, although this rarely showed through his gentle nature. Standing over six feet in height, with straight, jet black hair and dark eyes, the big man became angry slowly.

"I've left the missus. She's been having it off with some joker. I can't bear to be near her. Can you put me up for a while?" he pleaded, his eyes red from hours of miserable sobbing.

"Oh, shit. You poor bastard. Of course, I will. There's not much room, but you're welcome to have the little sitting room at the front," Terry commiserated, hurrying to re-arrange the tiny balcony room adjoining his lounge into a makeshift bedroom.

Although Noel's company was welcome, Terry's separation was an extremely bleak period, which occurred during the latter part of his second year in the Nelson A.O.S. It also coincided with a callout to an isolated Mauitipu farmhouse during the early hours of one typically cold winter's morning. Concerned by the sound of screaming and gunfire, neighbours had telephoned the Nelson police station.

Living only a short walking distance from the headquarters, Terry was first to arrive at the small outside vault containing their equipment and weaponry. Attired in his black uniform, comprising jumper, woollen trousers, ankle-length boots and beret, he commandeered two police vehicles, a patrol car and a Bedford prison van. Loading two heavy plywood boxes containing loud hailers, spotlights, teargas launcher and other assorted equipment in the van's rear compartment, he had only a few moments to wait before the first of his team arrived. Equipped with only limited information and lacking any knowledge as to the identity of the shooter, or the reason behind the gunfire, he briefed his stocky section commander and other team members.

They lost no time driving to the scene. Chubby commandeered the Upper Moutere community hall as his command post and directed Terry and his men to surround and contain the farmhouse.

The A.O.S. approached cautiously, dispersing to various points around the darkened dwelling. With no moon, the night was as black as pitch. Frost covered the paddocks and a low fog made the positioning of troops extremely difficult. Nevertheless, the elite black clad weapons and tactical experts crept along the hedgerows, closing in on the now silent building. Alert for the slightest foreign sound or movement, they positioned themselves, lying spread eagled beneath thickets, telescopic sighted rifles pointing toward the target zone.

Spreading his topographical maps in the dry warmth and relative comfort of the old hall, Chubby was a safe distance

266

outside the general duties personnel forming an armed outer cordon. Impatient for a quick resolution to the perilous situation, the despotic sergeant called for a SITREP.

Terry responded, whispering into the microphone of his small portable radio, "Scene Commander from Field. We have positioned ourselves around the subject dwelling. There is no sign of life and we are unable to distinguish anything from our various locations due to the darkness. In the absence of further information or developments, I recommend we wait until first light before we make any move." He could well imagine the dictatorial sergeant pacing agitatedly inside the hall. Inactivity did not sit easily with Chubby.

"Roger!" Chubby's dissatisfaction with his Field Commander's decision was evident in every syllable of his laconic response. However, with the responsibility for the safety of his team resting heavily on his shoulders, Terry was not about to engage in rash actions. To approach more closely across the open terrain without knowing what they might face, was to invite tragedy. There was nothing to lose by simply waiting. Terry's hushed communication by two-way radio with his front line men, confirmed this was the best course of action, despite the chilly dampness penetrating the thick material of their uniforms.

They had been in position for nearly an hour, when the sound of booted feet shuffling slowly along the nearby asphalt surface of the country road disturbed the nocturnal calm, alarming Terry. Using his radio, Terry called urgently to each of his men, confirming that the footsteps did not belong to an A.O.S. member. With the only policemen permitted so close to the danger zone being A.O.S. members, he asked himself, *is the person walking along the road friend or foe?*

Positioning himself to sight his rifle toward the approaching footsteps, Terry waited. Although he could not see his hand in front of his face, a pale moon, shining dimly through thick grey clouds, provided sufficient light for him to distinguish the black tip of his rifle's foresight silhouetted against the night sky. Flicking off the safety catch, he waited, index finger resting against the trigger guard. Suddenly, the silhouette of a darkly clad male figure loomed directly in front of him. Stopping within a few metres, the man seemed to sense Terry's presence and turned toward his position. Terry could distinguish that he held a rifle in readiness across his body. Poised to squeeze his trigger, there was no way Terry could miss his target at such a short range.

"This is the police. Identify yourself!" At the first sound of Terry's voice, the armed man stiffened. With his finger tightening on the trigger, it needed only one small hostile gesture for Terry to fire. With a chilling certainty, he knew in that split second, he would not hesitate to kill.

"It's alright Terry. It's only me." The inimitable, nasally, high-pitched voice of Constable Brian "Shudders" Ryan immediately defused that dreadful moment. Terry relaxed, lowering the barrel of his rifle.

"Shudders, you stupid bastard! What the hell are you doing inside the cordon? You nearly got yourself shot!" Relieved and angry at the skinny policeman's disobedience of procedures, Terry felt physically sick. "Get the hell out of here now," he commanded in an urgent whisper.

Unabashed, Shudders wandered off into the night.

"Christ," Terry muttered to Rod Curtis, who waited a few feet away with his police dog. "That was bloody close."

A few moments later the radio crackled into life, "Sergeant Flatley from Whatman. Over?" Chubby' patience had run out. "I want you to take your men and approach the farm house to find out what's happened there."

"It's alright for him," Terry muttered. "He's not going to run the risk of getting shot. Pressing the microphone switch, he replied, "Whatman from Flatley. Negative to your last. I say we wait until daylight. I do not deem it safe to approach the house until then."

Unbeknown to Terry, Whatman had been in touch by telephone, with his former friend and associate, Chief Inspector England, outlining his plan to storm the farmhouse. England, as acting district commander in McCarthy's absence, did not appreciate the danger to which Terry and his troops were exposed. He readily concurred with his A.O.S. Commander's decision.

"I am instructing you to take your men and clear the scene," Chubby repeated tersely.

"And **I** repeat; I do not deem that course of action safe. We will wait until daylight!" Terry reiterated stubbornly.

With no alternative other than to accept his field commander's decision, Chubby fumed at his loss of face. He wasted no time in reporting Terry's mutiny to the acting district commander, confident that retribution would surely follow.

With a faint blue tinge behind the low rolling hills, finally heralding the approach of dawn, Terry and his team cautiously crept to the still silent cottage. Pushing open the door, they found it empty and deserted. With no sign of blood, bodies or foul play, there was nothing to do but pack up and return to base. They decided to attribute the report of shots and screaming to a hoax, or perhaps, just trigger happy larrikins playing the fool.

On the squad's return to headquarters, they unpacked their gear and disbanded. Whatman still smarted from Terry's disobedience, refusing to discuss the matter with his counterpart or arrange the customary debriefing session despite Terry wanting an explanation for Shudders incursion into the dangerous area of the inner cordon. With two rostered days off scheduled, Terry leapt in his car and headed back to the little upstairs flat.

Noel was waiting for him. Employed as an inspector for the Apple and Pear Marketing Board, his quietly spoken friend had invited Terry to accompany him on a work related trip to the West Coast. Knowing Noel suffered terribly from depression following his wife's infidelity, Terry agreed to go. He was genuinely concerned his friend would do something foolish, such as, aim his car into a roadside tree in a tragic suicide attempt.

Terry's fears proved well founded, for Noel admitted on their return that he had intended to do just that, had Terry not accompanied him.

When Terry resumed work, Chief Inspector Holland summonsed him to the district commander's office. Although he suspected he was in for a torrid time, he had no idea just how torrid it would be.

Whether the chief inspector had ever worked undercover in his earlier career, Terry didn't know but England was one of those nondescript people with a forgettable face and a humourless personality. His clean-shaven, squarish features, below short-cropped greying hair and grey eyes, weren't exactly handsome, but they weren't ugly either. Without his immaculate police uniform and the ostentatious row of silver pips on their stiff shoulder boards, he may have been mistaken for a real estate or car salesman.

The acting commander didn't invite Terry to sit. Instead, he stared unsmilingly at the young sergeant his face impassive. Terry stood before the highly polished mahogany desk occupying most of the overly tidy Nelson's district commander office. *Here we go again. This is going to be another case of 'the little man syndrome',* Terry guessed.

"You wanted to see me, sir?" Terry asked, breaking the silence.

"Yes. Sergeant Whatman has complained that you wouldn't follow orders during the Mauitipu incident. We can't have this sort of thing going on during an armed offender's operation!" England accused Terry sternly.

"I presume you are referring to the fact that I refused to storm the house? Well, if that's the case, I am not prepared to jeopardise the safety of police officers in the field. We didn't know what we would be walking into. We had insufficient information and no idea of the layout of the house, which was in complete darkness. By barging in, we may well have placed the life of a hostage in jeopardy had it been a siege situation. I stand by my decision. It's all right for Sergeant Whatman, sitting back in his warm command post, to order us to clear a house because he's bored with sitting around, but he wasn't in a position to judge whether it was safe or not. I was."

Terry's rebuttal seemed to go straight over the little Chief inspector's stubbled head. *He's not even interested in what I've got to say,* he realised. *I might just as well talk to a deaf man because he's ready to hang me out to dry whatever explanation I offer.*

"I understand that when you got back to headquarters, you were in a hurry to rush off and weren't prepared to attend the usual debrief. It seems your heart isn't in the job."

Stunned by this accusation, Terry couldn't believe that Whatman would give such a distorted version of events to avenge himself. "That's absolutely not true. I am completely dedicated to the Armed Offenders Squad and will continue to give it everything I've got. It was Sergeant Whatman who didn't want to hold the debrief. The operation was over and I had arrangements in place to go away on my days off."

Terry's protests reminded him how he had felt when, as a schoolboy he had once been caught stuffing a potato up the exhaust pipe of a teacher's car. *For Christ's sake, I am not the one at fault here. England and Whatman have obviously conspired to make me the villain.*

England played his final ace. "I also understand that you have separated from your wife. I think your emotional stability is in question and that you should relinquish your position as second in command of the Nelson A.O.S."

The statement came with all the force of a punch to his lower abdomen. His jaw dropped in amazement. "Are you suggesting that I am so emotionally unstable that I am a danger to others?" His rage rose like a hot wave, spreading up the back of his neck and across his cheeks until he fought for self-control. "This is absolute bullshit!"

"We can't be too careful in cases like this. I want you to tender your resignation from the squad."

"You mean you're sacking me. I've never been sacked from anything in my life. I resent any inference that I have not been doing my job to the best of my ability and that I will not continue to do so. I also resent your inference that I am unstable. My private affairs have nothing to do with my position on the Armed Offenders Squad and in no way affects my performance. I am outraged and insulted. This is a slur on my character and reputation and is completely unjust. I hope Whatman has also informed you, that one of the constables on the outer cordon nearly got himself shot because he disobeyed instructions?"

England brushed Ryan's indiscretion aside. "That's not the issue here. sergeant, you are no longer a member of the Nelson Armed Offenders Squad."

"It's clear to me that you and Chubby have got together on this just because I bucked his rash and dangerous decision to send men into a potentially life threatening situation. Well, if that is the way *you* run things, its better that I am not involved with the squad, because I am never going to put lives at stake, no matter who orders me to do so." Without waiting for the customary dismissal, the irate N.C.O. turned on his heel and stormed from the commander's office.[33]

---

[33] Many years later, Terry learnt that after domestic troubles Whatman'

He took his sacking hard. Although he toyed with idea of appealing to John McCarthy when he returned from leave for an unbiased re-assessment of his handling of the Mauitipu incident, as he had come to call it, he dismissed the idea. He would seek vindication by other means. *Give the bastard enough rope. He'll eventually hang himself,* he decided of his rotund former A.O.S. compatriot.

Contrary to the opinions of England and Whatman, he wore the A.O.S. uniform and membership of the elite squad with considerable pride. He cared little for the gossip running rife among the police community surrounding his ignominious fall from grace. Had he known his decision not to storm the farmhouse would have such drastic consequences, he would have acted no differently. What rankled most were the injustice and Chubby smugness at his victory. He resolved to get on with his normal policing duties and put the painful episode behind him. He missed his children dreadfully and the added humiliation of his dismissal came as a body blow.

Unfortunately, further bad news lurked around the corner.

After one particularly harrowing afternoon shift, Terry looked forward to the quiet sanctuary of the little upstairs flat. His flat mate seemed on edge as he entered. The ex-pugilist sucked heavily on a hand rolled cigarette, expelling the pungent smoke noisily. "How was your day?" he enquired.

"Oh, the usual domestic disputes, drunks and pub fights. Just time consuming stuff and the frustrations of idiots who can't seem to exist without calling the police to solve their petty little problems. Honestly, I get sick and tired of handling this crap." Flicking the cap from a bottle of beer, he flopped into a chair. "Heard any more from the missus?"

"No. The vindictive bitch isn't going to make things easy for me. If I want to see the kids, I'm going to have to fight a battle for access through the Courts. She's doing everything she can to poison their minds against me." Noel stubbed his fag end viciously into an ashtray. "Terry, I can't stand this. I don't have the energy to waste on all this crap. She's got everything, the house, the car, the furniture... What more does the bloody

---

personal firearms were confiscated by police concerned that the gun happy N.C.O. would run amok following his own domestic problems.

272

woman want from me? I'm not the one who's been unfaithful. I can't take any more. It's eating me up."

Terry stared anxiously at his friend. "I know mate. At least I can see my kids. What are you going to do?"

"I've already done it. I've chucked in my job and I'm going to Christchurch. I'll live with my parents until I get back on my feet."

Noel's ageing parents would no doubt be glad to help their tormented son and Terry was pleased that Noel had their support. However, the news was another body-blow. "I'll be really sorry to see you go. We've got along really well over the past few months," he stated quietly, a sinking feeling churning at his intestines. Until now he had not appreciated how much he valued the companionship of his grieving friend. "Who's going to cook dinner for me now?" he joked.

They were both proficient in the kitchen and as each took turns at meal preparation, Noel immediately understood the comment was intended to distract Terry from becoming maudlin. "You'll have to go back to living on baked beans I 'suppose," he retorted

Having made the decision to leave, Noel lost no time in packing his few pathetic possessions into two battered suitcases. Having little money and no vehicle, he booked a seat on the Newman's coach, due to depart the following morning for Christchurch.

As he was rostered to start work at 5.00 am, Terry left the flat before his friend awoke. He penned a short note wishing Noel good luck and imploring him to keep in touch.

That afternoon, he dreaded returning to the empty flat, spending time walking along the grassy banks of the nearby Maitai River, reappraising his own situation. Too young to understand their father's pain in an unworkable marriage, his children were suffering badly from the separation, becoming withdrawn and falling behind in their schoolwork. Life would not be much fun for them now and he worried they would somehow see it as their fault that their father no longer lived at home.

After wandering, head down in a trance-like state for over an hour, Terry suddenly straightened his posture, setting his jaw determinedly. Noel's sudden departure had served as the catalyst for the unpalatable decision he had been postponing. *I must put the kids' needs before my own. I somehow have to find the strength to endure the bitter fruit of my stupidity in rushing in to a marriage that was always doomed. It's not the kids' fault.* He felt physically ill at the prospect of returning to the acrimony of his life before the separation. Turning slowly on his heel, he trudged lugubriously toward the nearest telephone box. He felt like an escaped prisoner returning to his cell.

Jane appeared to welcome him back, outwardly resolving to work with him again toward rebuilding their relationship. Terry mentally crossed his fingers, and his four children were overjoyed, tempering his pessimism for marital harmony with an unbridled demonstration of their affection.

However much he tried to reassure himself, Terry knew in his heart that it was only a matter of time before his relationship with Jane degenerated again. *We are just not compatible and should never have married. I'm not the person she needs or wants. She never got over being chucked out of the convent and doesn't love me and never has*, he mused. *I'll stick it out, at least until the kids are old enough to understand and fend for themselves*, he promised.

Although ethnic gangs had existed in New Zealand for decades, the seventies and eighties witnessed exponential growth of an underclass that flaunted normal conventions and scorned the country's laws. Often highly organised and funded through prostitution, drugs and burglary, the problem had become a serious threat to civilised society. Turf wars between various gangs resulted, with bashings and shootings terrorising the Nation's decent law abiding citizens. There were frequent clashes between gangs and the police. Although the problem was worse in the North Island, Christchurch and Dunedin experienced their share of particularly disturbing murders and fire-bombings. It seemed no community enjoyed immunity. Highly mobile, the gangs often joined forces with their affiliates in other centres, terrorising any small community in their path, as they moved about the country.

In response, the police established shadow patrols to follow the mass migration of bikies and other gangs, recording and documenting illegal activity and retaliating when prudent with appropriate charges against the miscreants. Often instituting impromptu searches for weapons, while simultaneously 'reading

274

the riot act' to gangs prior to embarking on their mass migration, the tactic, although highly effective, placed a heavy strain on police resources. Under normal circumstances, these sorely needed officers could have been deployed proactively on other crime fighting activities; however, the New Zealand police had little choice and knew no other effective method to counter the spreading cancer of organised gangs.

It was a period of immense civil disobedience. New Zealanders may have been excused from thinking they were but one step away from total anarchy. Although it was unlikely that the gangs would put aside their differences to rally en mass against their common enemy, the police, there was always the possibility that a perceived racial infraction or mishandled incident might ignite serious armed conflict.

Largely unarmed, except for small relatively ineffectual wooden batons, the worried police Association pressed the hierarchy in Wellington to better protect and train its members. After researching the various options, the boffins settled on the Monadnock PR 24 baton, a revolutionary device favoured by several United States law enforcement bodies. Constructed from either aluminium or hard plastic, the baton measured twenty-four inches in length and sported a six-inch handle a like distance from one end. In the hands of a trained officer the device could be used effectively in either defence or attack and if one could believe the advertising propaganda, it was a useful tool in all manner of circumstances, none the least being the destruction of wooden doors.

Gripping the handle lightly between the thumb and forefinger, a skilled exponent could rotate the weapon at lightening speed, striking an opponent from various poses, or jabbing and blocking as necessary. Worn on the belt, the PR24 baton was highly visible and blatantly offensive.

For the previously sedate and inoffensive New Zealand Police Service to switch from their warm and fuzzy image to one of open aggression, rightly worried the public relations conscious High Command. They decided to establish elite squads, not unlike the A.O.S. units, to be mobilised in the event of major riots, unrest, or other civil disobedience. Entitled Team Policing Units and comprised of officers skilled in various drill formations for riot control and mass arrest, the elite teams quickly sprang up throughout New Zealand. The new batons now formed an integral part of the police armoury, along with riot shields, groin protectors and Perspex helmets. In addition to these precautions every frontline officer would undergo PR24 baton training notwithstanding, the new baton was not issued for general use.

In the service's often ad hoc manner of implementing new ideas, the Nelson Police district high command chose Terry as its trainer for the new baton. Farcically, unlike other trainers in the new weapon, Terry did not receive the benefit of hands on instruction from the touring American police officer tasked with imparting his skills to the trainers to-be. After handing Terry a cardboard box full of the shiny black weapons, Bert Barber ordered him to read the instruction manual covering the various poses for striking, blocking and jabbing, and formulate a training package to be presented to the Nelson Police district's complement of some 140 frontline men and women. If he was successful, the program, although daunting, carried with it a certain amount of prestige.

First, he had somehow to convince himself of his proficiency with the weapon.

In the privacy of nearby antiquated sheds of the Naval Cadet Training School, Terry propped the book open to the photographs showing the stances favoured by exponents of the strange and unfamiliar device. Gripping the weapon as described, he endeavoured to attack a vinyl punching bag suspended from the rafters of the old drill hall. On his first strike, the baton simply flew from his grasp. *There is clearly more to this than meets the eye*, he decided, retrieving the baton, glad there was no audience to his excusable ineptitude.

After many hours of practice, he was at last able to spin the baton in the approved fashion and strike the punching bag in forward, backward, inward and outward strikes. Such was the speed of the weapon that each blow left melted green vinyl from the bag on the black tip of PR24. Feeling decidedly foolish, he then set about learning the various martial arts based offensive and defensive techniques, simultaneously exclaiming the appropriate grunts and aggressive cries. He was to learn later that the baton had its origins in Japan, where in the absence of other

276

suitable weapons, peasants in feudal times had adapted a simple rice-harvesting tool as an effective weapon against raiders.

Although the training sessions he conducted throughout the police district seemed to go off well and the majority of the regular members embraced the new crime-fighting tool, Terry never felt confident that he was imparting the skills correctly and would have been far happier had an expert in baton training vindicated his interpretation of the manual.[34]

With the local bikie gang, also growing in strength and daring, Honest John worried there would be a repeat of the mardis gras episode. Calling his crusty senior sergeants together, he sought their counsel. "We've got to clamp down hard on these thugs and somehow show them that they don't rule the day," he instructed. "I want to form a local team policing unit to deal with these louts and to handle any trouble, such as, pub brawls."

Each summer, the population of the pretty, bay side city, swelled threefold by holidaymakers from the colder parts of the South Island. There were inevitable fights fuelled by alcohol and illicit drugs in the region's plethora of hotels.

Bert Barber replied without hesitation. "I agree sir. I've got just the man to lead the unit. Sergeant Flatley's been putting a special licensing squad together each summer for the past few years and has been very effective in keeping the lid on violence and street offences."

"Good choice, Senior," McCarthy nodded. "After his removal from the Armed Offenders Squad, he's been at a loose end. I think this would display our confidence in him and bring him out of the doldrums. He seems to have handled the new baton training program well."

The following day, after dispatching his team to their various duties, Terry was striding purposefully through the watch-house on his way to the patrol cars parked in the station yard. Barber's small office adjoined the station's hub and the door as usual was open. Terry called, "G'dday senior," as he passed and received a "Got a mo sergeant," in reply. He detoured and stood expectantly before his superior's cluttered desk.

---

[34] Terry's concerns were without foundation however, as he and his newly formed Team Policing Unit used the new weapon to good effect on several occasions.

"I've got a request from the boss Terry," Ben stood up smiling good- humouredly.

"Oh. What might that be?" Terry was on his guard immediately. Anything emanating from the Superintendent invariably meant something tedious, unpleasant or it had been successfully handballed down the chain of command.

"The district commander thinks you would be the ideal person to head a local Team Policing Unit."

I suppose this is supposed to make me feel better about my sacking from the A.O.S. Terry deduced. *Oh well. At least it shows they still have some faith in me.* "I'd like to choose my own team if I may, Ben," he suggested confining his use of the tall senior sergeant's first name to those occasions when they were alone.

A mutual respect and liking existed between the two men who had spent some time together on social fishing trips. Although Terry was close to his senior sergeant, he also knew Ben would draw a very straight line in the sand over official police matters.

"Okay, I've no problem with that. Who do you suggest? I'll have to adjust the rosters and fill the gaps on the shifts."

Terry hesitated momentarily, "Tom Harvey, Chad Brough, John Pearson, John Hines and Bob York." Terry's choice encompassed the attributes of size, strength, fitness and maturity. Conscious of the recently relaxed physical entry standards for police recruits, he wanted a team who looked the part when thrown into situations where they would frequently be helplessly outnumbered. "I also want a free hand in training the team. I expect each member to be physically up to the task and that will mean daily workouts, preferably in the department's time."

Ben grinned, "You don't want much, do you?"

"I think team moral and confidence are vital. I want my group to feel special, and bond well, and know that they can depend on each other. That can't be achieved if we just take a bunch of blokes off each shift and throw them in a car to deal with pub brawls."

"It sounds as though you've already thought this through. Okay. You'll cop some flack from the rest of the troops." Ben was alluding to petty jealousy that was about to surface among those who thought they should be chosen.

However, with no time to spend on the niceties of correct staff selection techniques or political correctness, he would handle accusations of misogynous behaviour, favouritism, or racism, when, and if they arose. With the holiday season already upon them, the new squad needed to be on the road immediately.

None of the men on Terry's list hesitated or balked at their secondment to the new team. In fact, all were enthusiastic, welcoming the opportunity for the espirit de corps accompanying the specially chosen group.

During the 1970's, the New Zealand police had no physical fitness standards and no recognised methods for gauging fitness. In fact, the organisation considered physical fitness a matter for the individual. Although there were few officers in the front line in poor shape, the overall standard wasn't far from the optimal. However, the fitness required to perform routine duties fell far short of that needed to deal on a regular basis with mob violence. Terry set about bringing each member of his team to a common level, adopting the universally accepted and demanding physical fitness standards of the Royal Canadian Air Force.

Although he was aware Tom Harvey and Chad Brough would struggle to meet his targets, he remained optimistic their youth and peer pressure from other members of the group would work in his favour. Each day prior to commencing patrol, the team embarked upon a six-mile run, followed by a workout in a borrowed gymnasium. He documented each member's performance and reset targets at the end of each week.

A public-spirited local martial arts instructor volunteered his services free of charge and prepared a basic regimen for the team. Being "the old men" in the group, John Hinds and Terry were determined not to be beaten by their younger comrades, clocking superior times in their daily run and always managing to squeeze out extra push-ups and chin-ups.

Following their workout, the Nelson Team Policing Unit would shower and prepare for duty, feeling enlivened and eager to confront whatever the evening and their sergeant had in store.

With the lush green tinge of spring quickly fading from the Port City's many low hills, Nelson had shrugged off the sombre cloak of winter in exchange for the vitality of its seemingly endless and famous summer. Like gaily-coloured butterflies, a myriad of sails wandered aimlessly about the sparkling blue, safe and sheltered waters of Tasman Bay. In the business district, traffic slowed to a crawl as exuberant visitors in bright shirts, skimpy mini skirts, or ragged denim shorts, explored the retail district, pallid skin betraying their tourism status. The city's shopkeepers temporarily suppressed parochial impatience to play tuneless cash register choruses and fill till drawers from the short-lived bounty of soon to be-emptied, annual holiday savings accounts. Odours of suntan lotion, salty skin, sandy feet and ice cream blended with the general air of holiday indolence.

With the small town blossoming to the status of a small city, local motels, caravan parks, camping grounds and B and B's had, without exception, hung out their "Fully Booked" and "No Vacancy" signs.

As families retired to caravans and tents for evening games of scrabble, Pictionary, or Trivial Pursuit, pubs and taverns swung into action, plying young patrons with alcohol to the amplified cacophony of second-rate pop bands. Accompanying nightfall was the inevitable proliferation of human cockroaches, peddling their filthy trade in illegal drugs and preying on the unwary, like a rampant cancerous growth. Behind the drug scene, seemingly aloof, and mockingly untouchable, the illegal gangs fed vociferously from the spoils.

As well as quelling the alcohol fuelled pub brawls, which exploded with a volcanic suddenness, Terry and his team sought to deter the anti-social behaviour accompanying various forms of entertainment sponsored by the business community for the benefit of teenage holidaymakers. One such event was a large and well-advertised rock concert, held beneath the enormous domed roof of Nelson's barn-like Endeavour Centre.

Following several arrests for minor street offences, the Team Policing Unit were enjoying a well-earned mid evening break in the station meal room, when an undercover policeman advised them that drugs were being sold openly at the venue.

With a crowd of several thousand packing the huge dimly lit hall, Terry knew a raid needed ample resources, split second timing and a well-coordinated effort. With the sudden presence of uniformed officers, the potential for panic or major conflict was considerable. Conferring with his small team, he unhesitatingly decided to mount an operation on the dancehall, during which they would attempt to identify the principal drug dealers, while searching and arresting any persons believed to be in possession of illegal substances. Once again, the duty sergeant was Dave Allen and Bert Barber the station senior sergeant.

Briefing both NCO's with his hastily contrived Operation Order, Terry sought their co-operation and assistance. Fortunately, both men concurred with the plan, which included recruiting the assistance of the entertainment centre caretaker who would provide in depth knowledge of the building's layout, including entry points, toilets, staging, dressing rooms and the lighting system.

Terry held the briefing in the station's small mess as uniformed officers jostled to hear his words. "Dave, your men are to be positioned at all the exits. They are to prevent any persons entering or leaving the building during the operation. As soon as we enter the main hall, the caretaker will turn on all the lights. I will shut down the band and take over the sound system. The undercover officer will point out the main offenders to my team who will conduct searches and arrest procedures. At the same time, I will make an announcement for everyone attending the dance to remain where they are, while systematic searches take place. Now, as soon as the uniforms are spotted, I am sure pandemonium will break out. Anybody with drugs will try to dispose of them. We well may encounter resistance. There could even be a major disturbance and panic as people try to get away. We obviously won't be able to arrest everybody, so we are just trying to get the main culprits. For an operation of this size to be successful, we really need many more troops than we've got, but we can't wait to call out staff. We've got to go in immediately and make do."

In his quiet unflappable manner, the slightly built Irish sergeant left to organise his team. Terry knew he could depend on Dave and was grateful for the older man's maturity and efficiency. Taking the middle-aged, balding caretaker with him in the patrol car, he followed the Team Policing Unit prison van to the agreed rendezvous point behind the entertainment venue.

Dave Allen's crew were already in position at the centre's many fire exits as Terry's crew, dressed in their riot helmets, with the menacing PR24 batons swinging from the silver belt rings, slid undetected into one of the narrow passages leading to the stage area.

The central dance hall where the crowd stomped and shook in a drug-fuelled frenzy to the amplified beat of the emaciated rock stars had two main entry points. Dividing his crew equally, to storm the hall simultaneously through each door, the young N.C.O. nodded to the caretaker, whose hand was poised in readiness above the light switches.

They burst through the doors as the bright overhead lights flickered and bathed the packed assemblage in a yellowish glow. There were a few valuable seconds before the puzzled throng comprehended the situation allowing Terry time to mount the stage. Pushing aside a scruffy, lank haired, sweating musician, pounding a frenetic beat on his electric guitar, Terry seized the microphone.

The noise was almost unbearable. Terry lifted his hand, and on his cue, the caretaker killed power to the instruments, leaving the amazed rock band impotent without their guitars, keyboard and drums. Before he could utter the first words of command to the crowd, bodies dashed hither and yon as in a frantic effort, they headed to the toilets to ditch deal bags. Plastic bags, reefers and other drug paraphernalia, materialised beneath the feet of the stunned crowd as frightened drug users shed evidence of incrimination.

Rushing to head off the dealers at the toilet doors, the Team Policing Unit could hear the sound of numerous cisterns flushing. Grabbing the likely culprits and flinging them against the walls, unceremonious searches revealed small bags of cannabis, amphetamines and other illicit substances. Caught red-handed, some dealers resisted violently, effectively tying up Terry's small crew and enabling the escape of others into the crowd where prospects of their apprehension were dismal.

Fortunately, a major riot did not eventuate, as without cohesion, the crowd acted as frightened individuals rather than as an enraged mob. The total number of persons actually caught in possession of drugs and arrested numbered ten. This group included the dealers identified by the undercover operative. However, at least three times that number escaped arrest in the ensuing confusion. With so few resources, Terry lamented what he judged to be an ineffectual attack on a major drug event.

Despite the limited numbers arrested, the raid was a major talking point in the small town and established the T.P.U. as a major crime-fighting weapon in the Nelson police arsenal. The local community had never before experienced such a coordinated police response and the use of tactics previously seen only on television. For team members, there was only momentary glory, as the reality of what they had done hit home.

Prosecution files had to be prepared for the next day's court hearings, effectively removing the team from further duty. Terry guessed correctly that all ten of the prisoners would enter "not guilty" pleas. What he did not anticipate, was a raft of counter allegations against himself and every member of his team. With no obvious defence to the drug charges, the prisoners used the ploy of alleging that the police had planted the drugs found in their possession. Despite the obvious absurdity of their claims, the public relations conscious police hierarchy hastily dispatched a chief inspector and his lower ranked inspector side kick from the neighbouring Blenheim Police Station to investigate.

Encouraged by such success in muddying the legal waters, each defendant added allegations of police brutality to his spurious claims. The old ploy of deflecting attention from one's guilt to cast doubts as to the veracity of your accusers, was an old ploy but one that unfortunately still worked.

Stung by the injustice of the allegations, Terry nevertheless appreciated the police Department's need to show its officers had acted correctly and demonstrate its readiness to deal with all forms of corruption. However, he was unprepared for the officious manner and the obvious relish with which the investigating officers attended to their task.

The diminutive chief inspector heading the inquiry appeared oblivious to his uncomplimentary nickname, "Fitter." This title had been acquired because of his reputation for mercilessly persecuting officers who, through naivety or inexperience found themselves on the wrong side of the police Service's poorly explained and authoritarian General Orders and Instructions.

A slightly built individual with a round, clean-shaven, baby-face, mousy brown hair and nervous fidgeting manner, Fitter discovered a short cut to promotion very early in his career. He would happily travel the despised road of the internal investigator, even if that corpse littered path led to his own perdition.

The cherubic persecutor and his lower ranked lackey verbally attacked each member of Terry's team in separate interviews, hoping to exploit any discrepancy while assuming the guilt of their hapless victims from the outset. Fortunately, the combination of a well developed instinct for self-preservation, acuity, experience under skilled cross-examination and the knowledge that their actions were above reproach, enabled the T.P.U. to survive the innuendo and crafty mind games Fitter used to unseat his victims.

The internal investigation and court trials resulting from the drug charges had the T.P.U. tied up for weeks, successfully destroying Terry's plans for further impact on the provincial town's motorcycle outlaws and problems borne from the illicit drug trade.

With no substance to the allegations of corruption and assault, the internal investigation eventually petered out. Although the police Department rarely handed out praise, Terry anticipated that the very least Fitter would do, would be to acknowledge in writing that each of the Team Policing officers had acted correctly. However, it was clearly beneath the chief inspector to admit his misjudgement of the officers of the T.P.U. Although an apology and congratulations for diligence and initiative would have been appropriate, the investigation concluded with the words, "No charges will be laid against Sergeant Flatley or the officers involved!" The ambiguous conclusion seemed to suggest that the inquiry had faltered through lack of evidence and inferred some truth to the claims of impropriety.

The bitter gall of injustice persisting in the throats of the T.P.U. only needed the antacid of the simple words, "*the allegations are without foundation,*" to dissolve it.

Terry understood why so many older police officers were embittered, and cynically avoided any involvement with situations that might turn and bite back. With the growing perception amongst frontline officers that the service would not back its officers, he concluded grief to be the ultimate reward for diligence and enthusiasm.

As the acrimony subsided, the T.P.U. vowed to eradicate from their city, the scourge of gangs financing activities through the sale of drugs. In order to do so, they would devise strategies to shield themselves from their target's cries of, "we've been framed!" Henceforth, they would ensure every action was corroborated, substantiated and beyond reproach. Terry told them, "If the imposition of tedious procedures nullifies our effectiveness, so be it. Our integrity and survival is paramount."

In the drug world, others did the gang's dirty work, reducing any likelihood of major convictions. However, the tall T.P.U. Commander reasoned that the accumulation of many minor convictions might just bring about the gang's downfall. In future, whenever the Lost Breed ventured onto the streets, they were to become a major target for his team who would prosecute every infraction of the law, no matter how insignificant.

Traffic infringements appeared an especially effective way of harassing the gang from existence. Crazy George and his judicial cohorts would happily confiscate driver's licences if enough demerit points accumulated against gang members. Then, if they persisted in riding or driving motor vehicles, the police were empowered to arrest. Without mobility, the gang must eventually become impotent.

As the T.P.U. patrolled, they recorded movements of gang members, including the location of their motorcycles, their favourite watering holes, their associates and other regular haunts. Whenever a Lost Breed motorcycle moved, a T.P.U. vehicle amazingly appeared as its shadow, stopping and booking the rider at the first lawful opportunity. It was not long before the gang realised that they were targets of a specialised group and retaliated with abuse and threats.

Being threatened is part of the police officer's lot and T.P.U. members dismissed attempted intimidation casually. As the leader of the unit, Terry bore the brunt of the gang's anger. Even remarks such as, "you better watch out Copper. We know where you live. How would you like a fire bomb through your window?" and the possibility of retaliation against his family served only to make Terry more determined to squash the Lost Breed. He did not think for a moment the gang would dare follow through with such drastic retaliation against the family of a respected police sergeant. *They're just trying to get me rattled*, he told himself, brushing aside the remarks.

The alarm bells began to ring at last, when his wife began hearing prowlers around their quaint weatherboard cottage. Always nervous when Terry worked night shift, she was unaware of the Bikie's threats, as he could see no point in alarming her. In any case, he rarely discussed his work, having learnt early in the piece that she offered him no comfort to the stresses and strains of police work. Indeed, her unfathomable propensity to criticise and judge him harshly in times of strife, rather than share his burden, or offer words of comfort or advice, deterred him from making her his confidant. It appeared that he must shoulder the burden alone.

The holiday season had finished, and as the little town returned to quiet normality, the T.P.U. unit had been relieved of full time patrol duty, resorting to an "on call" status, along with other specialist sections such as, Search and Rescue and the Armed Offenders Squad. Although now leading his section of officers on general duties, Terry's pressure on the Lost Breed was unrelenting. Having learnt the effectiveness of the tactic for dealing with the gang, other Nelson police officers joined the campaign.

Wearing the patch of the Lost Breed had become a very unhealthy practice.

With physical fitness an important part of his life, Terry often jogged home from work along the winding Atawhai Drive with its' waterfront views. Sometimes if the exigencies of the Service permitted, he squeezed a training run into his work schedule, always advising his team the route he would take in case of trouble. It was during one of the latter occasions that Terry was running through the deserted Nelson streets at 3.00 am on a ten-kilometre run. Hearing the sound of an approaching vehicle, he turned to glance over his shoulder to see Ike Proctor, the stocky Maori policeman and the irrepressible Ian Etheridge, approaching hastily in a marked patrol vehicle.

As they pulled alongside, Proctor's head protruded from the driver's window like a hairy black cannonball. "Sarge, your missus just called to say she thinks there is someone prowling around your house again. We thought you'd like to come with us."

Dripping with perspiration from his half-completed run,

Terry snatched the rear door handle and slid quickly onto the back seat. "Let's go!" he commanded unnecessarily, hardly noticing his bare legs sticking to the vinyl. The rear wheels squealed their protest as the Holden's engine responded to the sudden pressure on the accelerator.

The trip to his Dodson's Valley home took mere minutes. With the city sleeping, there was little doubt the sound of the speeding police car carried to whoever had been skulking around the house long before they reached their destination. However, there was no alternative with the safety of Terry's family paramount. *It's better to scare them off than catch them in the midst of some heinous act,* he rationalised.

"Drop me here," the scantily clad sergeant instructed. They were adjacent to the street half a block from the rear of his rambling weatherboard cottage. He hoped by cutting through the houses behind his he might just come across the culprit. Ike and Ian sped off to approach from the front. Running quietly in his joggers, borrowed torch gripped firmly as a makeshift baton, Terry used his local knowledge in the darkness to navigate through a maze of shrubbery. He scaled a low hedge at the bottom of his garden and reached the back of the house just as the other two policemen climbed the last steps from Dodson's Valley Road at the front.

"See anything?" Ian Etheridge flashed his six-cell torch, the beam briefly illuminating a fibro cement shed, swimming pool and well tended vegetable garden.

"Nah! If there was anybody, they took off long before we got here." Terry's torch was on now as he scoured the soft earth beneath the windows for footprints or other sign of intrusion. "Look here!"

On the eastern side of the house, a large pohutukawa[35] hedge ensured the sun's rays never reached the ground. The bare dry earth revealed the unmistakable impression of a large commando boot. The fine hairs on the back of the young sergeant's neck bristled as if some unseen and evil presence had brushed past him. The ugly reality of the prowler's recent violation of his home seemed surreal and somehow more menacing than if he now hid in the darkness waiting to spring.

"Do you want to call Rod out?" Ike was staring intently at his sergeant.

---

[35] Pohutukawa is the Maori name for an indigenous flowering Christmas tree.

"No. It will be a waste of time. Our friend will be home with his scungy mates by now. We'll need more than a boot print to do us any good and I'm sure the track will only stop where he vamoosed on whatever set of wheels he used."

"Do you think it's the Lost Breed?" Ian Etheridge shook a cigarette from the packet he'd pulled from his tunic. Limp and unlit, it hung strangely white from the thin gash of his lips.

Terry's hands shook slightly as he nodded. "I can take anything these bastards want to dish out, but when they target my kids, that's a different story! I'd better go inside and make sure Jane's okay. Don't say anything to her about what we've found," he cautioned. "We'll play this down. I don't want her or the kids getting any more scared than they already are."

"What was it? Don't tell me it was nothing, because I am sure I heard someone open the side gate. The hinges creaked." Jane was sitting up in bed with the lamp on, shaking visibly. "What are you doing in your joggers and shorts at this time of the night? You must be mad running through the streets at 3.00 am!"

"What do you think? I have to keep fit and things were pretty quiet. The boys knew where to find me. Anyway, you've nothing to worry about. It was probably just somebody taking a short cut," Terry lied. "Whoever it was has gone now but we'll come passed in the patrol car several times between now and daylight. If you do hear anything, we'll be here in a flash. How are the kids?"

"They're still asleep."

"Okay. I'll see you in the morning. Leave the outside light on. I'll lock the door after me." He moved to give her a parting kiss, which landed on her cheek as she averted her face at the last moment. "Go back to sleep now."

"Fat chance of that."

That day, Terry set about devising a mantrap to deter future episodes. Secretly, he was very concerned. The words of the bikies resounded in his head and their angry faces haunted him. "We know where you live copper. How would you like a firebomb through your window?" Images of his terrified children screaming while trapped amid the raging flames of his home chilled him with fear.

In the parched malnourished soil where he had seen the boot print, Terry dug to the depth of his garden spade. Taking a plank of wood, he hammered six-inch nails through the timber, leaving the sharp points protruding several inches on the opposite side. As night approached, he buried the spiked board in the soft earth, confident in the knowledge that his children would not venture outside after their nightly baths. After brushing the dirt smooth to conceal evidence of his recent activity, he stood back to survey his handiwork. The rusty points of the nails were invisible and the earth showed little sign of disturbance. Next, he stretched a fine trip wire across the gap between the house and the hedge. With a locked gate at the other side of the cottage barring access, anybody prowling about the garden must walk across the mantrap to reach the front yard. On the frames of the partly open wooden bedroom windows, he tied various objects, so that should anyone attempt to enter the windows, the resultant noise would immediately awaken him.

The previous night had been the last night of his night shift and the fact that he would be home with his family provided some comfort. Whether the lurking menace from the previous night would return, was a matter for conjecture but Terry was taking no chances. With the family home set high on a knoll, he felt safe from any missile launched from a passing vehicle. Similarly, the high angle of trajectory of any weapon fired from street would render it harmless. If the disgruntled Lost Breed intended to hurt his family, they would have to be on foot.

Jane was unaware of the spiked plank and trip wire waiting for its victim. Terry assured her that the improvised burglar alarm on the bedroom window was just a precaution against the unlikely return of any harmless "Peeping Tom." "He won't come back. He's sure to have been scared off after the other night," he lied.

That night, they retired early. Despite severe sleep deprivation after a week of night shift, he was unable to sleep, for as usual, Jane kept the bedroom light on, reading until late in the night. He knew from previous experience that gentle pleas or cajoling to extinguish the light were to no avail. Any need he might have for sleep was never of concern to her and that fact caused immense irritation. He simply had to wait until the book slipped from her grasp as she fell asleep before reaching past her to switch off the bedside lamp.

It was close to midnight when the rustle of pages finally ceased. He lay in the darkness alone with his thoughts. *"What is the point of all this?"* he asked himself. *I'm in a job where I've placed myself and my family at risk. I'm stuck on shift work for the rest of my working life as long as I stay in Nelson. There's no point in sitting promotion exams because we'll be moved to Wellington or Auckland and that will wreck the marriage.* The fact the marriage was already on the brink of dissolution had not escaped him but he still held hopes of somehow patching up the relationship for his children's sake. Employment prospects outside the police Service were grim and the likelihood of Jane agreeing with any business venture as an alternative to his dead end police career was nil. No matter how promising the venture, any previous suggestions had been met with allegations of irresponsibility. Unable to see any way out of his dilemma, he finally dozed, tormented by nightmares.

Suddenly, he was wide-awake. It was a still night. Crickets chattered incessantly in the garden beneath the bedroom window. *Why am I awake? Has there been some movement outside or is it just my imagination playing tricks?* He lay there listening, eyelids beginning to droop as his body demanded sleep. Beside him, Jane slept soundly, lying on her side at the far edge of the mattress, her back to him as a deterrent to physical contact. No he was not mistaken! There was something or someone outside. The normally noisy crickets abruptly ceased their monotonous racket. Rolling over quietly, he prepared to sneak to Veronica's room and peak between the curtains. In the street below, a single mercury-vapour street lamp cast a harsh bluish white glare, sufficient to see the steeply sloping front lawn and the zigzag concrete garden path. Suddenly, a thump and a muffled curse of pain made him jump. There was a brief pause, followed by the sound of running feet. A wry smile of satisfaction crossed his face.

"That'll teach the bastard!" he muttered maliciously, before turning on the outside lights to indicate to the prowler that the commotion had awakened him. Dismissing any pursuit as pointless, he slid back beneath the sheets. He was surprised the next morning to find that after the prowler incident he had immediately fallen into a dreamless sleep.

Worried that his children or some other innocent party would stumble on the cruel device, he dismantled the mantrap. Making no mention of the nocturnal visitor, he preferred instead to await the Lost Breed' next move.

He didn't want to jeopardize his family safety further and decided secretly to suspend his vendetta against the gang. He hated himself for what he perceived as weakness in the face of evil. However, under no circumstances would he entertain placing his family at risk. Neither did he want to shirk his duty. What was he to do? His position as a devoted law enforcement officer had become untenable.

Events took a further turn for the worst in August 1978. Most small towns have at least one troublesome family who make life for the authorities very unpleasant and Nelson was no exception with the town's particular scourge being the Wood[36] family. Every member of Local Government, police, Fire Brigade or Government agency detested the notorious, professional troublemakers who frequently lodged spurious complaints, wasting the time and resources of every organisation with the misfortune to figure in their imaginative and mischievous acts.

As recipients of Social Security benefits, the Woods had ample time on their hands to invent grievances and research various laws surrounding their imagined wrongs. Obnoxious and undoubtedly inbred, they nonetheless possessed an innate and devious cunning, compounded by in depth knowledge of the internal workings of bureaucracy. There was little doubt the Government Ombudsman cringed every time another letter arrived to add to the copious raft of unfounded complaints.

The chief protagonists in the family were Laurie and Frederick. Having recently fallen foul of the law over a minor misdemeanour, Laurie engaged the services of legal counsel through the system of free legal aid for the underprivileged. With all the time in the world, he was determined to fight the case until he exhausted every avenue of appeal. If during the protracted legal process the police had the misfortune to stumble, he would seize upon any advantage to lodge further complaints.

---

[36] A fictitious name for obvious reasons.

Using the strategy of persistent complaining to aggravate the poor soul with the misfortune to be in charge of the case, the Wood family telephoned the Nelson Police Station at all hours of the day and night. They knew every perceived grievance, no matter how petty, would end up in the file basket of the same investigating officer as he was the one most familiar with their circumstances.

The hapless constable on this occasion was John Hayes. He had the heart felt sympathy of every Nelson police officer as they breathed collective sighs of relief at having escaped dealings with the Woods.

Terry and his team were working night shift when a spate of telephone calls from Frederick commenced over the triple one emergency line. Despite warnings not to tie up the telephones with frivolous matters, Freddy persisted, harassing the Watch house Constable, Steve Oakland, mercilessly. As the calls did not originate from the Wood family home, they did not know the source of the calls and were powerless to stop them. Finally, Freddy made the mistake of telephoning from a public call box. Terry instructed Steve to keep Freddy talking while New Zealand Telecom traced the call.

The Telecom technician receiving Terry's request had also suffered with the Wood family and could not wait to oblige. The result of the trace returned within seconds and indicated that the call originated from a public 'phone box approximately one block from the Wood's house. Terry, accompanied by policewoman, Gail Bennie drove straight to the call box, finding Freddy still on the telephone shouting abuse and nonsense to the frazzled Steve.

Wasting no time, Terry hauled Freddy from the box. "Frederick Wood, I am arresting you for disorderly conduct. Other charges will no doubt follow under The Telecommunications Act but that'll do for the present! You are not obliged to say anything unless you wish to do so, and anything that you do say will be taken down in writing and may later be used in evidence." Terry rattled off the familiar caution as required by The Judges Rules while manhandling the struggling serial nuisance toward the police car. Freddy resisted strongly but despite his lanky 194 centimetre frame, he was no match for the physically fit sergeant.

Realising the imminence of his incarceration, Terry's prisoner resorted to collapsing, feigning some sort of attack in the hope of delaying or complicating arrest. Terry and Gail fed the limp body into the rear of the Holden patrol vehicle, finding keeping Freddy upright in the seat was impossible. Gangly arms and legs splayed around the cramped confines of the rear seat, preventing any chance of a second person occupying the seat as a precaution against attack on the driver.

"You keep and eye on him while I drive back to the station," Terry instructed, judging that he would be able to stop the car in time should the prostrate man show sign of movement. "If he moves, let me know."

With Gail sitting side on in the front passenger seat so she could watch over the prisoner, Terry accelerated toward the police station only a few minutes drive away.

"Watch out. I think he's coming around," Gail warned quietly as they descended a steep section of Wainui Road. Terry withdrew his foot from the accelerator intending to pull over to the side of the road.

"Gaaa!" Freddy screamed, sitting bolt upright. There was no time to take evasive action. The prisoner's arms suddenly reached either side of Terry's head. He slapped both hands over the policeman's eyes. With the patrol car still moving at speed, the danger of collision with one of the many wooden light poles flashing by to their left was considerable. Emitting strangled sounds of rage, the maniacal Freddy pulled Terry's head fiercely backward.

Stamping on the brake pedal, while grabbing frantically at the hands obscuring his vision, the shocked sergeant located Freddy's little fingers. Yanking both fingers painfully downward, he broke his attacker's hold. The police car screeched to a halt, the front tyres leaving thick swathes of rubber on the road surface. The deranged prisoner changed his grip, encircling his victim's throat with both hands. Struggling for air as the pressure on his windpipe increased, Terry broke Freddy's grip a second time only to find Freddy yanking frantically at his hair. With his head forced backward over the seat, Terry was powerless and felt as though his neck would break at any moment.

"For Christ sake Gail, hit the bastard with your baton!" In his desperation, Terry forgot policewomen did not carry batons.

Gail beat ineffectually at Freddy's head, her tiny fists no match for the demented creature attacking her sergeant. Terry realised the slightly built woman was powerless to help him. If he were to prevail, he would need to muster all his strength and break free from the hands wrenching his head backward. Summoning all his strength, Terry forced his head forward against the hands clinging to enormous bunches of his hair. With a tearing sound, he heard the hair rip painfully from his scalp. Before Freddy could recover, he threw himself violently to one side, twisting to face his assailant. In the struggle, his foot had slipped from the brake pedal. The police car began rolling unchecked down the steep slope. Again, he rammed his foot hard down on the brake pedal as he glimpsed Gail rolling out the passenger door. Snatching open the rear door, she tried to grapple with Freddy as white flecks of saliva sprayed from his leering mouth. Flaying both arms wildly, he struck her in the face, warding off her futile attempts to control him.

"Right, you bastard!" Terry decided. *"This has gone far enough."* The high head-rests of the front seat provided hampered his attempts to reach his prisoner. There was no time to reach for the handbrake. His foot must remain on the brake pedal. With his body twisted awkwardly, he lined up Freddy's stupidly grinning face for the target of an enormous roundhouse punch. Never before had Terry felt such a mix of anger, desperation and frustration. Angry with himself for placing them in this predicament and angry at the stupid man for his senseless and dangerous attack, he focussed all his emotion into the energy behind the blow, firing his fist explosively while trying with all his might to knock the lunatic's head completely from his shoulders. Indeed, the rear window beyond Freddy's head became the actual target as he mustered a massive follow-through with the punch. His knuckles crunched sickeningly against soft flesh and brittle facial bones. Terry's relief and satisfaction was palpable as Freddy's head lolled to one side. This time there was no doubt as to his prisoner's state of consciousness. Handcuffing the unconscious offender, Terry traded places with the traumatised policewoman for the return journey.

Reaching the station yard, they found Steve Oakland waiting. Their dishevelled appearance and tense faces spoke volumes. By this time, Freddy was conscious, although blood poured from his smashed and broken nose. Angrily, Terry seized his prisoner by his shirt collar, dragging him unceremoniously from the car across the bitumen surface of the yard. A searing pain enveloped the sergeant's shoulder, neck and back. With adrenaline still coursing through his veins, he paid no heed to his injuries and propelled Freddy headlong into the charge room where he lay in a limp and tangled heap.

"We'll look after him from here if you like Sarge." Steve cast a knowing conspiratorial glance toward Wayne Fordham and Ian Etheridge who had returned from patrol to witness the spectacle of one of the despised Wood family in custody.

By now, the pain in Terry's shoulder and back had become almost unbearable. Grateful for the chance to seek respite from his pain, he retreated to the sergeant's office to commence his report.

Although strange shrieking sounds emanated from the charge room, filling the deserted corridors of the police station, Terry paid no heed, assuming Freddy was merely putting on a performance for the benefit of other prisoners.

That morning, the gaoler carted Freddy, battered and bruised to the Magistrate's Court. As expected, Wood entered a plea of "not guilty" and Crazy George, who was well acquainted with the Wood Family's antics, set a date for the trial.

Although several weeks passed between Freddy's incarceration and the Court hearing, Terry had still not recovered from his injuries. Wrongly diagnosed[37] as soft tissue damage to his neck, shoulder and back, his doctor decided X- rays were unnecessary.

Hiring a local barrister who had grown considerably wealthier from the Wood families exploits, Freddy alleged police brutality. His highly improbable story included allegations that Constable Jenson had stuffed the prisoner's woollen socks in Freddy's mouth during his search at the Watch-house, also drenching him with a fire hose to quieten him. As Terry had not been present during pre-incarceration procedures, he had no knowledge of

---

[37] Many years later, a bone scan for another matter revealed an old fracture to his shoulder. The injuries from Freddy's attack would bother him for the remainder of his life.

events in the charge room and said as much during his evidence. Fed up with the entire farce, "Crazy George" in his wisdom and impatience, dismissed Freddy's version of events, finding the town's most troublesome character guilty as charged.

It was not until several weeks after Wood's conviction that Terry's team revealed the truth of Freddy's story.

"The clown was performing like a deranged baboon. No matter what we said to him, he wouldn't shut up. We got sick of his nonsense. The noise he made reminded me of a shrieking peacock, so, I stuffed his socks in his gob!" Steve alleged laughing. "When we put him in his cell, he blocked the wash basin with toilet paper and flooded the place."

By this time, Terry was of the opinion that, although improper, Freddy's treatment was minor consolation for the pain and trauma the crazed man had inflicted. Unable to find an answer to the omniscient and palpable threat, which, hung pall-like, over his family, the rights of that particular prisoner assumed no importance.

"Guess whose due out of clink this week?"

Terry had only just dispatched his shift to their various duties and was passing through the watch-house when Pat Bickley fired the enigmatic question. He stopped in his tracks and turned to face his senior sergeant. "I've no idea Pat, but I'm sure you're going to tell me. Who is it?"

"Brian "Crazy" Mansell."

"The name doesn't mean anything to me, Pat. What's his claim to fame?"

"I forgot. He's a bit before your time. He's probably one of the worst crims this town has ever turned out. We put him away for ten years for attempted murder, aggravated assault and firearm offences. The Parole Board in their wisdom has decided to let him loose on the community. God help us." Bickley ran a leathery hand through his greying locks. "Take it from me. That bugger will kill somebody. He hates cops and has close links with the bikies. You might say he was their hit man before he went inside. If you want to know more about him, have a look in the police Gazette. It makes interesting reading and I'm sure yours and his paths will cross pretty soon."

"Thanks Pat. I will."

With a sudden heavy sense of foreboding, Terry sat at the watch-house computer. Guessing the birth date, he entered the name Mansell. Almost instantaneously, the electronic wizardry replied, flashing the notorious criminal's description, New Zealand police Gazette reference and an horrendous and extensive list of previous convictions onto the small screen. "Jees, this bastard started early. He first did time in Borstal, back in sixty-two for armed robbery, assault on police and escaping from custody," Terry muttered.

"Who's that?" Ian Etheridge, his watch-house keeper inquired.

"Some cove called Crazy Mansell."

"He's a real mean bastard. He hates cops and we've had several armed offender's operations involving him. Why the interest in him? He's doing time and shouldn't be out for years." Etheridge flicked a cigarette from its packet, lighting it with a Zippo lighter, a souvenir from his former navy career.

"Pat Bickley's just dropped the bombshell that Mansell is being released this week."

"Shit. Here we go again. Let me offer a word of advice. Steer well clear of him unless you've got plenty of backup. He swore that he'd kill a cop and I've no reason not to believe him."

"That's what the Gazette says. It also says that he's made threats against prison officers and was done for assault on other prisoners while he's been inside." Terry stabbed his index figure at the arch criminal's mug shot. "Mean looking sod isn't he?"

Although police photographs were sometimes a poor depiction of the characters arrested, the small black and white image somehow managed to convey the swarthy, tattooed convict's homicidal evilness. In his mid-thirties, Mansell's greasy black hair hung limply to his collar. 'Boob' dots on both cheeks and a large spider's web on his neck announced a recidivist criminal.

"Why would they let somebody like that out before his time?" Terry wondered aloud.

"I've given up trying to figure out the weird and wonderful processes of logic used by the bloody "do gooders" and dreamers that decide such things," Ian stated tersely.

"It's a pity that he isn't going to live next door to them on the outside. Perhaps, then they'd have a different point of view."

"Well, I guess we'll just have to see if we can put him back behind bars where he belongs," Terry reasoned.

"He's not afraid of gaol and he'll make it worth his while if you try. The only thing that will stop him ultimately, will be a bullet."

Just as Pat Bickley had predicted, Crazy Mansell wasted no time in renewing his affiliation with the Lost Breed who, recognising his impressive criminal record, powerful charisma, misguided organisation skills and desire for revenge, welcomed him back to their fold, charging him with their captaincy. Where previously the gang lacked a leader with enough courage to tackle the police head on, they now closed ranks behind him, becoming openly hostile and obstructive.

With the Lost Breed still harbouring resentment for gaoling of their members following the mardis gras riot, and the more recent incarceration of Michael Webber, the leader of the Team Policing Unit had little doubt that if he was to continue his campaign of gang harassment, the new regime they would now seek retribution. Unlike his police counterparts in the bigger cities who enjoyed a degree of anonymity, Nelson police officers, and in particular those holding rank, were public figures, whose homes and families were easy targets. Like a brimming pot reaching the boil, tensions simmered dangerously.

A police informant added further fuel to the fire when he revealed the gang was selling drugs from their Worthington Valley fortress, which he stated, also contained an arsenal of illegal firearms. Acting swiftly, the C.I.B. supported by the Armed Offenders Section and Team Policing swooped in a well-executed morning raid, once more marshalling gang members onto the front yard under armed guard. With most gang members mysteriously absent, and no sign of Mansell, the police could not establish ownership of several seized rifles, assorted baseball bats and motorcycle chains. It was the same tale for an insignificant quantity of illicit drugs, which suggested somebody had tipped off the gang in advance.

One sunny warm spring morning, Terry was patrolling alone in the Nelson central business district when Glenys Cooper whom he had detailed to duty in the watch house called urgently, "Is there any patrol near Endeavour Street? Over."

Snatching the microphone from its cradle, he answered immediately, "Roger. Nelson from Sergeant Flatley. I am heading west on Hardy Street at the moment."

"Sarge, we've had a call from a prison officer to say his prisoner has escaped and is running south on Endeavour Street. The escapee is one Johnny Tapawhera who is currently doing time for aggravated assault. Tapawhera is heavily tattooed, about five foot eight inches in height and of strong build. Can you assist?"

"Roger, Nelson. I know Tapawhera well. I am heading for the area now. If there are any other patrols in the vicinity, please assist also, over."

What on earth is Johnny Tapawhera doing in Nelson? He is supposed to be in Paparoa Prison, Terry wondered as he unbuckled his seat belt and scrutinised the crowded shopping area. Well known for his hatred of police and links to motorcycle gangs, Tapawhera was a violent part Maori criminal who had been sentenced to a lengthy term of imprisonment. Terry could not understand why he would be in Nelson under escort.

Terry slowed the patrol car to a crawl as he turned into Endeavour Street. A sudden movement on the crowded footpath caught his eye. "I think I've spotted him," he radioed, before turning off the engine and leaping from the patrol car.

Tapawhera, thinking he had outrun his escort had slowed to a fast walk and was attempting to blend with the crowd when he spotted the police vehicle turning into Endeavour Street across his path. Turning on his heel, the agile escapee again took flight as Terry alighted from his vehicle. Instantly forgetting the lethargy he felt from a 5.00 am start, Terry ran after him, dodging the ambling shoppers who stopped to gawk at the running policeman. Although the desperate prisoner had a start of at least fifty metres, Terry was gaining ground. Looking over his shoulder as he ran, Tapawhera realised his capture was imminent and darted swiftly through the parked vehicles lining the kerb. Attempting to vault the bonnet of an approaching sedan, he miscalculated its speed, crashing onto the windscreen and rolling heavily onto the road. Unhurt, he attempted to regain his feet but the few seconds he'd lost was all Terry needed. With the Maori's impressive history of violence foremost in his mind, Terry was not going to give him any advantage. Pouncing on the struggling criminal's back, he pinned him to the ground beneath his booted feet as he reached for his handcuffs.

I've got you, you bastard, he thought triumphantly. As he pulled the escapee's hands back and began to apply the handcuffs, Terry unexpectedly found himself lifted bodily by an enormous pair of hands.

"Get off him copper," snarled the owner of the hands. "I'll fucking kill you!"

With his own arms pinned to his side by whoever had interfered, Terry watched in dismay as Tapawhera began to get to his feet. "You're obstructing police. That man's an escaped prisoner. Let me go!" Turning his head, Terry recognised the massive bearded features of Nobby Hall, a member of the Lost Breed.

In the few seconds since he'd caught Johnny Tapawhera, a large crowd had gathered, encircling the police sergeant and his prisoner. Now a heavily set dark haired man pushed his way through the throng, perspiration dripping from his forehead. To Terry's enormous relief the man pulled a pair of handcuffs from his belt and unceremoniously slapped them on Tapawhera's wrists.

"Thanks, sergeant. I'll take over from here," he panted. "Let the sergeant go," he ordered Nobby Hall.

"You'll keep, cop," Hall spat, releasing his crushing hold.

Terry looked at the faces of the crowd surrounding him. Every countenance expressed extreme hatred and anger. He also noticed that without exception everyone wore dark suits and black ties.

Noticing his puzzled gaze, the prison officer explained. "Johnny was allowed out to attend his father's funeral. I think it all became too much and he decided to run off."

Terry had been on the point of arresting Hall for assaulting and obstructing police. The palpable anger of Tapawhera's mourning relatives was sufficient to convince him that to do so would provoke a riot. Apart from that, he felt some empathy for the prisoner despite his horrendously violent past. Swallowing his anger at having been lifted from Johnny's back by Hall, he answered, "Okay. As far as I'm concerned, there's been no real harm done. Take him away and do what ever you want. Under the circumstances I won't charge him with escaping."

His comment placated the milling mob of mourners. As the prison officer led his now subdued prisoner away, they dispersed, muttering angrily. Somehow, Terry sensed that he had narrowly escaped being mauled by the mob that obviously had no love for the police uniform.

Cliff Barron, the police photographer was the first to arrive as Terry's backup. "What was all that about?" He inquired looking at the retreating figures.

"It's all under control Cliff. Tapawhera's back in custody and no harm's been done."

"Do you realise how dangerous that man is? You took a hell of a risk tackling him on your own."

"Why do you think I jumped on his back with my size elevens? I wasn't taking any chances. I don't usually resort to such extreme measures when I make an arrest."

"Well, I'd watch my back if I was you. You saw the looks on the faces of Johnny's relatives."

The crash as the bottle smashed through the window resounded through the stillness of the night awakening him from the soundest sleep. Tyres howled on the road and the powerful sound of a V8 engine accelerating faded as the attackers sped off into the night. His daughters' screams chilled him to the bone. Racing down the hall a wall of flames beat him back. His beloved little girls' terrified faces appeared ghostly pale as they called pitifully to him before disappearing in the inferno. There was no sign of his sons. Using his arms to shield his face, he tried again and again to push through the hell that had been their bedroom. The hair on his head caught fire and he thought his eyeballs would melt. Huge watery blisters swelled his arms and the smell of burning flesh filled his nostrils. God let it be his flesh he could smell! Taking a mighty leap, he threw himself into the room. He was on the floor now, groping through the smoke and heat as he felt for Veronica and Helen's bodies. Suddenly, with a shower of sparks, the ceiling collapsed burying him and then everything went black.

He woke sweating and trembling, his chest heaving in paroxysms of uncontrollable sobbing. Unaware of his distress, Jane murmured quietly to herself in her own dream world. He knew it was just a horrible nightmare, a product of his troubled mind, but he had to seek reassurance at his little girls' bedsides.

Tip-toeing along the carpeted hall the horror of the nightmare still fresh, he entered the bedroom. He exhaled in relief, tears hot on his unshaven cheeks, watching as they slept soundly, breath whispering softly, faces angelic in the soft moonlight filtering through the net curtains. Peering at the deserted street below his house, he re-lived the terror. It had all been so terribly vivid and he understood at once, what he must do.

During the 1970's South Africa's apartheid policy alienated it from the remainder of the world, and many countries, New Zealand included became divided as to whether politics and sport were separate issues. As a fiercely proud rugby nation, many in New Zealand maintained that the countries All Black rugby team should compete with South Africa's Springboks. In the late 1960's the intensity of feelings in New Zealand was such that the government of the day interceded and cancelled a scheduled tour of the dual island nation by the Springboks. Ever since that time, the issue had continued to simmer with regular noisy and sometimes violent demonstrations.

With the pending tour by the Springboks, again on the drawing board for 1980, the National Government acceded to the demands of the powerful and vociferous rugby union lobby groups. Never before, had an issue been so controversial and the country was evenly divided. Tempers ran high and the issue threatened to split many families including those of police officers. Anti-tour groups vowed to disrupt rugby games through a planned program of civil disobedience. Knowing mobs would storm every game, various rugby groups found the erection of high wire fences necessary and called upon the government to provide police in sufficient numbers to maintain order. Still smarting from the anti-Vietnam War demonstrations, the New Zealand police Service stepped up crowd control training for its officers, intending to place various team policing units in the forefront of riot control. Terry and his team would be among them.

police officers by the very nature of their profession must put aside personal beliefs no matter how strongly they may feel on issues of the day. As with most policemen, Terry had been required on several prior occasions to arrest both pro and anti abortion protesters, with both sides accusing him of bias.

Although he tended to support the anti-abortion lobby, he understood the issue was not clear cut and could empathise with either side of the debate. His views during the anti-Vietnam War era had not been sufficiently strong to become a matter of conscience requiring him to take a stand for either side, and, causing conflict with his role as a law enforcement officer. It was perhaps just as well, for with substantial financial commitments and family responsibilities, a conscience was an expensive luxury he could not afford. Now with the anti-tour issue looming it was a completely different story. Although his financial and family responsibilities had not diminished, he was more mature and socially responsible. Despite the New Zealand Rugby Union hierarchy's assertion that sport and politics were separate issues, Terry categorically believed that apartheid was so deeply enmeshed in South African Sport as to be inseparable. He shared an opinion with many others, that playing sport with a country whose regime classified people with darker skins as sub-human was akin to courting the devil.

Some say that the Lord works in mysterious ways (his wonders to perform). Providentially, the Springbok tour provided Terry with an escape from the spectre of violent criminal elements bent on revenge. The major crisis of conscience he faced had become the catalyst for his resignation, allowing him to walk away from the war against evil gangs without guilt haunting him for the remainder of his days. *I wish there was some way, to finish what I started with the bikies, without risking my family,* he told himself. *On the other hand, I will not arrest courageous and decent citizens who stand against oppression. If I remain in the police, I must become a coward to save my family and a hypocrite if I compromise my beliefs by arresting people during the Springbok tour. If I tell Jane that my actions have made her and the kids targets, she won't understand what I was trying to do and will just condemn me. I can see no alternative but to resign despite her fierce opposition.*

Two years had elapsed since a heart attack in August 1978 claimed Tom Browning's life. Judy's regular letters from her Boyanup home, in Western Australia expressed her anguish, grief and depression. Although in her late fifties, Judy spoke of selling her home and placing herself in an old people's institution. Tom had been her soul mate and the very reason for her existence. Like a rudderless, storm tossed ship; she was aimlessly drifting through depression and grief toward her ultimate demise.

"I'm really worried about mum." Terry slid the letter he had been reading across the kitchen table to Jane. "She's far too young to be writing herself off. Can you imagine anyone putting themselves into an old folk's home at her age?"

"It's ridiculous. She seems to lave lost her reason for living. It's as if she's just longing for death so that she can be with him. What do you want to do?" Jane's face creased with concern.

"I'd like to go and visit her. I might be able to show her that she's still loved and needed. Perhaps I can help her find a new purpose in life. She's obviously very lonely in Boyanup, living on her own."

Jane thought for a moment. "We can afford it. You should go." Had she known the quandary Terry faced over his police career or had been able to foretell the future, her reply may well have been different.

It was late spring, in 1980 and with the weather still mild, the Western Australian countryside was only just beginning to turn brown. Judy drove from Boyanup to Perth to meet her son's flight from New Zealand due the following morning. Although only 180 kilometres south of the clean and thriving capital of Western Australia, she was a nervous driver and wanted to appear relaxed when she met him at the airport.

Terry was unprepared for the change in his mother since he had seen her last. Tom's lengthy illness and death on the operating table had taken its toll on the once vibrant woman. Although excited at the reunion, Judy's eyes exhibited a depth of sadness only seen in the grief stricken. Her once proud bearing had gone, her shoulders slumped and somehow she seemed smaller than he remembered. Enveloping her in a crushing hug, he felt the wetness of her tears through the thinness of his shirt.

"Hello mum." The simple greeting was sufficient for facial expressions and gestures conveyed love and compassion far more effectively than words ever could. With his arm around her shoulders, he let her lead him to her small white Cortina sedan waiting in the car park. Judy drove and prior to undertaking the short journey to Girrawheen, she made a detour to show him the sights.

"We're going to stay overnight with Kevin and Nina," she told him. Kevin Browning was Terry's stepbrother. Although they had never met, his mother had often mentioned Kevin and Nina in her letters. "It'll be a bit grubby but they do their best and they're looking forward to meeting you, so just try and overlook things. It's only for one night," she added.

Viewed from Kings Park, Perth bustled with activity below them. The Swan River's placid waters reflected a few woolly grey clouds floating in a startlingly blue sky. The abundance of skeletal metal cranes on top the new skyscrapers, advertised the city's obvious economic growth. With huge expanses of neat green parks, large homes and apparent lavish life style of its inhabitants, Terry could not help but compare life in New Zealand. There, the country he loved so much was undergoing a period of economic stagnation. With high unemployment and a lower standard of living, he worried about the limited opportunities for his children in a provincial town the size of Nelson. He pondered again, the limited options offered by his stalled police career, the risk to his family and the looming violence of the Springbok rugby tour.

One avenue of escape from the police, its associated shift work and Bikie gangs had been commercial tomato growing. When he'd confided in an elderly and understanding friendly real estate agent, the man had come up with a once in life time opportunity. Following a heart attack, Tony Angerami, one of Nelson's successful Italian tomato growers operating a thriving and lucrative business in the Wood area sought to lease his enterprise to make his retirement possible. Tony insisted that there was no need to pay anything until the first crop matured and placed his enormous expertise at Terry's disposal.

The proposition was very tempting. He had always loved horticulture and felt confident that the extensive research with other growers and representatives from the Department of Agriculture that he could succeed. *There were risks but weren't there always risks?* The chance of failure appeared minimal and the potential returns far exceeded his sergeant's salary. Almost bursting with enthusiasm, he presented the plan to Jane expecting her to be equally excited. Her negativity stunned him. No matter how he tried to convince her, she stubbornly refused to entertain the proposition insisting he should not risk the security provided by the police Service.

Jane's opposition had created a major turning point in his attempts at reconciliation. There seemed to be no escape from the spectre of eternal shift work, its associated health problems social pressures and the colossal strain upon his family. Increasingly, subjected to assaults in the course of his employment and with the omnipresent threat of attack from the lawless elements, he felt like a caged lion. The real estate agent friend had stood to make nothing from the arrangement was extremely annoyed that Terry had wasted his time. So annoyed was he, that he severed their friendship despite Terry's best efforts to explain Jane's opposition.

"We'd better get going, Ter!" His mother's use of the hated diminutive version of his name immediately brought him back to reality. Casting one last glance at the beautiful panorama below him, he smiled at his mother, "Okay. I was just daydreaming. Perth is certainly a lovely place."

They reached Kevin and Nina's brick and tile three bedroom home. Located in a working class northern suburb where the houses were predominantly Government owned and the yards littered with old car bodies, the streets appeared crowded with young urchins left to fend for themselves. As they drew into the driveway, Terry's stepbrother appeared holding the ubiquitous stubby of beer. A young woman of immense girth followed with two children. Their genuine warmth and friendship was almost overwhelming. "Hello little brother!" Kevin swapped the stubby to his left hand before offering a calloused paw for Terry to shake. "Christ mother! You told me he was a big bastard but I didn't know he was such a big streak of weasel piss."

Taking the proffered hand Terry shook it warmly. "Hello Kevin. It's nice to meet you," he offered politely.

"Nina, get the man a beer. Shit woman, what's wrong with you, you big fat useless tart!"

"Get him a beer yourself, you lazy bugger," Nina retorted.

Shocked by the language and crudity Terry was to learn that insults and bantering between the two were standard behaviour and relentless. Kevin's reference to him as, "His little brother," although slightly irritating at the outset was to become Kevin's catchcry. He knew Kevin meant well and although intended as a term of endearment, the title so easily bestowed by someone with whom he had no emotional attachment or shared memories, grated like fingernails drawn across a blackboard.

306

Nina announced proudly that she had cleaned the house especially for him. Judy cast him a sympathetic look as Terry tried to conceal his disgust at the squalid conditions and the mottled grey sheets on his bed, which clearly had not experienced the rigours of a washing machine and soap powder for some considerable time. "This is family," he told himself. "I've got to look past the dirt and Kevin's exaggerated "Ockerisms."

Conversation with his stepbrother appeared limited to matters surrounding motorcycles, trucks, booze and football. Unable to express himself without recourse to the use of four letter words, Terry squirmed uncomfortably each time Tom's only son uttered another expletive with scant regard for his mother's presence or gentility. "They're hardworking people and just battlers who have different standards to mine!" The mental incantations did little to help and Terry could not help but look forward to his departure the following day.

"Coming for a ride, little brother?" Kevin's head was poking around the door post of the room Terry was to occupy that night. The older man's tousled mane of thick grey hair was like a dirty halo around the wrinkled leathery face.

"Okay. Sounds good." Terry replied leaping off the grubby bed. His enthusiasm was real. Anything was preferable to enduring the odours of the unkempt house.

Three year old Rhys and his younger sister Jennifer whom Terry guessed was about five, bounced in the rear seat of Kevin's Fairmont. The V8 engine thundered noisily. "This little baby'll leave anything for dead at the lights!" Kevin beamed proudly at the powerful petrol-guzzling beast.

While heading along Wanneroo Road toward towering and distant office buildings, a Japanese motorcycle overtook them. Its helmeted rider gunned the engine to an angry scream, reminiscent of a horde of attacking wasps.

"Bloody Jap crap," Kevin muttered scornfully, before glancing in the rear vision mirror to where his cherubic snowy haired son now sat quietly. Kevin and Nina's third birthday present to Rhys had been a tiny, "Pee Wee" Honda motorcycle.

"Son," Kevin demanded, "What do your call a Yamaha motor bike?"

"I piece of ssit." Rhys slurred, on cue and giggled while his father applauded proudly with his laughter.

The following morning Terry accepted his mother's suggestion that he take over the driving. Waving a relieved farewell to Kevin and Nina, they headed south to Boyanup a quaint but expanding hamlet on the banks of the Preston River. After spending one night in the little flat roofed fibro house, they set off to explore the picturesque South West of Australia's largest State. Judy navigated, recounting tales of hers and Tom's travels to such places as Augusta, the historic Leeuwin lighthouse, Canal Rocks, Walpole, Denmark and Albany with its beautiful deep blue harbour and the old de-commissioned whaling station. Mother and son grew close during the trip, although they carefully avoided the still suppurating sores of the past's painful memories.

After ten days touring the South West, Judy appeared to shrug off her depression and loneliness. She refused to think about her son's departure knowing she must return to the empty house. Tom's presence had seemed so real and she often called out to him. She had been unable to come to terms with the fact that he was gone from her life forever. She expected him to somehow re-appear at any moment as if he had merely gone for a walk to the shop or pub as he did sometimes. The nights were always the worst. Sleep eluded her and she'd read, not absorbing the words, until in the small hours when at last the book fell from her grasp. Sometimes in her dream world, her beloved Tom would come to her smiling, arms outstretched, only to vanish cruelly before she could feel his loving embrace. Awakening to the black empty silence, her grief magnified a thousand fold and the aching vacuum that had replaced her heart would threaten to implode. *Oh God, let me go to sleep and not wake up,* she would pray each night but of course it was never that simple and she had concluded the pain must be His way of punishing her for her past misdeeds. *When will it end? How much can I endure?*

Terry had never believed in ghosts but there was something ethereal in the little fibro house. Several nights in succession, he awoke to the sound of someone or something moving through the cottage. At first, he rationalised that the sounds were merely the old timbers of the house contracting in the cool night air. On the third night, the creak of floorboards appeared consistent with somebody walking from his mother's bedroom to the back verandah. Quietly opening the bedroom door, he peered into the gloom but could see nothing to explain the noises. His mother's unbroken snoring discounted the possibility of her nocturnal wandering. He slid back into bed and settled down; telling himself that there had to be a logical explanation for the strange footsteps. His eyelids drooped as he drifted into the first stage of slumber.

Bang! The sudden loud retort as something struck the outside wall near his bed head made him sit bolt upright. Certain that someone prowling about the yard had struck the wall of the house with a hard object, he darted outside. The little hamlet slept peacefully and nothing moved about his mother's garden. The light dew covering the grass was undisturbed; there was no wind and no damage to the wall. He was at a loss to explain the explosive force with which something appeared to have struck the fibro wall. *There was no way that was just the house contracting*, he told himself.

At breakfast the next morning, he pondered how he could mention the inexplicable noises to his mother. He did not want to alarm her or have her think he was mentally unbalanced. "Mum, did you hear any unusual noises last night?"

"Why do you ask?" Judy avoided the question.

"Well, this house seems to emit some pretty strange sounds. The floors creak as if someone is walking through to the toilet and it sounded as if something hit the wall just outside my room."

"Oh, thank God you hear them as well!" Judy's relief was almost palpable. "I've been too afraid to mention the noises to anybody else for fear of them thinking I'm potty."

"It certainly doesn't sound like the house contracting. The noises follow a path just as if someone is walking through the house." Terry shook his head. "The imagination can play strange tricks. I'm sure there is a perfectly logical explanation."

"No!" Judy replied vehemently. "One night when the noises woke me up, I distinctly saw Tom standing beside my bed. I didn't imagine it. I was wide-awake. I got really frightened. It's happened several times since and in the end I said, Oh, Tom! Go away and leave me alone. He wouldn't mean any harm; it's just that he's worried about me on my own and he wants me to know he's watching over me."

The next night Terry waited expectantly but the house

remained quiet. After the conversation with his mother, the noises ceased. He found their absence just as inexplicable. *Surely, it was not possible that Tom could come back in another form? Why would the noises stop? Had he been trying to tell them that there was another world apart from the one they knew?*

Before leaving Perth, Terry visited Western Australian police Headquarters. The modern multi-storey police edifice occupied prime real estate overlooking the famous W.A.C.A. Cricket Ground and the Swan River.

Perhaps as a trained and experienced police officer, they will readily accept me into their organisation. My training and background must be worth something to them. I could make a new start without the threat from the gangs. . It would certainly get us on our feet if we were to come and live here, he mused.

Approaching the front desk from Adelaide Terrace, he produced his N.Z. police identification card and smiled warmly. "Good morning. I am a police sergeant from the New Zealand police on holiday in Perth. I am interested in speaking to someone about joining the Western Australian police Force."

The fresh faced young constable returned his smiled. "Hang on mate. I'll just be a tick. I'll see if there's anyone in recruiting."

Terry did not have long to wait. A man of medium build and height, wearing a crumpled baggy suit appeared a few moments later. "I'm Inspector Crabbe the officer in charge of recruiting. I hear you want to join the Western Australian police Force?" The inspector's lined and leathery face, down turned mouth and penetrating stare displayed no vestige of warmth or welcome.

"I'm visiting my mother from New Zealand. I am interested in the possibility but I'm just making inquiries at this stage to see if it's feasible."

"Well, you couldn't come in here as a sergeant you know," Crabbe almost spat the words.

Taken aback at the obvious hostility, Terry re-joined, "Well, I wouldn't expect to!"

"What makes you think we'd want you?"

"For a start, I've fourteen years experience. I was fully trained as a member of the New Zealand police Armed Offenders Squad. I have six years search and rescue experience and training. I'm also a qualified police Prosecutor and have been in charge of a

310

Team Policing Unit for the past two years. Surely, that's worth something?"

"How old are you?"

At thirty-four years of age, Terry was extremely fit. He considered himself to be in the prime of his life. "I'm thirty-four. Why?"

"You're too old!"

"What?" Terry scarcely felt like an old man. "What do you mean *I'm* too old?" The implication as he looked the older man up and down was obvious. A hot flush of anger now spread up his neck to his cheeks. Crabbe's rudeness and abrupt dismissal of his training and expertise was completely unexpected.

"Yeah." Crabbe sneered, his eyes like flint. "We don't want old cops here."

The man's attitude defied all logic. "Do you mean to tell me that you would rather take a rooky off the street who knows absolutely nothing, and then spend thousands of dollars and countless years training him before you can turn him into a useful copper?" Not waiting for the inspector's reply, Terry turned on his heel and strode toward the door, announcing in disgust, "All I can say to you *mate,* is, if that's how you buggers run the police here, then I wouldn't want any part of it!"

His next stop was the headquarters of the Australian Federal police located in a nondescript office building in the heart of Perth's business district. In stark contrast to the state's law enforcement body, "FEDPOL" representatives greeted him warmly.

"Yes sir. Welcome to Western Australia. It is always a pleasure to meet officers from other law enforcement agencies. Please take a seat and I'll see if the Commander is free to see you!"

Terry had scarcely sat down before the waiting room door burst open.

"Sergeant Flatley?" I'm, Commander Shepherd, the officer in charge of the Western Australian division of the Australian Federal police. Please come through to my office and take a seat." The statuesque physique of the middle aged senior Federal policeman suggested a man who looked after his personal fitness and appearance. "What can we do for you?"

Shepherd listened attentively as Terry summarized his police experience and the reason for his sudden visit.

"Well, we'd be very glad to have someone of your obviously fine calibre in the Federal police. Firstly, let me explain how our organisation works. We have two components. There is the uniformed division and the detectives. The former is split into two bodies. There is the Protective Service Division, which is responsible for guarding duties at Commonwealth Government establishments and the general duties component, which is responsible for everyday policing duties in the A.C.T. Someone of your experience would be bored and wasted in the Protective Service Division and should aim for normal policing or detective work. If you decide to join us, you would have to go to the Australian Capital Territory and serve a couple of years there before you were eligible to apply for a transfer to Western Australia. You couldn't join us and come straight here I'm afraid."

"That sort of defeats the purpose, really. I want to live in W.A. where I can be close to my mother to offer her support."

"I know but I'm unable to do anything about that."

"Thank you for taking the time to see me, sir. It's been very pleasant. I guess I'll just have to look for a new career."

Terry's impatience to return home and announce his plans made the flight home to New Zealand appear interminable. The wait for connecting flights from Auckland to Wellington and then finally to Nelson, frustrated him immensely. Jane and the four children were waiting for him at Nelson airport. The children's obvious excitement and glee compensated for his wife's subdued greeting.

"Daddy. Daddy. We've got a big surprise for you. What was Australia like? Is Nana coming to visit us soon?"

Not waiting for his answers, they squabbled over who was going to carry his bags and where each should sit in the car. Swallowing the lump in his throat, Terry hugged each child. *Oh, how I have missed them.*

After the short ride home, he parked the family's Kingswood sedan in the garage and allowed the children to drag him excitedly up the zigzag path to the house. As he entered, they grew strangely silent, watching his face expectantly. His jaw dropped at the site confronting him. "WELCOME HOME DAD," announced the large paper banners in childish scrawl. Balloons and streamers festooned the kitchen and tiny dining area. Hot stinging tears of love welled behind his eyes as he realised just how much his family meant to him. *Oh, if only, I never had to growl at them and I never lost my temper,* he mourned.

To his surprise, Jane raised no objection when he announced that he wanted to move to Western Australia. Despite the enormity of the decision, she was quite prepared to sell their home and all their furniture, sever friendships and travel to a new land with unknown prospects and no emotional or financial support. *Could it be that she craved the chance for a new beginning?* He mentally crossed his fingers, grateful for the lack of conflict.

"What are you going to do for a job?" Surprisingly, there was no hint of challenge in Jane's question.

"Basically, all I know is police work. I've got to somehow translate those skills to the private sector. I'd like to think we could buy some sort of business and run it together. With the money we get from the sale of the house, my holiday pay and superannuation payout, we should be able to find something. In the mean time, I'm quite prepared to have a go at anything. I don't care if it's working in a pub or driving a truck, as long as there's no shift work and we can manage. It will be great to get away from all the bloody crims and lead a life like normal people who have weekends off and sleep at night. In any case, do you realise that you have better qualifications and greater likelihood of finding employment than I do? You might have to be the bread winner for a while and I'll look after the kids."

Jane looked doubtful. "I haven't had a job for so long I've probably forgotten most of my skills."

"Rubbish. It'll be just like riding a bike. If you have to work, it will soon come back to you. Don't worry, we've lots of options!"

Upon his return to duty, Terry's work mates bombarded him with questions about Western Australia. Most expressed dismay at his plans to resign. He repeatedly encountered the same comments. "Don't be bloody silly. Take leave of absence. All you need is a good holiday. How can you bare to abandon so much? Don't burn your bridges. If, things don't work out, you can always come back here and take up where you left off!"

Terry wished he could reveal the full truth of his resignation but doubted their capacity to understand his quandary. "No. It's time for a fresh start. Neither my marriage nor I can survive police life for much longer. I've had enough of being a human punching bag, the terrible toll of shift work and defending myself against groundless allegations of impropriety. My career as a policeman is finished," was the best reply he could invent.

Some of his peers pushed him further with questions such as, "What do you mean? Why don't you sit your promotion exams? You don't have to remain in Nelson as a sergeant. You should pursue your career."

Visions of past encounters with Jane over the issue of study and promotion exams filled Terry's head. How could he explain to others the horrendous domestic disharmony surrounding that issue? Instead, he replied, "Promotion is pointless. Promotion means moving to Auckland or Wellington and prolonging working shift work. Do you know, that even at the rank of inspector, I would still be rostered on night shifts? On the other hand, if I stay here, I'll be walking the beat for the next twenty years. That's if some bloody bikie doesn't decide to fire bomb my house in the mean time. No. I've got to make a clean break and find a new life outside the police."

Thanks to the weekly flea market, disposing of their furniture and other items too bulky to transport, proved no problem. Eager for a bargain, the vultures swooped, snatching things from the trailer as Terry drove to their allotted space in a central city car park. Even the tattered and fraying rope used to secure the tables, chairs, wheelbarrow, boxes of children's toys and crockery disappeared.

With a burgeoning real estate market, the family home sold for a tidy sum and suppressing nostalgic misgivings, they waved a tearful farewell to the delightful town nestling between the quiet harbour and tree covered hills. They were on their way to a new life, which would bring some almost insurmountable challenges and test relationships to breaking point.

As Terry expected, finding work in Western Australia was not a problem. Locating well-paid and meaningful employment was, however, a very different story. Packed into Judy's tiny, flat-roofed fibro cottage, their arrival coincided with the commencement of Western Australia's wettest winter for forty-six years. Forced to cope with the uncertainty of their future and dwindling cash reserves, the magnitude of his decision shocked Terry like a bucket of ice water.

His first foray into the stark world of private enterprise saw Terry cast in the role of Bar Manager for Bunbury's Rose Hotel. As one of that country town's better hotels, "The Rose" was like a gracious old lady who had seen better days. Owned and operated by an unassuming publican with the most inappropriate name of John Drinkwater, the Rose catered for a motley collection of red nosed, ageing barflies who lacking the motivation or incentive to find other ways of wiling away time, propped up the long, chest high, beer soaked counter, on a daily basis.

With no concept of the rudeness with which the public treated persons employed in a servile work, Terry had thought the life of a barman might be quite fun. Like an aspiring amateur lightweight boxer who leaps into the ring with a heavyweight professional opponent, romance met reality.

Although it was one explanation, it was highly unlikely that the drinking holes' past employees possessed the gift of mental telepathy. Whatever the reason, the geriatric brain damaged alcoholic patrons were so used to staff anticipating their every whim and fancy, they deemed it either too hard, or unworthy of their status to engage their brains long enough to form a sentence. Slamming empty glasses noisily on the linoleum topped bar was their chosen form of communication with the lowly minions employed to serve.

Valued patrons or not, as far as Terry was concerned, the customer was *not* always right. "I'm not a bloody mind reader!" he advised one particularly obnoxious barfly loudly so that all could hear. "If you wish to be served, you will ask politely for your chosen poison, *and* you will thank me when I serve you. Now *sir,* what is it that you would like?"

Surprisingly, after the initial stunned silence, his abrupt no nonsense response worked well. Almost immediately, the atmosphere in the public bar changed to a jovial bantering between the new bar manager and the old codgers. Politeness became the norm, with both staff and patron treating each other with renewed respect.

Although Drinkwater harboured higher managerial aspirations for Terry, the poor remuneration was insufficient compensation for split shifts and unrelenting drudgery. Often commencing duty at 9.00 am, he worked until lunchtime before having an enforced six-hour break. Expected to return at teatime, he toiled until the last patron left the restaurant, which was often not until the early hours of the morning. Being tall, the low beer taps and sinks caused excruciating backaches and it was not long before the new bar manager handed the publican his notice.

Locating the old notebook in which he had hastily scrawled all possibilities for employment or business ownership, Terry explored each opportunity, avidly searching the businesses for sale and the situations vacant columns of the West Australian newspaper. The endless sea of possibilities compiled in the lush optimism of New Zealand had somehow evaporated in Australia's desert of actuality.

Together, he and Jane carefully evaluated numerous husband and wife enterprises, delving deeply to unmask the ugly and carefully disguised truth, masquerading behind valid but false reasons for sale. In every case, they revealed a major pitfall, deeming the purchase fraught with risk. In some instances, tax figures proved the owner's claims had been grossly exaggerated. On other occasions, the claims were tantamount to fraud. Sometimes, the landlord had substantial rent increases in store, or the Local Authority had plans to re-route traffic, with would impact substantially upon business viability.

Tired and despairing of ever finding a viable venture, Terry turned to the employment pages. Although Jane appeared well qualified for the numerous job opportunities, pay rates for women were much less than her male counterparts enjoyed. Obviously, Western Australia lagged behind New Zealand in such matters. It mattered not, that Jane displayed a marked reluctance to return to paid employment, quite simply, she would not be able to support the family financially.

During his search for meaningful employment, Terry concluded that Perth held the majority of opportunities or they needed to move further a field to the remote, incinerator hot, mining towns. With the desire to be physically capable of supporting his ailing mother and the need to provide a sound education for Liam, Veronica, Michael and Helen, any move to an isolated location was out of the question. Despairing and beginning to regret his rash plan to escape from the threat hanging over them in New Zealand, well meaning people advised him to apply for work in the security industry. Somehow Terry was not yet ready to exchange the police uniform and all its associated authority for the badge of commercialism and the stigmata of being a "hired gun." Possessing an almost overwhelming craving for anonymity and acceptance into a world of normal people, he knew uniforms of any description would serve as a constant reminder of his recently abandoned career and all its so bitterly sullied aspirations.

Desperate for independence and self-sufficiency, the depressed young man answered an advertisement for a sales representative. A small local company wanted someone to extol the merits of various forms of insulation and in his naivety, Terry laboured under the delusion that the general populace shared his high opinion of home insulation, happily parting with the dollars required to enjoy its merits.

"This will be a piece of cake!" he judged. It did not matter to him that his remuneration was solely commission based; his confidence in the product dispelled any doubts as to the size of his salary.

He should have been suspicious, when at interview, the company's sole proprietor; Joe Hodge dismissed his curriculum vitae with a wave of his hand. "I'm sure everything's in order. You'll do fine!"

Hodge- displayed a stack of cards bearing what he described as "red hot" leads. "You just need to visit all these people and we'll both be wealthy," his sapling thin, lanky prospective employer announced. "They're all literally crying out for our product. I've contacted them all by 'phone and they're expecting you!"

Purchasing a late model Holden HJ Belmont sedan, Terry attached the company's magnetic logos to both front doors. Loading a briefcase with samples and pamphlets, he mapped out a plan to tour all the country towns in the South West, believing prospective customers were anxiously waiting to part with thousands of dollars to enjoy greater protection from extremes of temperature variation.

Alas, as Terry worked his way through the so-called "hot leads," his happy optimism quickly gave way to monumental disappointment. Not one person on the list had heard from

Hodge or his company. He soon deduced the horrible truth. Acquiring lists of building applicants from various local Councils, Hodge frequently used their names as the basis for his marketing campaigns. The problem was his unscrupulous use of unsuspecting budding sales people to do the "leg work" at no cost to him. By the time most had worked out the alleged leads were an embellishment of the truth and resigned, it was too late. Despite the fact that it was not cost affective to chase names on a list on the off chance someone might purchase insulation, a percentage of the leads invariably paid a dividend for Hodge. It was just too bad, if the salesperson responsible for the groundwork was not around to pick up part of the proceeds. There would always be an unlimited supply of "suckers."

Somewhat wiser from the experience, Terry chose not to be embittered by the cold reality of the world of door-to-door sales and exploitative employers. A few more weeks later, and with so many mouths to feed, the substantial downward adjustment of the bank balance precipitated what was for him, a painful decision. He had little choice but to accept the only readily available employment as a security guard with all its unpleasant implications. *It's just for a little while, until we get on our feet,* he told himself. However, somewhere deep inside a little voice whispered, *"That's what you think!"*

In the 1980's Western Australia was riding high on the back of a resources boom. Fuelled by the World's insatiable demand for aluminium and other metals essential in the manufacturing sector, Worsley Alumina called for tenders to construct a major alumina refinery on the Darling Scarp, 65 kilometres to the east of Bunbury. As the principal contractor, Raymond Engineers, itself a subsidiary company of American construction giant Kaiser Engineering, had the task of completing the eleven hundred million dollar project.

While many unions held companies to ransom through the threat of strike action for higher wages, Raymond Engineers vowed to bar the most militant of unions, The Builders Labourers Federation from their site. In order to do so, it was necessary to screen every potential employee closely to check union affiliation. Ties to the barred BLF meant automatic disqualification from employment. With two-metre high cyclone

318

fences topped with barbed wire encompassing the site, security patrols, identification passes and gate checks, the principal contractors felt sure they could keep the site free from militancy and costly strikes. However, with a work force of four thousand requiring daily access this was never going to be an easy task. Each day representatives from the BLF held recruiting campaigns outside the gates in the hope of convincing construction workers to change their union allegiance.

As a new recruit to Raymond Engineers private police force, Terry did not receive a briefing as to his principle duties. The head of security, Gerry Fraser an autocratic former Victorian police detective sergeant, liked to keep as much information to himself as possible. His theorised that, by allowing his employees to know as much as he did, would threaten his own position. The fact that the dissemination of basic information to his hireling's would improve the functioning of his organisation and reflect favourably on his skills, as a manager seemed to escape him. Many of the routine tasks appeared pointlessly mind numbing and good morale non-existent.

Within a few days, Terry worked out for himself why he was there but with so many obvious flaws in the system, security procedures became farcical when placed under pressure. Each morning a seemingly endless stream of workers stormed through the main entrance, along with a sundry collection of vehicles. There was obvious resentment at the presence of guard's with abuse and open hostility being commonplace. Checking each person's face against a miniature photograph on an identification card was a physical impossibility for the two security guards on gate duty. Along with the many that forgot or refused to wear identification, there were always new starters whose identity required checking against lists left in the security office the night before. Among the workers, a percentage of troublemakers swapped passes or tried to get in without displaying identification, deriving some sort of perverse pleasure in testing the system.

Conditions for guards at the main gate were appalling. Overworked and stressed by an ineffectual system they were afforded no protection from the elements. Forced to endure blinding summer heat, swarming flies and choking red dust and in winter, freezing winds and driving rain which made life intolerable. While guards were supposed to rotate between gate duty and patrolling the construction site, the duration of each persons time at the gate was excessive, resulting in frayed tempers and the mind numbing pain of boredom. When construction crews left for the day, the situation eased, although lack of purpose produced the same unendurable boredom.

Tasked with providing emergency first aid and fire fighting duties, guards formed the basis for emergency response. It was on the rare occasion of a conflagration or injury that Terry finally found some degree of satisfaction putting to good use fire fighting and first aid skills acquired through company funded training programs. For the majority of the time, his frustration at under utilisation of police training and experience threatened to overwhelm him. As with most major construction projects, the employer sought to squeeze the most from each employee, deigning twelve hour shifts normal.

With a fifty minute drive to and from work each day, there was very little time for family life. Once again, Terry found himself caught in the trap of demanding shifts, sleep deprivation and unrewarding work. The strain of living too closely with his mother under trying conditions had begun to tell on them all and he shelved any aspirations for business ownership in the interest of expediency. After searching and examining the real estate opportunities befitting their budget, Terry and Jane chose a soon to be completed house in the new sub division of Clifton Park, to the north of Bunbury.

As the house was too small, they requested the builder to add an additional bedroom. So anxious were they for their own home, they moved in before Western Power connected the electricity. With the responsibility of a large mortgage weighing heavily on his already overburdened shoulders, Terry heard the door slam firmly shut on the cage of financial commitment.

Six months elapsed and with the strain of shift work once more threatening to destroy his fragile relationship with Jane, Terry answered one of the few employment advertisements in The South West Times. On this occasion, Solahart Hot Water systems needed an additional representative to service Bunbury. Always able to sell himself at interview, Terry became that company's representative on a small retainer and commission. Bursting with enthusiasm and gratitude for the lifeline rescuing him from certain marital destruction in shift work's pit of despair, there was little he could do when his new employer decided to change the deal offered at the initial interview.

"I've decided instead, to keep Bunbury for myself." Greg Chalk, the charismatic, tall, athletic company franchisee advised. "As a Bunbury boy, the locals prefer to deal with me, rather than someone they don't know. I was going to develop the whole of the South West and give all the Bunbury sales to you. Shaking his blond head, Greg smiled disarmingly; blue eyes sparkling as he ruthlessly cut the ground from beneath Terry's feet. "You can have the South West. I've got a display trailer with a solar hot water system on it that you can tow around the towns and set up in all the shopping centres. "I'll give you twenty percent of the sale price of every system that you sell as well as two hundred dollars per week retainer. How does that sound?"

Bugger! Terry swore silently. *I took this job knowing that I would have the benefit of all the sales generated through the shop front and local advertising. Now he tells me I've got to go cold canvassing! What else can I do, but make the most of it? I'll just get stuck in and give it my all. I'll show this bugger how good I can be.* "I guess that's okay," he replied aloud.

Once more, Terry hit the road, committing himself fully to the success of his new career. Almost immediately, his efforts paid dividends. Erecting the display trailer in supermarket car parks throughout South West towns, he bailed up everyone who would listen, handing out brochures and demonstrating the benefits of, "free hot water from the sun."

As the sales cheques rolled in, it appeared as if his newfound sales career would be successful. Enjoying the public contact and believing in the product, the life of a sales representative promised to be both financially rewarding and satisfying. Alas, the axe was about to fall once more.

"I've had complaints from all the plumbers in the South West towns," Greg advised. "I have plumbers appointed all over my franchise area who have the rights to any units sold in their towns. They all want a cut from every unit that you sell. They're actually pretty sore that you've been going into town and selling under their noses."

"What! That's what you told me to do." Terry's anger boiled over. "What right do they have to claim anything from the hard work that I've put in? I'm the one who has got off his arse, incurred the travel costs and generated the sales. No units would have been sold if it weren't for me. In any case, they're getting income from installing every unit sold by me. It's not fair."

"Sorry, mate. That's the way it is. I've got to keep them happy. In future you will have to give them half your commission!"

Like bloody hell, he thought savagely but bit his tongue. The need to service mortgage repayments and feed his family overrode his desire to express his displeasure in the crudest and most succinct way. "What about the solid fuel heaters that I sell. Do the bloody plumbers get the proceeds from those as well?"

In addition to hot water systems, Chalk sold wood heaters as a side-line. He had advised Terry he would receive commission from any sales in this area.

"Oh, no. There's no problem there. Go for it!"

Although the proceeds from wood heaters were minor compared with solar water heaters, Terry decided to redouble his efforts, making up any shortfall by additional sales. Several weeks elapsed before Greg summonsed him to a sales meeting.

"You've been going well. Solahart in Perth have decided to set targets for all representatives. He slid an A4 paper sheet across the desk. "This is what they say you should be selling in future."

Terry's eyes scanned the list. It appeared that sales representatives in the Perth area were far more successful than he was. With weekly sales averaging three or four units, he adjudged himself successful. "Bloody hell. They're selling five or six units a day! How the hell do they do that?"

"Population difference," Chalk replied laconically. "Ah, I see you've found your target."

Terry spluttered amazedly, "They are living in a dream world. There is no way that I can sell ten units each week!"

"That's why we're going to Perth next week for a sales motivational session."

"I don't see any way that we can do any better than we're doing at the moment. I'm as proactive as can possibly be and all the advertising in the world is only going to sell a certain number of units."

"I've got some other bad news for you."

Expecting to hear the end of his sales career, Terry replied quietly, "What's that?"

"Solahart have advised me that I have to take the solid fuel sales away from you so that you can concentrate on hot water systems!"

That's it. Terry decided secretly. *Every time I look like getting somewhere, they shift the bloody goal posts. What ever I do is never going to be good enough.*

Depressed, desperate and with no apparent alternative, he turned to the one source he knew could provide immediate employment. While he dreaded the prospect of returning to Worsley, he knew he could exploit contacts and talk himself into a job in Raymond Engineers Warehouse. By this time, winter had set in again. Torrential rain fell day after dreary day turning the Worsley construction site into a sea of sticky brown clay and deep treacherous holes. Winters on the Darling Scarp seemed interminable.

Led by the irascible and eccentric Alex Slater, Raymond Engineers employed forty or so personnel including office clerks, crane drivers, dogmen, forklift drivers and labourers. This workforce had responsibility for receiving, documenting, storing and distributing every single component essential for creation of a large alumina refinery. Items range from minuscule electronic components to massive steel pressure vessels.

Terry was to discover he was now part of the biggest team of reprobates and dysfunctional misfits ever to come together in one place. Team spirit, work ethic and industrial harmony appeared to be words missing from the vocabularies of the larger percentage of this eclectic bunch. Squabbling continually among themselves, while fracturing into disparate groups, they displayed a genius for avoiding work, greedily clutching every minute of overtime to inflate already excessively generous pay packets.

The lazy animal cunning of some individuals defied description. When allocated duties, many would simply disappear, hiding from the scrutiny of Worsley officials in the nearby forest. Others were so effective at wasting time they could spend the periods between authorised work breaks simply driving or walking as slowly as possible from the warehouse and their allocated work area. By the time they reached their destination it was time to start heading back again for morning tea or lunch!

Well known for his explosive bursts of temper, Slater had much to occupy his thoughts, with such a bunch of indolent troublemakers in his care. Terry had dismissed the reports as exaggerated until he experienced them first hand and could understand why his boss was so irascible. However, the smallest infraction or irritation could provoke volcanic rage. Bellowing like an enraged bull, the stocky warehouse manager would storm through the hanger-like structure, slamming doors and swearing angrily. So unpredictable were these displays of rage, everyone avoided him wherever possible and winced in sympathy for the targets of his abuse.

Terry had hoped for a physically active job in the warehouse. The warehouse manager had other ideas. Bestowing the lofty title of Expediting Officer upon his newest recruit, Slater directed Terry toward a one-metre high, teetering mountain of documents, piled in the corner of his jumbled office.

"The detail on every one of those forms must be copied by hand onto another form, photocopied 12 times and then distributed throughout Raymond's construction office," he commanded without elaboration

Terry was puzzled. "What information is on the documents?"

"They form a record of all the materials received on site for construction of the refinery."

"But, why do I have to write out everything again. Why can't they just be photocopied?"

Slater stared at Terry, a scowl seizing his face with the suddenness of a West African coup. "Because that's your bloody job. Now, get on with it!"

Terry could see he was not going to get any sense from his hostile manager. Deciding that other office staff could provide the explanation he sought, he picked up an armful of papers and made his way to a vacant desk. He was quickly disappointed.

"Oh, thank goodness they've given that job to you!" The comment came from a dumpy, plain faced girl of seventeen.

"Why is that?" Terry asked expectantly.

"Julie and I used to do that job but we hated it so much, we've just avoided doing it."

"What's the reason for having to handwrite all this stuff out again?"

"Dunno. It's stupid. That's why we don't do it any more!" Rosie turned away dismissively, her snub little nose directed huffily toward the ceiling of the over-heated office.

Terry tried several times to engage both girls in conversation. Giggling among themselves, they retreated to their partitioned enclave, shuffling paper into neat piles and they gossiped about their boyfriends.

Empty-headed little twits, Terry decided.

"I hear you were a policeman!" Sneered, a hatchet-faced clerk. "Bit of a bloody comedown for you, working here. Bloody cops are all the same. Think they know everything but only end up as coppers because they can't get jobs any other place!"

"It's nice to meet you too!" Terry replied sarcastically.

Most of the office staff shared a similar attitude toward him, rebuffing any attempts at friendship or polite conversation. In their minds, Terry was clearly an intruder in their environment. The animosity was no doubt due in part to their manager's Hitler-like personality and his propensity for rage, which filtered down through the hierarchical structure. However, the unwarranted contempt suggested to Terry that some had experienced less than pleasant encounters with the Australian law.

It was dark when Terry left home at 5.00 am and dark when he returned home again each evening. Confined to a stuffy overheated office performing mundane and senseless duties Terry thought he would go insane. A gigantic circular clock dominated one wall of the office, taunting him as its hands moved ponderously across the Roman numerals. "Why the hell do they call me an expediting officer?" he wondered. "I'm just pointlessly pushing bloody paper for ten hours a day."

Each Friday afternoon, the assistant warehouse manager Brian Sykes, walked slowly through the office and the warehouse asking each employee the same question. "Are you right for overtime tomorrow?"

Arriving at Terry's desk, Sykes opened his mouth to speak. Before he could utter the repetitious phrase, Terry looked up and spoke first. "No. I am not prepared to work another ten hours on this stuff when there is clearly no worthwhile work for me to do now!"

Sykes frowned, displeasure evident upon his normally genial features. He moved on without further comment.

"Why don't you want to work? Everyone is expected to work on Saturdays! The comment came from a painfully thin, red-haired young man occupying a nearby desk. Terry Radicci was one of the cop haters who took delight in baiting Terry at every opportunity. Skilled in identifying troublemakers and criminals from their mannerisms, attitude and appearance, Terry suspected Radicci was a drug addict and petty dealer. So far, he had successfully avoided Radicci and dismissed his barbed remarks with some inane and indifferent comment. This time he reacted angrily.

"What has it got to do with you? This place is full of lazy bastards who do nothing all week and when the weekend comes; they put their hand up for overtime. What is wrong with this bloody outfit that it can't find enough work to keep these buggers busy, can't supervise men properly and then wastes money paying overtime?

"Wake up mate! Haven't you worked it out yet? The more people on the payroll, the more money Raymond Engineers makes."

"How can that be?"

"Look! Raymond Engineers is employed on a cost plus ten percent basis to build this refinery. The more money they spend, the more money they make and they're making heaps! This job is money for old rope. Grab it while you can mate."

"No thanks. I'm used to being busy and deriving satisfaction from the fact that I earn my wages honestly. Fifty hours a week bored out of my mind is already more than I can bare and I need to see my kids sometime."

After the conversation with Radicci, Terry seriously questioned the value of the tedious and repetitious paper work that occupied his days. Unable to get any sense from Sykes or Slater he began telephoning all the persons who received the fruits of his labours. "What do you do with this information when you get it? Does it serve any useful purpose for you?"

In each case, the answer was the same. "No. We wonder why we get it. It ends up in the waste paper basket!"

"That's it," he decided. "I'm not doing this any more."

Each day he increased the length of time spent away from his desk, finding tasks within the warehouse to occupy his time.

Every time Slater noticed Terry's absence he screamed, "I've told you, you're not employed in the warehouse. I don't want to see you out here again. Get back to your desk!"

Knowing that he faced the risk of the sack, Terry waited until Slater left the warehouse, as he did frequently. He would then slip outside, extending his unofficial job description by driving forklifts and other useful tasks. The mountain of papers continued to grow. However, with no-one dependent upon the forms, there were no repercussions. Terry's conclusion that he was employed merely to increase Raymond Engineer's workforce thus adding to the costs charged to Worsley Alumina had been confirmed.

Within a few months of him returning to Worsley, Judy announced that she would sell the Boyanup house and move to Perth. "It's too much for me to look after and I need to be closer to doctors and hospitals. I'm not getting and younger and now I know you've got a good job and a lovely new house, I feel I can move away from you."

How little you know about my miserable life, he wondered but not wanting to worry her, replied, "That's nice, mum. It will give us a good excuse to go to Perth. I am sure it's the best thing for you."

Over a period of weeks, Terry completely altered his job description, volunteering to drive trucks and forklifts and helping to unpack crates of machinery components as they arrived on site. Enjoying the physical activity and at last feeling some degree of usefulness, he discovered his back was still vulnerable to injury following the attack by Freddy Wood. A persistent pain stabbed continually down the outside of his right leg. Choosing to ignore it, he soldiered on, expecting the pain to disappear in time.

Slater gave up trying to get his errant expediting clerk back to his desk, no doubt concluding that Terry's mutiny made no difference to the bottom line of the balance sheet. One day, after a particularly riotous display of temper the unstable warehouse manager mysteriously disappeared from the scene. Brian Sykes slipped into the vacant chair as rumours circulated that Slater's mental health was the reason for his sudden demise.

As the weeks dragged inexorably by, the refinery began to take shape, colossal ugly steel edifices rising from the mud. To the uninitiated, the vast structures were a jumble of pipes, tanks, valves and pressure vessels, a conglomeration of junk thrown together like something from a plumber's nightmare. However, its pending completion coincided with rumours that a bauxite glut would result in mothballing of the giant creation.

Gradually, the huge work force declined, as welders, concrete workers and steel fixers moved onto other projects. The boom which justified the refinery's existence vaporised into the black clouds of an economic downturn, making the employment prospects for local workers appear extremely bleak. With a population of slightly more than one million people, Perth could not absorb the flood of men seeking re-employment. Once more Terry and Jane turned to the business opportunity columns of the local papers but could find no viable alternative.

Concerned for the future of his family, Terry expected that he would be one of the first laid off by Raymond Engineers. Although he hated his tenuous position at the warehouse, the need for an income deterred his resignation. In any case, the long hours at the isolated location made the search for alternative employment nearly impossible. Deciding to seek reassurance, he requested an interview with Sykes.

"Oh, you have nothing to worry about, Terry. I assure you that you will receive adequate notice when we decide your services are no longer required," his grey-haired employer smiled benignly from behind his immense and untidy desk.

"Thanks, Brian. I need to know, because Jane and I have purchased a block of land in Perth and we plan to build a house there. I don't want to commit myself to another mortgage if I'm likely to be on the dole."

"Don't worry. You'll be okay for a while yet."

In anticipation of Worsley reaching its conclusion, Terry and Jane had sold their house at Clifton Park, moving into a rented brick home in Bunbury. They knew Perth offered better employment prospects and wanted to be ready for the move when Terry's job ran out. Although the rented house was up for sale, they did not anticipate much happening due to the depressed property market. With plans to build on a small orchard property purchased at Chidlow, Terry intended to live in single men's quarters at the construction site while Jane and the children moved into a caravan on their block.

Apart from Liam, Veronica, Michael and Helen not seeing their father during the week, the planned separation was of little consequence, as by this time, the marriage existed solely to provide a stable home environment for the children in whose presence they strove to maintain a charade of happy, well-adjusted parents. Unfortunately, when the bedroom closed each night, the situation was vastly different.

Within the space of a few days, the real estate company handling the sale of their rented home announced its sale and demanded they vacate almost immediately. While they were still reeling from this news, Brian Sykes called Terry to his office. "I have to give you a week's notice. Raymond Engineers is reducing its workforce."

"But you told me less than a week ago that I had nothing to worry about!" Flabbergasted, Terry could not believe Sykes could retreat on his promise so quickly.

"I'm sorry," he replied lamely. "If you like, I can put in a word for you for the gas pipeline project."

With the discovery of an enormous natural gas field near the north-western town of Karratha, the Western Australian State Government planned to pipe the valuable resource nearly two thousand kilometres to Perth.

"What bloody good is that to me? I want to build a house in Chidlow and live there with my family. You know that's my plan and I very nearly took out a mortgage on the strength of your promise of continued employment!"

Sykes merely shrugged. "Things changed a bit more quickly than I anticipated."

As much as he loathed the Worsley warehouse, the dysfunctional misfits that made up its workforce and the meaningless work, he felt shattered. In the space of a few short days, he could not provide either a home or income for his family. *My God! What are we going to do now?* Terry cried desperately.

Terry's anguish and feeling of abject failure was all encompassing. Fortunately, Jane did not rub salt into his wounds, maintaining a stoical cheerfulness that only served to increase his guilt at placing his family in such a predicament.

"I don't know what to do now. We can't go ahead with the house and we've spent all our money on the block at Chidlow," he muttered dejectedly after breaking the news of his sacking.

"Brian Sykes seems to think I can get a job at Karratha on the gas pipeline project. The only thing I can think of is for us to buy a caravan and drive up there in the hope of getting work. The prospects for work in Perth and Bunbury are pretty bleak."

"Let's ring Garry and Ruth. They might have a suggestion," his wife offered.

Terry and Jane's former neighbours from Clifton Park had become close friends. Having suffered from the economic downturn in a real estate partnership with his brother Neil, Garry and Ruth Scott moved to the remote aboriginal settlement of Halls Creek in the Kimberley Ranges. Employed by the Agricultural Department on the task of eradicating the evasive Nagoorah burr and feral donkeys, Garry and Ruth lived in Government housing and confessed to loving their lifestyle.

"Shit, I'm sorry to hear that," Garry swore when informed of their plight. "That's a real bastard. Look. If you come up here, I am one hundred percent sure that you would both get work within a week."

"Bloody hell Garry. Halls Creek is three thousand kilometres from Perth. I hear the heat is unbearable. Besides, where would the kids go to school?"

"There's a school here but you could always put your eldest into boarding school in Perth. You would qualify for Government assistance and would probably be given a State house."

"What's the town like. I hear the aborigines outnumber the white people and things are pretty primitive."

"It's not that bad. You make your own fun here and the white community are really friendly. There's about two thousand black fellas and about two hundred white people who are mostly employed by the Government. You get used to the heat and the place sort of grows on you. We wouldn't come back to Perth for quids!"

After hanging up the telephone, Terry turned to Jane. "What do you reckon?"

"At least we'd know where we stand. It's better than living on the dole and wondering if you're ever going to get a job. Besides, we might only have to go as far as Karratha. You will probably get a job there with Raymond's."

"I guess we don't have much choice. I'd better ring mum and ask her if Liam can board with her because there's no High School in Halls Creek."

The thought of splitting his family and leaving Liam behind made Terry feel ill. "I guess we'll have to treat this as an adventure and just make the most of it," he told himself, hoping that by viewing things from that perspective their situation would not appear quite so grim.

The following day, Terry told Brian Sykes that he did not wish to work out his notice. Having committed to a plan of action he did not want to spend any time reflecting on the wisdom of their choice. In any case, they had only a week to vacate the house.

"Here's a reference. When you get to Karratha, go to the North West Shelf project and tell them I sent you. You're sure to get a job there in the warehouse."

Oh no. Not the bloody warehouse. There's no way I'm going through that again! Terry could picture himself pushing paper all day in a boring unsatisfying job and returning to a caravan in a squalid camping ground each evening. *It's, Halls Creek, here we come, for better or worse*, he promised himself.

***

CHAPTER SEVEN
DIAMONDS, DUST AND DEPRESSION

With its front wheel nearly lifting off the ground from the weight of their hastily purchased caravan packed full with family possessions, they set off from Bunbury. Squashed in the rear seat with four children was the family mongrel dog, Muppy. The kids adored her and there was no way they could bare to leave her behind. Never having towed a caravan before, Terry knew he was going to undergo a steep learning curve over the next three thousand two hundred kilometres. He felt sure they would encounter every conceivable road hazard along the way.

Stopping briefly at Judy's Tuart Hill unit, they deposited Liam and waved him a tearful good bye. "Don't worry son, I promise to get us all back together again as soon as I can," Terry pledged, as Liam silently appeared to accept his lot. Liam was not one for revealing his feelings and Terry could only hope the unfortunate turn of events would not distress his eldest son.

Taking five days, the journey proved almost uneventful until they reached the tiny town of Roebourne. With a shortage of rental homes in Karratha, they immediately dismissed any lingering thoughts of setting up home in the red dusty town from which many commuted to the nearby natural gas project. They would have to live in the caravan and the outback hamlet offered few attractions. The red dust, broken glass, rubbish and snotty nosed half-naked aboriginal children squabbling in the otherwise deserted streets was too much for the travel weary family. After an overnight stay, they departed the next morning, eager to reach Halls Creek, which was still several days away.

Fitzroy Crossing marked the end of the bitumen. Ahead of them stretched nearly four hundred kilometres of rutted, corrugated and unsealed gravel. Talcum powder fine bulldust hid treacherously deep potholes, causing the little trailer home to bounce and rock cruelly as if it wanted to be free of the mud caked Holden. With the monsoon season only just over, numerous creeks swirled across what served as a road, hiding all manner of hazards. At each crossing, Terry waded through the muddy water to ensure they could safely negotiate a path to the far side.

Garry Scott met them half an hour's drive from their destination and piloted them to Scott's GEHA[38] cottage. His beaming smile and welcoming handshake did much to dispel their fatigue and despair.

The tiny former goldmining settlement seemed to embrace broad tree lined streets, aboriginal stockmen in wide hats, dirty urchins and road trains as its hallmark. Small groups of desert tribes' people sat in groups unmindful of the red dust, chattering loudly and swigging wine from cardboard casks. Everywhere, broken glass gleamed in the harsh sunlight. Mangy dogs snarled and ran lose, chasing dust caked, Toyota Landcruisers and steel mesh encased shop fronts bore testimony to less peaceful times. A police paddy wagon cruised quietly by, its uniformed driver and passenger waving a friendly salute and raising their spirits immeasurably.

As promised, both Jane and Terry secured immediate employment at the local hospital with its wide verandahs, wide oleander lined driveway and a small mortuary situated outside the main fence line. Terry was to learn that the superstitious native Australian population would not enter the hospital if they saw death as part of the hospital's entity.

With the recent resignation of the handyman, Terry's job description also encompassed the duties of ambulance driver, mortuary attendant, gardener and orderly. Being the only male in an otherwise exclusively female workforce, Terry rediscovered a surprisingly high level of job satisfaction. He immediately set about restoring the neglected gardens to their previous glory and took great delight in repairing anything he could find that was within his self acquired refurbishment skills.

On many occasions, he had to abandon the ride-on lawnmower or his workshop to drive the ambulance, attend motor accidents and meet the Royal Flying Doctor Service aircraft bringing seriously ill patients from distant stations or aboriginal settlements.

In many respects, the small hospital formed the backbone of the community with the local black population gravitating there

---

[38] GEHA Government Employees Housing Authority.

for treatment following drunken fights. It also served as a focal point and meeting place, with the wide verandah almost permanently occupied by aboriginal mothers picking nits from their children's heads as they gossiped the hours away. At one point, the Department of Health decided in their wisdom to downgrade the vital institution to the status of a nursing post. Under this category, the hospital could no longer hold patients overnight and closed its doors at 5.00 pm each afternoon.

The farcical situation resulting from the closure meant the poor individuals occupying beds during the daytime had to find alternative arrangements each evening.

Despite being above the twenty-sixth parallel, Halls Creek would become bitterly cold between the months of June and September. Situated on the edge of The Great Sandy Desert, biting winds squeezed the mercury down into single figures with pneumonia a common condition among desert people.

"Terry, I have a job for you this evening." The Hospital Matron, Elspeth's small frame cast a shadow into the workshop. "I want you to take one of the patients back to the river bed tonight. He is quite ill and can't get back there himself." Elspeth shook her head, curly brown hair bobbing, her stern face creased with concern. Noticing his surprise, she added, "I know. There's nothing we can do about it. These people are tough. He'll be alright."

Nightfall arrives quickly in the tropics. No sooner had the sun dropped below the horizon than it became pitch black. With a canopy of twinkling diamonds providing the only light, Terry carefully negotiated the dry creek bed with the F100 ambulance in four-wheel drive. The grizzled old black man leaned forward from his seat on the stretcher in the rear. "That's it boss! That's me camp."

A fat black lubra got to her feet slowly where she had been sitting in the gravel beside the embers of a dying campfire. Her back stiff from arthritis, she smoothed a tight grubby floral dress down over her enormous thighs and lumbered to meet the ambulance. Wheezing heavily, the ancient black man climbed unsteadily from the back of the vehicle and shuffled to the campfire. Terry scurried about in the darkness, gathering fuel and soon flames danced a yellow corroboree in the gravel. He placed a blanket around the old man's shoulders, incredulous that someone so ill could be cast out into the darkness.

He was preparing to leave and had asked if the old chap would be all right when gnarled parchment like fingers seized his wrist. "Come. I show you."

Reluctantly, he followed the ailing black man a short distance along the bone-dry riverbed. "Looky here boss!"

A neat round hole, approximately one and a half metres deep had been scraped from the gravel. Shining his torch into the depths, Terry could make out turbid water in the bottom of the well. "We got good water here, Boss. We be okay. Don't worry."

Hoping the aboriginal man would survive the night, Terry left him to the darkness and the care of his woman. He could not comprehend how the Health Care System could lavish all the care at its disposal during the day but be so neglectful and uncaring at the close of the hospital's doors each night.

After living in their caravan in Scott's backyard for two weeks, the Flatley family moved to the local caravan park, not wanting to wear out their welcome by abusing the Scott's good-natured hospitality. Veronica, Michael and Helen enrolled at the local school where they discovered to their chagrin the horrors of reverse racial discrimination.

"Hey, white girl! How'd ya like some of deese in your pretty white girl's hair?" More a statement than a question, the words emanated from an obese, filthy creature with dried crusts of snot prevalent upon the wide expanse of her upper lip. With skin so dark that it appeared almost blue, the teenage girl's matted hair was grey with a heavy infection of head lice.

Helen recoiled in horror as the girl pulled long strands of obviously infected hair from her scalp and thrust them at the pale faced white girl. Broad faces split in watermelon red grins, revealing piano keyboard teeth as the entire assembly erupted with laughter at the newest arrival's expense.

"Get away from me!" Helen slapped both hands protectively over her prized pristine brown hair. Her skin crawled and itched at the thought of the tiny crab like creatures violating her hygiene.

"Isadora! Leave her alone!" Arriving unannounced, the stern command from Miss Duncan, mercifully saved Helen from further abasement. "Class, this is Helen Flatley. She has just come to Halls Creek with her family and will be attending this school. I expect you to make her welcome." Turning to focus her attention on the class bully, Miss Duncan glowered. "I do not want to see that sort of behaviour again. Do I make myself clear?"

"Yes, miss." Isadora wiped her forearm across her face, smudging vestiges of green snot across one cheek, dumb insolence betraying her future intentions.

Although brief, Miss Duncan's intersession provided sufficient respite for Helen to formulate plans for her self-defence. At recess, she sought the company of other white children. "Pauline, how do you stand this?" Her question was directed toward Scott's youngest daughter who also attended the town's only school.

"They're not so bad. You just have to show them that you can be one of them and forget how things used to be."

"But they're so dirty and smelly and they don't want to learn. They're so far behind. I was doing this work in grade six!"

"It's a lot different here. The kids don't have to go to school. In fact, they get paid for attending. A lot of them just show up long enough so they'll get paid and then they take off. Their fathers are drunk most of the time and their mums get bashed just about every day. They live of Government pensions and often there isn't much food for them at home, 'cos it all goes on booze. You'd be pretty angry at white people too if you lived in the conditions they do."

"But it's not my fault. Why don't they wash and clean themselves up? Why don't the men get jobs and try and better themselves?"

"I don't know." Pauline shook her head. The complexity behind the woes of the town's aboriginal populace was beyond her understanding. "They're not all like Isadora. Look, dad's explained it to me like this. Here there are three levels in the social structure. There are the black fellas, the pure-bred aborigines who have only recently come in from the desert and tribal life. They haven't been able to adapt to the white man's ways and have learnt that they collect "sit down" money from the Post Office every fortnight instead of hunting for food. Unfortunately, they've got caught up with drinking and blow all the money on booze. Then there's the "yella fellas." They're half cast aborigines who have jobs and try and act like white fellas.

They are hated by the black fellas and don't really fit in with the white people. Then, there's us. We're the ones who have everything, the jobs, the nice houses, the money and other stuff. The black fellas know they can never make the grade and just give up and turn to the booze. It's no wonder some of them hate us."

"But, what do I do? I don't want to be here. I can't change things for them. Besides, we're pretty poor too!" Helen cried indignantly.

"Try and make friends with the ones that want to be friendly. Show them that you accept them for who they are. Pretty soon, they'll come around. I've got some really good black friends. In the mean time, stick with me and watch out for Isadora and her mates!"

"What are you doing?" Terry demanded upon arriving home that evening to find Jane minutely examining the children's heads one by one.

Jane looked up from what was to become a tedious almost daily routine "We're looking for head lice. I don't know how we're going to keep them out of the children's hair. All the kids seem to be crawling with knits. It's just awful! Tell your father what happened today!

As Helen retold the unpleasant experience of her first day at school, Terry felt a sickening ache in his stomach as the dagger of guilt twisted with each word. He knew the privations and hardships would help to mould strong character in his offspring, but feelings of colossal failure overrode all other emotions. He silently vowed to claw his way from the abyss of poverty and desperation created from his rash decisions.

Finding work had been the first hurdle. The second was to get out of the caravan and into a house. With the intense heat of summer imminent, a sixteen foot caravan without air conditioning or shade would be an unbearable hell. Lodging an immediate application with the Housing Commission[39], they crossed their fingers, hoping to be treated as an emergency case.

"Where will our house be when we get it, Garry?" Terry inquired of his friend during one of their regular barbecue dinners.

"It'll most likely be in the Garden Area. That's where all the

---

[39] Now Homes West.

Housing Commission houses are." Noticing Terry's surprise, he laughed. "Don't get too excited. The name might imply that its flash but its pretty ordinary. Still, it's better than a bloody caravan."

Known locally as The Garden Area and set to one side of the township, the collection of corrugated iron and fibre cement sheet houses provided accommodation for both white and black families. Unpainted, without guttering or downpipes and constructed on the rock hard red clay soil, the dwellings offered only basic comforts. As with most rental properties, few sported gardens. Separated by low wire fences and in close proximity to neighbouring homes, privacy was impossible and domestic disputes among the populace a continual problem. Used to green lawns, tree lined streets and the orderly quiet of suburbia, Terry's stomach lurched at the prospect of life among the squalor of old car chassis, mangy mongrel dogs and dry weed infested yards.

"Yeah, it will be better than a bloody caravan," he agreed despondently and failed to add the unspoken, "but not much!"

Although it was merely a few weeks, the wait for the ponderous wheels of bureaucracy to churn out its inexorable decision seemed interminable. With Garry Scott's intercession, the sole Government official responsible for the allocation of housing placed their application near the top of his pile. They vacated the Halls Creek Caravan Park, towing the by now sad looking caravan to the yard of their new home. With no furniture, the house supplied cooking and bathroom facilities while they slept in the van awaiting their furniture's lengthy trip from Bunbury.

With an aboriginal police aide and his family living on one side and a crowd of itinerants coming and going from the house on the other side, life was vastly different from any previous experience. With the setting sun, street fights between warring factions became a nightly occurrence. Hurling bottles and shouting drunken abuse at each other, the local inhabitants of the area created a siege mentality among the hopelessly outnumbered whites. Closing gates and doors and hiding behind drawn curtains, they prayed each night their dogs would deter and discourage attack.

Unused to living in white man's structures, the neighbours to one side slept in the dust outside the house, lit cooking fires in the backyard and tore down anything suitable for fuel while their undernourished and untrained dogs ran in and out of the vacant

338

house. On the other side, the police aide and his de-facto wife ignored the nightly conflict while their own dogs continued to multiply unchecked. On one occasion when a puppy died from neglect, in their desperate hunger, the other dogs fought over the carcass.

Not surprisingly, the relationship between Terry and Jane was at best, strained. While continuing to maintain an outward façade of normality for the sake of their children, conversation did not extend beyond that which was necessary for daily functioning of the family. There were now too many dangerous topics of conversation, which could instantly set alight simmering resentment.

While Jane left the hospital, securing a more lucrative clerical position with the Halls Creek Shire, Terry discovered to his dismay that his employment arrangements with the local hospital were to change. The appointment of a husband and wife team to cover the positions of matron and handyman meant Terry's relegation to the status of Gardener, also encompassing the duties of orderly and cleaner. The mini empire he'd created along with its associated job satisfaction and autonomy would exist no longer. What was worse was the fact that the new handyman would not direct him in his duties. One day of the new man's arrogance was sufficient for Terry to decide the arrangement was untenable.

"The Argyle Diamond Mine is looking for security officers." Garry advised. "You'd be a dead cert to get a job there. I hear the pay is excellent."

Although Terry had heard of the mine, which had been the subject of considerable political manoeuvring, the press articles had provided scant information on its exact location. "Where is the mine?"

"It's about two hundred and twenty kilometres from here. You head down the highway to Wyndham and Kununurra, through the aboriginal camp at Turkey Creek and turn off along a dirt road beyond the Ord River. The mine workers are mostly on twelve week shifts and live in single men's quarters. They fly from Perth to Kununurra and then the mine's 'plane flies them into the mine site. There's probably no reason why you couldn't drive home from there to Halls Creek on your days off. It wouldn't hurt to give it a go. With the sort of salaries they get you'd soon be on your feet again."

Despite the tenuous domestic situation, Terry's reluctance to live away from home was considerable. He feared for his family's safety with the onset of the Wet Season when desert aborigines embarked upon their traditional "walk about." Violent inter tribal clashes were as certain as the approaching monsoon. With many of the white populace deserting the town before the big rains, there was always the possibility of those remaining being unwitting victims in the violence.

"Thank God Veronica is out of it," he told himself. Divided even further by the need to send Veronica to boarding School in Perth, there was now only Jane, Helen, Michael and himself in Halls Creek. With the local black boys showing increasing interest in their pubescent eldest daughter and even resorting to hopping the front fence and tapping on her window at night, Terry and Jane feared that one of them might eventually persuade her to let him into her bedroom. Or worse still, she would fall victim to rape.

Heart broken at the thought of further family division, Terry flew to Perth with Veronica and enrolled her at St. Brigid's Catholic College in Lesmurdie where they believed the nuns would protect her innocence. The prospect of their beloved teenage daughter with an unwanted bastard child at such a young age was too terrible for words and outweighed any other considerations. He'd hugged her to him on the front steps of the College, their tears intermingling on sodden cheeks, his guilt and sorrow once again, unbearable. On the long flight home, his mind churned with schemes and wild ideas for family reunification but nothing feasible emerged from his grief.

"What do reckon?" Garry's question brought Terry back to the present with a jolt.

"I don't think there's any alternative. I guess if I can put up with that sort of life for a while we might be able to afford to build that house we want at Chidlow."

Nestling on the side of a jagged mountain range and overlooking the Spinifex plains of the Ord Valley, the Argyle Diamond Mine seemed an incongruous intrusion in the timeless land. Ugly steel structures and tumbling cylindrical screens, broad rubber conveyor belts and unsightly piles of tailings bore testimony to man's greed and his indifference to nature's savage beauty.

340

"See that big hill over there? There's about two hundred million tonnes of rock that we're going to cut away to get to the diamonds lying in the pipe beneath! That hill will cease to exist soon." Gary Watters[40] the mine's security manager shouted above the din from the rocks crashing together on the gigantic vibrating screen. All this stuff is trucked in from Smoke Creek and Limestone Creek and is alluvial material. The true wealth of this mine lies somewhere beneath that mountain.

The temperature was forty six degrees Celsius. Reflection from the corrugated iron sheds and roofs hurt the eyes. Red dust rose in clouds, hanging above the mine, visible for miles and staining everything with its fallout. Haul pack mine trucks tore maniacally along broad dirt roads, ferrying huge loads of rich ore for sorting, crushing x-ray examination, further separation and final sorting. That these huge loads could be reduced to the contents of two milk churns amazed Terry. A helmeted and goggled female diamond sorter, clad in dusty red shorts and T-shirt emerged from a building surrounded by a mesh enclosure. Escorted by the khaki uniformed figure of an Argyle Diamond Mine security guard, the woman made her way to the base of the tower housing the X-ray equipment. Unlocking the milk churn, she stooped and dragged it free, replacing it with an empty container.

"That churn contains uncut diamonds," Watters said unnecessarily. "They are mostly industrial diamonds, but a small percentage will be gem quality. Argyle diamonds are rapidly becoming famous for their colours and purity."

Negotiating a steel platform alongside the mine plant, they descended to ground level. Watters nodded to a patrolling security guard and leant on the buzzer beside the electronically controlled security gate. High on a pylon above their heads, closed circuit television cameras relayed their image to the Control Room operator. A second camera swung on its mounting nearby as the unseen guard panned and zoomed in on their faces. The gate clicked as the guard recognised and acknowledged their credentials. Inside the sorting room, Terry removed his helmet, grateful for the comfort air conditioning. Four women sat on high stools, each with a pile of glistening diamonds through

---

[40] (Fictitious name.)

which they meticulously scratched, carefully separating quality stones from the dross.

"Every week we fly the diamonds down to Perth. We choose a guard at random to escort the aluminium cases and right up until the last moment, no-one knows who will escort the diamonds. Each shipment is worth many millions of dollars. It is an offence for anyone to be in possession of diamonds without authority and the Argyle Diamond Mining Act carries heavy penalties of imprisonment," he added ominously.

"How many security guards does the mine employ?" Terry asked.

"We have about thirty six. Everyone works twelve hour shifts and there's approximately ten officers on duty at any one time. There will be two staff at the main gate along with the Supervisor controlling access into the mine proper, one in the sorting area where we are now, one on foot patrol outside the compound, one on mobile patrol and one each at Smoke Creek and Limestone Creek and one in the Control Room. Your duties as a security officer are to prevent the theft of diamonds from the mine. You have the legal powers to stop and search anyone and to arrest if you believe someone has stolen diamonds or is attempting to steal diamonds."

"But diamonds being so small, anyone could hide them inside the body or throw them over the fence and pick them up later!"

Watters ignored Terry's statement. "When the workers leave the mine compound they all have to pass through a turnstile where we institute random searches. The same system of random searches is practised at the Limestone and Smoke Creek compounds."

The shortcomings of the Mine's Security Management Plan were immediately apparent to Terry. However, it was clear that any suggestion or criticism of the system would not be welcome. "Button your lip and just collect your pay!" he told himself.

Consisting of former Armed Service personnel or ex police officers, the security force was very authoritarian. Hard faced and obviously lesbian women with a dislike for males, two of the female supervisors delighted in asserting their power over unfortunate male subordinates. For his part, the male security manager enjoyed creating division and dissension within the ranks, openly stating that it was his policy to "divide and rule." Watters harboured the misguided philosophy, that by discouraging friendships or alliances better-qualified members of his crew were unlikely to threaten his position. "Keep them bickering among themselves, seemed to be his silent catchcry and morale never lifted above rock bottom.

The tedious nature of a guard's duties provided ample time for reflection, fuelling further discontent. The most dreaded of shifts were those at the huge fenced compounds of Limestone and Smoke Creek. At these locations, a guard could sit for twelve hours with no communication and nothing to relieve the boredom. Dismissal being mandatory for those caught in the act of reading, the hours dragged remorselessly. With only the occasional brief interlude to hold out a tin of white marbles to the rare visiting employee in the hope that one would choose a red marble, thus providing the opportunity to conduct a vehicle and body search, there was nothing else to do. Any one of the many Haul pack trucks thundering in and out had ample opportunity to smuggle the prized stones but with nothing allowed to slow production, the trucks continued unchecked.

The situation was equally tiresome in the close confines of the sorting compound. Conversation with the female sorters was prohibited and with other mine workers heavily involved in their duties, there was nothing to do but amble slowly in endless circuits of the tiny yard as the blistering sun threatened to bake one's brain to the point of madness.

Terry had never realised how slowly could be the passage of twelve hours. The expression, "bored out of your brain," took on a new meaning. "Jesus John!" he blasphemed one day to the newest addition to the security force. "I swear this is driving me nuts. The other day at Limestone Creek, I found myself outside screaming at the sky just to relieve the frustrations. This entire security thing is a joke. I could run a double decker bus through the loop holes. With nothing better to do, I've actually mapped out an alternative plan, which would address the issues. I bet there's a small fortune walking out the door with the change of each shift."

John Larenzo smiled. "Hang in there mate. We'll stick this out together; we both need the job and the dough."

A slightly built but extremely fit man, with a head of thick black hair, Larenzo originated from New Zealand and had instantly built a rapport with Terry. A former butcher by trade, he had slipped into the security industry as a temporary measure, following the sale of his butcher shop in Auckland. John's marriage had dissolved and with three children to support in Perth, he and Terry empathised with each other's domestic troubles.

"When I came here John, I thought I could put up with a lot for the money. It's much easier to say that than actually do it. I really miss the kids. Halls Creek is a hot bed of trouble at the moment, and I am worried that the drunken lunatics that run wild everywhere with "The Wet" coming on will attack the family in the house one night! As soon as I can arrange it, I'm out of here. This whole move to Western Australia has been a total disaster. I'm planning on going back to New Zealand if I can line up a job there. I've put advertisements in the Christchurch newspapers for employment. I hope someone in the security industry over there will offer me a job. Fourteen years as a policeman and working here and at Worsley must count for something."

"I wish you luck mate. Your problem is you are too family orientated for a place like this. There's a lot of people here who love the life and wouldn't have it any other way."

"Yeah, I know. I've seen them at night time, flitting between each other's "dongers. It's like Peyton bloody Place. You never know who's shagging who from one day to the next. With free accommodation and meals provided and no financial worries, it's no wonder they love it."

"Which reminds me, how are you getting on with Maria? She's sure got the hots for you!"

"Lay off John. That little Italian sheila is always flirting and she makes it so obvious what she's after. It's bloody embarrassing. Just because half the camp is sleeping with the other half, there's no way I'm going to get mixed up with her. I know only too well, what it feels like to be betrayed. As far as I'm concerned, anyone who cheats on his partner has sunk about as low as you can sink."

"When are you going home again?"

"I've got three days off next Wednesday. I'll have worked nine of these twelve hour shifts without a day off by then. I hope the rains hold off because there are twenty two creeks to cross between the mine and the highway."

With ominous thunderheads looming on the distant horizon, Terry accelerated along the dusty gravel track to the highway. If the rains beat him he could easily be caught between creeks and stranded. On the other hand, if he managed to reach Halls Creek he could well be trapped there when the flooded rivers cut off the town as they so often did during the Wet Season. Lighting flashes were distinguishable among the huge black and white woolly monsters. Somewhere off behind him he could see smoke rising from burning spinifex ignited by the nature's fireworks. Breathing a huge sigh of relief he at last bounced off the gravel onto the sealed roadway as darkness suddenly descended. By now, the enormous magnesium bright explosions of electricity were almost continuous. With the pitch blackness of night chased away every few seconds, the country's stunted snappy gums seemed to jump out at him from all directions like twisted white skeletons. All around lighting bolts crashed to the bare red earth, setting alight t the tinder dry scrub.

With the Holden's headlights on full beam, Terry pressed the accelerator to the floor in a desperate chase from an unseen hand throwing all it's might at him. He knew the unfenced country allowed cattle to stray across the road and only the foolish travelled at night. A cow lying on the bitumen would not be seen until the last moment and kangaroos frightened by the storm might bound in front of the car at any moment. Laying his hand on the horn in the plaintive hope of scaring livestock off the road, he peered into the blackness beyond the headlight's range. Suddenly, in his peripheral vision he glimpsed big red cows either side of the car. Instinctively, his foot went to the brake pedal. A split second later the lumbering body of a massive bull loomed in the path of the car. With acrid blue smoke spurting from the tyres and rubber howling in protest, he steered around the bull as it turned to look stupidly at the mechanical invader with glaring white eyes.

Abnormally large wet droplets splattered against the Holden's windscreen. With the wipers smearing the red Kimberley dust to a thick brownish paste, Terry stuck his head out the driver's window. His hands shook as the adrenaline retreated from his system and he breathed deeply of the heavy warm air to calm his pounding heart. The rain increased in intensity forcing him to wind up the window. As his vision improved he pressed on, the slip slap of the wipers and the drumming of the rain a constant reminder of the floods, which inexorably followed the Big Wet.

Already causeways and culverts ran darkly with murky brown torrents. At the mighty Ord River Terry could make out the marker posts along the edge of the long narrow concrete causeway. Water gushed over boulders, spurting high into the air and the shadowy shapes of dead trees moved sluggishly in the racing current, nudging the road edge as if anxious to hurdle the man made obstacle, which could only stop them temporarily. He knew he could cross in safety but turning back would be out of the question once he got beyond a few kilometres. "Look's like you'll be flying back to the mine when your days off finish!" he told himself grimly, pressing on.

Glancing at the luminous dial of his wristwatch he noticed that an hour had gone since the rain began. The windscreen wipers were no longer necessary. He had managed to outrun the storm and with his confidence growing, he urged the car to go faster although the memory of his near miss was still fresh in his mind. At last, he descended the long straight section of the highway north of the little town, grateful that the Elvire River had not yet begun to run. Dry for most of the year, the Elvire could quickly become a treacherous. It was known occasionally to sweep away the giant road trains, which plied the highway daily bringing essential supplies to the remote communities.

The town's lights seemed blurred in the falling rain as the majority of its inhabitants sheltered from the storm. Stooped figures of the black population could be seen shambling along the otherwise deserted streets, ignoring the rain in their quest for something more important to them than sleep. Outside his house, a tiny Datsun 120Y sedan sat sadly, its steeply sloping roof concave where the local children had used it as a makeshift trampoline. "Bugger!" Terry swore. The car's owner was one of the mine security force's supervisors who had asked Terry to try and sell the car for her in Halls Creek where the ever present demand for second hand motor vehicles meant it would be snapped up quickly. "Bridget's not going to be happy about that."

Although the children were in bed, Jane was still awake as Terry turned his key in the door. "I didn't think you'd try and drive home with The Wet on the way," she said sounding almost disappointed.

"There's some mail for you from New Zealand." She averted her head, offering a cheek as an alternative for his greeting kiss.

Terry's heart skipped a beat. Could this be an answer to his advertisement in the Christchurch Star? The letter proved to be from a small security company offering him a position as a sales representative for their products. Although Terry suspected that the job would not meet his expectations and was most likely to be a commission sales position, he clutched the opportunity like a drowning man thrown a lifeline. "This could be our chance to get out of this mess," he told Jane. "I'm going to give in my notice at Argyle and fly to New Zealand. While I'm there, I'll look up Bob Crooks and Trevor Joy. They might be able to get me into the airport security."

Jane was noncommittal. She knew it was no use to challenge her husband's decisions made under extreme duress. Nothing she could say would dissuade him.

For the three days Terry spent in Halls Creek, unrelenting rain swelled the rivers making return by road impossible. He'd travelled as far as the Ord in a vain attempt to get back by car but finding the river had become so deep even the marker posts along the causeway had disappeared, he camped on the river bank hoping the waters would recede enough to attempt a crossing. Placing pebbles at the water's edge, he erected a tarpaulin as shelter from the searing heat and settled down to wait. With plenty of water and food in an emergency kit he always carried, he knew he could last days if necessary. The rain had ceased and with no clouds in sight, he reasoned that the river should fall. The better part of a day went slowly as he swatted the ubiquitous and annoying swarms of bush flies, which seemed determined to crawl into his eyes, nose, mouth and even his ears. Each time he checked his pebble markers he found the river even higher than before. "It must be still raining somewhere backup in the hills," he muttered to himself. Somehow, the sound of his voice seemed foreign in the stillness of the vast countryside.

No other vehicles turned up to wait with him. From this, he assumed nothing could move very far on the Kimberley's great empty roads. Throwing dirt on the campfire he'd lit more for distraction than actual need, he pulled down the shelter and spun the nose of the faithful Holden back toward Halls Creek. He knew the only way back to the mine was by air and he'd purchase a seat on the tiny single engine Cessna that flew daily to Kununurra.

Although he'd travelled in every type of aircraft including Iroquois helicopters, giant Hercules transport 'planes, tiny aero club gliders and even the plexiglass bubble cockpit of the diamond mine's little chopper but nothing compared to the exhilaration of the trip from the remote outback airstrip to Kununurra. Terry knew Outback pilots were in a class of their own and would not take to the air unless they were confident of safely completing their journey. He settled in his seat beside the pilot and prepared to enjoy the ride.

To describe the flight as bumpy was an understatement. Once more, giant thunderclouds filled the sky. Majestic and frightening in their enormity, they concealed enough energy within the billowing mass of grey, white and pitch black water vapour to supply a small city's electricity needs. Distant flashes of lightning provided a free fireworks display and the flimsy aircraft bucked and pitched, as if tossed carelessly in the hands of some unseen giant.

As the little engine's unbroken roar filled the cockpit, the pilot pointed below. Like piles of red pancakes, the spectacular formations of the famous Bungle Bungle Ranges seemed to reach up to grab at the manmade intruder. Silver threads of a thousand waterfalls contrasted beautifully against the ochre of time worn rocks. Beyond this maze created by nature, the seemingly endless plains were no longer the harsh burnt brown to which Terry had become accustomed. Vast tracts of land transformed by life giving rains were now a soft emerald green and countless lakes dotted the countryside sparkling in the sun's rays.

Terry marvelled at the awesome beauty of this cruel yet captivating land. Somewhere deep within him something seemed to move nostalgically and a little voice seemed to whisper, *Stay here, this, is your true home.* However, mentally shook himself bringing common-sense to bear. *It wouldn't work. The heat and conditions are just to harsh,* he told himself.

Now he had made up his mind to leave Terry was impatient to be on his way but first he had to fulfil his contractual obligations to the Diamond Mine. With no car, Jane had to drive from Halls Creek to the mine with Michael and Helen to collect her husband when he finished working there. On his last day, Terry arranged for the security patrol vehicle to transport him to the highway where he would wait for Jane's arrival.

Standing alone in the darkness with his suitcase, he prayed Jane would make the trip without incident. In a careless and tragic accident, Jane had lost one eye as a child. Although she coped well, she was unused to driving such vast distances in the Outback. She would also need to negotiate swollen rivers and wandering livestock.

As the prearranged meeting time came and went, Terry paced nervously and his imagination produced many horrific scenarios. She's probably broken down. Maybe she's hit a cow. Maybe she's collided with a road train. Perhaps she's been swept away by a swollen river. Sick with worry there was nothing he could do but wait and hope. Tired from the endless pacing and a twelve hour shift, he sat on a rock, pitching stones into the night while he tried to assure himself that there was an innocuous explanation for his wife's non-appearance. Occasionally headlights reflecting off the low clouds heralded an approaching vehicle long before it came into view. He'd jump to his feet ready to flag down the driver. However, on each occasion a road train thundered by without stopping.

It was approaching midnight before another set of headlights signalled the approach of another vehicle. He'd almost given up hope when the juggernaut began to slow, the driver using his gears to bring the brightly lit monster to a halt. Terry's heart jumped as he realised another vehicle had been following close behind. Climbing down from his cabin the truck driver called to him, "You can stop worrying now mate. Your missus is okay! She got stuck at The Ord and I had to pull her through the river but she's okay now."

Terry did not know how to express his thanks to the Good Samaritan and the simple, "Thanks mate," he uttered seemed hopelessly inadequate. Tears of relief stung his eyes and he silently admonished himself for risking his family's safety. He wanted to hug his wife and tell her how sorry he was but she greeted him as coolly as a stranger might.

Christchurch in May was bitingly cold after the heat of The North West. Terry had forgotten how icy the easterly wind blowing in from the Tasman Sea could be. "Beasterly Easterlies" they had always called them. The neat and orderly garden city seemed caught in a time warp as nothing much appeared to have changed since his last visit. The city's relaxed pace, immense parks and pretty gardens were all part of the charm that evoked comparisons with such places as Oxford and Cambridge in England. Ancient motor vehicles still plied the streets and its citizen's friendly nature contrasted with the bustling and introspective natures of such places as Sydney, Melbourne and to a lesser extent, Perth.

Jane's mother Betty Trafford welcomed Terry and could not contain her pleasure at the prospect of her only daughter returning to Christchurch. "It's about time you got all that nonsense out of your head and came back! You should never have left such a good job and a lovely home. Perhaps you'll settle down now," she admonished.

Terry smarted at the rebuke but refrained from comment. The stern faced woman had never forgiven him for not naming Michael after his grandfather. With thoughts only for her daughter, she would never understand the events, which had precipitated his decision to go to Australia. He wished he'd arranged accommodation elsewhere as he no longer felt comfortable in the old Urunga Avenue house. He remembered the cottage in it's hey day before Jane's brothers had married and left home. In those days, the house seemed about to burst at its seams, with four athletic and noisy young men seated around the long dining table, laughing and swapping tales at meal times. Jane's brothers had always done their utmost to make him feel like one of the family despite his mother-in- law giving him the impression that she merely tolerated him as her daughter's chosen partner. Now, with the old lady living alone, the weatherboard house had all the warmth of a mausoleum. He felt momentary pangs of pity for the ageing widow and knew he could never appreciate the loneliness she must endure following the loss of her husband and her children's departure.

After a meal eaten in awkward silence with his brooding mother in law, Terry excused himself saying he wanted to go for a walk. In reality, he was very tired. With the five hours time difference between Western Australia and New Zealand taken into consideration, it had been a long day, but he needed solitude to collect his thoughts. The worries of his divided family, a wife who obviously no longer loved him, no employment and how he was going to sort out the mess he'd created bore down heavily upon him.

With needle sharp sleet stinging his face, he turned up his coat collar. Thrusting his hands deeply in the pockets, he wandered the dark still streets of Bryndwr. Several hours past and by the time he returned, the old lady had gone to bed leaving her bedroom door ajar so she could hear his return, he slipped silently into the spare bedroom. The chilly room smelt strongly of mothballs and its emptiness palpable. Wishing for the unity of his family and salvation of his marriage, he fell asleep between the cold sheets of the bed, which had not felt human warmth for many years.

The next morning he reluctantly contacted the manager of the security company who had replied to his advertisement. As he suspected, the salary was purely commission based. Although he knew a simple telephone call from Western Australia would have elicited that information and saved him the cost of an airfare, the letter of offer had provided the excuse he needed to resign and return to New Zealand. In a way, his resignation based on the spurious job offer, had been dishonest but desperation had driven him. It had been desperation to unite his family and desperation to be free from the mind numbing boredom. Any way, he reasoned, if I hadn't resigned, how could I find another job living three thousand five hundred kilometres from civilisation?

"Hello, Terry. It's good to see you after so many years. What brings you to Christchurch?" Bob Crooks had been Terry's police In-Service Training Instructor. A slightly built, dark haired man with almost black penetrating eyes and a small oval face, Crooks had left the police to establish the New Zealand Civil Aviation Security Service along with Trevor Joy. On initial secondment from the police, Joy now headed the service.

"Well, Bob, it's like this," Terry launched into a lengthy discourse on events since his resignation while Crooks listened intently for several minutes until Terry concluded; "I have had enough and just want to get my family together. I realise now that I should have taken a lengthy sabbatical but at the time I was so burnt out I couldn't see what others were trying to tell me."

"Why don't you re-apply? I'm sure the police Service would give your application serious consideration."

"No, I can't see myself going back. I've become really interested in security work as a profession and would like to remain in that field."

"Okay. I'll run it past Trevor and you could probably get in on the next intake."

"When would that be?" Terry sense of enormous relief was short lived, as Crooks brow creased with a sudden thought.

"I have no idea. We have to wait until there are sufficient vacancies to make running a recruit course worthwhile. It could be quite some time. Of course, you realise that you probably wouldn't be posted to Christchurch as there are rarely any vacancies here. You would almost certainly go to Auckland; however, a government house goes with the job. We'll contact you when where ready!"

When Terry announced his plans to return to Perth, Betty Trafford took the news hard. She looked suddenly very old and tired. "What are you going to do back there? Why don't you stay here until you get the job in Auckland?"

"I'm sorry. I really am, but I can't just wait around indefinitely. I've got to try and get something happening now so that we can all be together as soon as possible. I'll go to Perth and look for work there because it might be many months before I can get into Aviation Security. On the other hand, Trevor Joy might decide that he doesn't want me in the service. My recent track record hasn't been too good!"

Terry flew to Perth the next day. With a small nest egg saved from his Argyle employment, he searched the business opportunities columns once more. A small advertisement for a fish and chip shop caught his eye. It was the right price and he reasoned optimistically that he would be able to build up the run down business with hard work. He imagined Jane and him running the business together and building the house they wanted on their Chidlow block.

"You've done what!" Jane's astonished anger flooded from the telephone handset. "If you think I'm going to run a fish and chip shop with you, you can think again!"

"But, there's no work in Perth. I might not get into the security service and this gives us the opportunity to build on our block and get all get back together."

"What makes you think I want to come back to Perth?"

Terry reeled from the unexpected response." Because we're supposed to be a family. Because we're all living at three different locations. Because Halls Creek is such a dreadful place and I thought you wanted to build a house at Chidlow."

"Well, I'm not so sure I want to leave. I've got a good job here and I don't mind Halls Creek. It's really not that bad."

The rumours he'd tried to ignore seemed to make sense. Acquaintances in Halls Creek had told him that his wife and the Shire Clerk were having an affair but he would not let himself entertain what he thought was a ridiculous notion. *It's just malicious small town gossip*, he'd told himself. *Could there be any foundation in the whispers? Why else wouldn't she want to do everything in her power to unite the family?* Still, he refused to believe. *She's just angry because I didn't consult her before I made the decision to buy the shop. She'll come around.* Although he knew it had been foolish not to get her opinion, he didn't want to risk anything coming between him and his burning desire for family reunification.

The little fish and chip shop proved to be yet another disaster. Situated in a depressed area among other struggling businesses, no amount of hard work or imagination seemed to improve the meagre income. Each week as Terry struggled to run the business alone, he counted the few notes and coins remaining after meeting the rent and other outgoings. Judy helped him during the rare busy periods but for much of the time he sat expectantly hoping customers would come through the doors. His greatest consolation was being able to see Veronica regularly as St. Brigid's College was only a short drive from the East Victoria Park shop.

After letter drops and advertising failed to expand the struggling business, he finally admitted defeat placing the business in the hands of a broker. For once Lady Luck smiled on him and the broker found a buyer quickly. Feeling incredibly mean and guilty knowing his shop would never provide a good income; he cashed the cheque quickly before the new elderly owner could change her mind.

With no news from Bob Crooks, Terry wrote directly to

Trevor Joy imploring him to help. As he disconsolately searched the employment pages applying for anything remotely within his expertise, he plummeted into the abyss of depression. Never before had he felt so powerless. Judy tried to keep him occupied playing board games and crossword puzzles as he waited for some positive response. The hours dragged, the days unbearable and the weeks seemed eternal.

With the State's economy falling into recession as a direct result of Government corruption and entrepreneurial greed gutting the wealth of previously affluent corporations. Job applicants vastly outnumbered vacancies. Dole queues grew longer and with too many applicants to process, most employers deemed acknowledging unsuccessful applicants too expensive and time consuming. Along with the decency of a polite rejection, the hopes and dreams of desperate people had become mere flotsam on the hard steps to the temple of greed.

The weeks rolled by without success until one morning Terry spread "The West Australian" newspaper on the kitchen table to sift through the job vacancies. "Mum, listen to this," Terry's sudden excitement was palpable. "This looks like my cup of tea. The Department of Administrative Services is to establish an organisation known as, The Australian Protective Service. The APS is to take over the role of Commonwealth Security formerly handled by The Australian Federal police. Suitable applicants will possess previous police or military service. The role consists of providing security patrols and appropriate response to incidents at Commonwealth Government establishments and custodial services for the Department of Local Government and Ethnic Affairs at various Immigration Detention Centres. I wouldn't want to be a screw. I had enough of dealing with prisons when I was in the police to know that I couldn't stand being locked behind bars all the time. However it says here that the detention centres are in Sydney and Melbourne, so I wouldn't have to worry about that in Perth. Mum, I've got to apply for this."

"Where do you apply," Judy asked silently praying that her son's struggle might soon be over.

"It says prospective applicants should present themselves next Saturday, for a pre entry test at the Leederville TAFE"

Terry arrived at the allotted time to find a crowd gathered

354

outside the technical college. "Surely, all these people can't be here for the same thing!" His amazement turned to despair as he began to doubt his ability to succeed with so many seemingly able people chasing so few positions. Eavesdropping on conversations made him realise just how well qualified some of the applicants were.

"Damn it! I'm here now and I've nothing better to do. I may as well go through the test."

Intended to last three hours, the examination questions seemed ridiculously easy to Terry. The majority of the questions appeared to mimic those he answered so many years for when he'd applied to join the New Zealand police. Completing his examination paper within less than an hour, he checked it and left after handing it to the examiner. "I must have missed something. It couldn't be that easy," he told himself.

As with government institutions almost everywhere, weeks went by and he heard nothing from the Australian Protective Service. In the mean time, a letter arrived from New Zealand. The envelope carried the logo of the Aviation Security Service and Terry's hand trembled as he slit the envelope. Accompanying official looking application forms was a personal letter from Trevor Joy.

Dear Terry,
I am sorry to take so long to reply to your letters. I am sorry that things have not worked out for you and Jane in Western Australia. However, I am pleased to offer you a position with the Aviation Security Service.

Please complete the enclosed forms and return them along with the necessary measurements for your new uniform. A departmental house has been allocated for you at Auckland International Airport and you will need to present yourself for the recruit course on 1 October 1984. Please acknowledge this application at your earliest convenience.

Yours sincerely,
Trevor Joy.

Terry's elation took him straight to the telephone to break the good news to Jane. She did not share his enthusiasm responding with a verbal bombshell, "I don't know whether I want to live in Auckland!"

Terry exploded, "Well, that's too bad. The kids need us to get back together and this is the only way I know to do it! In the mean time, if I hear from the Protective Service that I've got a job with them, I can cancel the New Zealand one. It would obviously be much easier to stay in W.A."

"What about the block at Chidlow?"

"We'll just have to put it into the hands of an agent until it sells.

"What are you going to do until October?"

"I'll drive back to Halls Creek as soon as I can and just wait away the time."

The brilliant red of Sturt's Desert pea provided a spectacular show all through The Pilbara's vast empty countryside as Terry coaxed the old Holden Belmont on what he hoped would be his last trip to Halls Creek. Purchased for a few hundred dollars, the old car overheated whenever he drove over eighty kilometres per hour. Determined to get back to his family he drove without stopping until unable to keep his eyes open any longer and beginning to hallucinate, fatigue forced him to a halt.

After dozing for a couple of hours, he pushed on into the baking arid country of Sand Fire Flat. Late in the afternoon of the second day, he reached the isolated Sand Fire Roadhouse. Refuelling the faithful old car, he decided to check the radiator before tackling the next leg of his journey to Broome. He was unprepared for the pressure beneath the radiator cap. A scalding geyser of rusty water drenched his right arm, neck and face. Cursing his stupidity, there was no alternative but to push on. Tipping water over himself every few minutes in a futile attempt to lessen the agony, he drove into the night, tears of pain coursing down his cheeks. Stopping briefly at the Roebuck Roadhouse to refuel again, he wondered why other travellers stared at him. Getting back into the car, he caught sight of himself in the rear view mirror. All down one side of his head the skin had bubbled into a huge blister.

By the time Terry reached Halls Creek on the third day, the pain had subsided but his right arm and shoulder had blistered to match his face. Jane showed little concern for his burns with the laconic comment, "You better go to the hospital."

The nursing sister sprayed an aerosol substance over him, which formed quickly into an artificial skin. "That should keep any infection away," she stated simply. "I don't know how you drove all this way like that. You're a very silly boy!"

Knowing the future was brighter, Terry settled down to wait each day hoping he'd hear something from the Protective Service. While Jane continued to provide financially, he adopted the role of house husband. As the weeks vanished and the deadline drew nearer, he became increasingly anxious. Long distance telephone calls to Canberra elicited the unhelpful response, "We expect to make a decision any day now!"

With only two days remaining before he must catch the coach to Perth and travel on to Auckland, he demanded a definitive answer from the faceless woman in Canberra. "Look! I would rather stay in Western Australia and work for the APS but unless you can tell me now that I have a job, I am afraid I must go to Auckland."

The woman refused to be intimidated, however, her reply after weeks of bureaucratic procrastination stunned Terry, "Mr Flatley, we are able to offer you a position in Perth. You will attend the second Australian Protective Recruit Course in Adelaide on 20 October 1984."

Terry's relief almost overwhelmed him. He did not know whether to laugh or cry and at first thought that he had misheard or that she was playing a cruel joke on him. He felt like falling to his knees and thanking the God who had appeared deaf to his prayers for so long.

Run along lines very familiar to Terry, the APS recruit course had obviously been adapted from the Federal police training. With his background and knowledge of law and policing procedures, Terry excelled and often discovered he knew far more than those tasked with imparting knowledge to the eager recruits. With virtually no reference to work at detention centres and heavy emphasis on Commonwealth law and the security of sensitive government institutions Terry naturally assumed he would be looking after the Government's Perth based establishments. Despite the prospect of shift work he was excited to be assuming a quasi police role once more. The course directors waited until his graduation to drop the bombshell, "Protective Service Officer Grade One, Terry Flatly, you'll be posted to the Immigration Detention Centre at Perth Airport."

"What do you mean?" Flabbergasted, Terry could not believe what they were telling him.

"That's right. We only have a small contingent in Perth and they look after the Detention Centre."

"But, no-one ever told me the APS were prison officers. Everything I've been told has been connected with guarding and security duties. If I had known I was going to be a "screw" I would never have joined this organisation. What about the security of Commonwealth Government facilities and buildings in Perth?"

"There are no Commonwealth facilities in Perth which warrant protection and you are not going to be "a screw" as you so rudely put it," the elderly ex Federal policeman retorted harshly. "Detention Centres are not prisons! Are you telling us you don't want the job now?"

Exasperated, Terry tried to explain, "What I am saying is, I have been recruited under false pretences. I should have been advised at the outset what my role would be so that I could make an informed decision. I've turned down a worthwhile career in New Zealand only to find I'm now stuck in a role for which I have an intense loathing. Because I have a family to support, I have no viable option left open no but take the job."

It was no consolation for Terry to find that of eight hundred applicants for two positions in Perth, he and Tanya Armitage were the successful applicants. It was as though the bottom had fallen out of Terry's world once more.

After graduating, Terry arranged to rent house in the Perth hillside suburb of Mundaring as he tried to resign himself to his new role as a custodial officer at the cramped detention centre. He scurried around buying second hand furniture and doing his utmost to create the most comfortable home his limited budget allowed as he eagerly anticipated the reconsolidation of his family.

"I've got everything set up. We've a quite nice house in Mundaring, which will do until we can build at Chidlow. You can come down to Perth whenever you're ready," he advised Jane proudly.

"Who says I'm coming back to Perth."

Oh, God. Not this crap again. What will satisfy this woman? "I do," he retorted angrily. "Get yourself down here!" He slammed the telephone down in disgust.

With his family re-united Terry prayed that Jane would work with him to re-build their relationship for the sake of their four children. They researched building companies and plans with the hope of finding something affordable and finally settled on an A-frame two-storey timber and iron cottage. The house came in kit form and lacked many of the niceties they had previously enjoyed. The upstairs area was one large room and with the only bedroom on the ground floor Terry set about constructing partitions creating four separate sleeping areas for each of the children. Although they were dirt poor, the Chidlow house signified a new beginning and Terry was overjoyed that they were all together again. He knew it was only a matter of time before they clawed their way back to a decent living standard. After so much hardship a dream had come true and Terry knew that good times could be ahead if he and Jane adopted a united front and forgave each other's failings and past mistakes.

Built on their two and a half acre block which had once been an orchard; their cottage overlooked the neighbour's dam and enjoyed semi rural setting. Surrounded by navel orange and Granny Smith apple trees, the property boasted two plentiful bores, peace and quiet and ample space for a vegetable garden and chooks. Although they were some distance from Perth, the rural atmosphere, nearby forests and beautiful Lake Leschenaultia more than compensated for the absence of big city life. Always ambitious, Terry knew it was only a matter of time before he would use the land to good advantage, producing a modest income from blueberries while fully embracing his new career.

Although his new role brought with it all the stresses of shift work, he could see the chance to rise quickly within the ranks of a fledgling organisation that lacked personnel with dedication, training and experience. Although the Perth Immigration Detention Centre was far from Terry's ideal workplace, he envisioned the APS expanding to become a more law enforcement focussed body. Although the hierarchy at that time did not share Terry's vision he was undeterred by their short sightedness and knew in his heart that the day would come when these things would happen. To him, it seemed a natural progression if the organisation was to survive so he set about lobbying the hierarchy and those within the ranks working on the premise that by sewing enough seeds in the right places something would eventually happen. He was not surprised to find that a few rising stars in the eastern states shared his dream and were already pressuring the sluggish leadership to act. Although the tyranny of distance largely negated Terry's efforts APS management awoke to the possibilities and cast their net for the necessary expertise. In a whirlwind visit to Perth to familiarise himself with working conditions at the Perth Immigration Detention Centre, the new Director of the APS, Peter Dawson found himself cornered by Terry. "Sir, I know you will probably tell me that it isn't going to happen but I see the APS taking over airport and diplomatic security from the Federal police. I can also see us providing for the security needs of all Commonwealth Government Departments. We could establish an alarm monitoring station and security patrols who would respond to incidents and alarms. The Federal police are under utilised in their role at airports at present and would be more effective if they were to focus their efforts away from security aspects into crime prevention."

"It's not going to happen, Terry. I admire your enthusiasm and vision but the Australian Protective Service will never take over airports from the Federal police. For a start, we don't have the necessary legislation or the powers and it is simply not the government's plan for us."

Terry smiled. "I sincerely hope you are wrong sir. It would only take the stroke of a pen to give us the necessary powers. If this organisation is going to survive it must expand or it will regress. Within our ranks you will surely find all the expertise and knowledge to accomplish those goals. I have spoken to some highly qualified and knowledgeable individuals at the rank of P.S.O. Grade 1 who have enjoyed success in their previous police and military careers who are just longing for the chance to make things happen. The APS must tap into that expertise."

The APS Director frowned. He was not used to such frankness from those at the bottom of the organisation. He adjusted his thick-rimmed spectacles. His lean features and straight grey hair gave him a bookish appearance. "It's just not going to happen Terry. I am sorry to disappoint you. Perhaps you've chosen the wrong career path," he added tersely.

"I don't think I have sir. I am sure the APS will move into the areas I have suggested. It's just a matter of time. Thank you for listening to me." Although Terry knew the senior public servant was well regarded in clerical circles, he doubted the man's ability to successfully steer a body comprised of so many former police and military personnel who resented the public service mindset. *Does he know the two cultures are diametrically opposed?* Terry wondered as he escorted the Director to the carpark.

Although somewhat deflated by the head man's negative attitude and apparent lack of vision, Terry was determined to climb the promotional ladder. He resolved to become a Shift Supervisor within two years and within five to hold the rank of senior sergeant. The latter position would eliminate the need for him to work shift work while providing a healthy income and job satisfaction.

With their four children at High School, the financial pressures on Jane and Terry became intolerable. They struggled to make ends meet on Terry's meagre wage and Jane's overwhelming need to serve her Catholic faith meant she would not countenance any suggestion that the children attend Government Schools. "Terry, I insist the kids all go to Catholic secondary schools."

"It's impossible! On my wages, there is no way I can pay school fees. There is nothing wrong with the education they will get at Eastern Hills High School. You're expecting a champagne lifestyle on a beer income." Terry argued exasperatedly.

"It doesn't matter that we can't pay the fees. The Catholic Education Board will always waive the fees for special cases," Jane retorted, unmoved by the economic argument.

"I am not going to become a bloody charity case. As far as I am concerned, if you can't pay your way, then you should send the kids to a State school!"

"They are going to a Catholic school and that's final."

"I think it's totally reprehensible to put kids into a private school knowing that you will not be able to meet your financial obligations. If you insist on it, don't expect me to go cap in hand

and ask for La Salle College to accept the children on that basis. You can do it and let it be known that it is totally your decision."

Jane's determination to run up bills of thousands of dollars, which Terry could not repay, was tantamount to fraud. Coming on top of a heavy financial burden, which had been considerably exacerbated by her deeply ingrained, cavalier approach to all financial matters, Jane's stubborn refusal to yield on the issue of Catholic schools drove a deep rift in Terry's efforts to rebuild their fragile relationship. Terry finally reached the end of his patience and resourcefulness. "I am at my wit's end as to how we are going to make ends meet!" Terry waved a fistful of bills, which he'd already shuffled several times over the preceding weeks, paying the critical ones first. Now, they were all critical. "I am afraid, you are just going to have to go out and find some sort of work, because I can't manage any more."

"Who's going to give me a job?" Jane's reluctance to seek employment stemmed from a lack of self-confidence, despite having recently held down a responsible position at the Shire of Halls Creek.

"Don't sell yourself short. You are well trained and qualified. With the experience in Local Government at Halls Creek, you will have no problem finding a good job."

"And, how may I ask, am I going to get there each day?"

"We'll cross that bridge when we come to it. "I'll find a car we can afford when you find the job. I'm sorry Jane, but we are at crisis point."

The ongoing arguments over financial problems seemed to drive the final nail in the coffin of their fragile relationship. Jane's resentment over the enduring hardships since leaving New Zealand and Terry's insistence she find work turned to a palpable hatred exhibited through savage verbal attacks, insults and glaring anger.

"You're mad! You're insane!" she'd often tell him, contemptuously seeking the ultimate verbal sword to plunge deep into his fragile self esteem.

The enormity of her hatred astounded Terry. *How is it that we can experience so many tough times together, raise four beautiful children and be on the verge of triumphing over adversity and enjoying better days, yet she wants so desperately to destroy me? Can't she see that I have always done the best I can and everything I've done has been with the family in mind? How can I live with*

362

so much hatred and resentment? he wondered. "Come with me to counselling again. Let us see if we can work through this together," he implored her to no avail.

"There's nothing wrong. You're imagining it. You wear your heart on your sleeve too much. What exactly do you expect this marriage to be like? It's not some fairy tale romance!"

"Well, clearly my expectations are different from yours. If you think this is what marriage should be like, then you have a strange sense of what normal is. We need an unbiased mediator to help us. We cannot go on like this."

"If you think you're going to get me in front of some counsellor so that you can manipulate me, you've got another thing coming!" she told him bluntly.

Any hope Terry had of rebuilding the marriage evaporated at that point. With so many past issues, conversation was akin to walking through a verbal minefield. Anything beyond requests such as, "Please pass the salt." somehow always degenerated into seething resentment. In a shaky but hostile truce they both limited communication to that which was necessary for the family to continue functioning. Although they shared the same bed, there was no intimacy. Jane took to sleeping in her underclothing, waiting until she thought Terry had fallen asleep before she slid beneath the blankets, taking great care to lie on the very edge of the mattress with her back to him.

Dreading every moment that he must spend with Jane, Terry hung on, hoping some miracle might yet redeem the marriage. Spending long hours of soul searching, he re-lived the past as if he was replaying a video recording of their lives, attempting to understand when or how he had failed her. *What had he done or neglected to do that drove her to that point where she had sought comfort elsewhere?* He finally concluded that she had never really loved him. Il-suited and both on the rebound, she from her rejection by the Catholic Church and he desperately seeking love and stability, they had been doomed from the start.

One night he awoke in the throes of a frightening nightmare. With both hands around her throat, he had tried to strangle her. Although the incident terrified him, the nightmares became more frequent and in them, he always killed her in some horrendous manner.

Although in his waking moments, he could never commit such a heinous act, he knew severe depression and hopelessness had seized his subconscious mind. Increasingly he found himself dismissing unwanted thoughts of his wife's demise, emanating from somewhere deep within the recesses of his mind over which he had no control. He knew he must seek immediate help before he became the insane creature his wife described.

"Let me assure you, there is nothing wrong with your sanity despite what your wife tells you. "You are perfectly sane. You are just a man under enormous stress. If your wife refuses to agree to counselling, then you need to get out of the relationship as soon as you can," a psychologist advised.

Still, Terry hung on. *How can I desert the kids?* he cried inwardly.

Finally, after one of Jane's particularly acrimonious outbursts, Veronica turned to him one evening, and shaking her head sadly, told him quietly, "Dad, you don't have to put up with this for our sake."

His beautiful daughter could see his agony and understood! For a brief moment, the unbearable load lifted from his shoulders.

***

EPILOGUE
A NEW BEGINNING

"John, I don't know whether I want to go on a blind date."

Nearly twelve months had slipped by since Terry had summoned up sufficient courage to leave home. He had advanced to a supervisory position within the APS, achieving the first goal he'd set well within the allotted time. Although he missed his children deeply, life seemed worth living once more.

His close friend John Larenzo now lived in Perth having left the Argyle Diamond Mine. Dating a fiery Irish lady with two boys, John offered to introduce Terry to her friend Chris, suggesting the four of them spend an evening together. "Come on mate. She's a very nice lady. I'd go out with her if I wasn't going out with Pat."

"Oh well, I suppose it's only for one evening. I can be polite for that long."

Travelling together in John's car, the foursome headed to Fremantle where the Port City throbbed to a new vitality following the injection of much needed monies from the America's Cup yacht race. Terry had been impressed with his first impression of Chris. The slim, blonde haired woman seemed very quiet and shy but John's description of her as "an attractive lady" had failed to do her justice. *"She's too good looking to be interested in me,"* Terry thought dejectedly.

Terry and Chris had to endure Pat and John's constant bickering in the front of the Kingswood leaving little opportunity for them to become acquainted. The foursome visited several hotels and their more extroverted friends dominated the conversation. For that reason, the evening was not as pleasant as Terry had hoped and as they parted at the end of the night Terry shyly thanked Chris for a good time. So out of touch with social niceties was he that he neglected to ask her out a second time and they parted, both assuming that was the end of the matter.

With Christmas due, Terry found himself thinking increasingly of the quiet woman with the curly blond hair and sad blue eyes. Mustering his courage to telephone, he expected to be rebuffed and was not surprised by her response. "I am sorry, but I am busy that night."

In for a penny, in for a pound, he thought. *I'll see if she's really not interested.* "What about the following week?"

"I'd love to!" Totally unexpected, her reply seemed to make his heart skip a beat.

He could hardly wait for the Saturday night date. Collecting her from her Balcatta home they drove to Cicerello's Mexican Restaurant in Mount Lawley. Never had Terry enjoyed a woman's company so much. It was if they were soul mates. Both had endured so much unhappiness in their lives they chatted for hours and could scarcely bear to end the evening. With the following day off work, they met again early the next morning and from that, point became inseparable. Almost intolerably happy, Terry could not believe he could find someone so sweet and caring and was terrified that the sweet gentle-natured woman would vanish or be plucked from him by the cruel hand of fate.

Married on 15 May 1988, in the company of close friends, Terry's choice of John to be his best man was obvious as he was eternally grateful for his friend's insistence he accept a blind date with someone who turned out to be his soul mate.

With Chris's enormous love and support, Terry advanced quickly within the APS, attaining the rank of APS Inspector. His faith in the organisation was very strong. Despite opposition from short-sighted union elements within APS ranks, he worked diligently to ensure the future of the fledgling, security and quasi-law enforcement body establishing an alarm monitoring station and mobile response for Commonwealth Government Departments, diplomatic and consular protection, cultural property escorts and protective security risk reviews for both state and federal government departments.

Terry was instrumental in the APS expansion nationwide and chosen by its leaders in Canberra to establish Perth Airport as the model and front runner for counter-terrorist-first-response and security for all Australian International Airports, the very thing the APS director had said would never happen.

Unfortunately, the APS Western Region lost its commander with the sad death of his wife from breast cancer. The new appointee systematically dismantled most of Terry's work and under his control the APS lost the custodial role at the Perth Immigration Detention Centre.

Morale within the APS had always been low despite Terry's best efforts to duplicate the team spirit he'd enjoyed with the troops under his control in the NZ Police. APS officers simply enjoyed too many "perks" and many exploited an abundance of overtime, even engineering "sickies" to create staff shortages which sometimes resulted in a few money hungry PSOs working 24 hour shifts to collect the incredible penalty rates resulting from such a long stint of duty. Recruiting standards were inadequate for what was supposed to be a uniformed, disciplined body responsible for protecting the travelling public from terrorism. However, under the new commnader morale sank even lower, discipline was virtually non-existent and Terry's appeals to his commander to back him by bringing the recalitrant officers to heel fell on deaf ears.

Deciding he could not bear to see his work dismantled and discipline shrink to an abysmal level he decided on a new challenging career path. Appointed as the first security manager for Parliament House Westerrn Australia he trained a small team to protect the iconic institution and its inhabitants. He also conducted a comprehensive security review from which he developed a security system and management plan, although after 12 months he could no longer tolerate the world of egomaniacs and moved to the private sector where he ran a succession of small businesses before retiring.

"Terry" still lives in Perth enjoying many grandchildren with the love of his life, Chris. Unable to remain idle he founded a men's shed in the northern suburbs to help combat social isolation, loneliness and depression and is actively involved in establishing a second such shed.

*****